DOUBLE

LIBERTY RUN/
HOUSTON RUN
DAVID ROBBINS

LEISURE BOOKS   NEW YORK CITY

Dedicated to...
Judy and Joshua and the one in the oven,
& Socrates,
George Gordon Lord Byron,
and Mighty Mouse.

A LEISURE BOOK®

October 1991

Published by

Dorchester Publishing Co., Inc.
276 Fifth Avenue
New York, NY 10001

LIBERTY RUN Copyright ©MCMLXXXVIII by David Robbins
HOUSTON RUN Copyright ©MCMLXXXVIII by David Robbins

Printed in the United States of America.

LIBERTY RUN

Blade stepped over the cot and reached the officer while the Russian was still on his knees. He flicked his right foot up and out, connecting, slamming his instep into the Russian's ribs, knocking the officer onto his back.

"Blade! Stop!" Plato cried.

Plato went to grip Blade's arm, but Geronimo quickly stepped between them, shaking his head.

Blade drew his right Bowie and pressed the tip into the Russian's genitals.

The officer squirmed and thrashed, wheezing, his eyes bulging.

Blade paused, his gray eyes boring into the officer's.

"You killed two of my Family, you son of a bitch!"

HOUSTON RUN

"Damn!" Blade fumed, and burst from the stairwell, activating the whip. He plunged into the mass of troopers, swinging the whip like a madman, cracking it left and right, sparks flying as the whip crackled and sizzled.

Blade whirled in one direction, then another, his right arm constantly in motion, knowing he couldn't afford to slacken his pace for an instant. The muscles in his right arm bulged as he flicked the whip every which way. He slashed a trooper's neck open and sent the trooper hurtling into those nearby. To the left he seared a trooper's eyes. The trooper was flung backwards, plowing into others.....

Other titles in the *Endworld* series:

LIBERTY RUN

ENDWORLD
Warrior Roll

ALPHA TRIAD
Blade
Hickok
Geronimo

BETA TRIAD
Rikki-Tikki-Tavi
Yama
Teucer

GAMMA TRIAD
Spartacus
Shane
Bertha

OMEGA TRIAD
Ares
Helen
Sundance

ZULU TRIAD
Samson
Sherry
Marcus

1

Three women emerged from the compound.

"Look!" exclaimed the stockiest of the five soldiers hidden in the forest to the west.

"I see," said the leader of the quintet, a lean lieutenant with angular facial features. His brown eyes narrowed.

"Do we take them, Lieutenant Lysenko?" asked the third of the five men. Each of them wore a brown uniform; each of them was a seasoned professional; each carried an AK-47.

Lieutenant Lysenko nodded.

"It is big, is it not?" commented another soldier, a handsome, youthful trooper wearing his helmet cocked at an angle.

Lieutenant Lysenko, keeping his attention fixed on the trio of women 150 yards away, nodded. "The Home embraces a thirty-acre plot," he noted absently.

"The Home!" The stocky soldier snickered. "What a stupid name!"

"I don't know about that," Lieutenant Lysenko remarked. "I sort of like it. The man responsible for constructing that walled compound knew what he was doing. His name was Kurt Carpenter, according to the files our informant turned over to us. Carpenter was no fool. He foresaw the inevitability of World War Three and took appropriate action. For an American, he was most unusual. Not at all like the typical capitalistic swine of his time. He used his wealth to build this place he called the Home, then gathered a select group here shortly before the war. He dubbed them his Family."

"The Home! The Family!" the stocky soldier said, his tone laced with scorn. "I still think it's stupid!"

Lieutenant Lysenko cast a disapproving glance at the trooper. "Were your feeble intellect the equal of your flippant mouth, Grozny, the Party Congress would hail you as a genius," he stated acidly.

Private Grozny frowned, but held his tongue. He knew better than to match wits with the cerebral Lysenko. He also knew what would happen if he riled the officer.

The approaching women were 125 yards off.

"Was it stupid of Kurt Carpenter to surround his compound with twenty-foot-high brick walls?" Lieutenant Lysenko demanded. "And to cap those thick walls with barbed wire? Or to install a sturdy, massive drawbridge in the center of the west wall as the only means of entering or exiting to minimize hostile penetration? Was it stupid of him to initiate the practice of designating certain Family members as Warriors, superbly trained individuals responsible for preserving the Home and safeguarding the Family?"

"No," Grozny admitted.

"It was very smart of them to clear the fields all around their Home," interjected the youngest soldier.

"True," Lysenko said. "Our task is that much more difficult."

Grozny nodded at the women. "The mice come to the cats, eh?"

Lieutenant Lysenko studied one of the women. "But one of the mice sports fangs," he observed.

One of the women was armed. She was a tall blonde with prominent cheekbones, thin lips, and an intent expression. A brown shirt and green pants, both patched in several spots, covered her athletic form. Moccasins adorned her small feet.

"What kind of guns are those?" asked the youthful trooper.

"I don't know," Lysenko acknowledged.

"They arm their women?" Grozny inquired.

"What is so surprising about that?" Lieutenant Lysenko countered. "We have female soldiers in our army."

"Do you think the blonde is a Warrior?" queried the young soldier.

Lieutenant Lysenko scratched his chin, reflecting. He

had not considered the possibility of the woman being a Warrior, and he mentally chided himself for his neglect. An officer could not afford to overlook any eventuality. The mission's success and the lives of his squad depended on his perception and judgment.

"Orders?" Grozny questioned him.

The five soldiers were concealed behind trees and brush a few yards from the edge of the forest, from the end of the field.

"Move back," Lysenko instructed them. "You know the drill. And remember. General Malenkov wants a live prisoner. We will take the blonde."

"And the other two?" Grozny mentioned.

"Kill them," Lysenko directed.

The quintet melted into the foliage, Grozny and the young trooper drawing their bayonets as they blended into the bushes.

The unsuspecting women neared the tree line, the blonde in the lead. Her alert green eyes scanned the forest, probing for mutates, mutants, raiding scavengers, or any other menace. She detected a slight movement deep in the trees and stopped.

"Is something wrong?" asked one of the women behind her, a brunette wearing a faded yellow blouse and tan pants.

"I'll tell you what's wrong," quipped the third woman. She was exceptionally slim and wore a blue shirt and pants, both garments having been constructed for her by the Family Weavers. "Sherry's a Warrior."

"What's that have to do with anything?" inquired the brunette.

The third woman ran her right hand through her black hair. "Warriors are walking bundles of nerves," she said. "They have to be, in their line of work. She probably heard a twig snap, and can't decide if it's a bunny rabbit or a monster!"

"Quiet," Sherry declared.

"Give me a . . ." the black-haired woman started to speak, but the brunette gripped her right arm and motioned for silence.

Sherry raised her M.A.C. 10, listening. All she could

hear was the breeze rustling the leaves of the trees, an unusually warm breeze for an October day. The leaves were red and yellow and orange, resplendent in their fall colors. She couldn't see anything out of the ordinary, but her intuition was nagging at her mind, and over the years she'd learned to rely on her feminine intuition. It was seldom wrong.

"Should we return to the Home?" whispered the brunette.

Sherry bit her lower lip and glanced over her right shoulder at the Home. Blade's orders had been specific: escort a pair of novice Healers into the forest and guard them while they searched for wild herbs. The assignment was far from critical. But how would Blade react when he learned she'd aborted the search because of a vague troubling premonition? She decided to proceed, but cautiously. "We'll keep going," she informed the pair behind her. "But stick close to me. Don't wander off."

The brunette nodded.

The third woman rolled her brown eyes skyward.

Sherry advanced toward the woods. She could feel the comforting pressure of her Smith and Wesson .357 Combat Magnum in its holster on her right hip.

Somewhere in the depths of the northwestern Minnesota forest a bird chirped.

Sherry paused when she reached the end of the field, peering between the trunks of the trees and into the shadows of the pines.

"Let's get this over with," said the black-haired woman. Like the brunette, she was 20 years of age. Unlike the brunette, she had applied to become a Healer at her mother's insistence and not due to any innate sense of altruism.

Sherry stared at the impatient neophyte. "When I tell you to be quiet," she informed her, "you'll shut your mouth or I'll shut it for you. Understand?"

The black-haired woman bristled. "Who do you think you are, talking to me like that?"

"As you pointed out," Sherry said, "I'm a Warrior, Claudia. And as such, in times of danger, what I say goes."

"Danger?" Claudia scoffed. "What danger? Are we going to be molested by a moth?"

"Claudia!" the brunette spoke up. "Sherry is right, and you know it."

"Nobody tells me what to do, Jean!" Claudia snapped. Before Sherry or Jean could intervene, she angrily stomped into the forest.

Jean stepped up to Sherry. "Don't take her outburst personally. Claudia is upset because she knows she won't be accepted as a Healer. Our apprenticeship, our probationary period, is over in a week. And there's no way Claudia will be certified."

Sherry watched Claudia disappear behind a broad pine tree. "Why did the Elders even accept her as a trainee? She's too damn immature to be a Healer."

Jean shrugged. "You know the Elders. They probably wanted her to at least have a chance at it."

"And her mother is real close to Kant, and Kant was the Elder who recommended Claudia for Healer status," Sherry stated.

Jean seemed shocked by the implication. "The Elders would never allow anyone to unduly influence their judgment."

Sherry started walking into the woods. "The Elders aren't infallible," she said over her left shoulder.

Jean stayed on Sherry's heels. "If you'd been born in the Family, you'd never make such an accusation."

Sherry's lips tightened. True, she'd been born and raised in Canada, in a small town called Sundown located across the border from Minnesota. True too was the fact her nomination and acceptance as a Warrior could be attributed to the influence exerted by her husband, the Family's preeminent gunfighter, the Warrior known as Hickok. Perhaps, if she had been reared in the close-knit Family, she wouldn't presume to question an Elder's integrity. Jean's mild rebuke stung her, and for a few moments she was distracted, weighing the validity of the reproof instead of concentrating on the vegetation around them, on their immediate situation.

The mistake cost her.

"Where did Claudia go?" Jean asked.

The query brought Sherry out of herself. She searched the landscape ahead. "Claudia! Where are you?" she called out.

Claudia didn't answer.

"Knowing Claudia's temper the way I do," Jean mentioned, "she might just ignore you."

"She does," Sherry said, "and she'll live to regret it."

"Claudia!" Jean shouted. "Come back here!"

Sherry moved past a large pine, then up a low incline. She reached the top of the mound and glanced down. And froze.

Claudia was lying on her back at the base of the grassy mound. Her throat was slit, and blood was gushing from her neck and flowing down the front of her blue shirt and spilling over her shoulders. Her wide, lifeless eyes gaped at the azure sky.

Jean bumped into Sherry, then spotted the corpse. "Dear Spirit!" she exclaimed, horrified. "Claudia!"

Sherry twisted and shoved Jean from the mound. "Run!" she ordered. "Head for the Home!"

Jean hesitated, too stunned by Claudia's death to realize her own danger.

But Sherry knew. Her intuition had been right! Some menace was lurking in the woods! And whoever had slain Claudia had to be nearby, ready to pounce again! She crouched, cradling the M.A.C. 10.

Not a moment too soon.

A soldier in a brown uniform burst from the brush seven yards to her right.

In the instant Sherry spied him, she recognized the uniform as belonging to a Russian trooper, and knew the gun in his hand was an AK-47. Hickok had told her all about his experiences in the Capital, when he'd been captured by the Russians. Her mind processed the information in the split second it took her to react, and her finger squeezed the trigger when the Russian was still six yards off.

The Soviet soldier was stopped in midstride as the

slugs tore through his chest. His ears never heard the metallic chattering of the M.A.C. 10, because he was dead before the sound could reach them. He toppled to the hard ground without uttering a word.

Sherry swiveled, knowing there would be more, and there was another one, coming at her from her left, holding the barrel of his AK-47 as if it were a club, his legs pounding up the mound, and she fired when he was only two feet from her. The M.A.C. 10 caught him in the face, and he was flipped backwards by the impact, sprawling onto his back and sliding to a halt against a tree.

Jean!

Sherry spun, hoping the Russians hadn't gone after the aspiring Healer, but she was too late.

A stocky soldier had grabbed Jean from the rear. His left arm was clamped around her neck, while his right plunged a bayonet into her body again and again and again.

Sherry was about to let him have it in the head, when she heard the padding of rushing feet behind her. She whirled, but before she could complete the turn someone plowed into her and bore her to the earth. Strong arms gripped her wrists, preventing her from using the M.A.C. 10. She glimpsed a youthful face above her, and then something was pressed over her nose and mouth, something soft with a slight odor. Sherry heaved and strained, attempting to buck her captor, but another set of hands grabbed her shoulders and held her fast.

"We have her!" someone exulted.

Sherry's senses were swimming. She tried to focus, to use the martial fighting skills taught to her by Rikki-Tikki-Tavi, but her sluggish mind refused to obey her mental commands. Gasping, she made one last valiant effort to rise, then lost consciousness.

"We have her!" Grozny repeated, still holding her shoulders.

The young trooper, straddling her waist, nodded.

Lieutenant Lysenko, crouched to her right, removed the chloroform-soaked white cloth from her face and stood. "We must leave right away!"

"What's the hurry?" Grozny asked. "Shouldn't we bury our comrades first?"

"Fool!" Lysenko barked. "Do you want to end up like them?" He pointed to the two dead men. "The Family will have heard the shooting in the Home! They will send their Warriors after us!" He paused and gazed at the unconsious blonde. "She is quite formidable. If the other Warriors are half as good as her, we are in trouble! Come! Grozny, you carry her. Serov, you take the lead. We must reach the rendezvous point and signal for the copter to come and pick us up."

Serov grabbed his AK-47 from the ground where it had fallen, then hurried to the southeast.

Grozny grunted as he draped the blonde's body over his left shoulder. He retrieved his AK-47, clutching it in his right hand.

"Go!" Lysenko directed. "I will cover you." He picked up his AK-47 and waited while Grozny hastened into the trees. So far, so good. They had the live captive General Malenkov wanted. Leaving the dead men behind was regrettable, but it could not be helped. The Family would learn who was responsible for taking one of their vaunted Warriors, but what could they do about it? Nothing. According to the files relayed by the spy in Denver, the family only numbered about seven dozen members. Only 15 of them were Warriors. And 15 fighters, no matter how adept at their craft they might be, could hardly hope to oppose the military might of the Union of Soviet Socialist Republics.

Loud voices arose from the direction of the Home.

Lysenko followed his men, constantly surveying the foliage behind him, alert for any hint of pursuit. He thought of the reception awaiting him in Washington, and he was pleased. This mission would definitely boost his career, perhaps lead to a speedy promotion. Maybe an assignment on General Malenkov's personal staff. The prospect was exciting. General Malenkov was a man of considerable stature in the North American Central Committee, responsible for administering the occupational forces in America. The Soviets had been

fortunate during the war; they'd been able to invade and
hold a sizeable segment of the eastern U.S. New
England, a portion of New York, southern Pennsylvania, Maryland, New Jersey, southern Ohio, southern
Indiana, parts of Illinois, Kentucky, Virginia, and West
Virginia, as well as sections of North and South
Carolina were all under Soviet hegemony. The Soviets
had intended to conquer the entire country, but their
drive through Alaska and Canada had been stopped.
And their push into the deep South had been resisted
every step of the way, and eventually halted, by the
determined Southerners.

Now, over a century since World War III, the status
of the Soviet occupation was still the same. Slightly over
30 years ago, the Russians in America had lost contact
with their Motherland. Ships sent to investigate the
reason had never returned. Planes had vanished.
Communications had gone unanswered. To maintain
their military rule, the American-based Soviets had
instituted a program of forcibly impregnating selected
American women, then training and educating their
children, indoctrinating them, creating devoted
Communists every bit as loyal as any ever born on
Russian soil.

In other areas, the Russians had encountered severe
problems. Much of American's industrial might had
been crippled during the war, and the Soviets suffered
shortages in everything from food to military hardware.
Their expansion plans to the west had been thwarted by
the Civilized Zone Army. During the war, after a
neutron bomb was dropped on Washington, what was
left of the United States Government had withdrawn to
Denver, Colorado, and reorganized under the direction
of a man named Samuel Hyde, the Secretary of Health,
Education, and Welfare. Hyde had implemented
Executive Order 11490, a law few Americans had ever
known existed, enabling him to assume dictatorial
control of the area under his domination, the area sub-
sequently dubbed the Civilized Zone. Hyde's bloodline
had ruled the Civilized Zone for a century.

Then the incredible had happened. The tiny Family

had defeated the last of the dictators and his cohort, the infamous scientist known as the Doktor, and precious freedom had been restored to the people of the Civilized Zone. According to the files Lysenko had read, the Family had been aided in their epic struggle by several factions. One was an army of superb horsemen from South Dakota called the Cavalry. Another contingent of fighters had come from the subterranean city designated the Mound, located many miles east of the Home. Refugees from the ravaged Twin Cities of Minneapolis and St. Paul, calling themselves the Clan, had abetted the Warriors, as had the Flathead Indians from Montana. Afterwards, these six groups had formed into the Freedom Federation, pledging to present a united front to any adversaries and to work toward wresting the country from the savage barbarism prevalent since the collapse of civilization.

Which worried the Soviets no end. General Malenkov and the other Russian leaders viewed the Freedom Federation as their primary enemy, to be eliminated at all costs, no matter what steps might be necessary. The Family was considered to be the soul of the Freedom Federation; they were the smallest numerically, yet they exerted the greatest influence in the Freedom Federation councils. The files the spy had sent contained extensive information on the Family, but not enough to satisfy General Malenkov. He'd ordered a squad sent to capture a Family member, and then truth serum could extract pertinent information detailing the Family's exploitable weaknesses.

And here I am, Lieutenant Lysenko mentally noted as he hurried after Grozny and Serov.

Several sparrows suddenly flew from a dense bush 20 yards to the rear.

Lysenko stopped, training his AK-47 on the bush, waiting.

Nothing else happened.

Lieutenant Lysenko jogged to the southeast. He knew General Malenkov viewed this assignment as being critically important, especially in light of the recent fiasco in Philadelphia. The Soviets could not afford to conduct campaigns on two fronts. The Family's destruction was imperative. The Family was the unifying element in the Freedom Federation. Without the wise guidance of the Family, the Freedom Federation would fall apart. Or so General Malenkov believed. But how to accomplish the Family's elimination? Lysenko had participated in two policy sessions. Some high-ranking officers had wanted to send in a large force and wipe out the Family in one fell swoop. But this had been tried before, and it had signally failed. Others had advocated bombing the Home or using long-range missiles, but this idea contained crucial flaws. Soviet planes and jets were in disrepair, incapable of flying the tremendous distance involved. Their helicopters were marginally functional, too unreliable to undertake a full-scale assault of the compound. None of the aerial means, including missiles, could deliver a payload guaranteed to demolish a 30-acre expanse. And General Malenkov did not want any survivors, any martyrs to stir up the Freedom Federation. So Malenkov had proposed using deadly chemical weapons. To be completely effective, the Russians needed to know the layout of the Home, something their spy had been unable to uncover.

All of this passed through Lieutenant Lysenko's mind as he sprinted up a low hill. Fate had smiled on him. If he could pull this off, General Malenkov would be duly impressed. And when an officer was in Malenkov's favor, the sky was the limit as far as his career was concerned. Lysenko grinned. He would give anything to please his superior.

Lysenko reached the top of the hill and stopped, glancing back. He thought of the sparrows, and he wondered if they were being pursued. Except for the startled birds, there had been no other indication of anyone on their trail. The Warriors might be exceptionally competent, but it was doubtful they could chase someone through the thick forest without making *some* noise. The muted snap of a twig, or the faint rustle of a branch, could betray the stealthiest of professionals. Perfect silence, at the speed Serov, Grozny, and him were maintaining, was virtually impossible.

Or was it?

Lieutenant Lysenko started down the far side of the hill, bothered by a fact from the files he had neglected in the excitement of the moment.

What about the genetic deviates?

The brilliant Doktor had specialized in genetic engineering, in creating unique test-tube offspring, creatures combining human and animal qualities, aberrations endowed with bestial senses, yet governed by a rational intellect. Three of these genetic deviates, according to the files, now resided with the Family, had actually joined the Family in its fight with the Doktor, rebelling against their demented creator. Lysenko had heard other tales about the deviates, about their grotesque appearance and extraordinary abilities, even reports the deviates consumed humans. He quickened his pace.

The minutes dragged by.

The helicopter had deposited the squad ten miles to the southeast of the Home, in a spacious clearing in the woods. Lysenko had hidden their radio before departing for the Home. The helicopter had returned to Decatur for refueling and to await their transmission signifying their mission was completed.

Lieutenant Lysenko spotted Grozny and Serov 40 yards ahead, waiting. He ran to join them.

Grozny was on one knee, breathing heavily, the blonde on the ground beside him.

Serov was leaning against a tree, scanning the nearby vegetation.

"Why have you stopped?" Lieutenant Lysenko demanded as he reached them.

Grozny looked up. "I have carried her eight miles, sir. I am fatigued."

Lysenko frowned. "You can rest when we get to the rendezvous point. Not before. On your feet!"

Grozny slowly stood, his left hand held to his side. "So sorry, comrade, but I have a pain."

"You are becoming soft, Grozny," Lysenko snapped.

Grozny resented the insult. "Soft? Who else could carry over a hundred pounds for eight miles?"

"I could," chimed in a new voice.

The Russians whirled.

There were three of them, calmly standing between two trees, not more than ten yards to the west. The one on the right was the tallest, about five feet ten, and humanoid in aspect. The creature was naked except for a brown loincloth. Its skin was gray and leathery. A hawklike skull dominated its squat neck. Its nose was pointed, its ears no more than tiny circles of flesh on either side of its bald head. The mouth was a thin slit. The eyes contained bizarre, bright red pupils. Its expression reflected its nervousness.

The one on the left wore a black loincloth, and its feral features radiated sheer animosity. This deviate only reached four feet in height, and couldn't have weighed more than 60 pounds. Brown hair, about three inches in length, covered its entire body. Its head was outsized for its diminutive form. A long, tapered nose almost resembled a snout. Beady brown eyes shifted from trooper to trooper.

In the center was the smallest deviate, just shy of four feet tall, but weighing about as much as the feral one. A thick coat of short, grayish-brown hair or fur encased his wiry physique. A gray loincloth protected his genitals. His eyes were vivid green and slightly slanted. His ears were pointed. He resembled, for all the world, a living cat-man. Pointed nails capped his bony fingers. Amazingly, his posture conveyed a supreme nonchalance. He was even grinning, exposing his needlelike teeth. "Hi, there, chuckles!" he said to Lysenko in a high-pitched, lisping voice. "We're the Three Musketeers. I'm Athos. This"—he indicated his tall companion—"is Aramis. And this"—he nodded at the feral one—"is Porthos. We're here to shish-kebab your gonads!"

Lieutenant Lysenko recovered quickly. His initial stupefaction subsided, and he leveled his AK-47 and squeezed the trigger.

Too late.

The three . . . things . . . darted from view, taking cover behind the trees, moving with astonishing speed. One moment they were there; the next they were gone.

Lysenko's burst struck the two trees, splintering the wood, sending chips flying. He ceased firing, glancing at Grozny, jerked his head to the left.

Grozny nodded and crouched, stepping to the left of the trees.

Lysenko motioned for Serov to do likewise to the right. He waited while his men cautiously neared the trees from opposite sides, prepared to catch the genetic deviates in a cross fire.

Grozny and Serov paused, exchanged glances, and swept around the trees, weapons at the ready.

"Well?" Lysenko barked when they failed to fire.

"They're gone!" Grozny exclaimed.

"Gone? Where could they go?" Lysenko queried in disbelief.

Harsh laughter sounded from the wall of forest beyond.

Grozny and Serov backpedaled to Lysenko's side.

"What are they?" Serov hissed.

"Mutants," Lieutenant Lysenko answered. "Man-made mutants."

"They're dead mutants if they show their faces again," Grozny vowed.

From in the woods came a low, raspy question: "Should I be scared now, or later?"

More laughter.

"What do we do?" Serov asked in a soft whisper.

"You can drop your guns and give up!" ordered the one with the high, lisping voice, the cat-man. "And we'll let you live!"

"You are insane!" Lysenko shouted. "You don't even carry guns!"

The cat-man snickered. "I don't need a gun, bub! My nails will slice you open like a rotten melon!"

Grozny was peering into the vegetation. "Where the hell are they? I can't see them!"

Lieutenant Lysenko looked at the blonde. Inspiration struck. "I know you come from the Home!" he sh outed. "I know what you are!"

"I think we've just been insulted," said the low, raspy voice, seemingly coming from a tangle of brush to the left.

"If you don't come out now," Lieutenant Lysenko warned, "I will kill our prisoner!"

"I wouldn't do that, dimples, if I were you!" yelled the cat-man. "Her hubby is after your ass, and he's one mad son of a gun. His name is Hickok. Maybe you've heard of him? He's got quite a rep. I expect he'll jam his Colt Pythons up your butt and keep pullin' the triggers until the cylinders are empty!"

"I'm serious!" Lysenko repeated his threat. "I'll kill her!"

The cat-man uttered a peculiar trilling sound. "Not nice, chuckles! Not nice at all!"

Silence descended.

"Do you think they've gone?" Serov asked hopefully.

"Come out!" Lysenko bellowed.

"Please!" cried a new voice, coming from directly ahead. "Surrender, yes? Avoid bloodshed, no?"

Lieutenant Lysenko was stymied. He could hear the deviates, but couldn't see them. And he couldn't shoot what he couldn't see. He was bluffing about killing the blonde, because General Malenkov needed her alive. Lysenko suspected the damn mutants were deliberately delaying their escape, hindering them until the Warriors could arrive.

"What do we do, sir?" Serov asked anxiously.

Before Lysenko could reply, a high-pitched voice, from directly behind them, answered, "I say we play peekaboo!"

The Russians soldiers spun.

The cat-man and the feral one were already in motion. The cat-man leaped onto Grozny, burying the tapered tips of his right fingernails in Grozny's eyes, even as his left hand, his fingers pressed together, forming a compact point, speared into Grozny's throat. Grozny screamed as the cat-man tore his eyeballs from their sockets and ripped his neck from chin to chest.

Serov bravely endeavored to bring his AK-47 into play as the feral creature landed on his chest in one bound. Snarling, the deviate placed a hairy hand on either side of Serov's astounded face, then brutally wrenched Serov's head to the left. There was a distinct popping noise, and Serov slumped to the ground.

Lieutenant Lysenko had retreated several steps, unable to fire without hitting Grozny and Serov. He aimed at the feral one as Serov fell, but before he could shoot, the third mutant intervened. Steely gray arms encircled him, lifted him from the ground. The pressure was unbelievable. He felt like his chest was on the verge of being crushed. His AK-47 clattered to the earth.

The feral one was standing with its arms folded, smirking, staring at Serov.

The cat-man suddenly rose from Grozny's body, its hands soaked with blood, dripping crimson. It grinned, then glared at Lysenko. "Put the Red down, Gremlin," he said. "I want to have some fun."

Gremlin twisted his torso, holding the soldier away from his feline friend. "No, Lynx! Blade wanted them alive, yes? Must spare this one, no?"

Lynx shook his head, his ears twitching. "I just want to have a little fun with him."

"Bet me!" interjected the feral one in his low, rasping tone. "I've seen that look in your eyes before. You've got the blood lust."

"Who asked you, Ferret?" Lynx quipped.

"I know what I'm talking about," Ferret persisted. "All of us are prone to it. Maybe its part of our genetic constitution. You know as well as I that the damn Doktor designed us as his personal assassin corps."

"Yeah," Lynx concurred. "The Doc was always braggin' about being the only person able to edit the genetic instructions encoded in DNA, or some such garbage. Odds are, he intended for us to live to kill."

Gremlin shook his leathery head. "Gremlin has never had blood lust, yes? Must not be true for all of us, no?"

Lynx snickered. "Gremlin, you're such a goody-goody, you'd never kill anyone or anything just for the thrill of it."

Gremlin frowned. "There is a thrill in killing, yes?"

"For some of us," Lynx confessed. He nodded at the Red. "You're real lucky, pal. If I hadn't of given my word to Blade, you'd be mincemeat right about now."

"Listen!" Ferret exclaimed.

There was a crashing in the underbrush, and a man dashed into view, breathing heavily from the strenuous exertion of having run eight miles. He was a lean blond, with a sweeping handlebar mustache. Buckskins and moccasins covered his muscular frame. Strapped around his waist were a pair of pearl-handled Colt Python revolvers.

"Hickok!" Lynx declared. "We're having a pajama party! Care to join us?"

The gunman ignored the comment. His blue eyes swept the area, and locked on the unconscious figure of his wife. He ran up to her.

Lynx glanced at Ferret. "Is this what they mean by true love?"

Hickok knelt by Sherry's side and cradled her in his arms. He carefully examined her but couldn't find any visible injury.

"Sherry is fine, yes?" Gremlin asked hopefully.

"She'd best be," Hickok growled. He took her in his arms, then stood.

"Do you need some help?" Ferret asked.

Hickok shook his head. He walked over to the Russian officer, his seething eyes pinpoints of fury. "If you've hurt her, you bastard, you're dead! Nothing will keep me from you! No one will stop me! I'll kill you inch by miserable inch, until you beg for mercy! You understand me?"

Lieutenant Lysenko scowled.

Lynx looked at Ferret, beaming. "I love it when he talks like that!"

Hickok leaned toward the Russian. "You wipe that off your face, or I'll kill you right now!"

"Hickok!"

The speaker was new to the scene, a giant of a man, striding toward them, his massive arms and legs bulging with raw power. His hair was dark, his eyes a piercing gray, his complexion rugged. He wore a black leather vest and green fatigue pants, as well as moccasins, the typical Family footwear. A pair of Bowies, his favorite weapons, rested in their sheaths, one on each hip.

"Uh-oh!" Lynx declared. "The party-pooper is here!"

"I need him alive," the big man said to Hickok.

Hickok's lips compressed. He glanced at the giant, then nodded. "Fine by me, Blade, but I want him when you're through."

"That's not up to me," Blade said, "and you know it."

Hickok gazed at the soldier. "I'll be seein' you." He walked off, Sherry nestled in his arms.

Blade studied the dead men, then stared at Lynx. "I thought I told you I wanted them alive."

Lynx shrugged. "Couldn't be helped. Besides, we did save you one of them."

Blade moved over to Gremlin. "I'll take him from here."

"Gremlin can carry to Home for you, yes?" Gremlin asked.

"Thanks," Blade responded. "But the Warriors will take over now." He drew his right Bowie.

Gremlin released the Russian.

Lieutenant Lysenko dropped to the ground, landing on his knees. The razor edge of a Bowie was abruptly applied to his neck.

"You give me any trouble," Blade stated, "and I'll let Hickok have you! Stand up! Move!"

Lysenko obeyed.

Blade started ushering the Russian in the direction of the Home.

"Hey!" Lynx called.

Blade paused. "What?"

"What about us?" Lynx inquired. "No 'thank you'? No pat on the back? No parade in our honor?"

"I'm sure Hickok will thank you personally," Blade said. "I appreciate what you did. You three caught up with them much faster than we could have—"

"You got that right," Lynx commented.

"—but I must get this one locked up, and see how Sherry is doing, and send out a detail for the bodies of Jean and Claudia. Talk to you later," Blade remarked. He took another step, prodding the Russian officer with his Bowie.

"What about these dead troopers?" Ferret inquired. "Want us to leave them here?"

"No," Blade replied over his right shoulder. "They might attract a mutate, or something worse. Bury them."

Lynx watched the Warrior chief and the Red disappear in the trees, then turned, gesturing angrily. "How about that? We pull Sherry's fat out of the fire, and this is the thanks we get! Bury them? I say we leave 'em for the worms!"

"Blade wants them buried," Ferret said.

"So who is he? Our fairy godmother? Why do we have to listen to him?" Lynx retorted.

"You know why," Gremlin mentioned. "The Family has been nice to us, yes? Given us a place to live, when no one else would, no? We owe them, yes?"

Lynx sighed. "Yeah, I guess we do. But I've got to tell you guys something." He placed his hands on his hips. "I'm gettin' real tired of this life. I mean, I'm bored to tears! Oh, sure, the Family is as sweet a bunch of people as you'd ever want to meet. And they've been real nice to us. Feedin' us. Treatin' us like one of their own."

"What's wrong with that?" Gremlin wanted to know. "Is pleasant, yes?"

"Yeah," Lynx agreed, "but it's also a pain in the butt! Look! We were just talkin' about the good Doktor, about how he created us to be killing machines. Well, I don't know about you two clowns, but I'm dying for some excitement in my life! Something to get the blood flowin', if you know what I mean."

"I do," Ferret said, listening attentively.

"Wasting these morons was the most fun I've had in ages," Lynx went on.

"I did . . . enjoy . . . myself," Ferret acknowledged.

"See?" Lynx said. "I'll be honest with you. The

Family is so devoted to the Spirit, so involved with loving one another and being kind and courteous and all, sometimes they make me want to puke!''

Gremlin appeared to be shocked. "You exaggerate, yes?''

"A little,'' Lynx confessed. "But you get my drift.''

"So what can we do about it?'' Ferret asked.

"There's nothing we can do, no?'' Gremlin stated.

"We could leave the Home,'' Ferret suggested.

Gremlin's mouth dropped. "Ferret not serious, yes?''

"Why not?'' Ferret countered. "I like the Family too. But there might be somewhere else in the world where we'd fit in even better.''

"Gremlin never leave Home,'' Gremlin stated.

"Neither would I,'' Lynx agreed.

"But you just said—'' Ferret began.

"I said,'' Lynx replied, cutting him off, "I was bored to tears. Not stupid! We've never had it so good. The Family are our friends. We'd be idiots to cut out on them.''

"Then how do you plan to inject some excitement into your life?'' Ferret inquired skeptically.

"There has to be a way,'' Lynx declared.

"I don't see how,'' Ferret said.

"Me neither,'' Gremlin remarked.

Lynx sighed. "Well, let's get to plantin' these jerks.''

Gremlin scoured the earth for a likely spot. "Too bad we're not Warriors, yes?'' he commented absently, squatting.

Lynx's ears perked up. "What? What did you say?''

Gremlin began scooping some soft dirt from a small grassy patch. "Too bad we're not Warriors, yes? Then we could do like Blade and the others, no? Lynx have more excitement than he'd know what to do with, yes?'' Gremlin chuckled at the preposterous notion.

Lynx reacted as if he'd been zapped by a lightning bolt. He straightened, his eyes widening and gleaming from a dawning revelation. His hands shook with excitement. "That's it!''

"That's what?'' Ferret asked.

"That's how we'll do it!'' Lynx, unable to restrain his

enthusiasm, jumped up and down several times, cackling.

Ferret and Gremlin exchanged glances.

Lynx ran over to Gremlin and, before Gremlin quite knew what he was about, gave him a fleeting hug. "You did it!" he shouted in delight. "You're brilliant!"

Gremlin was flabbergasted.

"What are you babbling about?" Ferret demanded.

"Don't you see?" Lynx replied ecstatically.

"All I see," Ferret said, "is you acting like an idiot."

"You don't get it?" Lynx gazed at both of them.

"Get what?" Ferret inquired.

Lynx shook his head, grinning. "Look. I'll spell it out for you dummies! Who's responsible for the security of the Home?"

"The Warriors," Ferret answered.

"And who's pledged to protect the Family?" Lynx queried.

"The Warriors," Ferret responded.

"Exactly! And who's always gettin' involved in a fight of some kind or another in the performance of their duties?"

Ferret pursed his lips and glanced at Gremlin. "Is he leading up to what I think he's leading up to?"

Lynx smiled contentedly. "The solution is simple! If we want some excitement in our lives, some thrills to alleviate the boredom, then"—he paused—"we become Warriors!"

Ferret snorted and shook his head.

Gremlin laughed.

Lynx was offended. "What's the matter with you two? It's a great idea!"

"The only way you'll ever come up with a great idea," Ferret said, "is if you have a brain transplant."

"Very funny!" Lynx said stiffly.

"I'm not trying to hurt your feelings," Ferret stated. "But think about your proposal."

"What's wrong with it?" Lynx asked.

"Everything. For starters, the Family already has enough Warriors. Fifteen, isn't it? Divided into five Triads of three Warriors apiece. They don't need another Triad," Ferret said.

"How do you know?" Lynx countered. "Plato might like the idea."

"I'm not finished," Ferret remarked. "Being a Warrior isn't a post you take lightly. It's a major responsibility. All of those people are relying on you to safeguard them from harm. Their lives are in your hands." He paused. "It's not a job you take for the fun of it."

Gremlin snickered.

"Who said I'd take the job lightly?" Lynx demanded.

"Ferret is right," Gremlin chimed in. "Being a Warrior is very important, yes? Without Warriors, the Family would not survive in this world, no?"

"So who said I'd take it lightly?" Lynx reiterated angrily.

"Forget it," Ferret suggested.

"Who died and appointed you leader?" Lynx rejoined.

"Lynx forget it, yes?" Gremlin said, adding his opinion.

Lynx looked from one to the other. "I'm not givin' up that easily. I'll find a way to convince you."

"I don't take bribes," Ferret quipped.

Lynx's shoulders slumped dejectedly. "You know, it's true what they say."

"What do they say?" Ferret asked, walking over to assist Gremlin with the digging.

"Nobody really appreciates a genius," Lynx commented seriously.

Ferret chuckled. "Show us a genius, and we'll appreciate him."

Gremlin stared at Lynx. "Genius help us dig, yes? Or maybe genius is too good for manual labor, no?"

Lynx vented his frustration by hissing. "Ingrates!" he muttered.

Ferret nudged Gremlin. "If he's acting this crazy today, we'd best keep a close eye on him tonight."

Gremlin's forehead creased. "Why?"

"The moon will be out."

2

The Family was in an uproar by the time Blade returned to the compound. Everyone was gathered near the drawbridge, anxiously watching the Warriors and the Elders go about their business. News of the deaths of Claudia and Jean had already spread and was the main topic of discussion, along with the implications of the Soviet attack.

Blade, his prisoner in front of him, came across the drawbridge. He spotted the man he needed, a stocky Indian dressed all in green, armed with a genuine tomahawk angled through his brown belt, and an Arminius .357 revolver in a shoulder holster under his right arm. "Geronimo!" Blade called.

Geronimo shouldered his way through the throng. His brown eyes studied the Russian. "Spartacus said you wanted us to stay here until you returned," he commented.

"I'll explain everything later," Blade said. He scanned the compound. "Did Hickok make it back with Sherry?"

"Just arrived a bit ago," Geronomi replied. "Hickok wouldn't let anyone touch her. He took her to the infimary."

Blade indicated the Red soldier. "Take him there too. And don't let Hickok kill him."

"Will do." Geronimo drew the Arminius. "Let's go!" The crowd parted to permit their passage.

A diminutive man with Oriental features, dressed all in black and carrying a katana in its scabbard in his right hand, dashed up to Blade. "Orders?" he asked.

Blade sheathed his Bowie, then pointed at the forest. "Take your Triad, Rikki, and retrieve the bodies of Jean and Claudia. They're about ten to fifteen yards into the trees. You'll also find a pair of dead Russians. Strip them and bury their bodies. Bring me their belongings."

Rikki-Tikki-Tavi nodded. "We're on our way," he said, and raced off.

A tall man with his blond hair in a crew cut, wearing buckskin pants and a brown shirt, with a broadsword attached to his wide leather belt, jogged up to the head Warrior. "I kept them all back, just like you wanted," he stated.

"You did a good job, Spartacus," Blade said. "Now I want you to notify every Warrior we're on alert status. I want Gamma, Omega, and Zulu Triads on the walls within five minutes. Got that?"

"Consider it done," Spartacus responded, and left.

Blade started toward the concrete structure that housed the infirmary.

"Blade!" someone cried.

Blade turned.

It was the Family leader, Plato. His long gray hair and beard were stirred by the breeze as he approached. His wrinkled features conveyed his apprehension. He was dressed in faded jeans and a baggy blue shirt. "I need your report," he stated. "The Elders will be meeting in emergency session as soon as you provide the essential details."

"Come with me to the infirmary," Blade suggested. "I'll fill you in along the way."

Plato fell in beside Blade, and they headed in the direction of the concrete blocks.

The Home was a model of utility and conservation. The eastern half was preserved in its natural state and used for agricultural purposes. A row of log cabins for the married couples and their children occupied the middle of the 30-acre compound, extending in a line from north to south. In the western portion of the Home, grouped in a triangular configuration, were six huge concrete blocks, each designated by a letter. The Family armory was A Block, located at the southern tip of the triangle. The founder, Kurt Carpenter, had personally supervised stocking the armory with every possible weapon and insured adequate ammunition, where needed, was stockpiled. One hundred yards to the northwest of A Block was B Block, the domicile for single Family members. Another hundred yards to the northwest of B Block was the infirmary, C Block, managed by the Family Healers. An equal distance to the east of the infirmary was D Block, the spacious workshop outfitted with thousands of tools and other equipment. One hundred yards east of D Block was E Block, the gigantic Family library. Carpenter had crammed its shelves with hundreds of thousands of books, encompassing every imaginable subject. Finally, a hundred yards to the Southwest of E Block was the large building used by the Family Tillers, F Block.

"Enlighten me," Plato said.

"I was on the west wall with Hickok and Spartacus," Blade elaborated. "I'd just sent Sherry out as an escort for two new Healers."

"Yes," Plato commented. "Jean and Claudia. They were conducting their herb identification test."

"There was shooting," Blade continued. "We ran down the stairs. I found Lynx, Ferret, and Gremlin standing near the drawbridge, so I enlisted their help. Spartacus was left behind, to keep everyone back. We raced to the woods and found the bodies of two dead Russian soldiers, and"—he paused, frowning—"the bodies of the two Healers."

"What then?" Plato asked.

"I sent Lynx, Ferret, and Gremlin on ahead. They can move a lot faster than we can. They caught up with three Russians, trying to cart Sherry off. Two of the Russians were killed, but we do have an officer prisoner. That's about it," Blade succinctly concluded.

"And Sherry?"

"We'll know in a minute," Blade said.

They hurried toward C Block.

"What do you think Nathan will do if Sherry has been harmed?" Plato asked, referring to Hickok by the name his parents had bestowed upon him at birth. Each Family member, on their 16th birthday, was formally rechristened during a special Naming ceremony. Kurt Carpenter inaugurated the rite. The Founder had worried that subsequent generations might neglect their historical antecedents, might forget about the history of

humankind and the factors leading up to World War
Three. Carpenter had tried to insure his followers never
lost touch with their roots. He had persuaded them to
have their children search the history books, and when
the young men and women turned 16, they were
permitted to select the name of any historical figure they
admired as their very own. This practice became known
as the Naming, and it survived Carpenter's death. The
Family expanded on it, allowing the youths to take a
name from any book in the library. Compliance was not
mandatory, but most members adhered to the
observance. A few retained the names given them by
their parents. Even fewer created a new name of their
own. In every case, the name chosen was supposed to
reflect the personality of its holder. Thus, 16-year-old
Nathan became Hickok. The strapping Michael picked
an entirely new name, predicated on his preference for
edged weapons, and became known as Blade. Lone Elk
became Geronimo. Clayton became Plato. And 16-year-
old Chang, aspiring to achieve perfection as a martial
artist and devoted to the ideal of conserving spiritual
value and protecting the Family, became Rikki-Tikki-
Tavi.

"I expect Hickok will declare war on the Soviets,"
Blade predicted.

"At least they would be evenly matched," Plato commented.

They reached the enormous concrete block and
entered the front door. Only five people occupied the
building. Seated on a cot to the right of the entrance was
the Russian officer. Geronimo stood three feet from the
cot, his .357 trained on the officer's head. Dozens of
cots, aligned in two rows, filled the middle of the
infirmary. Medical cabinets were dispersed at prudent
intervals. On one of the cots in the center was Sherry.
Beside her knelt Hickok. Standing on the far side of the
cot was one of the Healers, a brown-haired woman
dressed in white.

Blade walked over to Sherry's cot. "How is she,
Nightingale?" he asked the Healer.

"I can answer that for you," Sherry unexpectedly

responded, and sat up. "I'm fine," she told Blade.

Hickok held up a white cloth smelling of chloroform. "Geronimo found this in one of the bastard's pockets. I reckon they wanted her alive and unhurt. Thank the Spirit!"

Sherry stared into Blade's eyes. "I let everyone down. I'm sorry."

Blade knew what she meant. "You were ambushed and outnumbered. There was no way you could have prevented the deaths of Jean and Claudia."

Sherry frowned, her profound inner turmoil evident. "Yes, there was," she said slowly. "I sensed something was wrong. I should have acted differently."

"Believe me," Blade assured her. "No one will blame you for what happened."

Sherry's green eyes mirrored her emotional agony as she replied. "Yes, there is someone. Me."

Hickok glanced up at Blade, his mouth downturned.

"I need to interrogate the Russian," Blade said. "But I want to talk with you about this later. All right?" he queried Sherry.

Sherry nodded. "I'll come see you," she promised.

Blade smiled encouragingly, then turned, Plato still at his side.

"Sherry is adversely affected by her experience," Plato commented when they were beyond hearing range.

"I know," Blade agreed. "We've both seen the same symptoms many times before. If she doesn't conquer her doubt, if she doesn't realize she didn't fail in her duty, she'll be washed up as a Warrior."

"Curious, isn't it?" Plato thoughtfully remarked. "A Warrior can be in superb physical condition, can be supremely skilled with a variety of weapons and in hand-to-hand combat, and yet, if the Warriors lacks the proper mental attitude, all the conditioning and skill in the world are wasted."

Blade nodded. They were nearing the Russian's cot. The officer was glaring at them. This one wasn't going to be easy to crack. Drastic measures were called for. "Has he given you any trouble?" Blade asked

Geronimo as they reached the cot.

"He's been a good little boy," Geronimo answered. "From the way he's been squirming, I think he needs to go potty."

"Is that right?" Blade asked. "Would you like to relieve yourself?"

The officer nodded.

"Tough," Blade snapped, and before anyone could gauge his intent, before Plato could hope to stop him, he lashed out with his right fist, catching the officer in the mouth and sending him head over heels from the cot.

"Blade!" Plato yelled.

Blade stepped over the cot and reached the officer while the Russian was still on his knees. He flicked his right foot up and out, connecting, slamming his instep into the Russian's ribs, knocking the officer onto his back.

"Blade! Stop!" Plato cried.

Blade's left hand grabbed the gasping officer under the chin. He squeezed and lifted, his arm bulging, hauling the Russian from the cement floor and into the air.

Plato went to grip Blade's arm, but Geronimo quickly stepped between them, shaking his head.

Blade drew his right Bowie and pressed the tip into the Russian's genitals.

The officer squirmed and thrashed, wheezing, his eyes bulging.

"Now that I've managed to stimulate your interest," Blade said, "I'm going to tell you how it is." He paused, his gray eyes boring into the officer's. "You killed two of my Family, you son of a bitch! I'd end your murderous career right now, but I need information. So here's how it is. I'm going to ask you some questions. If you refuse to answer them, you're dead. If you hesitate, you're dead. If I suspect you're lying, you're dead. You can tough it out and die, or you can cooperate and live. If you follow me so far, nod."

The officer nodded. Vigorously.

"Good. I want you to think about something. If you

refuse to answer, if you value loyalty more than your life, no one is ever going to know how brave you were! Your buddies, your comrades, will never know how you died! You'll have died in vain! Think about it. And about this. If you cooperate, I'll give you a canteen and some jerky and let you go. My word on it. We've released prisoners before. We're not butchers, like you. We don't kill innocent women. But, as the Spirit is my witness, I will gut you like a fish if you don't give me the answers I need." Blade unceremoniously dumped the Russian on the cot.

The officer landed on his left side. He coughed and sputtered, rubbing his neck, gaping at the giant Warrior.

Blade held the right Bowie out, slowly moving his wrist back and forth, allowing the light to gleam off the blade. "What's your name?"

"Lysenko," the officer instantly replied. "Lieutenant Frol Lysenko."

"Why were you sent here?" Blade demanded.

"To capture one of your Family alive and transport them to Washington," Lysenko responded.

"How were you going to get back?" Blade asked.

"By helicopter," Lysenko said.

Blade pondered a moment. "Is this helicopter waiting for you or are you supposed to signal it?"

"Signal," Lysenko disclosed.

"How are you to signal it?" Blade queried. "Be specific."

"We have a portable radio transmitter stashed about ten miles southeast of here," Lysenko answered.

Blade contemplated his next question. He was excited about the transmitter. If the radio could be retrieved, the Family would be able to monitor the Soviet broadcasts and perhaps learn information crucial to the continued safety of the Freedom Federation. "How did you discover the location of the Home?"

Lysenko almost laughed. He hesitated for a fraction, then recoiled in fear as the Bowie slashed toward his abdomen. "The spy!" he screamed. "The spy!"

Blade   halted   his   stroke   inches   from   Lysenko's stomach. His brow creased. "Spy? What spy?"

"We have a spy stationed in Denver," Lysenko revealed.

Blade straightened. A spy in Denver? In the capital of the Civilized Zone, one of the Family's allies? "What's the name of this spy?"

"I don't know," Lysenko said. He saw Blade's arm tense. "Honest! I really don't! General Malenkov never told me. All I know is a spy infiltrated the government of President Toland about a month ago, and has been feeding us classified information ever since."

Blade and Plato exchanged glances. President Toland was the duly elected leader of the Civilized Zone, and one of the few people aware of the Home's *exact* location. Many persons knew the Home was in Minnesota, but Minnesota contained almost 80,000 square miles. Anyone searching for the compound could waste a decade in the hunt and still come up empty.

"You mentioned General Malenkov," Blade noted. "Is this the same Malenkov Hickok encountered when he was in Washington, D.C.?"

Lysenko nodded. "Hickok's escape embarrassed the general. It was so public . . . so spectacular. And so many lives were lost! The general hates your Family. He wants you eliminated."

Blade nearly grinned. General Malenkov's reaction was understandable. Hickok, with his usual flair for mayhem, had stirred up the proverbial hornet's nest in the former American capital. "All right. You stay put. I'll be back to question you some more later." He glanced at Geronimo. "Escort him to the bathroom. Then park him here until further notice."

"You've got it," Geronimo said.

Blade looked at Plato, then nodded toward the doorway.

Plato followed the Warrior chief outside into the bright sunlight.

"Is there anything you want me to ask him?" Blade inquired.

"Not offhand," Plato said. "We are already familiar

with the Soviet system, and cognizant of their logistical
and industrial problems, thanks to Nathan." He
paused. "We must contact Toland and inform him
about the spy. Perhaps this secret agent can be apprehended." He paused again, frowning. "But there is
something I would like to discuss with you."

"What is it?"

"Before I proceed," Plato stated, "I must qualify my
complaint." He adopted a paternal air. "Blade, I know
the Founder had his reasons for organizing the Family
the way it is. I know Carpenter believed it was necessary
for the head of the Warriors to be permitted to override
the Family Leader in a time of crisis. I comprehend the
wisdom of the arrangement. And I know interrogating a
prisoner is your province." Plato sighed. "But I really
must protest your treatment of Lieutenant Lysenko."

Blade went to speak, but Plato held up his hand.

"Bear with me," Plato said. "Lysenko isn't the first
prisoner you have treated so brutally. I doubt he will be
the last. And, yes, I can recognize the validity of the
psychology behind your methods. But I want to pose a
moral issue for your consideration. Don't answer me
right away. Meditate on this." He cleared his throat.
"We, the Family, believe in the guidance of the Spirit in
our lives. We believe in exalted concepts of love and
brotherhood, don't we?"

"Yes," Blade replied.

"We are, after a fashion, symbols for those still
languishing in a squalid cultural darkness, are we not?"

"I never thought of it that way," Blade admitted.

"You should," Plato said. "Talk to some of your
friends in the Freedom Federation. You'll be surprised
at how favorably they view our accomplishments."

"What's this have to do with my methods?" Blade
asked.

"Simply this. If we claim to be living on a higher
moral and spiritual plane than those unfortunates still
suffering from the delayed ravages of the nuclear war,
don't we have a certain responsibility to them and
ourselves to conduct our behavior according to our
highest spiritual dictates?"

Blade studied his mentor. He'd always admired Plato's wisdom, and reciprocated Plato's abiding affection. But in this instance, he felt, the Family Leader was wrong. "So what you're getting at," he deduced, "is that I should treat our prisoners differently. Not be as hard on them. Is that it?"

"Precisely," Plato said, smiling. "You see my point?"

"I see it," Blade declared.

"Excellent."

"But I don't agree," Blade commented.

"Why not?"

Blade raised his right hand and pointed at the west wall. "On the other side of that wall is a world filled with evil, a world where people are murdered over trifles, a world where survival of the fittest is the norm. Oh, there are a few exceptions. The Civilized Zone. The Flathead Indians. The Cavalry. Us. But by and large, a lot of folks out there take each day as it comes, never knowing if they'll still be alive at the end of it or not. There's no peace of mind, no security. Existence is hand to mouth." He swept the compound with his hand. "Well, that's never going to happen *here!* I won't allow it! The only reason we're able to live on a higher moral and spiritual plane, as you put it, is because those walls, and the Warriors, keep all the killers, all of the degenerates, all of the power-mongers, and every other type of social parasite conceivable *outside* the Home. Not everybody lives on the same plane we do. A lot of people are outright evil. Wicked. Living to harm others." Blade leaned toward Plato. "The only methods those vermin understand are the same methods they employ. Violence. And more violence. And if that's what it takes to preserve the Family, then those are the methods I'll employ!"

This time it was Plato's turn to open his mouth to speak; instead, he mutely scrutinized his protegé. Plato had taken Blade under his wing after the death of Blade's father, had even let it be known he wanted Blade to succeed him as Family Leader after his demise. He knew Blade was an outstanding Warrior, perhaps the best the Family had ever seen. Oh, Blade wasn't as deadly as, say Hickok or Rikki or Yama. But Blade's overall temperament, despite his tendency to brood periodically, qualified him to be the top Warrior. One day, Plato hoped, if his tutelage was successful, Blade would also qualify to hold the post of Family Leader.

Blade gently placed his right hand on Plato's left shoulder. "I'm sorry if my methods disturb you. But it simply can't be helped." He somberly gazed at the west wall. "You haven't been out there, Plato. You haven't seen what it's like. The constant killing, the senseless slaughter. You must stay on your guard from the moment you leave the Home until the moment you step back inside. It's sheer hell."

"True, I haven't journeyed beyond the Home as extensively as you have," Plato acknowledged. "But I'm not naive either. I've survived attacks by a variety of mutations, the clouds, and wild animals. I saw the carnage the Trolls wrought when they invaded the Home and abducted some of our dearest friends and loved ones. If you'll recall, I readily assented to sending Alpha Triad to Fox to save the kidnapped women. I also lived through an all-out assault by the Civilized Zone Army while you were in Denver. I wasn't born yesterday. I know the postwar era is rife with bloodshed, and violence rules. I only wish we didn't need to subscribe to it."

"We have no choice," Blade stated.

Plato sighed wistfully. "I'm reluctant to admit it, but apparently you're right. It's so distressing, though, to see us pulled down to their level."

"When dealing with trash," Blade philosophized, "you have to expect to get a little dirty."

Plato scrunched up his nose. "I wish you wouldn't define it in quite those terms."

"Just thank the Spirit there's a big difference between them and us," Blade mentioned.

"Which difference do you mean?" Plato inquired.

"We may slip into the muck now and then," Blade said. "But at least we can climb out again." He paused. "Bastards like Lysenko, and the Trolls and the Doktor too, live in it. Wallow in it. Enjoy it.''

Plato deliberated for a minute. "I never considered the matter in that light."

"Try it sometime," Blade recommended. "You'll sleep better at night.''

3

Morning of the next day.

Six men and a woman were gathered near the open drawbridge in the west wall of the Home. Lieutenant Lysenko stood meekly in the middle of the group. The gunfighter, Hickok, was to his right. The Indian, Geronimo, to his left. Three other Warriors ringed him. One of them, a tall blond man in buckskin pants and a green shirt, armed with a broadsword, was familiar. Lysenko had seen Blade conversing with the man the day before in the infirmary, after Blade had returned to continue his interrogation. The Warrior with the broadsword was named Spartacus. But the other two were new to Lysenko.

One was a beautiful dusky woman with an Afro. She wore a green fatigue shirt and pants, black boots, and carried an M-16. For some mysterious reason, she couldn't seem to keep her eyes off Hickok.

The other newcomer was a youth, obviously shy of his 20th birthday, possibly even younger. His hair and eyes were brown, his eyebrows bushy. Whether deliberately or not, he wore his long hair in the same style as Hickok. His clothing was all black, and patterned after a cut Lysenko was unfamiliar with, incorporating wide lapels and tight pants legs. A revolver was strapped to his right thigh.

Blade was four feet away, arms at his side, glancing from one to the other. "You have your instructions. Any questions?"

"Yeah," Hickok said. He grinned at Lysenko. "If

this cow chip makes a break for it, can I perforate his noggin?"

"Do whatever is necessary," Blade advised, "but keep him alive until after you retrieve the radio transmitter. I don't care what happens to him afterwards."

Lysenko frowned. "You promised I would be set free if I helped you!" he protested.

"And you will be," Blade assured him.

Lysenko nodded toward Hickok. "How do I know he will do as you say? How do I know he won't decide to kill me on the way back?"

"Hickok is a Warrior," Blade stated. "He follows orders."

Hickok leaned toward the officer, smirking. "Which makes you the luckiest hombre alive."

"It's only ten miles there, and ten back," Blade addressed them. "I expect you here before dark."

"No problem," Geronimo said. In addition to his tomahawk and the Arminius, he carried a Marlin 45-70.

Blade glanced at Hickok. "All of you should take rifles or automatics," he commented.

Hickok nodded, then looked at the youth in black. "Shane, I want you to run to the armory and grab a rifle or whatever, and pick one up for Spartacus."

"I prefer a Heckler and Koch HK93," Spartacus said to Shane.

Shane started to run off.

"Whoa!" Hickok called.

Shane stopped and turned.

"Swing by my cabin, will you, and ask Sherry for my Henry?" Hickok said, referring to his cherished Navy Arms Henry Carbine.

Shane grinned, eager to please his acknowledged hero. "I'll be back in a jiffy," he promised, and sprinted to the east.

The black woman laughed. "That boy'd lick your boots clean if you asked him!"

"I'm not wearing boots," Hickok rejoined.

"Moccasins. Boots." The black woman shrugged. "It wouldn't make no nevermind to Shane. Ain't you noticed how he's put you up on a pedestal?"

"I've noticed, Bertha," Hickok said, sighing.

"Shane isn't the only one," Geronimo interjected, winking at Bertha.

"And what's that supposed to mean?" Bertha demanded.

"Oh, nothing," Geronimo responded, grinning mischievously.

Blade smiled. Bertha's long-standing crush on Hickok was common gossip around the Home. She'd been interested in the gunman ever since they'd met in Thief River Falls. Even Hickok's later marriage to Sherry hadn't dampened Bertha's ardor. Although she was regularly seen in the company of several Family men, Bertha had never taken a mate. Some said she was holding out, saving herself in the forlorn hope Hickok might one day become available. Hickok, Blade knew, was extremely uncomfortable over the situation, but didn't seem to know what to do about it. Sherry appeared to tolerate Bertha's affection for her husband, as long as the affection was kept at a distance.

There was a sudden commotion to the north.

Blade looked to his right, puzzled. There they were. At it again. Lynx, Ferret, and Gremlin. The trio had spent every waking moment since their return yesterday, arguing. He couldn't imagine the cause of their dispute, but it was evident Lynx was constantly remonstrating with the other two over something.

"I'll be back in a bit, pard," Hickok declared, and walked toward the bickering mutants. He could see Ferret and Gremlin shaking their heads, and Lynx gesturing angrily. A few of the words Lynx was saying became audible.

" . . . morons . . . couldn't find your butts . . . broad daylight . . . !"

Ferret spotted the gunman when he was still ten yards off, and quickly whispered to the other two.

The argument abruptly ceased.

Hickok chuckled as he neared them.

All three faced the gunfighter. All three were smiling serenely. All three smiles were patently phony.

"What's with you bozos?" Hickok greeted them.

"You've been spattin' like three stallions over a mare on the make!"

Lynx stretched his fake grin even wider. "Spattin'? Us? No way. We've been havin' an intelligent discussion."

Ferret snorted.

Lynx ignored him. "What can we do for you, Hickok?"

Hickok stared at each of them. "I plumb forgot yesterday. I owe you boys a debt."

"No, you don't," Lynx said.

"You saved my missus from those pricks," Hickok stated. "I wanted to thank each of you, personal-like. And let you know I'm in your debt. If there's ever anything I can do for you, just say the word."

"There's no need," Lynx declared.

"Yes, there is," Hickok disagreed.

"You're our friend," Lynx elaborated. "You've always treated us with respect. We just returned the favor."

Hickok put his right hand on Lynx's shoulder. "I'm serious about this. I'll never be able to thank you enough. Anything I can do for you, I will."

"Thanks," Lynx said, "but you don't . . ." He stopped, blinking rapidly.

"What's wrong?" Hickok asked.

"Nothin'," Lynx replied, beginning to smile again.

"I'll be seein' you," Hickok said, and began to turn away.

"Just a minute!" Lynx said, a look of triumph on his face.

Hickok paused. "What is it?"

"Can you clarify somethin' for me?" Lynx inquired.

"If I can" Hickok answered. "Shoot."

Lynx beamed at Ferret and Gremlin, then faced the gunman. "I need some info about the Warriors."

"What about them?" Hickok replied.

"To become a candidate for consideration by the Elders," Lynx said, "doesn't a person have to be nominated by a Warrior?"

"Uh-oh," Ferret interjected.

Hickok glanced at Ferret, perplexed, then answered Lynx. "We call it being sponsored. A candidate for Warrior status must be sponsored by an active Warrior before the Elders will vote on admittin' them to the Warrior ranks. Why?"

"Oh, just curious," Lynx lied. "Tell me somethin'. How many candidates can a single Warrior sponsor?"

"I don't follow you," Hickok said.

"For instance," Lynx detailed, "let's pretend two people want to become Warriors. Could a single Warrior, like yourself for example, sponsor both of them?"

Hickok pondered for a moment. "It's never been done that way before, but I reckon it would be okay."

"And what about if three people wanted to become Warriors," Lynx went on. "Could you sponsor all three?"

"I could give it a shot," Hickok said. "And I could always talk Blade, Geronimo, or one of the others into sidin' with me. Why?"

"No reason," Lynx stated. "Like I said. I was just curious."

"Are you thinkin' of becoming a Warrior?" Hickok asked.

"No, he isn't!" Ferret responded before Lynx could answer.

"Must excuse Lynx, yes?" Gremlin added. "Received bump on head yesterday, no?"

"I did not!" Lynx declared testily.

Hickok saw Shane racing from the east, his arms laden with the requested weapons. "I'll be seein' you," he told them.

"I'd like to talk to you when you get back," Lynx said.

"No, he wouldn't," Ferret remarked.

Hickok shook his head and ambled toward the drawbridge. Behind him, Lynx, Ferret, and Gremlin started up again in hushed tones.

" . . . idiots!" Lynx snapped.

" . . . not asking him!" Ferret responded.

Hickok could only distinguish a few more words as he

moved away.

" . . . had a brain . . . be dangerous!" came from Lynx.

" . . . over my dead body!" came from Ferret.

". . . be arranged!" was part of Lynx's rejoinder.

And then Hickok was out of hearing range. He wondered if Lynx did, indeed, want to become a Warrior. Hickok favored the notion. He'd seen Lynx in action during the Battle of Armageddon, as the Family liked to call the fight in Catlow, Wyoming, and he judged Lynx to be prime Warrior material. If the runt wanted sponsorin', he'd be right proud to oblige.

"Here you go!" Shane exclaimed, out of breath, holding the guns in his arms.

Spartacus took his HK93.

Hickok grabbed his Henry.

Shane was left with a Winchester Model 94 and his Llama Comanche .357 Magnum on his right hip.

Blade was standing next to Spartacus. "What was that all about?" he asked Hickok, while nodding toward the trio still debating to the north.

"Beats me, pard," Hickok admitted. "I think Lynx wants to become a Warrior, but Ferret and Gremlin don't cotton to the idea."

"Lynx a Warrior?" Blade said thoughtfully. "That's a good idea. Come to think of it, all three of them would make great Warriors."

"Maybe you should let them know," Hickok suggested.

"I'll talk to them when I get the chance," Blade said. "Right now I must find Plato." He surveyed their group. "Take care out there. May the Spirit be with you." He departed.

Hickok waved his right arm toward the drawbridge. "Let's move out! Spartacus, take the point. Shane and Bertha—the rear. Stay in sight at all times!"

The Warriors assumed their formation, and their retrieval party departed the Home. Some of the Family members ceased their activities to watch the group leave.

"You said to the southeast, right?" Hickok asked

Lysenko.

Lysenko nodded.

"Spartacus!" Hickok yelled. "Bear southeast. We'll guide you with hand signals. Stay alert!"

Spartacus nodded, moving to a position 15 yards in front of Hickok, Geronimo, and Lysenko. Bertha and Shane were an equal distance behind them.

"I hope I can find the clearing again," Lysenko commented as they crossed the field to the south of the compound.

Hickok wagged the Henry barrel in the Russian's face. "You'd best find it, you four-flushin' coyote!"

Lysenko glanced at Geronimo. "Excuse me. Is it permissible to ask you a few questions?"

"Why are you asking me?" Geronimo replied.

Lysenko motioned to Hickok. "I know he would not talk to me."

"You're not as dumb as you look," Hickok stated crisply.

Geronimo nodded. "I guess it would be all right. Blade says you've been cooperating fully with us. What do you want to know?"

"Several things," Lysenko said. "For starters, why does Hickok talk so strangely?"

Geronimo laughed. "Everybody asks the same thing. Have you ever heard of the Wild West?"

"The Old American West?" Lysenko said. "I read a little about it in one of my history classes. As you probably know, we are versed in both cultures. We study Russian and American history. And we become bilingual, speaking English and Russian fluently."

"So Hickok told us after his visit to Washington," Geronimo stated.

"Hickok talks the way he does because he likes the Old West?" Lysenko queried.

"Because he admires a man who lived way back then," Geronimo explained. "A man by the name of James Butler Hickok. The dummy in the buckskins talks the way he thinks the real Hickok would have talked."

"Most peculiar," Lysenko remarked.

"I've been saying that for years," Geronimo quipped, and laughed.

Hickok ignored them. They reached the edge of the forest and entered the trees.

"Some other aspects of your Family puzzle me," Lysenko said.

"Like what?" Geronimo responded.

"Your informal attitude, for one thing," Lynsenko stated. "You are all so relaxed in your relations. Plato is your Leader, yet not once did I observe anyone accord him any special respect. And you Warriors! Blade is your chief, yet you talk to him like you would anyone else. There is no saluting, no drill, no regimentation in your Warrior organization. You don't even wear uniforms!" he marveled.

"Why should we?" Geronimo replied.

"Regimentation promotes discipline," Lysenko commented.

"No," Geronimo corrected him, "regimentation promotes subservience. We deliberately shun formality. Our Founder was a wise man. He saw what happened to the prewar society. Everyone was required to fit into a certain mold. Behave in an acceptable manner. Wear fashionable clothes. Even trim their hair in faddish styles. If they didn't, they were considered outcasts or weird. People were denied the opportunity to express themselves, to assert their individual personality. They were manipulated by the power-mongers at every turn." He paused. "Carpenter wanted to discourage formality, so he instituted a policy allowing Family members one name, and one name only. No Mr. So-and-So. No Miss or Ms. or Mrs. He thought last names bred a sense of false civility. And he felt the same way about titles. Titles were used to make people inferior to the one with the title. There was 'Mr. President,' or 'Your Honor,' or 'Your Majesty.' Carpenter despised that practice, so he implemented a policy where each and every Family member receives a title. Whether it's Tiller, Healer, Empath, Warrior, or whatever, we're all equal socially. No one lords it over anyone else. And that's the way we prefer it."

"Amazing," Lysenko mentioned.

Hickok abruptly stopped and glared at Geronimo.

"What's wrong with you?" Geronimo asked.

"Why the blazes are you being so nice to this prick?" Hickok demanded.

"What's the harm in a little conversation?" Geronimo retorted.

Hickok stabbed his right thumb toward Lysenko. "This bastard killed two of our sisters!"

"I know that," Geronimo said slowly.

"Then how the hell can you be so friendly toward him?" Hickok queried angrily.

"Just because I'm talking to the man doesn't make me his friend!" Geronimo stated defensively.

"It does in my book!" Hickok snapped, and marched several feet ahead.

They walked in an uncomfortable silence for several minutes.

"I know it's not any consolation," Lysenko said in a restrained voice, "but I deeply regret what happened to the two women."

"Sure you do, you mangy varmint!" Hickok barked over his left shoulder.

"I do!" Lysenko insisted. "I was merely following orders—and I know that's no excuse—and I see that it was wrong."

Hickok snorted.

Lysenko glanced at the stocky Indian. "You believe me, don't you?"

Geronimo laughed. "Doesn't matter what I believe."

"But I'm sincere!" Lysenko said. "I've never felt like this before. Never felt remorse over the slaying of an enemy."

"Enemy!" Hickok exploded, whirling. "They were Healers, you Red scum! They were devoted to helpin' others! They wanted to relieve suffering and pain! And you and your rotten henchmen killed 'em!"

Lysenko blanched.

Hickok's right hand dropped near his right Python. "Not another word out of you, you hear? Don't speak unless you're spoken to! You got that?"

Lysenko nodded.

Hickok wheeled and stalked off.

Geronimo studied the broad back of his best friend, worried. He had never seen Hickok so emotional over the death of a Family member, or in this case two, before. The gunman was hotheaded at times, even reckless on occasion. But he rarely permitted his feelings to impair his better judgment. So why was Hickok acting so temperamentally now? Was it because Sherry had nearly been abducted? Was Hickok regretting having agreed to Sherry becoming a Warrior? Or was it something else? Hickok had loved another woman before Sherry, a Warrior named Joan. Joan had been slain in the line of duty, despite Hickok's efforts to protect her from harm. Had the unsettling incident with Sherry and the Russians rekindled his anxiety? Was the gunman tormented by the prospect of losing Sherry too? Geronimo increased his speed, caught up with his friend.

"What do you want?" Hickok barked. "Why don't you stick with your Commie buddy?"

Geronimo's brown eyes narrowed. "That crack was uncalled for, and you damn well know it!"

Hickok didn't reply.

"Nathan," Geronimo said, "I'm sorry."

"You should be!" Hickok said.

"Not for talking to Lysenko," Geronimo stated. "You know as well as I why I did it."

"Oh? Do I?" Hickok rejoined acidly.

"Yeah. We covered it in our Warrior Psychology Class, remember? How if you engage an enemy in idle chitchat, sometimes they'll let an important fact slip without realizing it," Geronimo elaborated.

"Whoop-de-do for psychology!" Hickok commented.

Geronimo frowned. "Cut the crap and listen to me! I said I was sorry. Not about Lysenko. But about you."

"Me?"

"Yeah, dimwit. I should have realized sooner how upset you were about Sherry. I should have been more sensitive to the hurt you're feeling inside. For that, I'm sorry," Geronimo declared.

Hickok glanced at the man who knew him better than anyone else, except perhaps Blade. His blue eyes were troubled. "I almost lost her!" he exclaimed in a tortured whisper.

"But you didn't," Geronimo reminded him.

"I would have," Hickok said, "if it hadn't been for Lynx and the others. They could trail the Russians by scent, and do in minutes what would have taken us hours tryin' to find tracks." He paused, then visibly shivered. "I almost lost her, Geronimo!"

"Don't be so hard on yourself," Geronimo advised. "It wasn't your fault."

"You know," Hickok said softly, for once neglecting to use his Wild West jargon, "I don't know if I could stand to have it happen again. Losing Joan was terrible, the worst experience in my life. When Sherry first told me she wanted to become a Warrior, I really came close to telling her we were through if she did. But I decided I couldn't put a leash on her, couldn't make her live the kind of life I figured was right for her. She has a mind of her own. She can make her own decisions."

"I think you did the right thing," Geronimo remarked.

"I thought so too," Hickok concurred. "But now I'm not so sure." He stared into Geronimo's eyes. "If I lose her, I don't know what I'll do."

"Why worry about it?" Geronimo asked. "Like you said, Sherry has a mind of her own. You couldn't have stopped her from becoming a Warrior, even if you wanted to. The best you can do now is to hang in there, to be there when she needs you, and pray nothing happens to her."

"I reckon you're right," Hickok observed. He exhaled noisily. "Danged contrary females!"

"Look!" Geronimo suddenly exclaimed, pointing directly ahead.

Hickok looked.

Spartacus was hiding behind a tree trunk, motioning for them to take cover.

Hickok whirled. He saw Bertha and Shane, about 15 yards off, watching him intently. He waved for them to go to ground.

Geronimo grabbed Lysenko's right arm and pulled the officer around a dense bush.

Hickok spotted a low boulder five yards to his left. He ran to the rock and crouched. What in the blazes was it? he wondered. He cradled the Henry and peered over the top of the boulder.

Just in time.

The cause of Spartacus's alarm plodded into view. Once, the monstrosity might have been a whitetail buck, hardly a menace to humans. But now the hapless buck had been transformed, changed into a hairless, pus-covered horror by the regenerating chemical clouds, one of the many biological-warfare elements employed during World War Three. Ordinary mammals, reptiles, and amphibians could undergo the same revolting meta-morphosis. Hair and scales would fall off, and be replaced by blistering sores. Green mucus would spew from their ears and nose. Their teeth would yellow and rot. And they would become rabid engines of destruc-tion, existing only to kill every living thing in their path.

The buck had stopped ten yards from Spartacus's tree loudly sniffing the air.

Hickok hoped the critter wouldn't detect their scent. This buck sported a huge rack, six points on one side alone, more than enough to inflict a fatal wound. And he knew the mutate would charge at the slightest provocation.

The Family employed different, but similar, terms to describe the various mutations proliferating since the Big Blast, as they called World War Three. The pus-covered chemically spawned creatures were known as mutates. The mutations resulting from the massive amount of radiation unleashed on the environment, producing aberrations like two-headed wolves and snakes with nine eyes, were simply labeled mutants. Insects were subject to inexplicable strains of giantism. And, finally, there were the scientifically manufactured mutations, the genetically engineered deviations. The nefarious Doktor had been responsible for Lynx, Ferret, and Gremlin, and a horde just like them. But the Doktor hadn't been

the only one to tamper with nature. Hickok had read
books in the Family library, books detailing the experiments conducted by dozens of scientists shortly before
the Big Blast. Experiments intended to create new life
forms. Better life forms. They hadn't always worked as
designed. Hickok remembered reading about one such
experiment in particular, one conducted in a laboratory in
New York City. The genetic engineers had endeavored to
bring into being a superior chimpanzee by fusing a chimp
and human embryo; the resultant insane deviate had murdered 14 innocent people before it was brought to bay. The
gunman ruminated on all of this as the mutate advanced
several steps in his direction, still sniffing the air.

Spartacus was flat against the trunk of the tree.

The buck was now five yards from the tree, eyeing the
surrounding vegetation.

Hickok glanced over his right shoulder, but he
couldn't see any sign of Bertha and Shane. Perfect! The
mutate would wander off if they stayed concealed.

Someone sneezed.

The sound emanated from behind the bush screening
Geronimo and Lysenko.

Instantly, the mutate bounded toward the bush.

Geronimo stepped into sight, his Marlin 45-70 pressed
against his shoulder, and the big gun boomed while the
mutate was in midair.

The mutate was struck in the left shoulder, pus and
skin spraying in every direction. The impact of the 45-70
twisted the mutate to the left, deflecting it from its
course, and it landed on all fours, tensing for another
leap at the human in green. But it was now two yards to
the left of Spartacus's tree, in a clear line of fire.

Hickok rose up from behind the bounder, his Henry
thundering, once, twice, three times in all, and each shot
rocked the mutate as it was hit in the side.

Spartacus joined in with his HK93, the automatic
chattering, the slugs ripping the mutate from its tail to
its neck.

The mutate trembled as it was blasted again and
again, uttering a harsh gurgling sound as it sank to its
knees. The firing stopped.

That's when Shane dashed up to the mutate and jammed the barrel of his Winchester into its left eye. He squeezed the trigger, and the mutate's brains and an ample quantity of pus and mucus blew out the right side of its head.

The mutate dropped to the ground.

In the ensuring quiet, someone sneezed again.

Lieutenant Lysenko walked around the bush, the fingers of his right hand pinching his nose.

Hickok stepped up to the Russian. "What the blazes were you doin'? Tryin' to get us killed?"

Lysenko removed his fingers from his nose. "Sorry."

"Sorry don't make it, polecat!" Hickok said.

"I tried to prevent it," Lysenko stated.

"If it happens again," Hickok assured him, "you won't have a nose left to sneeze with!" He spun. "Let's move out!"

Geronimo fell in beside the Russian as they resumed their trek.

Lysenko looked over his right shoulder at the dead mutate. "I've heard of them, but I've never seen one before. They're horrible!"

"My Family calls them mutates," Geronimo noted. "They're all over the forest."

"We've cleared any mutations out of the cities and towns," Lysenko revealed. "But we still receive reports of them from the rural areas."

"Yep. They're all over," Geronimo reiterated. "I hope you can run fast."

Lysenko glanced at the Indian. "Why do you say that?"

"Blade's planning to release you after we retrieve the transmitter, isn't he?" Geronimo innocently asked.

"Yes," Lysenko replied slowly.

"And he'll supply you with a canteen and some jerky, right?" Geronimo said.

"Yes. So?"

"So a canteen isn't much of a weapon when it comes to facing a mutate, or any of the other . . . things . . . in the woods," Geronimo declared, suppressing a grin.

Lieutenant Lysenko stared at the trees and brush

around them. His forehead furrowed and he chewed on
his lower lip. "Surely Blade will allow me to take a
firearm," he said hopefully.

"Nope." Geronimo shook his head. "Sorry. But it's
not our policy to arm our enemies. We've taken
prisoners before, and we've always let the ones leave
who wanted to leave. We've supplied them with a
canteen and jerky, enough for a couple of days."
Geronimo deliberately pretended to be distracted by a
starling winging overhead. He feigned a yawn. "Funny,
though."

"What is?" Lysenko immediately inquired.

"We don't think any of them ever made it to
civilization," Geronimo mentioned.

"How would you know that?" Lysenko asked.

"We've followed a few of their tracks," Geronimo
fibbed.

Lysenko leaned forward. "And?" he goaded the
Warrior.

"And they just up and vanished into thin air,"
Geronimo said guilelessly.

Lieutenant Lysenko frowned.

"Oh! Wait!" Geronimo exclaimed.

"What?" Lysenko prompted.

"There was one we found. Well kind of. All we
located was his torn, bloody shirt." Geronimo looked
away so the Russian couldn't behold the twinkle in his
eyes.

Lieutenant Lysenko began chewing on his lower lip in
earnest.

4

"You wanted to talk to me?" Blade asked.

"Yes," Lieutenant Lysenko said, sounding irritated.

The retrieval party had returned at dusk with the
radio transmitter. They had reached the clearing, found

the radio, and returned without mishap. Once, in the distance, they'd seen a huge . . . thing . . . moving through the trees, but it hadn't seen them. Hickok, following Blade's instructions, had carted the radio to Plato's cabin. Spartacus, Shane, and Bertha had gone to B Block for their evening meal. Geronimo, with Lysenko in tow, had found Blade in the open area between the blocks and informed the Warrior chief that the Russian "wants a few words with you." Now, Geronimo stood eight feet away, his hands folded behind his back, whistling.

"What about?" Blade inquired.

"You know damn well what about!" Lysenko snapped. "Did you really think you'd get away with it?"

Blade, completely mystified, glanced at Geronimo. He noticed Geronimo seemed to be on the verge of laughing aloud. "Get away with what?"

"Don't play innocent with me!" Lysenko said. "I know all about it! Geronimo gave it away!"

"Oh, he did, did he?" Blade replied.

"Yes! And I'm telling you now that I won't leave here without a weapon!" Lysenko declared.

"Is that so?"

Lysenko mustered the courage to square his shoulders and face up to the giant Warrior. "Yes! I cooperated with you, didn't I? I led your people to the transmitter, didn't I?"

"Yes," Blade conceded.

"Then how can you send me out there to die?" Lysenko queried belligerently. "I know you said you've give me a canteen and jerky, but that's not enough! I've seen what's out there! I wouldn't last two days without a weapon!"

"I don't know . . ." Blade said.

"You don't have to give me one of your weapons," Lysenko stated. "Just hand over one of the AK-47's my men and I brought here."

Blade raised his right hand and scratched his chin.

"Listen!" Lysenko said, lowering his voice and inching closer to the Warrior. "Would you give me one of the AK-47's if I provided you with some classified information? How about it? The information in exchange for an AK-47?''

"What information could you possibly have?'' Blade remarked disinterestedly.

"Something important,'' Lysenko answered.

"We already know General Malenkov wants us dead,'' Blade said. "And you've told us all you know about the spy in Denver. Unless''—his eyes narrowed—"you were holding back on us.''

"No! I told you the truth about the spy!'' Lysenko declared. "This is something else. Something of possible value to you and the entire Freedom Federation!''

"I'll listen to it,'' Blade stated.

"And do I get an AK-47?'' Lysenko asked eagerly.

Blade sighed. "Tell you what I'll do. If the information is of value to the Freedom Federation, you'll get an AK-47 and all the ammunition you can carry. But if it isn't . . .'' He let the sentence trail off.

"It will be!'' Lysenko promised. He glanced around, then looked at Blade. "We were attacked.''

"Attacked? By who? The Southerners?''

"No!'' Lysenko responded, scoffing. "Not the wretched Rebels!''

"Then who attacked you?''

The Vikings!'' Lysenko whispered.

"The what?'' Blade replied skeptically.

"Hear me out,'' Lysenko said. "Two weeks ago Philadelphia was attacked. As you undoubtedly know, Philadelphia is under our control. It wasn't razed during the war like New York City. Our naval forces established a beachhead at Philadelphia at the outset of the war, and it was spared a nuclear strike. There are two million people residing there now. We have a major training center there for our officer corps. It's one of the few cities on the East Coast still resembling the kinds of cities they had before the war. The rest were extensively damaged or obliterated.''

"What's this about Philadelphia being attacked?'' Blade asked, goading the Russian.

Lysenko nodded. "They came in on ships. *Wooden* ships! Just like the ancient Vikings! There were thousands of them, and they were well armed. The design of their ships might have been antiquated, but their weapons were modern, at least the type prevalent before the war."

"There were thousands of ships?" Blade repeated doubtfully.

"No!" Lysenko said impatiently. "There were thousands of these Vikings. Our intelligence experts estimated there were no more than fifty ships in their fleet, with about one hundred Vikings for each ship. They came in under the cover of a heavy fog, and they were ashore before we knew it."

"Where were your ships?" Blade casually asked. "Weren't they patroling the port area?"

"Our ships?" Lysenko said, chuckling. "If you'd seen the condition of our navy, you wouldn't ask such a foolish question."

"In pitiful shape, huh?" Blade said.

"Worse than that," Lysenko disclosed. "Most of our ships were dry-docked decades ago. We lack the necessary repair facilities, and our manufacturing capability is practically nil. The few functional vessels we did have departed for the Motherland and then never returned. Several other vessels have ventured out to sea over the years, but they disappeared without a trace, just like your prisoners Geronimo told me about."

Geronimo began whistling a bit louder.

"Tell me about these Vikings," Blade urged.

"I only know what I saw detailed in the report," Lysenko said. "Approximately five thousand of them plundered and pillaged eastern Philadelphia for several hours, before our forces were mustered and pushed them back to the sea. They escaped in their ships, along with hundreds of captives and booty. Over six hundred of our men were killed, and seventy-four officers. I think the report said there were over fifteen hundred civilian casualties."

"Where did these Vikings come from?" Blade inquired.

"We don't know," Lysenko admitted. "We captured a dozen of them, and they're being held at a detention facility in Philadelphia while the Committee for State Security interrogates them."

"The Committee for State Security?"

"Yes. I believe the Committee was better known to America as the KGB," Lysenko stated.

"I recall reading about the KGB," Blade said.

"Yes," Lysenko commented proudly. "The KGB will elicit all the information we require on these Vikings, as they call themselves."

"And as far as you know," Blade stated, "the Vikings you captured are still alive?"

"So far as I know," Lysenko responded.

Blade pursed his lips.

"Do I get an AK-47?" Lysenko asked hopefully. He was mentally congratulating himself on his cleverness. It was true the information concerning the Vikings was classified, but he couldn't see where it was of any value to the Family or the Freedom Federation. They were hundreds of miles from any ocean. And should the Federation undertake to contact the Vikings, the outcome would be dubious. An alliance between the Vikings and the Freedom Federation was inconceivable. Essentially, he had just provided worthless information in exchange for a valuable weapon, a weapon he would need if he was to return to his unit. "Do I get an AK-47?" Lysenko repeated.

Blade nodded. "You were right. This information is important. You'll receive an AK-47 and all the ammo you can carry. Fair enough?"

Lysenko was beaming. "Fair enough."

"You must be hungry," Blade said. "Why don't you head toward B Block"—he pointed at the concrete structure—"and I'll be right behind you."

Lysenko nodded. "I can hardly wait to leave tomorrow." He took a step, then stopped. "It will be tomorrow, won't it?"

"It looks that way," Blade said.

Lysenko strode toward B Block.

Geronimo strolled over to Blade, and together they

slowly followed the Russian, staying about ten yards to his rear.

"He fell for it," Blade mentioned.

"So I noticed," Geronimo said, smirking.

"You overheard?" Blade asked.

"Every word," Geronimo confirmed.

"My compliments," Blade stated. "I expected him to willingly supply additional information, but I didn't expect the bit about the Vikings."

"I did exactly as you wanted," Geronimo commented. "You should have seen the look on his face when I told him about the alleged bloody shirt we found!" He laughed.

"There was no need to tell him we always allow anyone who leaves to take arms," Blade said. "He was right about that. No one would last two days out there without a weapon."

"You're going to inform Plato?" Geronimo inquired.

"Of course," Blade replied. "I want you to keep an eye on our Russian 'friend' while I go to Plato's cabin."

Geronimo stared into Blade's eyes. "You know what's going to happen, don't you?"

Blade sighed. "Yep. Plato will call a council of the Elders, and the Elders will decide to send the SEAL to Philadelphia."

"You don't have to go, you know," Geronimo said.

"Yes I do," Blade said disagreeing. "I'm the head Warrior. It's my responsibility. Besides, I've had the most experience driving the SEAL."

"Hickok can drive it," Geronimo remarked. "And I've practiced a few times."

"I appreciate the thought," Blade noted, thanking him, "but we both know Plato will want me to go."

"I get the impression you don't like these extended trips," Geronimo commented.

"I don't like being away from my family," Blade said sadly. "Jenny and little Gabe are my life. I don't get to see enough of them as it is. These long runs only make the situation worse."

"You could always relinquish your post and become

a Tiller," Geronimo suggested. "Or maybe a Weaver. You'd be real good with a needle."

Blade chuckled. "I'd belt you in the mouth, but I need you to watch Lysenko while I confer with Plato and the Elders."

"Will Hickok and I be going with you?" Geronimo asked.

"I don't know. Why?"

"Nathan isn't in the best frame of mind right now," Geronimo explained. "I had a talk with him today. He's pretty rattled over what happened to Sherry. He might be too distracted to perform effectively."

"Thanks for telling me," Blade said. "If that's the case, I'll have the Warriors draw lots. The two short straws will go, regardless of Triad affiliation."

"Like you did when you went to St. Louis," Geronimo commented.

"You've got it." Blade started to veer off toward the east.

"Hey!" Geronimo said.

"What?"

"Where do you think you'll be this time tomorrow?" Geronimo queried him.

Blade mused for a moment. "Probably the Twin Cities."

Geronimo grinned. "Your favorite vacation spot in all the world!"

5

As it turned out, Blade underestimated. The SEAL stopped for the night just south of what was once Mason City, Iowa. Like many cities and towns, Mason City had been abandoned during the war when the government had evacuated all citizens into the Rocky Mountain and Plains states. Now, Mason City was comprised of darkened ruins, situated in no-man's-land, with the Civilized Zone to the west, the Soviet-occupied territory to the southeast, and Chicago far to the east.

Blade had pushed the SEAL the first day. The SEAL had been the Founder's pride and joy. Kurt Carpenter had expended millions on the transport. Carpenter had foreseen the collapse of mass transportation and the public highway system. Accordingly, he'd provided for the Family's transportation needs by having a special vehicle constructed to his specifications. The scientists and engineers he'd employed were all experts in their chosen fields, and they'd given Carpenter his money's worth.

The SEAL was a prototype, revolutionary in its design and capabilities. The Solar Energized Amphibious or Land Recreational Vehicle—or SEAL, as it became known—was, as its name indicated, powered by the sun. The light was collected by a pair of solar panels affixed to the roof of the vanlike transport. The energy was converted and stored in unique batteries located in a lead-lined case under the SEAL. The floor was an impervious metal alloy. The body, the entire shell, was composed of a heat-resistant and virtually shatterproof plastic, fabricated to be indestructible. Four huge puncture-resistant tires, each four feet high and two feet wide, supported the vehicle.

Carpenter had wanted additional features added to the transport, and to incorporate them he'd turned to weapons specialists, to hired mercenaries. The military men had outfitted the vehicle with an array of armaments. Four toggle switches on the dashboard activated the SEAL's firepower. A pair of 50-caliber machine guns were hidden in recessed compartments under each front headlight. When the toggle marked M was thrown, a small metal plate would slide upward and the machine guns would automatically fire. A miniaturized surface-to-air missile was mounted in the roof above the driver's seat. Once the toggle labeled S was activated, a panel in the roof slid aside and a missile was launched. The missiles were heat-seeking Stingers with a range of ten miles. A rocket launcher was secreted in the center of the front grill, and the rocket was instantly fired if the R toggle was thrown. And finally, Carpenter had had the mercenaries include a flamethrower in the SEAL. It was an Army Surplus Model with an effective range of 20 feet. Located in the middle of the front fender, surrounded by layers of insulation, the flamethrower was activated when the F toggle was moved.

Blade gazed out the windshield at the night. The SEAL's body was tinted green, allowing those within to see out, but anyone outside was unable to view the interior. He stared up at the starry sky, then twisted in his bucket seat to check out his traveling companions. A console was situated between his bucket seat and the other bucket seat in the front of the transport. Behind the bucket seats, running the width of the vehicle, was another seat for passengers. The rear of the SEAL, comprising a third of its inside space, was devoted to a large storage area for spare parts, tools, and whatever provisions were necessary.

"We're makin' good time, ain't we, Big Guy?" Bertha asked. She was seated in the other bucket seat, her M-16 snuggled in her lap.

"So far, so good," Blade acknowledged. He glanced at the two passengers occupying the wide seat. "How are we holding up?"

Lieutenant Frol Lysenko was seated behind Bertha. His face conveyed his intense misery. Arms folded in front of him, hunched over dejectedly, he glared at the giant Warrior behind the wheel. "You lied to me!" he whined for the umpteenth time that day.

"No I didn't," Blade rejoined.

"Yes you did!" Lysenko snapped. "You promised me my freedom! You said I could have an AK-47 and ammo. Not to mention the canteen and jerky."

Blade smiled. "I beg to differ. I told you that you would be able to leave the Home, and you left it at sunrise this morning. There are several canteens and five pounds of venison jerky stored in the back of the SEAL. Take your pick."

Lysenko glowered at the Warrior.

"As for the AK-47," Blade went on, "we gave you one, remember? It's not our fault you didn't want it."

"Damn you!" Lysenko spat. "What good would it have done me? Sure, you offered me an AK-47 this morning! And you also offered me ten magazines of ammo . . . but it wasn't AK-47 ammo!"

Blade shrugged. "I kept my word. I promised to give you an AK-47 and all the ammunition you could carry. I never said the ammo would be for the AK-47."

"You devious son of a bitch!" Lysenko said.

Bertha glanced at Blade. "Do you want me to bop this sucker for you?"

"No need," Blade replied.

"I wouldn't let him talk to me that way," Bertha commented.

Lysenko made the mistake of leaning forward, sneering. "Oh? And what would you do, woman?" He accented the last word contemptuously.

The M-16 was up and around in the blink of the eye, the barrel rammed into Lysenko's nose.

The Russian gulped and blinked.

Bertha smiled sweetly, her brown eyes dancing with mirth. "You ever talk to me like that again, honky, and I'll waste you on the spot. Got that, ugly?"

Lysenko nodded.

Blade grinned. He enjoyed Bertha's company immensely. They had shared many an adventure over the years, ever since Alpha Triad had rescued her from the Watchers in Thief River Falls. She had assisted them in the Twin Cities, and later had been of inestimable help in the Family's fight against the wicked Doktor. Although she had been born and reared in the Twin Cities, and spent most of her life involved in the bitter gang warfare there, Bertha had been accepted as a Warrior based on her prior service to the Family. Blade, Hickok, and Geronimo had appealed to the Elders to approve her nomination. Hickok had made a rare, yet oddly eloquent speech calling for her installation as a Warrior, saying at one point, as Blade recalled: "If Bertha ain't fit to be a Warrior, then neither am I, or Blade, or Geronimo, or Rikki. Bertha may not have been raised in the Home, but she's as Family as can be. And, more importantly, she's a born Warrior in her heart. That feisty female can whip her weight in wildcats. So you'd best approve her application, or she'll most likely storm in here and punch you out." Blade could still remember the amused expressions of the assembled Elders.

Bertha turned toward the fourth member of their little group. He was seated behind Blade, dressed in a fancy gray shirt and trousers, both tailor-made for him by the Family Weavers. The shirt had wide lapels and black buttons; the pants legs were flared at the bottom. He wore a wide black belt with a silver buckle. Nestled in a black shoulder holster under each arm was an L.A.R. Grizzly. The Grizzly was an automatic pistol with a seven-shot magazine, chambered for the devastating .45 Winchester Magnum cartridge. Its grips were black, but the rest of it was shining silver. The man wore his black hair neatly trimmed around the ears, and a full black mustache added to his strikingly handsome appearance. "What's with you, Sundance?" Bertha asked. "You've hardly said a word this whole trip so far."

The Warrior called Sundance shrugged. "What did you want me to say?"

"Anything would've been nice," Bertha remarked. "You sure ain't the talkative type, are you?"

"Guess not," Sundance responded in his low voice.

Bertha pointed at the Grizzlies. "I've been meanin' to ask you. Are you any good with those pistols of yours?"

"Fair," Sundance laconically answered.

"You as good as Hickok?" Bertha inquired.

"Maybe," Sundance said.

Bertha threw back her head and laughed. She reached over and tapped Blade on the shoulder. "Did you hear this idiot? He thinks he's as good as White Meat!" White Meat was her pet term for Hickok.

"I've seen Sundance practice," Blade mentioned. "He's real fast, Bertha."

"Maybe so," Bertha stated, "but there ain't no way he could beat White Meat, and you know it."

"That depends," Blade said.

"On what?" Bertha retorted.

"On how you mean it," Blade explained. "If you mean fast on the draw, then I'd have to agree with you. I've never seen anyone who can draw as fast as Hickok. But, on the other hand, if you mean fast in firing a gun, then Sundance might have the edge."

"What?" Bertha said skeptically.

Blade nodded toward Sundance. "He uses automatic pistols, Bertha, Hickok prefers his Colt Pythons, and they're revolvers."

"So?" Bertha responded.

"So have you ever compared a pistol and a revolver?" Blade asked.

"No," Bertha admitted.

"You should sometime," Blade recommended. "We have a lot of books in the Family library on guns. Dozens and dozens of books, covering everything from bullet-making to replacing busted stocks. We know pistols and revolvers were popular before the Big Blast, and we also know there was considerable controversy over whether a pistol or a revolver could fire faster."

"What do you think?" Bertha queried.

"I'm getting to that," Blade said. "The experts debated the pros and cons of both types. Automatic pistols, as a rule, hold more rounds than a standard revolver. Sundance's Grizzlies, for instance, hold seven rounds in the magazine, while Hickok's Pythons usually hold five."

"Five?" Bertha said, surprised. "But the cylinders in the Pythons can hold six bullets."

"True," Blade conceded, "but Hickok seldom keeps a round under the hammer. Most professionals don't. Less chance of an accident that way." He paused. "The revolver is normally thicker and slightly bulkier than a pistol. But in reliability, when it comes to things like jamming and dud rounds, the revolver is considered superior. In the accuracy department, both are even when used by a skilled gunman. Revolvers can handle broader load ranges than most pistols, and that's a plus."

"But what about bein' fast?" Bertha interrupted

impatiently.

"I'm getting to that," Blade reiterated. "When it comes to speed, you have to keep in mind the type of revolver we're talking about. With a single-action revolver, you have to pull back the hammer before squeezing the trigger, and that definitely slows you down. Hickok's Pythons, on the other hand, are double-action, meaning he can fire either way, by squeezing just the trigger or by pulling back the hammer and then shooting. Double-actions have an edge over single-actions in that respect."

"But what about bein' fast?" Bertha asked, sounding peeved.

"I'm getting to that," Blade repeated again.

"This year or next?" Bertha rejoined.

Blade grinned. "In our last trade exchange with the Civilized Zone, we received two stopwatches."

"Two what?" Bertha inquired.

"Stopwatches," Blade said. "You know what a watch is, don't you?"

"Of course!" Bertha stated. "Do you think I'm a dummy? I saw a lot of watches on the Watchers . . ." She stopped, then laughed. "Watches on the Watchers! Get it?"

Blade sighed. "I get it."

"I know the Family didn't use watches years ago," Bertha mentioned. "But I've seen a few around since you started tradin' with the rest of the Freedom Federation. So what's a stopwatch?"

"It can measure how fast someone moves," Blade detailed.

"Really?"

"Really," Blade affirmed. "And Geronimo used one to time Hickok, to see how fast Nathan could draw and fire five shots."

"How did White Meat do?" Bertha asked him.

"Hickok drew and fired all five shots in his right Python in two-fifths of a second," Blade answered.

"Is that fast?" Bertha asked.

"Let me put it to you this way," Blade said. "If you'd blinked, you would have missed it."

"That fast, huh?" Sundance interjected.

"Yep," Blade confirmed.

Bertha smiled triumphantly. "So that means White Meat would beat Sundance's cute butt no problem, right?"

"Not necessarily," Blade said.

"Cute butt?" Sundance interjected again.

"Now what the hell does that mean?" Bertha demanded of Blade.

"Cute butt?" Sundance repeated.

"It means," Blade said, "Hickok can draw his Pythons faster than Sundance can draw his Grizzlies . . . ."

Bertha stuck her tongue out at Sundance.

" . . . but I don't think Hickok can empty his guns faster than Sundance can empty his," Blade concluded.

"What?" Bertha stated. "But you just said—"

"I wish you would listen to me," Blade said, cutting her short. "Yes, Hickok is faster on the draw, but only by a fraction. And yes, his double-action revolvers are the equal of most pistols. But I've seen both men shoot, and I believe Sundance can empty his Grizzlies a teensy bit faster. Does that answer your question?"

"It doesn't answer mine!" Lieutenant Lysenko snapped.

Blade turned in his seat. "You have a question?"

"Yes!" Lysenko snapped. "When the hell are you going to turn off the overhead light and let me sleep in peace and quiet? All this babble is extremely annoying!"

Bertha looked at Blade. "*Please* let me bop him in the head!"

"We need him," Blade told her.

"Need me?" Lysenko said. "For what? You won't get any more information out of me, not after the way you tricked me. I don't see why you brought me along!"

"Consider yourself our tour guide," Blade commented.

"You made the biggest mistake of your life when you screwed me over," Lysenko warned.

"Oh!" Bertha exclaimed. "Somebody catch me! I

think I'm goin' to faint from fright!" She tittered.

"Have your fun while you can," Lysenko said.
"What goes around, comes around."

"Blade," Sundance said.

"Yeah?"

"Can anyone see inside when the overhead light is
on?" Sundance inquired, staring out his side of the
SEAL.

"No. No one can see inside, no matter what. Why?"
Blade replied.

Sundance motioned with his head. "Because we have
company."

Blade stared into the night. "Where?"

"At the edge of trees. Keep your eyes peeled,"
Sundance said. "You'll see them moving from trunk to
trunk."

Although he knew they were invisible inside the
transport, Blade reached up and switched off the
overhead light anyway. If they had to open the doors,
the light would reveal them to any foes outside. He
scanned the row of trees on his side of the transport.
The SEAL was parked on the shoulder of U.S. Highway
65 two miles south of Mason City. Like the majority of
highways and roads, U.S. Highway 65 was in
deplorable, but passable, shape. Potholes dotted the
highway, intermixed with ruts, buckled sections, and
even stretches where the road had been totally destroyed
by the twin ravages of time and nature. The SEAL, with
its colossal tires, impervious body, and amphibious
mode, could circumvent virtually any obstacle. And
knowing the SEAL was bulletproof and fire-resistant,
Blade hadn't hesitated to park the transport in the open,
on the side of the highway. They hadn't seen a single
soul, not one other vehicle, the whole day. The
likelihood of being ambushed was extremely remote. Or
so Blade had thought.

"I see them!" Bertha exclaimed. "Lordy! There's a
lot of them!"

Blade could see them too. Dark shadows flitting from
cover to cover, slowly advancing toward the transport,
illuminated by the half-moon in the eastern sky.

"What do we do?" Bertha asked.

Blade deliberated. They could stay put and trust to the SEAL to protect them from harm. But what if one of those shadows was armed with a hand grenade? What if the grenade was tossed under the SEAL, where the transport was most vulnerable? Or what if they had a bazooka? Blade considered simply driving off, but the act of starting the engine might precipitate an assault. The SEAL's firepower was nullified by the angle the shadows were using to approach; the machine guns, the rocket launcher, and the flamethrower were all aimed to the front of the vehicle, while the shadows were coming up on the driver's side. He had to make a decision, and he had to do it quickly. "We need a diversion, something to draw their attention while I start the SEAL."

"Leave it to me," Sundance said, and he was in motion even as he spoke, flinging the door open and diving to the ground.

The shadows detected the movement of the door, and a fusillade of gunfire erupted from the trees, handgun and rifle fire, the slugs striking the SEAL, many of them whining as they ricocheted.

Sundance rolled on his shoulders as he struck the earth, and he came up with a Grizzly in each hand as the shadows charged from the forest. The Grizzlies thundered, one shot after another, eight shots in swift succession, and with every shot a shadow dropped, some screeching in agony as they fell.

Blade clutched at the ignition and twisted the key, and as the engine turned over there was a peculiar smacking sound from behind him and something wet sprayed onto his right arm and the back of his neck. He glanced over his shoulder.

Lieutenant Frol Lysenko was dead. Two of the wild shots fired by the onrushing shadows had narrowly missed Sundance and entered the open door. Lysenko had been struck in the forehead and the chin. The top slug had blown out the back of his head, splattering hair, brains, and blood over the seats. The chin shot had shattered his mouth; part of his tongue and four teeth hung by a thread of flesh from the ruined hole of his mouth.

"Sundance!" Blade bellowed. "Now!"

Sundance fired once more, downing a screaming shadow, and then he spun and vaulted into the SEAL, through the flapping door, as Blade accelerated, flooring the pedal, and the SEAL lurched ahead. Sundance landed on the floor, crouched over, his right elbow on the seat in a pool of Lysenko's blood. He twisted and slammed the door shot.

The shadows peppered the transport with gunfire as it sped off.

Bertha stared over the pile of supplies, out the rear of the SEAL. "We're leavin' them turkeys in the dust!" she exclaimed.

"We'll go another twenty miles, then stop for the night," Blade said, abruptly noticing he'd failed to turn on the headlights, an oversight he immediately remedied. He looked over his right shoulder at the Russian. "Damn!"

"What's the big deal?" Bertha asked. "It couldn't have happened to a nicer asshole!"

"We needed him," Blade stated.

"We can get by without that dork," Bertha said.

Sundance rose to a sitting position in the seat.

They drove in silence for several minutes.

Blade flicked on the overhead light and glanced in the rearview mirror at the dead officer. "Damn!" he fumed again. He slammed on the brakes and the transport slewed to a top. "Get him out of here!"

Sundance reached across Lysenko's body and unlatched the far door. He eased the door open, placed his right brown leather boot on Lysenko's chest, and kicked.

The mortal remains of Lieutenant Frol Lysenko pitched head-first into the night.

6

Four days later.

"What's the name of the town ahead?" Blade asked.

Bertha consulted the map in her lap. "It's some dinky place called Huntsburg." She checked the population index on the reverse side of the map. "The map doesn't say how many people lived there before the Big Blast."

They were in Ohio. The SEAL was idling on top of a low rise. A cluster of buildings was visible about a quarter of a mile ahead on U.S. Highway 322.

"How am I doing?" Bertha queried Blade. "Am I readin' this sucker okay?"

"You're doing just fine," Blade complimented her.

Bertha grinned. "Lordy! It sure is fine knowin' how to read!"

"You've come a long way," Blade said. "I know how hard you've applied yourself over the past year or so, taking all of those classes. It must have been very difficult."

"It wasn't easy," Bertha acknowledged. "But the Elders are good teachers."

The Elders were responsible for the Family's educational regimen. They taught classes on the basics, on history, geography, math, reading, writing, and more, to the family children. The Elders also offered advanced courses based on their individual expertise. The Home was unique in this respect. For most of America, public education, like all other cultural institutions, was nonexistent.

Bertha ran her left hand over the map, delighted at her progress. When she'd first arrived at the Home, she'd been illiterate. Now, thanks to the Family, she could read and write quite well. She took particular delight in signing her name, and had developed a flamboyant flourish as a token of her pride.

"Huntsburg doesn't appear to be big enough to pose any problems," Blade mentioned. "But stay sharp! We can't take any chances! We learned that the other night." He glanced in the rearview mirror at Sundance. "I know this is your first run away from the Home. You did real well against those goons, but you still don't have any idea how rough it gets out here. You never know when something will pop out at you. So keep your eyes open."

"You don't have to tell me twice," Sundance said.

Blade slowly drove toward Huntsburg. The four days since the last incident had been relatively uneventful. As on all his previous trips, Blade had deliberately avoided cities and large towns. Even smaller settlements, when there was any indication of habitation, were skirted. From prior harsh experience, Blade had learned the futility of foolishly relying on receiving a friendly reception *anywhere*. There were too many savage bands, too many scavengers, raiders, and worse roaming the landscape to permit the needless taking of any risks. Blade prevented trouble by avoiding it. The SEAL was capable of navigating any terrain, so bypassing cities and towns by swinging a loop through the contryside was an easy task. If the town or hamlet was a small one, lacking any evidence of being inhabited, Blade would gamble and drive straight through to save time. Usually, his instincts in this regard were reliable.

But not this time.

A small business section appeared ahead. A dilapidated restaurant was on the right, a crumbling bar on the left. Ancient signs, too faint to read, adorned some of the other ramshackle structures.

"Looks like nobody's home," Bertha remarked.

Blade scanned the cracked sidewalks and the shattered windows. Huntsburg seemed to be a ghost town.

"Think we can stop and stretch our legs?" Bertha asked. "It's almost noon, and we've been drivin' since dawn."

"I don't see why not," Blade replied. He angled the SEAL up to the curb in front of the restaurant. "It looks like the looters tore this town apart during the war," he noted.

"Sure is a dump now," Bertha agreed, leaning out her open window.

Blade braked, then shut off the engine.

Bertha opened her door and dropped to the sidewalk, her M-16 in her hands. "I'm gonna take a look around."

"Just be careful," Blade advised her.

"If you don't mind," Sundance spoke up, "I'd like to go with Bertha. My legs are getting cramped from all this sitting."

"Go ahead," Blade said. "I'll stick with the SEAL."

Sundance climbed out his side of the transport, closed the door, and joined Bertha.

Bertha cocked her head, scrutinizing him. "Why'd you want to come with me?"

"Do I need a reason?" Sundance inquired.

"Just so you ain't got the hots for my body," Bertha said. "It's already spoken for."

"So I heard," Sundance stated.

Bertha's jaw muscles tightened. "What's that crack supposed to mean?"

Sundance started walking along the pitted sidewalk, bearing to the east. "It means I don't have the hots for your body."

Bertha quickly caught up with him. "You don't?" she asked, sounding surprised.

"Nope," Sundance told her.

Bertha looked down at herself. "Why not? What's wrong with my body?"

"Nothing," Sundance said, surveying the street ahead. "It's one of the nicest bodies I've seen."

Bertha beamed. "It is? Really?"

Sundance glanced at her. "I don't lie."

They strolled in the sunshine for several moments.

"What do you mean by nice?" Bertha asked.

Sundance suddenly stopped. "Did you hear something?"

"No." Bertha studied the nearby buildings. "Why?"

"I don't know . . ." Sundance said, and resumed walking.

"Mind if I ask you a question?" Bertha mentioned.

"No."

"Why'd you pick the name Sundance? I know White Meat took the handle Hickok 'cause he's wacko about Wild Bill Hickok. What about you?" Bertha probed. "Was there some old-time gunfighter named Sundance?"

"There was," Sundance replied.

"Ahhh!"

"But he wasn't exactly a gunfighter," Sundance explained. "His real name was Harry Longabaugh, and he was an outlaw in the Old West. I read about him in a book called the *Encyclopedia of Western Gunfighters.* He was nowhere near as famous as Wild Bill Hickok, and far less deadly."

"Then why'd you pick his name?" Bertha asked.

Sundance grinned and looked at her. "Because I like it. The name has a certain ring to it."

"Sure does," Bertha agreed. Sundance cocked his head, listening.

Bertha glanced over her left shoulder. They were a block from the transport. "Maybe we shouldn't stray too far from the SEAL," she suggested.

Sundance stopped. "Fine by me." He gazed up at a broken second-floor window across the highway. "There it is again."

"There what is?" Bertha queried.

"Didn't you hear it?" Sundance asked.

"Hear what?"

"A sort of low whistle," Sundance said, moving to the edge of the sidewalk. "I've heard it several times already."

"It must be the wind," Bertha speculated.

Sundance held up his right hand. "But there's no breeze," he pointed out.

That was when Bertha heard it too: a low, warbling whistle coming from the empty office to their right. She peered into the inky gloom of the interior, trying to perceive movement. What could it be? she asked herself. A bird of some kind? A small animal?

But it was neither.

Bertha was just beginning to turn, to head back to the

SEAL, when she discerned a bulky shape materializing out of the darkness shrouding the office building. A stray shaft of sunlight glinted off a metallic object. "Sundance!" she shouted in alarm, not waiting to determine if the figure was friend or foe. The M-16 snapped up, and she fired from the waist, on automatic, her rounds chipping away the jagged pieces of glass remaining in the front window of the office and striking the shape inside, propelling it from sight.

Someone screamed in agony.

And all hell broke loose.

Over a dozen attackers burst from the buildings lining U.S. Highway 322, charging through doorways and bounding over windowsills, some with guns blazing, others armed with knives, swords, hatchets, and whatever else they could get their hands on. All of them were bestial in aspect, with unkempt, bedraggled hair and apparel. Most wore tattered clothing or filthy animal hides and skins. They jabbered and yelled as they surged from hiding.

Sundance was in motion even as the first scavenger rushed from a doorway across the highway. His hands flashed up and out, leveling the Grizzlies, and his first shot boomed while the scavenger was raising a rifle, the impact of the .45 Winchester Magnum slug lifting the scavenger from his feet and slamming him against the wall. Sundance swiveled as a filthy raven-haired woman appeared on a balcony on the other side of 322, a crossbow in her hands. She was aiming at Bertha when both Grizzlies thundered, and the top of her head imitated the erupting of a volcano. The female scavenger dropped the crossbow, tottered, and fell, crashing into the balcony railing and through the railing as the rotted wood splintered and gave way. Sundance never saw her fall. He had already spun to the left, finding a trio of scavengers sprinting toward them, spilling from the mouth of the alley, blocking their retreat to the SEAL. One of the scavengers was armed with a spear, and his hand was sweeping back for the throw when Sundance shot him in the right eye, jerking his head to the right, and sending the scavenger tumbling to the sidewalk.

Bertha was firing her M-16 as rapidly as targets presented themselves. "We've got to get the hell out of here!" she shouted.

"To the SEAL!" Sundance replied, squeezing both triggers, both Grizzlies bucking in his hands, and the two scavengers between the SEAL and them went down in a jumbled mass of flaying arms and legs.

Bertha took off, blasting a tall scavenger shooting at them with a revolver from the roof of the bar. His head whipped back and he vanished from view.

Sundance followed Bertha, covering her, killing two more scavengers sprinting across the street. Bullets smacked into the wall behind them. Something tugged at his left sleeve. They were still three-quarters of a block distant from the SEAL when he heard the loud pounding to his rear. He whirled.

A mob of maddened, bloodthirsty scavengers was pounding toward them, bellowing their rage and brandishing their assorted weapons. A grungy character in the lead was sighting a Winchester.

Sundance fired both Grizzlies, and the grungy scavenger was hurled from his feet to collide with another scavenger coming up behind him.

Bertha shot a scavenger on the other side of the street.

"Bertha!" Sundance yelled as an arrow streaked past his right cheek.

Bertha glanced over her right shoulder, spying the maddened throng pursuing them. "Shit!" she exploded, turning to support Sundance.

Sundance risked a look toward the SEAL, and he was surprised to see the transport roaring from the curb and racing down the center of the highway. The front end suddenly swerved toward the sidewalk, and Sundance leaped, his left arm catching Bertha around the waist. "What the hell!" she blurted, even as his momentum carried both of them over the lower sill of a demolished window and onto the hard wood floor of a deserted building.

Outside, the 50-caliber machine guns opened up, almost drowning out the shrieks of the decimated scavengers. The chatter of the machine guns was followed by a tremendous explosion. Screams and wails punctuated the din. And then there was a sibilant hissing, and smoke wafted from the nearby structures.

Sundance and Bertha slowly rose, coughing, their nostrils tingling with an acrid odor.

Sundance stepped over the windowsill, the Grizzlies leveled, prepared for more combat.

But there wouldn't be any.

Bodies seemed to be everywhere. Scorched, blasted, bloody bodies and body parts littered the highway and the sidewalks. Gray smoke hovered overhead. Whimpers and cries rose on the air.

The SEAL was idling in the middle of the street, not ten feet away. Tendrils of smoke rose from the front fender and the grill.

Sundance saw a scavenger with shredded stumps below the waist flopping on the ground and whining. Near the front end of the SEAL was a blackened, smoking pair of boots, minus their owner. On the sidewalk to the right was a severed right arm, the fingers still twitching. The tableau was grisly, ghastly beyond belief. Sundance felt sick to his stomach and grimaced.

Bertha grinned. "When it comes to wastin' chumps, Blade is almost as good as White Meat." She had seen the Seal in action before, and knew firsthand the havoc it could wreak.

Sundance stared at the twitching fingers, simultaneously fascinated and repulsed.

Bertha looked at the Warrior in gray, startled by the loathing reflection in his expression. "Ain't you ever seen the SEAL kick butt before?" she asked.

Sundance shook his head.

"You must of seen worse than this," Bertha stated. "How about when the Home was attacked while Blade was off in Denver? I was told the Home was knee-deep in bodies."

"I wasn't a Warrior then," Sundance replied absently. "I took a hit early on in the siege and missed most of the action. They had the mess cleaned up by the time I was released from the infirmary."

"Well, don't let it get to you," Bertha advised. "It

was them or us."

A door slammed, and Blade came around the front of the SEAL, a Commando Arms Carbine in his hands. "Are you two all right?" he inquired. His eyes alighted on Sundance. "Sundance?"

Sundance grimly nodded. "I'm fine." The right corner of his mouth twisted upward. "If I can't take this, I don't deserve to be a Warrior."

"We've got to get out of here," Blade said. "We don't know who might come to investigate all the firing."

Bertha nudged Sundance. "Let's go! Get your cute rump in the SEAL."

Sundance glanced at her in disapproval. "I wish you would stop that."

"Stop what?"

"Stop talking about my . . . rump," Sundance said, walking toward the transport.

"I'm just returning the favor," Bertha said.

"What favor?" Sundance asked as he opened the door.

"You said I had a nice body. Can I help it if I feel the same way about your buns?" Bertha stated.

Blade grinned and ran to the driver's door. He clambered into the SEAL and deposited his Commando on the console.

Sundance and Bertha took their seats.

"Here we go," Blade said, gunning the motor, weaving between the corpses as he bore to the east. "If all goes well, we should reach Philadelphia in two days at the most. Possibly sooner. It all depends on what we run into along the way. I've managed to keep well north of the Soviet lines, but we could still run into one of their patrols. Even the Technics."

"Aren't the Technics those bozos in Chicago?" Bertha queried. "The ones who forced you to drive the SEAL to New York City?"

"They're the ones," Blade confirmed. "I imagine the Family hasn't heard the last of them."

They drove past the rusted wreckage of a bus.

"You were right about one thing, Blade," Sundance

commented, in the process of reloading the clips in his Grizzlies.

"What was that?" Blade asked.

"You never know when something or someone will pop out at you," Sundance stated. "You have no warning whatsoever." He paused. "I think the next time I take a leak, I'll do it with a gun in one hand."

7

The SEAL wheeled off the road, its huge tires pulverizing all the weeds, bushes, small trees, and every other minor obstruction in its path. The transport cut across a field and into a dense forest.

Blade, carefully negotiating a path between the larger trees, glanced at Bertha. "We did it!" he said, elated.

"We've been lucky," Bertha declared.

"Either that, or there aren't as many Russians in this area as we were led to believe," Sundance chimed in.

The afternoon sun was in the western sky. White clouds floated on the air. A rabbit, startled by the mechanical behemoth plowing through the woods, hopped off in fright.

"If this map is right," Bertha said, hunched over the map in her lap, "then we're in what was once called Valley Forge National Historical Park."

"This was a park?" Blade queried, braking under an immense maple tree.

"That's what the map says," Bertha insisted.

Blade turned the engine off. He thought of their good fortune since the firefight in Huntsburg. Two days of travel, two days of sticking to the secondary roads and bypassing every town, no matter how small, and they were now close to their goal, to Philadelphia. Twice they'd spotted helicopters in the distance. In both cases, the copters were flying on the southern horizon. Both times, Blade had pulled the transport into nearby trees until the helicopter disappeared.

"So what's the plan?" Sundance inquired.

"We hide here until dark, then start walking," Blade answered.

"We're leavin' the SEAL here?" Bertha queried.

"We don't have any choice," Blade said. "Even at night, the SEAL would stand out as being completely different from anything the Reds have. We'll leave it here and commandeer a jeep or truck or a civilian vehicle if necessary."

"Why didn't we run into any roadblocks in the last hundred miles or so?" Sundance asked. "We know the Soviets control southern Pennsylvania. Why didn't we bring that radio along to monitor them?"

"It's too valuable to the Family to risk our losing it," Blade said. "As for any roadblocks, they'd be on the highways, and we've stuck to the less-traveled roads. Maybe, as you said, there aren't many troops in this area. Maybe they're concentrated in Philadelphia. Or maybe they don't use roadblocks anymore. Remember, it's been a century since the war. This area has been under their thumb for a hundred years. Resistance probably died out long ago. They haven't been attacked here in decades. Maybe security is lax because they don't have any need for it."

"I hope you're right, Big Guy," Bertha said. "It'll make our job a little easier."

"How will we find where these Vikings are being held?" Sundance questioned.

"We'll find a way," Blade stated.

Bertha snickered. "I love a person with confidence!"

Which explained her affection for Hickok, Blade mentally noted as he turned in his bucket seat. "Sundance, look in the rear section, in the right-hand corner."

Sundance shifted and began climbing over the top of his seat. "What am I looking for?"

"Find a green blanket," Blade directed. "It's folded in half."

Sundance, on his hands and knees, gingerly moved over their mound of supplies. "I see it," he said.

"Lift up the green blanket," Blade directed. "What do you see?"

Sundance raised the folded blanket. "I see uniforms." He leaned closer. "Russian uniforms."

"Bring them here," Blade ordered. "There should be one for each of us."

"Russian uniforms?" Bertha said. "Did the Weavers make them?"

"We took them from the bodies of the four soldiers killed near the Home," Blade detailed. "The Weavers did a rush job on them the night before we left. Washed them. Patched up the bullet holes and tears. The hard part was constructing a serviceable uniform for me. All of them were way too small. The Weavers had to sew two of the uniforms together, and they did a dandy job."

Sundance clambered into the middle seat, the uniforms under his left arm. "Here." He handed one to Bertha. "And this looks like the big one," he said, extending the uniform toward Blade.

"Thanks." Blade took the uniform. "This is it. We'll change into these."

"Now?" Bertha asked.

"Just so you get it done before dark," Blade replied.

"Why?"

"I don't know," Bertha said uncertainly. "I think I'll change outside."

"Whatever you want," Blade commented. "Or we can change outside and you can stay here."

"No. No need." Bertha opened her door, put the Russian uniform under her left arm, and grabbed the M-16 in her right hand. "I'll be back in a sec." She slid to the grass, then closed the door behind her.

A squirrel stared at her from the top of a nearby tree.

Frowning, Bertha moved away from the transport. What the hell was wrong with her? Since when did she become bashful about her naked body? She'd never cared one way or the other before. Before joining the Family.

The squirrel started chattering.

Bertha walked around a large trunk. Off to her left

was a thicket. She slowly stepped toward it, musing. The Family had changed her, that was for sure. And she didn't know if she liked all the changes. Being able to read was terrific, the thrill of her life. But what about the rest of the changes? What about being more subdued, about being less prone to speak her mind when something or someone bugged her? What about being embarrassed to change her clothes in front of two men? Two friends!

Or were they?

Blade was a friend. There was no doubt about that. One of the best she had. But what about Sundance? She hardly knew the man well enough to call him a friend. And if he wasn't a friend, then what was he? A fellow Warrior, of course. But beyond that? She had to admit to herself she was attracted to Sundance, and the disclosure bothered her. A lot. She had intentionally avoided becoming involved with anyone for ages. After what had happened with Hickok, who could blame her? she asked herself. She had given her heart to the blond gunman, and he had inadvertently hurt her to the depths of her soul. Her heart had been crushed. She'd never let on, never let Hickok or anyone else know how torn apart she felt. Surprisingly, the ache hadn't diminished with the passage of time. Every time she saw Hickok and Sherry together, she wanted to run off somewhere and cry. The "old" Bertha would have punched Sherry's lights out and forced herself upon the gunfighter.

What had happened to her?

Was it really the influence exerted by the Family? Or was the cause some quality inside of her? Had she matured? Was that it? She remembered Plato saying once that a person had to mature to grow. Was she becoming wiser, or dumber? What woman in her right mind would allow the man of her dreams to slip through her fingers?

Bertha sadly shook her head.

There were so many questions, and never enough answers.

Bertha stopped, concealed from the transport by the

dense thicket. She dropped the uniform onto the ground, then leaned the M-16 on a low branch. Preoccupied with her reflection, she removed her green fatigue shirt and her belt.

The underbrush to her rear rustled.

Bertha scooped up the M-16 and twirled, her alert eyes scanning the vegetation.

Nothing.

Her nerves must be on edge, she decided, and lowered the M-16 to the ground. It served her right for acting like a damp wimp, for leaving the SEAL to change her clothes. She stooped and picked up the shirt to the Russian uniform.

Footsteps pounded on the earth behind her.

Bertha released the uniform shirt and bent over, grabbing at the M-16. Before she could grip it, arms encircled her waist and drove her to her knees. She instinctively rammed her left elbow back and up, and was gratified when she connected and someone grunted. The arms encircling her slackened slightly, and she repeated the move with her right arm. At the same time, she butted her head backwards.

Both blows landed.

There was a gasp, and the arms holding her slipped away.

Bertha lunged for the M-16, sweeping it into her hands and rolling to her feet, her fingers on the trigger. She glimpsed her assailant and froze. "Son of a bitch!" she exclaimed.

It was a kid!

Her attacker was a boy of 12 or 13, a pudgy youth dressed in tattered rags. He was on his hands and knees, blood trickling from his nose, peering up at her in abject fear.

Bertha started to lower the M-16.

The boy bolted. He was up and gone like a panicked colt, racing back the way he came, heading into the brush.

"Wait!" Bertha called.

The youth ignored her. He darted between two trees and disappeared.

"Damn!" Bertha muttered, starting after him. She took three steps, then realized she was naked from the waist up. "Doubledamn!" She turned, spied her fatigue shirt, and snatched it from the grass. What the hell was a kid doing out here in the middle of nowhere? She jogged after him, donning her shirt as she ran, reaching the two trees and pausing to button her front.

Where was he?

Bertha studied the ground, wishing she could read tracks like Geronimo. A twig snapped, and she looked up in time to see the boy duck around a boulder ten yards in front of her.

There was no way she was going to let him escape!

Bertha took off, sprinting to the boulder and around it, but the boy was gone.

Now where?

The youth came into view 20 yards to the right, visible as he passed a tree and scurried into a patch of high weeds.

Bertha ran to the weeds and stopped, surveying the terrain. The weed patch was 15 yards in diameter, and the weeds were 3 to 5 feet in height. A hill rose on the other side of the weeds, its slope covered with trees and brush.

The boy appeared about ten yards up the hill. He glanced over his left shoulder at Bertha, then kept going.

The sucker sure could run! Bertha hurried after him, crossing the weeds and reaching the base of the hill. Close up, the hill was a lot steeper than it had seemed. She hurried up the slope, her powerful legs churning.

The fleeing boy became visible again, this time near the crest of the hill. He stopped, watching her ascend.

"Wait!" Bertha yelled.

To her surprise, the boy grinned.

"I won't hurt you!" Bertha shouted. "I just want to talk to you!"

The boy flipped her the finger.

"Wait there!" Bertha cried.

Instead, the boy turned and continued over the crest

of the hill.

Smart-ass kid!

Bertha chugged up the slope, halting when she reached the top. The other side of the hill was an eerie landscape. A fire, probably caused by a lightning strike, had fried the vegetation to a cinder. Dozens of blackened, charred trunks dotted the hillside.

The boy was almost to the bottom. He stopped, gazed up at her, and laughed.

What the hell did he think this was? A game? Bertha pounded down the slope after him. Below the hill was a field, and she saw the boy reach it and accelerate. For a pudgy kid, he sure could move! Her black boots crunched on the brittle burnt grass as she raced to the bottom of the hill. A sudden pain in her left side caused her to check her pursuit. She doubled over, breathing heavily.

Pudgy was nearly to the far side of the field.

Bertha inhaled deeply, trying to alleviate the discomfort. How far was she from the SEAL? she wondered. Too far. She couldn't keep following this kid, not when Blade and Sundance might become worried and come looking for her. If the brat didn't want to talk to her, that was his business. She was on a mission.

Besides, her chest ached like crazy!

Bertha slowly straightened.

The boy was on the other side of the field, simply standing there, his hands on his hips, watching her.

Bertha flipped him the finger.

The boy's mouth dropped.

Bertha turned, grinning. That ought to teach the little snot! She began retracing her path up the hill.

There was a loud scream from across the field.

Bertha spun.

The boy was gone.

Bertha frowned as she moved to the edge of the field. For some reason, the fire had not scorched the weeds and brush below the hill. She squinted, trying to see the trees on the far side clearly.

There was no hint of what had happened to the boy.

Bertha hesitated. She should get back to the SEAL,
return to Blade and report. But what if the kid was
really in trouble? She couldn't just leave. If the brat was
trying to fake her out, she'd give him a lesson he'd
never forget.

Like a bust in the chops.

Bertha jogged toward the woods, constantly scanning
for movement. The farther she went, the more
concerned she became about the boy. The forest was too
dangerous, what with all the wild animals and the
mutants, for a young boy. His threads had been pitiful.
He must be on his own, wresting an existence from the
land as best he could.

A shadowy shape materialized in the forest ahead.

Bertha halted, raising the M-16. Whatever it was, the
thing was enormous. She waited for it to move. And
waited.

What the hell was it?

Bertha cautiously advanced. She suddenly realized
the shape wasn't that of a monstrous creature.

It was a log cabin!

The cabin was situated approximately 30 yards into
the trees. The surrounding forest served to render it
invisible except at close range. Two windows, both with
their glass panes intact, fronted the field. Between the
windows was a door.

An open door.

Bertha tensed, suspecting a trap. Maybe the boy had
deliberately led her here. She stepped toward the cabin,
determined to get to the bottom of this. Her boots eased
forward, step by step.

The cabin seemed to be uninhabited.

Bertha reached a cleared space, a strip about ten
yards wide, forming a semicircle in front of the door.
She advanced toward the cabin, proceeding cautiously.
Her M-16 at the ready, she would take a pace, then
pause and survey the cabin and the trees. Take a step
and pause. Take a step and pause. She was on her
fourth step, her left boot about to contact the ground,
when she realized her mistake, when a startling insight
flooded her mind. If there was a cleared space in front

of the cabin, someone must have cleared it! Someone who used the cabin on a regular basis! And anyone who went to all the trouble to clear the vegetation around the door would hardly leave the cabin unattended with the door open! So if the door was open, then someone *must* be inside!

Bertha placed her left foot on the soil, intending to spin and race for cover. But she never made it. Her left boot touched the ground and didn't stop, sinking into the earth, into a gaping hole, almost spilling her off balance. She caught herself before she could plunge forward, and she was on the verge of pulling back from the edge of the hole when something slammed into the small of her back.

They had her.

Bertha received a fleeting glimpse of figures dashing from the cabin and the woods surrounding her, and then she pitched into the hole, into a large pit, crashing through a layer of dirt supported by a framework of branches and woven reeds and weeds.

Someone was laughing.

Bertha tried to clutch the rim of the pit, but her fingers slipped, unable to retain a purchase. She was aware of falling, of darkness, of dirt stinging her face and eyes, and then she landed with a jarring crash on her right side, the M-16 flying from her hands.

More laughter and giggling arose above her.

Stunned, Bertha rolled onto her back, gazing up at the rim of the pit seven feet away. Faces were looking down at her, but she couldn't focus on them. She shook her head, trying to correct her vision, and struggled to rise to her hands and knees.

"Not so fast, bitch!" shouted a harsh voice.

A hard object struck Bertha on the forehead, and she sprawled onto her face. Her last mental image before passing out was of Sundance.

8

"She should have been back by now," Blade declared, impatiently scanning the forest.

"Should we go look for her?" Sundance asked.

"You go," Blade said. "I'll stick with the SEAL. Take the autoloading rifle you brought from the Home with you."

Sundance twisted, leaned over, and retrieved his automatic rifle from the rear section. It was an outstanding piece of military hardware, an FN Model 50-63. The rifle featured a folding stock, an 18-inch barrel and 20-round magazine, and was chambered for the .308 cartridge. The FN 50-63 had initially been a semi-automatic, but the Family Gunsmiths had coverted it to full automatic. Next to his Grizzlies, Sundance preferred the FN over any other weapon in the massive Family armory.

"Be careful," Blade advised.

Sundance nodded, and exited the transport. He felt uncomfortable in the Russian uniform. The Grizzlies were in their shoulder holsters, nestled under the uniform shirt. He would need to unbutton the shirt to reach the Grizzlies, and he didn't like having them tucked away. Frowning, he hefted the FN and moved away from the SEAL. He had last seen Bertha walking to the west, and he hurried to a tree he remembered seeing her near.

There were her boot tracks, in the soft soil near the base of the tree.

Sundance searched the forest, then jogged to a thicket to the left of the tree. If Bertha had wanted privacy while she changed, the thicket would have screened her from the SEAL. He rushed to the far side of the thicket.

Bertha's Russian uniform was lying on the ground behind the thicket.

Sundance stopped, his penetrating green eyes sweeping the woods. Bertha was nowhere in sight. He grabbed her uniform and raced to the SEAL.

Blade was waiting for him outside the transport, standing near the front grill.

"I found this," Sundance announced as he approached, holding aloft the Russian uniform.

Blade took the uniform, scowling. He glanced at the woods.

"Do you want me to go look for her?" Sundance inquired.

"No," Blade replied.

"You're going to look for her?" Sundance asked.

"No," Blade said.

"We're not just going to leave her out there?" Sundance demanded, his tone rising.

"That's exactly what we're going to do," Blade stated.

"Like hell we are!" Sundance stated.

Blade stared at Sundance. "You'll do what I tell you to do."

Sundance gestured toward the trees. "But how can we just up and leave her? She could be in trouble! She could be counting on us to help her!"

"There's no doubt in my mind that she's in trouble," Blade said. "She wouldn't walk off and leave this uniform. But whatever fix she's in, she'll have to get out of by herself."

"Since when do Warriors desert their own?" Sundance asked bitterly.

"Normally, we don't," Blade said.

"Is this a special case?" Sundance queried.

"It is," Blade responded.

"You mind telling me in what way?" Sundance persisted.

Blade sighed. Sundance was obviously furious. "Our mission takes priority. Every run we go on, the mission is our primary consideration. We're under a time constraint on this run. We don't know if the Vikings the Russians captured are still alive, but we're operating under the assumption they are. Who knows what shape the Vikings are in after being questioned by the Soviets for over two weeks? We know the Reds don't go easy on their prisoners. The Vikings could be on their last legs.''

Sundance opened his mouth to speak.

Blade held up his right hand. "I'm not finished. We know the Vikings were definitely in Philadelphia about two weeks ago. They could have been moved, but then again, they might still be there. In any event, the sooner we reach Philadelphia, the better.''

"But Bertha—" Sundance began.

"I said I wasn't finished," Blade stated, cutting him off. "There's one more aspect to bear in mind. You're well aware of how close the Family came to being destroyed by the forces of the Doktor and the dictator ruling the Civilized Zone. You know we barely scraped through intact. And we could find ourselves in a similar situation real soon. The Soviets aren't to be trifled with. We might have strong allies in the Freedom Federation, but all of us combined are no more powerful than the Russians.'' Blade paused. "We have a chance here, Sundance, to turn the tide. If these Vikings are mortal enemies of the Russians, then we might be able to forge an alliance with them. The Soviets would be caught in a vise, between the Vikings on the east and the Freedom Federation in the west. Together, we might be able to defeat the Russians and drive them from the country.'' He paused again. "Knowing all of this, what do you think we should do about Bertha? Should we go after her? Where do we start looking?''

"Where I found the uniform," Sundance said.

"Okay. But we can't go waltzing through the forest yelling our lungs out for her. The Russians, or the damn mutants, might hear us and come to investigate. Which means we'd have to track her. Are you an expert tracker?''

"No," Sundance replied reluctantly.

"Neither am I," Blade said. "Geronimo is, but he isn't here. I'm a fair hand at it, but tracking takes time. Lots and lots of time. And time is the one thing we don't have to spare.''

"I know," Sundance said, averting his eyes.

"I'd let you go after her," Blade stated, "but what if something happens to you? What then? I can't complete our mission by myself.''

"And the mission is our primary consideration,'' Sundance quoted, his facial muscles tightening.

"Exactly,'' Blade affirmed.

"So we do nothing,'' Sundance snapped.

"We wait,'' Blade corrected him. "If she returns by nightfall, fine. If she doesn't, we leave for Philadelphia without her.''

Sundance squinted up at the sun. "That doesn't give her much time.''

"I know,'' Blade acknowledged.

Sundance studied his giant companion. "You know, I don't envy you.''

"Don't envy me? Why?'' Blade asked.

"I don't envy the responsibility you have,'' Sundance confessed. "I don't envy the decisions you must make. I don't think I'd ever want to be top Warrior.''

Blade chuckled.

"What's so funny?'' Sundance inquired.

"I was just thinking of something Hickok once said,'' Blade revealed.

"What did he say?''

"It was shortly after Hickok's son, Ringo, was born,'' Blade recalled. "Hickok said that being a Warrior is a lot like being a diaper.''

"A diaper?'' Sundance responded, surprised. "What in the world do Warriors and diapers have in common?''

Blade grinned. "We both get shit on a lot.''

9

Ohhhhhh! Her aching head!

"She's comin' around!'' a voice yelled.

Bertha slowly opened her eyes. Acute agony racked her, spreading from her forehead to her chin.

"She's awake!''

Bertha grit her teeth and turned her head, seeking the speaker. The last thing she remembered was falling into the damn pit. She found herself on a wooden table, flat on her back, her hands and feet securely bound. A sticky sensation prickled her forehead and face.

The table was surrounded.

There were over a dozen of them, kids of varying ages, boys and girls, all dressed in rags, all filthy.

Bertha blinked several times, wondering if she was dreaming. She could see a lantern hanging on a wall next to a closed door, and she realized she must be in the cabin.

"About time you woke up!" declared the oldest boy in the room. He was about 16, and wore a crudely fashioned, torn brown shirt and shredded jeans. His hair was red, his eyes green.

Bertha went to reply, but the mere act of moving her lips sparked an intense spasm in her head.

"I told you she's been hurt bad," said the eldest girl, a youth of 14 or 15 with stringy brown hair and brown eyes. She wore a patched, lopsided green shift.

"So what?" the oldest boy retorted. "Hunters are scum! She deserves what she got."

Bertha managed to elevate her head several inches from the table top. "Who . . . are you?" she mumbled.

The youngsters stepped back at the sound of her voice.

"Shut your mouth, Hunter!" the oldest boy barked.

"Hunter? I'm not hunting game," Bertha said. She closed her eyes as vertigo engulfed her.

"Game?" said one of the younger children, a girl of five or six. "Can we play a game?"

"Shut up, Milly!" the oldest boy ordered.

"Don't talk to Milly like that, Cole!" interjected the eldest girl.

"Butt out, Libby," Cole rejoined.

All of them began arguing at once, their commingled voices rising, filling the cabin with their clamorous dispute.

Bertha was too woozy to comprehend their squabbling. She rested her head on the table and closed her eyes. What was going on here? she asked herself. She'd been captured by a bunch of kids!

Someone prodded her on the left shoulder.

Bertha twisted to her left.

A young boy, not much over ten years of age, with long blond hair and big blue eyes, smiled at her. "Are you a Hunter?" he inquired in a high-pitched voice.

"I'm a Warrior," Bertha answered.

"What's a Warrior?" he wanted to know.

Bertha tried to answer, but her mouth refused to open. She grimaced as a throbbing twinge pierced her skull.

"What's a Warrior?" the boy repeated.

Bertha's eyelids fluttered, and she sank back, unconscious.

10

"What is it?" Sundance asked.

"Let's find out," Blade said.

Bright stars dominated the heavens. A cool breeze was wafting from the northwest. Before them, perhaps a hundred yards distant, was a huge archlike structure.

"I don't see any lights," Sundance whispered.

"Me neither," Blade commented. He moved toward the arch in a stooped-over posture, his Commando in his hands. The Commando Arms Carbine was one of his favorite guns. It came with an automatic or semi-automatic captibility, and only weighed about eight pounds. The Commando was about three feet in length, and used a 90-shot magazine. Blade had insured the magazine was fully loaded with 45-caliber ammunition before they had departed the SEAL. His last Commando had been lost in Chicago. Fortunately, there'd been another one in the extensive Family armory.

Somewhere off to the west an owl hooted.

Blade forced his mind to concentrate on the matter at hand. He was extremely worried about Bertha, and he couldn't allow his concern to affect his effectiveness.

They had waited at the SEAL until well after dark, with Sundance pacing back and forth the whole while, and Bertha had never appeared. Wherever she was, she was now on her own.

They reached a row of trees bordering the structure and stopped. Without the moon, the night was murky, and visibility was restricted. They could see for about ten yards; beyond that, only shadows.

Blade inched nearer to the arch. He discovered the ruins of a road and squatted, taking his bearings. They were traveling in a southerly direction, which meant the SEAL was parked in the forest about a mile to the north of the arch. The arch, whatever it might be, would serve as a landmark to guide them back to the SEAL. He glanced both ways, then sprinted to the base of the structure.

Sundance joined him.

The arch was rough to the touch, as if it had been constructed of stone. It rose high into the night, blocking out a section of the sky.

"What is it?" Sundance queried, running his left hand over the sandy texture.

"Maybe a monument of some kind," Blade deduced. "We studied about Valley Forge in school, remember?"

Sundance pondered for a moment. "Yeah. Didn't it have something to do with the Revolutionary War in America and George Washington, their first President?"

"This is the place," Blade affirmed. "This arch must be a memorial. Why else would they have put it in the middle of a field? I'm amazed it's still here after all this time."

Sundance motioned toward the field. "Didn't Bertha say this area was a park?"

"It was once," Blade said, "but I seriously doubt the Russians would have bothered to maintain a shrine to American liberty."

"Which explains why the place is overgrown with weeds," Sundance mentioned, "and why the road is a wreck."

"Let's go," Blade stated, leading off to the south.

They traversed another field and entered another stretch of woods.

"There's a light," Sundance said in a hushed tone, pointing.

Blade glanced to their left. A solitary light glowed approximately 400 yards to the southeast. "We'll take a look," he told Sundance.

The two Warriors bore to the southeast. The forest ended, and the Warriors discovered a quiet residential neighborhood. They crouched near a street curb and scanned the houses on both sides.

Blade felt his left Bowie hilt gouge his side. He had concealed the big knives under his uniform shirt, aligning the sheaths under his belt, with one Bowie on each hip. He shifted to alleviate the discomfort.

"Where is everyone?" Sundance murmured.

Blade was wondering the same thing. Except for the second residence on the left, all of the homes were dark, evidently uninhabited. And there was not a solitary soul in sight. He rose and ran across the street toward the first home on the left. The yard was a tangled jumble of weeds and brush, obviously neglected for years. Blade raced up the front porch, then stopped.

The home was a shambles, its door busted and hanging from the top hinge, its windows shattered. The pale yellow paint on the exterior was peeled and flaked.

Blade turned toward the next house. Sundance at his side, he jogged over to the north wall of the structure. The interior of the home was black, except for a flickering ball of light at ground level near the front door. The walls of this house, like the first, badly needed a paint job. Bits and pieces of broken glass from the windows lined the cement foundation.

The front door was located on the west side of the residence. Blade eased around the corner, bent down, and moved closer to the flickering light.

The glow was emanating from a busted basement window.

Blade dropped to his hands and knees, then inched to the edge of the window. He peeked past the metal lip.

The basement had a tenant. An elderly man with gray

hair and a long gray beard was seated on a wooden stool, hungrily gnawing on a roasted rabbit leg. A small fire was burning in the middle of the concrete floor. Dust and dirt covered the antique workbench, table, and chair positioned along the south wall, and the washer and dryer along the east wall. Cobwebs dotted the beams in the ceiling. A flight of stairs on the north side of the basement provided access to the first floor.

Blade examined the window, comparing its frame dimensions to the width of his shoulders. He decided he could do it.

Sundance was waiting behind him.

Blade twisted, motioned with his right arm toward the front door, then pointed at the basement window.

Sundance nodded his understanding. He crept past Blade and reached the door. The FN 50-63 in his left hand, he tried the doorknob with his right.

The door swung open with a slight creek.

Sundance grinned and disappeared inside.

Blade peered into the basement. The elderly man was still chewing on the rabbit leg, striving to strip every last vestige of meat from the bone. He wore a blue shirt and brown pants, both garments exhibiting more holes than fabric. His brown leather shoes qualified as relics; on both of them, his toes protruded from the ends.

Blade lowered himself onto his abdomen, then positioned his body so he was perpendicular to the window. He slowly counted to ten, and on the count of ten galvanized into action. Using his elbows, he slid his arms, head, and shoulders through the window. He aimed the Commando at the man eating the rabbit.

The man in the basement was almost as spry as the animal he was consuming. He was on his feet and darting for the stairs in an instant, but he halted after only five steps and raised his arms in the air, dropping the rabbit leg.

Sundance was standing on the stairs, the FN pointed at the elderly man's head.

Blade eased through the window, letting his body drop the seven feet to the floor. He executed an acrobatic maneuver in midair, jerking his feet down and swinging his torso upward, and alighted upright with the Commando trained on the man with the rabbit.

The elderly gentlemen glared from Sundance to Blade. "All right!" he snapped, displaying a gap where four of his upper front teeth had once been. "You caught me, you Commie bastards! Go on! Get it over with!"

Blade glanced at Sundance, who grinned.

"Get it over with!" the man demanded. "You finally caught old Nick! But it took you slime long enough, didn't it?" He cackled.

Blade walked toward the man called Nick. "What are you babbling about?" he asked.

Nick cocked his head and scrutinized the giant. "Damn! They're growin' you sons of bitches big nowadays, ain't they?"

'I think you're laboring under a misapprehension,'' Blade said.

Nick did a double take. "Damn! You pricks are speakin' better English all the time!"

"You have us confused with someone else," Blade stated.

"Oh? Who?" Nick replied.

"The Russians," Blade explained.

Nick laughed and shook his head, his beard swaying. "You morons! Do you really think old Nick is as gullible as that? I won't fall for your crock of shit!"

"We're not Russians," Blade said.

"You're not?" Nick responded in mock astonishment. "Then those must be ballet costumes you're wearin'!" He snickered.

Blade lowered the Commando barrel. "I'm serious. We're not Russians. We confiscated these uniforms."

"Yeah. Right. What are you tryin' to pull? Are you with the KGB?" Nick queried.

"What must I do to convince you we're not Russian troopers?" Blade inquired.

Nick tittered. "Sprout wings and a halo."

Blade indicated the smoldering fire with a wave of his left hand. "Why don't you have a seat? There are a few questions I'd like to ask you."

"I'll bet there are!" Nick declared, smirking. "I don't know what kind of game you're playin', but I'll go along with it. I don't have any choice, do I?"

Blade stepped aside as Nick walked to the stool and sat down. Sundance came down the stairs and moved to the right. He leaned against the wall, his automatic rifle cradled inis arms.

"I ain't never seen guns like yours," Nick mentioned, admiring the Commando in Blade's right hand.

"You see? Don't these guns prove we're not Russians?" Blade asked.

"They don't prove diddly," Nick retorted.

Blade sighed. "What are you doing down here all by yourself?"

"Jackin' off," Nick answered, and chuckled.

"Can't you give me a straight answer?" Blade queried.

"Why the hell should I?" Nick rejoined. "I hate all you Commie sons of bitches!"

"But I told you we're not Russians," Blade reiterated.

"Oh, you may not be from Russia," Nick said, "but you're still a Commie bastard! I know you're forcin' some of our women to have kids for you! I know you're raisin' the kids like they would have been raised in your rotten Motherland! I know!" His voice vibrated with the intensity of his emotion.

Blade frowned. This was getting them nowhere. He'd hoped to glean important information from their conversation, information which might aid Sundance and him in the attainment of their goal.

Sundance noted the expression on Blade's face. "Let's get out of here," he suggested. "This crazy old coot won't help us fight the Russians."

"I guess you're right," Blade admitted reluctantly. He smiled at Nick. "Be seeing you. Take care of yourself."

Blade and Sundance started toward the stairs.

Nick watched them cross the basement, his blue eyes narrowing suspiciously. "You're just gonna leave?"

"Yep," Blade confirmed.

"You ain't gonna kill me?"

"Nope," Blade answered.

"This is some kind of trick!" Nick exclaimed.

"Nope." Blade reached the bottom of the stairs.

"I don't get any of this," Nick muttered. "Why'd you bust in here, if you don't intend to kill me?"

Blade reached the third step. "I wanted to ask you a few questions."

"What questions?" Nick asked.

Blade paused. "You'll help us?"

"I still don't believe any of this," Nick said. "I think you're jerkin' me around. Then again, there's no way a pair of Hunters would walk off and let me live."

"Hunters?" Blade repeated.

"Don't tell me you don't know what Hunters are!" Nick stated.

"Of course we do," Sundance said. "Hunters kill game. I've hunted plenty of times. Deer, bear, ducks, you name it."

Nick squinted at Sundance. "Either you're the biggest idiot this world's ever seen, or you're the biggest liar."

Sundance turned. "I wouldn't make a habit out of calling me a liar."

"Touchy, ain't we?" Nick retorted.

"Will you help us?" Blade interjected.

Nick nodded. "You got me curious now. I'll answer your questions."

Blade and Sundance returned to the fire.

"So what are you doing down here all by yourself?" Blade asked again.

"Eatin' a rabbit I conked on the head with a rock," Nick said. "The homes around here were abandoned ages ago. I figured I could hide out here for a spell. No one ever comes around here, except the Hunters, of course. Valley Forge is off-limits."

"What are these hunters you keep talking about?" Blade inquired.

"Hunters are murderin' slime! The Commies train some of their soldiers in trackin' and night-stalkin', and everybody calls 'em Hunters. They hunt us down. Get a bounty for every Freeb they kill. Double the bounty if its a Packrat,'' Nick detailed.

Blade's brow furrowed in perplexity. "I don't understand. What's a Freeb? And a Packrat?''

Nick seemed surprised by the question. "I'm a Freeb, dummy! And the Packrats are the kids, the ones hidin' out in Valley Forge.''

"You're a Freeb?" Blade said. "I still don't understand.''

Nick stared up at the giant, amused. "They sure grow 'em stupid where you come from!''

"I told you we're not Russians," Blade stated sharply. "And we're not from around here. We don't have the slightest idea what a Freeb is. Or a Packrat.''

Nick pursed his lips. "You know, I'm beginnin' to believe you turkeys. Well, Freeb is short for freeborn. Anyone who ain't been printed and mugged by the Commies is called a Freeb 'cause the Commies ain't got no record of 'em. You understand that?''

"So far," Blade said. "But why do the Russians mug people? To rob them?''

Nick gazed at the washer and dryer. "Dummies! I'm dealin' with dummies here!''

"Who are you talking to?" Sundance asked.

Nick pointed at the appliances. "Them.''

Sundance glanced at Blade. "This geezer is nuts.''

"*I'm* nuts?" Nick said. "Tell me somethin', boy. Do you know which end of a horse the shit comes out of?''

"Why are we dummies?" Blade queried.

"Because you don't know what it means when I say the Commies mug folks. They take mug shots for their files. Get it? Photographs. Pictures. You do know what a photograph is?" Nick said.

"I've seen some," Blade answered. Actually, he'd seen thousands. Kurt Carpenter had stocked the Family library with hundreds of volumes depicting a pictorial history of humankind. Photographic books on every subject were represented, from sailing to spaceships. "But how is it you haven't been . . . printed and mugged . . . by the Soviets? Don't they mug everyone?''

"They try to," Nick stated. "But they don't catch

everybody. Their Admin Centers are concentrated in the cities and towns, and they have trouble keepin' tabs on all the rural folks. I was born nearly seventy years ago, on a farm in western Pennsylvania. My mom and pop never took me in to be mugged.''

"How long have you been hiding out like this?'' Blade inquired.

Nick sighed. "Too damn long. I'm gettin' tired of all the runnin' and hidin'. I've been in these parts for about a year. There are a lot of abandoned homes around Valley Forge, and I keep movin' from one to the next. Like I said, no one ever comes here. It's illegal to be caught in Valley Forge. Oh, I bump into the Packrats now and again. But they keep their distance, and I keep mine. Besides, I ain't got nothin' they'd want.''

"What are the Packrats?'' Blade asked.

"The kids, dummy.''

Blade looked at the window. "There are kids out there?''

"Bunches of 'em,'' Nick answered. "They live in gangs, and spend their time foragin' for food and fightin' each other. When they're not hidin' from the Hunters, that is.''

"Where do these kids come from?'' Blade queried.

"Everywhere,'' Nick replied. "But mostly from the big cities, like Philly. They're orphans, usually. Their parents get killed by the Commies, and they have nowhere else to go. So they hoof it. If they don't hit the road, the Commies will use 'em in their slave-labor camps. A lot of the runaways wind up here, or places like Valley Forge. They hear about it through the grapevine.''

"Kids,'' Blade said, feeling an overwhelming revulsion for the Russians, and thinking about his little son Gabe.

"Don't feel sorry for 'em,'' Nick declared. "They're mean, the Packrats. They'd slit your throat for the clothes off your back. They trap folks from time to time, then torture 'em before they kill 'em.''

"What happens to these kids when they grow up?'' Blade asked.

"Few of 'em live that long," Nick said. "Those that do, just wander off to make a go of it someplace else."

Blade reached up and scratched his chin. "I know a lot of towns were evacuated during the war for one reason or another. Some were destroyed. So the map I have isn't completely reliable. And I need to know where the nearest inhabited town is located. What would it be?"

"King of Prussia is nearby," Nick revealed.

"Are there Russians there?" Blade queried.

"Commies? Why do you want to find the Commies?" Nick asked.

"We need to borrow one of their vehicles," Blade declared.

Nick chuckled. "You don't say! Well, in that case your best bet would be Norristown. The Commies have a large garrison stationed there. Where are you guys headed?"

"I'd rather not say," Blade said.

Nick shrugged. "No skin off my nose. This way, if I'm caught, I can't talk, huh?"

Blade nodded.

Nick stared from the giant to the one with the mustache. "You know, I may be gettin' senile, but I believe you two. I don't think you're Commies. No Commie could play dumb that good."

"Thanks," Blade said. "I think."

"Do you know where Norristown is?" Nick inquired.

"No," Blade replied. "We'll find it. I have a map with me."

"But the map won't tell you where the Commies like to post checkpoints, and which areas to avoid and which ones are safe." Nick silently debated for a minute. "Tell you what I'll do. I'll go along with you. Guide you. How about that idea?"

Blade shook his head. "It would be too dangerous."

"Dangerous?" Nick cackled. "I didn't live this long by takin' it easy, boy! Danger don't mean a thing to me."

"No," Blade said. He walked toward the stairs, Sundance at his side.

"I could show you some shortcuts," Nick persisted. "I know this area like the back of my hand."

Blade paused, reflecting. Since speed was of the essence, any shortcut would greatly facilitate their assignment. "Do you promise to do exactly as I tell you?" he asked.

Nick snickered. "Of course!"

"Then you can come," Blade said. "But only as far as Norristown. Once we've acquired a vehicle, you're on your own."

"I'm always on my own," Nick replied. He rose and hurried to the stairs. "Say! I never did catch your names."

"I'm Blade," Blade said introducing himself. "And this is Sundance."

"Sundance?" Nick chuckled. "Ain't never heard a name like Sundance before. What's your last names?"

"We don't have any," Blade answered.

Nick squinted at them. "No last names? Never heard of such a thing."

"Nobody has last names where we come from," Blade revealed.

"And where might that be?" Nick casually inquired.

"Sorry," Blade said. "We'd best keep that information to ourselves."

Nick shrugged. "Fine by me." He glanced from Blade to Sundance. "You know, I think we're goin' to have a real fun time together!"

11

Bertha slowly regained consciousness. She became aware of an acute pain in her wrists and arms. A cool breeze was blowing on her face. She could smell the fragrant scent of pine and dank earth. And she realized she wasn't on the table in the cabin; she was suspended by her wrists, her body dangling in the air.

What had happened?

Bertha opened her eyes, confirming her assessment. A rope secured her wrists. She glanced up, and found the rope was looped over the stout limb of a tree. Looking down, she discovered her feet were swaying about three feet above the ground. And she wasn't alone.

Six of the youngsters were facing her, three of them holding lanterns. The other three each held an AK-47.

Bertha recognized the oldest boy, the one called Cole. She also saw the girl with the stringy hair, Libby, and the little girl named Milly. The 10-year-old boy with the blonde hair was there, as was old Pudgy Butt himself, the brat who had led her into the trap. The other two she didn't know, a boy and a girl, both about 12 years old.

"Glad to see you joined us, bitch!" Cole greeted her.

Bertha glared down at him. Her headache had subsided, but her forehead was sore. "That ain't no way to talk to a lady, you snotnosed shithead!"

Cole bristled, leveling his AK-47 at Bertha's belly. "I should waste you right now, bitch!"

"While my hands are tied?" Bertha taunted him. "Ain't you the brave baby!"

Cole took a step toward her. "I'm not a baby!"

"Could of fooled me!" Bertha retorted.

Cole jammed the AK-47 barrel into her gut. "Damn you!"

"Cole! No!" The girl called Libby cried.

"Why not?" Cole demanded, glowering up at Bertha. "She's a damn Hunter! Who cares if it's quick or slow?"

Bertha remembered the squabble in the cabin. She glanced at Libby. "What's a hunter?"

"Don't you know?" Libby responded.

"Nope," Bertha said.

"Bullshit!" Cole exploded. "You expect us to believe you?"

Libby gazed at Cole. "She might be telling the truth."

"Are you going to let her trick you?" Cole snapped. "You know what the Hunters are like! They'll do anything to catch one of us! Lie! Wear disguises! Shoot us in the back! Anything!''

Libby stared at Bertha, her youthful face betraying her doubt.

Bertha recognized a possible ally in the girl. "Look. I ain't no lousy hunter! I'm a Warrior.''

"What's a Warrior?" Libby asked.

"A Warrior protects others from harm,'' Bertha explained.

Cole laughed. "Can it, bitch! Nobody is going to believe a word you say!''

"I wasn't talkin' to you!" Bertha stated stiffly. "I was talkin' to Libby.''

"You're not here to hurt us?" Libby inquired.

"Nope,'' Bertha answered.

Cole turned on Libby, waving his AK-47. "Come on, Libby! You're not falling for this shit, are you?" He spun toward Bertha. "If you're not here to harm us, then why'd you chase Eddy?''

"I thought he was in trouble,'' Bertha answered.

"Yeah! Right!" Cole rejoined.

Bertha looked at Eddy. "Didn't you attack me, Fatso?''

Eddy seemed confounded by the unexpected query.

"Didn't you attack me first?" Bertha prompted him. "Wasn't I mindin' my own business, and you jumped me from behind?''

"I wanted your gun!" Eddy blurted.

"And wasn't I turnin' back when you screamed?'' Bertha asked.

"Yeah,'' Eddy admitted.

"There!" Bertha glanced at Cole. "I thought he was in trouble. If I'd wanted to waste Fatso, I could have shot him anytime!''

"It doesn't mean a thing!" Cole stated defiantly.

"Yes, it does,'' Libby chimed in.

"What?" Cole said.

"I believe her, Cole,'' Libby declared.

"Give me a break!" Cole quipped.

"I think she's telling the truth,'' Libby stated.

"Why?" Cole wanted to know.

"Lots of reasons," Libby said. "Have you ever seen a woman Hunter before?"

"No," Cole answered reluctantly.

"And have you ever seen a Hunter dressed like her?" Libby asked.

"No," Cole said, "but they wear all sorts of disguises!"

"What about her gun?" Libby pressed him. "Ever seen a Hunter packing a gun like hers?"

Cole's forehead creased. "No, can't say as I have. They always use an AK-47 or a pistol."

"And," Libby added triumphantly, pointing at their prisoner, "have you ever seen a *black* Hunter before? Ever *heard* of a black Hunter before?"

Cole slowly shook his head, studying the woman swinging from the rope.

"Cole . . ." said the little girl named Milly.

"Not now, Milly," Cole barked irritably.

"You finally seein' the light?" Bertha asked him.

"What's your name?" Cole inquired.

"Bertha."

"You gottta see it my way, Bertha," Cole said. "I'm the head of the Claws. Fifteen Packrats depends on me. If I make a mistake, they'll die."

"I'm not here to hurt you," Bertha reiterated.

"But I don't know that for sure," Cole mentioned. "If I go easy on you, cut you down, we could all wind up dead. I can't take the chance. Somebody is always after us. If it ain't the Red Hunters, then its one of the other Packrat gangs, or the mutants."

"Cole," Milly said, interrupting.

"Not now!" Cole told her. He gazed up at Bertha and shook his head. "Sorry, lady. But I can't let you live. You could be lying through your teeth for all I know. You could be some kind of new Hunter. We're just gonna have to leave you here for the mutants."

"Cole!" Milly cried.

Cole turned toward Milly, clearly annoyed. "Haven't I told you before not to butt in when I'm talking to someone else? What the hell is it now?"

Milly extended a trembling finger to their right.

"Eyes."

"Eyes?" Cole repeated, starting to pivot in the direction Milly was indicating.

Bertha glanced to the right, and she saw them first. A pair of reddish orbs, balefully staring at the youngsters from the stygian depths of the forest.

"A mutant!" Cole shouted. "Get to the cabin! Quick!"

The Claws responded to his order, dashing past Bertha toward the log cabin 20 yards away. One of them dropped a lantern.

Bertha glanced over her left shoulder and spotted the cabin, and saw Libby leading Milly and the others in a mad sprint for the cabin's front door. She swung her head around, just in time to see the mutant burst from cover and charge Cole.

The mutant was a canine, or would have been had its parents not been affected by the widespread chemical and radiation poisoning of the environment and given birth to a defective monstrosity. It was four feet high and covered with brown hair, and its features resembled those of a German shepherd. Its jaws slavering, its six legs pumping, its two tails curved over its spine, the mutant pounced.

Cole stood his ground. He crouched and fired, the stock of the AK-47 pressed against his right side. His shots were rushed, but effective.

The mutant staggered as the heavy slugs ripped into its body. It was wrenched to the right, but immediately recovered and renewed its attack.

Cole never let up. He kept firing as the mutant took a bounding leap, and he was still firing as the mutant slammed into him and knocked him to the ground.

The mutant recovered before Cole, and slashed at him with its tapered teeth.

Cole, flat on his back, brought the AK-47 up to block those cavernous jaws.

Enraged, the mutant clamped onto the AK-47, snarling as it strived to wrench the weapon from the human's hands.

Cole was clinging to the Ak-47 for dear life.

Bertha, suspended five feet from the savage struggle, saw her chance. She whipped her legs forward, then back. Once. Twice. Gaining momentum with each swing. And on the third try she tucked her knees into her chest, then lashed her legs out and down, hurtling at the combatants.

The mutant's senses were incredible. Furiously engaged as it was in attempting to tear the AK-47 loose and rip into its opponent's neck, it saw the woman sweeping toward it and tried to evade the blow. But in doing so, the mutant released the AK-47 and drew back, its head momentarily elevated.

In that instant, Bertha struck. Her black boots plowed into the mutant's face, into its feral eyes, and it was propelled for a loop, catapulted through the air to crash onto its left side six feet from Cole.

Cole took immediate advantage of the situation, rising to his knees, aiming the AK-47, deliberately going for the mutant's head, squeezing the trigger and holding it down.

The mutant twisted as it was struck, frantically scrambling erect. But the heavy slugs drove it to its knees, its left eye exploding in a spray of hair and blood. It reared back and howled as it was hit again and again and again.

The AK-47 went empty.

The mutant flopped onto its right side, its body convulsing. It whined once, then lay still.

Cole slowly stood, his eyes riveted on the mutant.

There was a commotion from the direction of the cabin, and the seven oldest Claws ran up, all of them armed.

"You got it!" shouted the pudgy Eddy.

Cole simply nodded.

Libby was with them, carrying an AK-47. She glanced at Cole, worry in her eyes. "It almost got you," she stated.

Cole exhaled loudly.

"You came close," Libby said.

"I know," Cole agreed in a soft voice.

"I saw the whole thing," Libby mentioned. "You'd

be dead right now, if she hadn't helped you!" And Libby pointed at Bertha.

Cole pivoted, gazed up at the Warrior.

"I couldn't let that freak eat you," Bertha said. "You might of given it indigestion!"

Cole almost grinned. He glanced at Eddy. "Cut her down."

"But I thought you said—" Eddy objected.

Cole whirled on the startled Eddy. "Cut her down! *Now!*"

"Thank goodness!" Bertha exclaimed. "I've really got to weewee!"

12

Blade had to hand it to Nick. The old Freeb was as good as his word. Nick seemed to know every alley, every ditch, every unfrequented street, within 20 miles of Valley Forge. His endurance and agility were remarkable for a man his age. He maintained a steady pace, never flagging, and they reached their destination two hours before dawn. They approached Norristown from the north. Nick guided them through the fields and across yards adjacent to Highway 363, then parallel to Egypt Road until they reached Ridge Pike. They continued to the south, sticking to the shadows, to the alleys and the side streets, skirting Jeffersonville, until they reached Norristown.

Blade was amazed by his first glimpse of Soviet-occupied territory. People appeared to be going about their daily business without hindrance. Traffic on the main arteries was light but steady. Civilian and military vehicles shared the roads. A checkpoint was posted between Jeffersonville and Norristown, but the Russians stationed at the checkpoint performed their duties in a desultory fashion. Squatting behind a hedgerow a block to the west, Blade saw the soldiers joking and laughing, and only occasionally stopping vehicles to verify papers. Again, he had to remind himself of the time frame involved. The Soviets had controlled this area for over 100 years. They were bound to be complacent after such a protracted interval. Which suited him fine, because their careless attitude increased the odds of successfully completing the run to Philadelphia.

Four times the trio inadvertently encountered civilians, and each time the civilians took one look at the Russian uniforms on Blade and Sundance and promptly made themselves scarce.

Once in Norristown, Nick increased their pace. They bore south on Lafayette, then turned left on Hawes Avenue, and dashed across Main Street to the far sidewalk. A military truck appeared in front of them, and Nick hastily led them into a side street. They traversed a succession of side streets and alleys, on the alert for patrols, until Nick abruptly stopped.

"There it is," the Freeb whispered.

They were standing at the end of a side street. Before them were railroad tracks, a wide avenue, and an imposing structure. Floodlights rimmed its roof. A barbed-wire fence enclosed the perimeter. Soldiers patrolled the length of the fence, some with guard dogs on a leash. A gate in the northwest corner of the fence was closed.

"What is it?" Blade asked.

"The Norristown garrison," Nick disclosed. "About eighty soldiers are headquartered there on a regular basis. There's a motor pool in the rear. The place used to be a newspaper. The *Times*-Something-or-Other. But the damn Commies took it over, like they did all the media."

"You know a lot about it," Sundance idly mentioned.

"You pick up bits and pieces here and there," Nick commented.

Blade was appraising the garrison's fortifications. "There's no way we can break in there to steal a vehicle."

"Maybe you won't have to," Nick said.

"What do you mean?" Blade inquired.

"Look," Nick said, pointing.

A guard was unlocking the gate in the northwest corner of the fence. He pushed the gate open and stepped aside, waiting. A moment later, a jeep drove around the corner of the garrison, evidently coming from the motor pool. The jeep braked at the gate, the driver exchanged a few words with the guard, and the jeep accelerated. It took a left.

"Hide!" Nick said, and before the Warriors understood his intent, he moved from the cover of the side street, out into the open, in clear view of the jeep's driver.

Blade grabbed Sundance's right arm, and they retreated into the shadows.

"What's he doing?" Sundance queried.

"I think I know," Blade said.

Nick was wobbling on his feet, staggering, seemingly inebriated. He glanced at the jeep, then put his left hand in the crook of his right elbow and snapped his forearm up, his right hand clenched into a fist.

The jeep slowed, then swerved, wheeling toward Nick.

Nick laughed and backpedaled, tottering.

The jeep was bearing down on the side street.

Nick stayed on the sidewalk, stumbling away from the wide avenue, leading the jeep further up the side street, out of sight of the garrison gate.

The jeep screeched to a stop, and two Russian soldiers climbed out, leaving the vehicle running.

"Hey, you bloodsuckers!" Nick called and snickered.

"Hello, comrade," the driver greeted Nick. He was stocky, his complexion florid.

"I ain't your lousy comrade!" Nick retorted.

"You are drunk, comrade," stated the second Russian.

Nick laughed. "What was your first clue, butthole?"

The driver and the other Russian exchanged glances.

"You will need to come with us," the driver said.

"Like hell I will!" Nick rejoined belligerently.

"You must come with us, comrade," the driver persisted.

"Why?" Nick inquired.

The driver and the second soldier walked toward the old man. They believed he was intoxicated, harmless, and in one respect they were correct. But in another, they were wrong.

"Please," the driver said, "do not resist! Public drunkenness is not permitted."

Nick straightened. "What about dyin'?"

The driver detected a movement to his left, and he spun, going for the automatic pistol on his right hip. His fingers were closing on the grips when other fingers clamped onto his neck. Powerful fingers, with a grip of steel. He caught a glimpse of a giant in uniform, and then he was bodily lifted from the sidewalk.

The second trooper saw the giant spring on the driver, and he went for his own gun.

Sundance sprang from the shadows, his arms swinging the FN barrel up and around, ramming the barrel into the second soldier's throat. The soldier gagged, doubling over, and Sundance smashed the barrel against his head twice in swift succession. The soldier gasped and fell to his knees. Sundance drew back his right leg, then planted his right foot on the tip of the soldier's chin. The soldier flipped onto his back, blood spurting from his crushed teeth, oblivious to the world. Sundance glanced at Blade.

The head Warrior, his Commando slung over his left shoulder, was holding the driver's neck in his right hand and the driver's midsection in his left, while supporting the trooper in the air above his head. The Russian was kicking and wheezing, his brown eyes bulging. Blade suddenly brought his massive arms straight down, and the driver's head produced a sickening crunching sound as it struck the sidewalk.

"Nice job," Nick complimented them.

Blade glanced at the mouth of an alley 20 yards off. "Let's stash them in there," he suggested. Suiting action to words, he stooped over and gripped the driver by the collar. "Hurry."

The two Warriors hastily deposited the soldiers in the

alley, secreting the Russians behind a row of trash cans.

"That should do it," Blade said. "Let's get out of here."

Blade and Sundance jogged to the idling jeep. As Blade was about to slide in, he stopped and looked around. "Where's Nick?"

Sundance swiveled. "I don't see him," he said.

"Damn!" Blade spat in annoyance. What the hell had happened to the Freeb? "We can't wait!" He eased into the jeep.

"Move it, dummy!" declared a voice from the rear. Blade twisted.

Nick was hunched over in the narrow back seat. "You'd best take off! We've been lucky so far! I didn't see anyone lookin' out their window. Haul ass before we're spotted!"

Sundance climbed into the jeep.

"We can't take you with us," Blade said to Nick.

"What's with you?" Nick demanded. "One second you're actin' like you're goin' to piss your pants because you can't find me, the next you're bootin' me out on my can."

"I told you before," Blade reminded the Freeb. "We agreed you could come with us as far as Norristown and that was it."

Nick leaned forward. "I didn't agree to nothin! And I haven't had this much fun in years! I'm comin' with you, unless you up and toss me out. And you'd best get your ass in gear. Someone's liable to peep out at us at any moment. And that Commie on the gate might be wonderin' what happened to this jeep."

Blade glanced at Sundance.

"Bring him," Sundance recommended. "He might come in handy."

Blade, annoyed, executed a tight U-turn and drove to the wide avenue. True to Nick's prediction, the gate guard was standing near the northwest corner, gazing in their direction. Blade waved at the guard, hoping his features were invisible in the dark interior of the jeep.

"That's a nice touch," Nick commented. "He'll think you're his buddy."

Blade took a right.

"Don't forget to stop at the red light," Nick stated.

Blade braked at the first intersection.

"So where are we goin'?" Nick asked.

Blade sighed. "Philadelphia."

"Philly?" Nick chuckled. "I know Philly like the back of my hand."

"I thought you would," Sundance interjected, grinning.

"What's in Philly?" Nick inquired.

Blade twisted and glared at the Freeb.

"Fine," Nick remarked. "I can take a hint. Go straight."

The light turned green, and Blade drove straight.

"Don't worry about a thing," Nick said. "I'll direct you to the turnpike, and we'll be in Philly before you know it."

"How long will it take?" Blade asked.

"We should be there by dawn," Nick replied. "Of course, it would help if I knew exactly where you want to go."

"I'm not exactly sure," Blade confessed.

"Oh, that's brilliant!" Nick scoffed. "You go to all the trouble of infiltratin' the Commie lines, you swipe one of their jeeps, and you don't know where the hell you want to go? What do you boys use for brains? Sewage?"

Blade's hands tightened on the steering wheel. He felt uncomfortable for several reasons. First, he didn't like having Nick along. But the elderly Freeb had served them well, so far, and he might really know Philadelphia like the back of his hand. Secondly, he felt awkward driving the jeep. He'd used a vehicle with a manual shift before, when he'd driven some of the trucks and jeeps the Family had appropriated during the war with the Doktor and Samuel II. But he usually drove the SEAL, and the vast difference was oddly discomfiting. Finally, a vague, worrisome sensation was nagging at his mind. Something was subliminally bothering him, and he was peeved because he couldn't isolate and identify the reason.

"Don't you have a clue what you're lookin' for?" Nick queried.

"Did you happen to hear about an attack on—" Blade began.

"Those hairy weirdos in the wooden ships?" Nick exclaimed. "Yeah. Everybody was talkin' about 'em for a while. They had the Commies pretty rattled, I heard."

"I'll bet," Sundance commented. He gazed out the rear window.

"So what about 'em?" Nick asked.

"We want to find them," Blade said, then elaborated. "We know the Soviets captured twelve of those invaders, those Vikings. We know the Russians are holding them at a detention facility in Philadelphia. And we want to find them."

"How'd you learn all this?" Nick inquired.

"That'll have to be our secret," Blade responded.

"Well, I don't know as I can be of much help," Nick said. "I don't have the slightest idea where the Commies are holdin' the ones you want."

"Do you know where they might be held? Where the detention facilities are located?" Blade probed.

Nick contemplated for a minute. "I might be of some help, after all. I know the Commies built a big detention place in northwest Philly, in Fairmont Park, right off the Schuykill Expressway. It's near the Schuykill River."

"Then we'll try there first," Blade said.

"I don't get it," Nick stated. "What are these Vikings to you guys?"

"Nothing," Blade answered.

"Then why do you want to find them?" Nick asked.

Sundance twisted in his seat. "You sure are the curious type, aren't you?"

Nick shrugged. "Sorry. Didn't mean to be nosy."

Sundance jerked his thumb toward his window. "What was that bridge we just went over?"

"It goes over the Schuykill River," Nick revealed.

"The same river near the detention facility?" Blade queried.

"Yep."

"Any chance of us following the river into Philadelphia?" Blade inquired.

"Nope."

"Why not?" Blade pressed.

"Because the roads don't follow the Schuykill, dummy," Nick disclosed. "Our best bet would be to take the Schuykill Expressway all the way in. It sticks close to the river most of the way."

"Can you direct us there?" Blade asked.

"No problem," Nick asserted.

"We do have one problem," Sundance remarked.

"Oh? What's that?" Blade replied.

"We're being tailed," Sundance said.

Blade glanced in the rearview mirror. A pair of headlights was in their lane, perhaps 500 yards distant.

"They pulled out of the garrison as we were going over the bridge," Sundance said. "They didn't even stop for a red light at the intersection."

Nick chuckled. "Sharp eyes you've got there, Sundance."

Sundance looked at Nick. "I don't miss much."

"We've got to lose them," Blade stated.

"Whatever we're going to do," Sundance declared, "we'd better do quickly."

"Why?" Blade asked.

Sundance was gazing over his left shoulder. "Because they're gaining on us."

13

"You should get some sleep," Bertha said.

"I'm too excited to sleep!" Libby stated happily.

"Me, too," Cole added.

They were seated at the wooden table in the cabin, a lantern in the center of the tabletop diffusing a soft yellow light throughout the room. The rest of the Claws were asleep, curled up on blankets on the floor.

"Do you really think they'll take us?" Libby queried in a low voice.

"They took me, didn't they?" Bertha replied. "Believe me, girl. The Family are the nicest bunch of folks you'd ever want to meet. We may have to cram the SEAL to the max, but Blade will agree to take you to the Home. I promise you."

"This Blade you've been telling us about," Cole said. "What's he like?"

"He's a righteous dude," Bertha stated. "One of my best friends. He's got more muscles than anyone else I know. And he's tricky."

"Tricky?" Cole repeated.

"I don't know how else to describe him," Bertha said. "He doesn't look like the brainy type, but he fools you. Just when you think you've got him figured out, he catches you off guard. I guess clever is the word for Blade."

"I'm looking forward to meeting him," Cole said.

Libby scanned the sleeping Claws. "But will there be enough room in this SEAL of yours for all of us?"

Bertha surveyed the children. "I don't know," she acknowledged. "We might need to throw out some of our supplies. But we'll find a way. Trust me."

Libby stared at Bertha. "I haven't trusted anyone for years."

Bertha frowned. "How do you make a go of it? Where do you find your food?"

"We do a lot of hunting and fishing," Cole detailed. "And we steal whatever we can get our hands on. We raid the nearby houses. Scrounge here and there."

Bertha nodded at a row of eight AK-47's leaning against the wall near the front door. "Where'd you get all the hardware?"

"Hunters," Cole answered.

Bertha whistled. "You Claws must be real good if you wasted that many Hunters."

"We get lots of practice," Cole stated. "They send in about a Hunter a month." He paused. "Funny."

"What is?" Bertha asked.

"The Hunters," Cole said. "Why do the fucking Russians only send in a Hunter at a time? Why not send in an army, and clean up Valley Forge in one day? And why do the Hunters only kill one Packrat, then split?"

"What?" Bertha leaned on her elbows on the table.

"That's what they do," Cole clarified. "They rack one Packrat, then leave. Four months ago Milly and Tommy were out picking berries. A damn Hunter popped up and blasted Tommy. Then he walked over to Milly, tickled her under the chin, and left."

"Why would he do that?" Bertha queried in surprise.

"Cole has an idea," Libby said.

"What is it?" Bertha prompted Cole.

The Claw leader gazed fondly at the slumbering Claws. "I think the Russians are using us as some kind of training exercise for their soldiers. I don't think they want to wipe us out. I think they're playing games with us, killing us off one at a time. Hell! They know we're here! And they don't usually let rebels keep on living. I know! They butchered my father and mother because my parents hated their guts!"

Bertha considered the theory. In a perverse sort of way, it made sense. The Russians knew the orphaned, homeless kids were flocking to Valley Forge, yet did nothing to stop the influx. Cole had said earlier that the Russians used disguises, even befriended some of the Packrats before slaughtering them. Why else would the Soviets go to so much trouble, unless the soldiers, probably their top commandoes, were honing their deadly skills on the lives of the Packrats? She stared at Cole with new respect.

"If we can get them out of here," Cole said, motioning toward the Claws, "I'll be the happiest man alive."

Bertha almost laughed at his use of the word "man." She stopped herself, though. Cole's parents, as Plato would say, had passed on to the higher mansions. Rather than submit to the Soviets, Cole had opted to resist. And now he was responsible for the lives of 15 others, for insuring they didn't starve to death and weren't killed by the Hunters, the mutants, or other

Packrats. Perhaps he did qualify as a man, after all. "How many other Packrat gangs are there in Valley Forge?" she asked him.

"Four I know of," Cole replied. "Maybe a few more. We each have our own turf to protect. The Bobcats are the closest to us, to the south a ways. We have run-ins with them all the time."

"Why don't all of you band together?" Bertha inquired. "There's strength in numbers."

"Band together?" Cole said. "I don't know. No one's ever thought of it, I guess. Besides, everybody shoots first and asks questions later. If I tried to make the peace with, say, the Bobcats, I'd be shot before I could even open my mouth."

"Sounds to me like you Packrats are playin' into the Soviets' hands," Bertha mentioned.

"There's nothing I can do about it," Cole stated. "It's been this way since before I came here."

"How long have you been here?" Bertha asked.

"Three years," Cole answered. "I wandered into Valley Forge after splitting from Phoenixville."

"How'd you hook up with the Claws?" Bertha probed.

"They were the first Packrats to find me," Cole said. "That's the way it usually works. Strays are taken in by the first group they come across."

Bertha shook her head. "I'm telling you! You bozos would do a lot better if you got organized. I used to belong to a gang in the Twin Cities, and I know what I'm talkin' about."

"You were in a gang?" Libby asked.

"Shhhhh!" Cole abruptly hissed.

Bertha glanced at the windows. Daylight was still an hour or two away, and the forest outside was shrouded in inky gloom.

"What is it?" Libby queried nervously.

Cole turned in his wooden chair and stared at the closed door. "I don't know. I thought I heard something."

"Could one of the other gangs, like the Bobcats, be sneakin' up on you?" Bertha inquired.

Libby shook her head. "No one goes out in the woods at night. It's too dangerous. The Packrats always hole up after dark."

"What about the Hunters?" Bertha remarked.

"Sometimes they come after us at night," Libby revealed. "But not often."

"Shhhh!" Cole shushed them. He stood and walked to the left window, cautiously standing to the right of the glass and peering out.

"Anything?" Libby asked in a whisper.

"No," Cole whispered back.

"I'll go have a look," Bertha proposed, rising. Her M-16 was propped against her chair. She grabbed it and moved to the doorway.

"If anyone's going out there, it'll be me," Cole said.

"I can take care of myself," Bertha informed him, her left hand on the doorknob. "You stay put and watch your Packrats."

"Bertha!" Libby said.

Bertha hesitated. "What?"

"Be careful!" Libby advised. "We can't afford to lose you! Not now!"

"Nothin' will happen to me," Bertha assured her. She opened the door, stepped outside, then closed it.

A strong wind was blowing in from the west, rustling the leaves on the trees. Above the cabin stars were visible.

Bertha faced into the wind, enjoying the cool tingle on her skin. She was feeling fatigued, and was glad dawn was not far off. Cole, Libby, and the rest could go with her to the SEAL. She hoped Blade and Sundance were still there.

A twig snapped.

Bertha was instantly on guard, warily raising the M-16 and searching the woods for an intruder, human or otherwise. She advanced toward the trees, bypassing the re-covered pit near the front door. The light from the cabin windows provided a faint glow to the edge of the trees. Bertha reached the tree line and stopped, crouching.

The wind was whipping the limbs, creating a subdued

clatter, mixed with the creaking of branches and the swishing of leaves.

Bertha strained her senses.

An audible scraping arose from the forest directly ahead.

Was it two limbs rubbing together? Bertha craned her neck and tilted her head, believing she could hear better.

Instead, she exposed her neck to the unseen lurker in the woods. A rope suddenly snaked out of the darkness, and a loop settled over her head and neck. Before she could react, Bertha was hauled from her feet and onto her stomach, the loop tightening about her neck, forming a noose, even as whoever was on the other end of the rope gave it a tremendous tug.

Bertha landed with the M-16 underneath her abdomen. She rolled, expecting her assailant to charge, but her attacker had another idea. The rope was yanked taut, and it felt like her head was being wrenched from her neck. Her breath was cut off, and she gagged as she struggled to her knees and released the M-16, clutching at the noose, her fingers urgently striving to pry the rope loose.

A burly man burst from cover, a 15 inch survival knife in his right hand, the rope in his left. He was dressed all in black, and his head was covered with a black mask. The knife extended, he rushed from behind a tree five yards away.

Damn! Bertha knew he had been waiting for her to drop the M-16! She let go of the rope and dived for the M-16, but her foe was already upon her.

The man in black launched his hefty body into a flying tackle, dropping the rope, and his left arm caught Bertha around the neck and drove her back, her desperate fingers inches from the M-16, and slammed her to the ground, onto her back, with him on top of her.

Bertha grunted and jerked her head to the right, and the survival knife plunged into the ground next to her left ear.

The man in black swept the knife up for another blow.

Bertha bucked and heaved, unbalancing her opponent, causing him to teeter to the right. She brought her right fist up and cuffed him on the cheek.

The man in black slashed at her face.

Bertha turned her face aside, but felt the keen edge of the survival knife slice open her right cheek.

The man stabbed at her right eye.

Bertha narrowly evaded the knife. Her left hand clutched his right wrist and held on fast.

He clamped his left hand on her throat.

Bertha was in dire straits. She was tiring, and tiring rapidly. She needed to do something, *anything,* to gain the advantage, or she was lost. Her years of street fighting served her in good stead. She jabbed her right hand upward, burying her forefinger in her attacker's left eye.

The man in black yelped, and his grip on her throat slackened.

Exerting her strength to its limits, Bertha surged her hips and stomach off the ground, tumbling the assassin over her head. She scrambled to her hands and knees, twisting to confront her foe.

He was superbly trained. Even as he landed on the dank earth, the man in black tumbled, coming out of the roll and straightening, whirling toward the woman in green.

The cabin door unexpectedly opened, spilling more light outside, bathing Bertha and the man with the survival knife.

The man in black spun, anticipating a threat from the cabin. For a fleeting moment, his back was to Bertha.

In a twinkling, Bertha struck. She shoved off from the ground, bringing her right foot up and around, executing one of the karate kicks taught to her by Rikki-Tikki-Tavi, the Family's supreme martial artist. It was a basic roundhouse kick, a Mawashi-geri, and it connected with the man in black between his shoulder blades.

The man in the mask was knocked forward by Bertha's kick. He tripped and toppled onto the makeshift latticework covering the pit. The limbs and reeds rent with a resounding crash, and the man in black sank into the pit.

Cole ran from the cabin, a lantern in his left hand, an AK-47 in his right. He halted at the pit rim.

Bertha saw the fury on Cole's features, and she surmised his intent at one glance. "Cole! No!" she shouted.

To no avail.

"Here, bastard!" Cole barked, and squeezed the trigger.

Bertha froze in midstride. She looked down, unable to prevent the inevitable.

The man in black was just scrambling to his feet when the slugs plowed into his chest and flung him against the pit wall. His body twitched and thrashed as more and more rounds were poured into him. A linear pattern of crimson geysers erupted across his torso, then angled higher, stitching a red path from his chin to the top of his head. The firing ceased, and the man in the mask pitched onto his face.

Cole gazed at his handiwork, smirking.

"You didn't have to do that!" Bertha exclaimed, panting.

Cole glanced at her. "Yes, I did."

"We could of questioned him!" Bertha stated. "He was a Hunter, right?"

"Without a doubt," Cole said.

Bertha doubled over, her ribs aching. "You didn't have to do that!" she reiterated.

Cole stared at the startled Claws emerging from the cabin, a few rubbing their sleepy eyes. He looked at Bertha, the set of his jaw determined and straight, and then at the corpse in the pit. "Yes, I did," he insisted softly.

This time, Bertha didn't argue.

14

"What the hell are they trying to pull?" Blade snapped.

"Beats me," Sundance admitted.

"Maybe they weren't after us at all," Nick commented.

The headlights behind them, after trailing the jeep for several miles, had turned off the highway.

"I don't get it," Blade said. "First, they almost catch up to us. Then they fall back and follow us for a while. Now, they're taking off. It doesn't make any sense."

"Who said the damn Commies have to make sense?" Nick asked.

Blade sighed. He was still experiencing a premonition of danger. But why?

"Take a left up ahead," Nick directed. "Stick with me, boys, and old Nick will guide you right up to the detention facility's front door."

"You'd do that for us?" Sundance queried.

"Hey! What are friends for?" Nick remarked light-heartedly. He patted Blade on the back. "Right, Warrior?"

And suddenly Blade recognized the source of his apprehension. The trifling inconsistencies accumulated into a plausible explanation, the only explanation possible under the circumstances. He smiled at Nick in the rearview mirror. "Right, Freeb," he replied.

Nick grinned. "Glad to see you're comin' around to my way of thinkin'!"

"I may be slow," Blade said, "but I catch on eventually." He glanced at Sundance.

Sundance grinned and nodded. "About time."

Blade realized Sundance had beaten him to the punch. How? What were the clues he had missed?

They drove to the southeast, Blade heeding Nick's infallible directions, using back roads until they reached the Schuykill Expressway.

"Just follow this south," Nick instructed them once

they were on the Expressway. "We'll be there before you know it."

"I can hardly wait," Blade mentioned. There were few vehicles on the road at such an early hour, and he maintained the speed at 50 miles an hour. Twice military transports passed on the opposite side of the Expressway traveling to the north.

"Look for the City Line exit," Nick advised.

"Will do," Blade stated.

The jeep reached the specified exit within minutes.

Blade wheeled onto City Line Avenue, moving to the southwest. A bakery truck approached from the other direction, conducting its morning deliveries.

"You want to make a left on Belmont Avenue," Nick disclosed.

Blade did, and a sign loomed ahead.

"The Vladimir I. Lenin Ministry of Psychological Sciences," Sundance read aloud. "Two miles."

"That's it!" Nick declared. "That's the place you want!"

"That's the detention facility?" Blade queried.

"That's it," Nick confirmed.

"You're sure?" Blade persisted.

"Of course I'm sure!" Nick retorted, annoyed. "Have I lied to you yet?"

Sundance began scratching at his chest. He idly started unbuttoning his uniform shirt.

Blade glanced over his right shoulder. "I doubt I could count all the lies."

Nick bristled angrily. "What the hell are you ravin' about?"

"Just this," Sundance stated, spinning in his seat, a gleaming Grizzly in his right hand.

Nick's eyes widened. "Hold on there, boy! What is this?"

"You tell us," Blade said.

"I don't know what you're talkin' about," Nick averred.

Blade looked at Sundance. "Why don't you do the honors?"

"Gladly," Sundance agreed. He leaned toward Nick.

"If you don't cut the crap, right now, I'm going to plant a bullet right between your eyes."

Nick was gawking from Sundance to Blade in bewilderment.

"The next words out of your mouth better be truthful ones," Sundance warned. "What's your real name?"

Nick's shoulders slumped. "Georgii Bakunin."

"Your rank?"

Bakunin frowned. "Captain."

"You're out of uniform, aren't you, Captain?" Sundance asked sarcastically.

Bakunin motioned with his left hand toward his face. "May I?"

"Only if you do it *real* slow," Sundance cautioned. "Twitch the wrong way and you're history."

Bakunin slowly raised his left hand and gripped the top of his long gray beard. He tugged on the upper right corner and his "beard" flopped to the floor.

"What about the hair?" Sundance queried.

"Dyed," Bakunin revealed. He ran his hand over his face, removing his "wrinkles."

"And the missing teeth?" Sundance said.

Bakunin reached his fingers into his mouth, scraping and pulling, and a minute later extracted a gummy black substance. His four upper front teeth miraculously reappeared.

"Pretty clever," Sundance conceded.

"What did I do wrong?" Bakunin asked in a pained tone.

"You figure it out for yourself," Sundance said.

"I'd like to know," Bakunin stated.

Sundance wagged the Grizzly barrel. "Don't press it. I'll pose the questions. What were you doing in that abandoned house?"

"Waiting for Packrats," Bakunin answered.

"You're a Hunter," Sundance deduced.

Bakunin nodded.

"You kill kids for a living," Sundance growled.

"No!" Bakunin said hastily. "It's required for all officers in Elite Branch."

"There's something I'd like to know," Blade interrupted, concentrating on his driving. "Why'd you string us along? Why'd you help us get this far? Why didn't you turn us in back at the garrison in Norristown?"

"I wanted to discover the reason you were here," Bakunin explained. "Find out what your connection to the Vikings might be."

"So you let us jump your comrades in Norristown," Sundance commented. "Didn't it bother you, knowing they could be hurt, or worse?"

"We must all make sacrifices for the cause," Bakunin said.

"The cause?" Sundance repeated quizzically.

"For the greater glory of Communism," Bakunin stated proudly.

"How did you know we were Warriors?" Blade interjected.

"You told—!" Bakunin started to reply, then angrily smacked his right palm against his forehead. "What an idiot I've been!"

"I wouldn't say you're an idiot," Sundance said. "Stupid, maybe, but not a complete idiot."

"How did you know we were Warriors?" Blade repeated his question.

Bakunin stared at the giant Warrior. "Your name was vaguely familiar. Something about it rang a bell. And then I remembered the incident in Washington, the one involving another Warrior named Hickok, I believe. And I recalled seeing an intelligence report on your Family."

"The information the spy in Denver uncovered," Blade speculated.

"We have a spy in Denver?" Bakunin asked innocently.

"What did this intelligence report say?" Sundance queried.

"It was merely a brief rundown on your Family," Bakunin replied. "A capsule summary of your Family's known history, organization, and leadership. It included a section on the Warriors, and contained a paragraph on the head of the Warriors. A man of gigantic proportions. A man named Blade."

Another sign materialized ahead, displaying an arrow indicating the direction they should travel to reach the Ministry of Psychological Sciences.

Blade took a left.

"Uh-oh," Sundance commented.

Five hundred yards to the southeast was a huge stone wall, 15 feet in height, capped with another 4 feet of barbed wire. A latticed iron gate, now closed, provided the only means of entering the Ministry. Four soldiers stood outside the gate.

Blade spotted a turnoff to the right and took it. The jeep lurched as he spun the steering wheel sharply, and then they were on a quiet side road. A stand of trees and brush screened the jeep from the guards at the iron gate. He braked the jeep.

"Now what do we do?" Sundance inquired.

"We proceed with the mission," Blade said.

"But how do we know this jerk was telling the truth about this place?" Sundance asked. "How do we know it's even a detention facility? Bakunin never said the Vikings were here for sure."

Blade glanced at the Russian. "No, he didn't. But so far, all the directions he's supplied have been right on the mark. Oh, he lied about who he was and lied to gain our confidence. But he told the truth about the garrison in Norristown, and about how to get to Norristown from Valley Forge. He didn't want us to know he was a soldier, didn't want us to discover his secret before he discovered ours, so he gave us accurate directions, expecting us to trust him, hoping we would blurt out the information he wanted. He couldn't come right out and say he definitely knew where the Vikings were being held, because that would have been too obvious, too suspicious. But he could, and did, give us a viable lead. I could be wrong, but I think he was telling the truth about the Ministry. The Vikings might well be there."

Sundance nodded toward Bakunin. "What do we do about him?"

Blade studied the captain. The wisest recourse was to kill Bakunin and dump his body in the weeds. Leaving the Russian alive needlessly invited trouble. If they tied him up, Bakunin might escape and alert the Ministry guards. A true expert could always slip free of constraints if given enough time. Blade seriously considered slitting Bakunin's throat, but then his conversation with Plato concerning excessive brutality flashed through his mind and he frowned. "We'll tie him up," he stated.

"You're the boss," Sundance said, "but if it was up to me, I'd waste the son of a bitch right now."

Blade nodded. "I agree with you."

"What? Then why are we going soft on him?" Sundance responded in surprise.

"It's something Plato said," Blade revealed. "About us not stooping to their level."

"Plato isn't a Warrior," Sundance stated cryptically.

Blade knew Sundance was right, but he didn't want to debate the issue. His affection for his mentor overrode his seasoned inclination. Just this once, he told himself, he'd do it Plato's way. Give Plato's outlook a chance. And hope he wouldn't live to regret it.

But he did.

"We don't have any rope," Sundance mentioned.

"We'll improvise," Blade said. He slid his right Bowie from under his shirt.

"What's that for?" Bakunin asked when he saw the big knife.

"I thought I'd carve my name on your forehead," Blade quipped. He shifted in his seat, examining its fabric. The back of the seat was covered by a leather-like, durable material. He inserted his knife into the fabric and began slicing wide strips from the seat.

"Cup your hands together and hold your arms out toward Blade," Sundance directed the captain.

Bakunin complied.

Blade swiftly bound the Russian, applying the strips to the officer's wrists and ankles, cutting additional strips as needed.

"You are cutting off my circulation," Bakunin said at one point.

"Should we cry now or later?" Sundance retorted.

Blade applied two strips around Bakunin's mouth,

effectively gagging the Soviet officer. "This should keep you comfy until we return." He eased his Bowie under his shirt.

Bakunin's eyes were simmering pools of hatred.

Blade accelerated, seeking another turnoff. He found a field after driving 60 yards, an overgrown patch of weeds and brush to his left, and he angled the jeep into the densest undergrowth. He stopped when he was satisfied the jeep was concealed from passersby on the road. "This will suffice," he announced, and switched off the ignition, placing the keys in his right front pants pocket.

Sundance replaced his Grizzly under his shirt. "What's our first move?" he queried as he buttoned up.

"We'll see how close we can get to that wall," Blade said. "Check out the layout."

Sundance grabbed his FN 50-63 and exited the jeep.

Blade verified the strips binding Bakunin were tight, then patted the captain on the head. "I want to thank you for your assistance. We couldn't have done it without you." He chuckled.

Bakunin vented his anger in a string of expletives, his words muffled by the gag.

"Be nice," Blade baited him. "And make yourself right at home. We'll be back in a bit." He climbed from the jeep, clutching the Commando in his right hand.

Sundance was waiting at the front of the vehicle.

Blade took the lead, moving off into the brush, heading for a row of trees close to the wall. Bright lights were discernible through the trees.

A tinge of faint light rimmed the eastern horizon.

"We'll have to hurry!" Blade remarked. "Dawn isn't far off."

Sundance nodded.

The two Warriors jogged to the row of trees and took cover behind two maple trunks, Sundance to Blade's right.

Blade peered around the bole of the tree, scanning the landscape ahead.

A field, 20 yards in width, separated the trees from the stone wall. Brilliant spotlights were attached at regular intervals along the top of the wall, aligned toward the field. A half-dozen towering structures reared skyward on the far side of the wall.

Sundance uttered a low whistle.

Blade glanced to the right.

Two soldiers were strolling along the base of the wall, AK-47's slung over their shoulders, coming toward the Warriors.

Blade ducked from sight. Gaining entrance to the Ministry promised to be extremely difficult. Crossing the field unseen, if guards were posted on the wall, would be impossible. And sneaking in the front gate was a ludicrous notion.

Or was it?

Blade waited until the two guards passed and were 50 yards off, nearing the gate. He waved to Sundance, then followed the guards, staying behind the trees.

The guards ambled at a leisurely pace.

Sundance caught up with Blade. "What are you doing?" he whispered.

"There's no way we'll get over that wall," Blade responded. "Not with all the lights and the barbed wire and the guards."

"So how do we get inside?"

"I'm working on that," Blade informed him.

The pair of patrolling guards reached the gate and halted, engaging the quartet of soldiers already there in conversation.

Blade edged to within 20 yards of the front gate, then squatted in the shelter of a large oak.

Sundance joined the head Warrior.

The light on the eastern horizon was increasing.

Blade scrutinized the wall, at a loss for an idea to penetrate the Ministry's defenses.

A muted rumble sounded from the northwest.

Blade glanced over his left shoulder.

A truck was slowly approaching the gate, still about 400 yards distant.

Blade squinted, striving to identify the truck. He wasn't worried about being observed by the truck's occupants; the trees were plunged in murky shadows.

The truck drove nearer.

Blade perceived the truck wasn't a military vehicle. It was white, with a small cab and a square body.

The truck was 350 yards off.

Blade glanced at the gate, then the truck.

The truck reached the 300-yard mark.

Blade turned to Sundance. "I don't have time to explain. I want you to stay here, right here, until I signal you or return."

"What? Where are you going?" Sundance asked.

"No time," Blade stated, and rose. He ran to the rear, keeping in the darkest areas, racing parallel with the road. His plan was perilous, but if he succeeded, he would be inside the Ministry in a matter of minutes. But he had to reach the 100-yard mark before the white truck.

The truck was 250 yards from the gate.

Blade sprinted full out, his eyes glued to the inky section of road next to an enormous willow tree. If he could reach that spot before the truck, and if his estimation of the truck's size was accurate, he could carry it off.

If.

The white truck was now 200 yards from the front gate.

Blade almost stumbled over a root. He recovered and sped toward the willow.

One hundred eighty yards.

Blade wished there had been time to detail his intent to Sundance. He knew Sundance would chafe at being left behind, but both of them trying for the truck was unrealistic, increasing their risk of detection. And as the tallest, Blade stood the best chance of accomplishing the maneuver.

One hundred sixty yards.

Damn! His legs ached! Blade ignored the pain, pounding forward, breathing deeply.

One hundred fifty yards.

If he tripped again, he was lost.

One hundred forty.

Blade slowed, slinging the Commando over his right shoulder.

One hundred thirty.

Blade reached the cover of the willow and pressed against its rough trunk, the bark scraping his right cheek.

One hundred twenty.

He would only get one try. If he blew it, they could forget locating the Vikings in the Ministry. If the Vikings were even there.

If again.

One hundred ten.

Blade tensed, watching the tires turn as the white truck neared the willow tree. He estimated the truck was moving at 30 miles an hour.

The white truck reached the spreading willow, was abreast of the trunk for an instant, and then was past the willow, proceeding toward the gate.

Blade was in motion as the truck came even with the willow. He darted around the trunk and dashed the five feet to the road, reaching the rear corner, his legs churning to keep pace, his arms outstretched, his fingers grasping for a purchase. For a second, the outcome was in doubt. And then his fingers closed on the corner, his nails gaining a slight hold on the metal, but it was enough for him to exert his tremendous strength, to tug on the corner, to pull his body that much closer to the rear panel of the vehicle, and there was a door handle in the center of the white panel. His left arm swung out, and he grabbed the handle and held on for dear life. The strain was incredible. His feet left the road, and for a moment he was hanging by one hand as his right was wrenched from the corner. He clawed at the handle with his right hand, gripping the cool metal, and used his added leverage to haul himself onto the rear fender.

The truck was 80 yards from the iron gate.

Blade glanced up. The roof was eight feet above his head. He steeled his leg muscles and leaped, his arms straight overhead, and his hands clasped the lip of the roof as his knees banged against the rear panel. He grimaced as he clung to the roof, knowing he must keep moving or he would falter and fall to the asphalt. His arms bulged, his neck muscles protruding, as he pulled himself up onto the roof.

Fifty yards from the dull horizontal and vertical iron bars.

Blade rolled to the middle of the roof. Two of his fingers were bleeding and his left knee was throbbing. But he'd done it!

The small white truck was reducing its speed. There was a slight squeaking noise from the cab, from the driver's side, as if the driver was rolling his window down.

Only four guards were at the gate. The two on patrol, Blade reasoned, must have resumed their rounds.

The truck came to a halt in front of the gate.

"Hi, Tim," said one of the guards. "You're late."

"I had to wait for them to get their asses in gear at my last stop," the driver, evidently the man named Tim, stated. "They couldn't find a bag of dirty aprons from last night."

"There's a note attached to my clipboard," the guard said. "They want you to pick up a load from Penza Hall."

"All right," the driver responded. "But I hope they have it all on the loading dock. I hate going into that place. It gives me the creeps."

"Just be thankful you're not in there as a permanent resident," the guard remarked, grinning.

"Don't even joke about a thing like that," Tim said. "I'm not an enemy of the State."

The guard snickered. He motioned toward the gate. "Open it!" he ordered.

The three other guards obeyed.

Blade, lying as flat as possible on the roof, felt the truck vibrate as it passed the iron gate. He'd made it! He was inside the Ministry of Psychological Sciences!

Now what?

The white truck took a right, along a narrow, tree-lined road. Few people were abroad.

Blade could hear the driver whistling as he drove. What was this Tim picking up at Penza Hall? And why was the driver so leery of the place? What was it Tim had said to the guard? "I'm not an enemy of the State."

Was Penza Hall a prison? Hardly likely, if the complex was devoted to the Psychological Sciences. Unless, Blade speculated, Penza Hall was devoted to psychological manipulations instead of simple physical incarceration. He recalled a portion of his Warrior course at the Home, a study of the psychological-warfare techniques employed by the superpowers and others before the Big Blast. The Russians, in particular, masters of mind manipulation, and at extracting important data from recalcitrant subjects. Perhaps Penza Hall was where such "extractions" were made. If so, then Penza Hall might be where the Vikings were being interrogated.

The truck took a left, driving between two high buildings, each over ten stories in height.

Blade peered up at the windows, hoping no one was gazing through them at the road below.

The white truck turned to the right, slowing.

Blade rose on his elbows and scanned the road ahead. They were entering an expansive parking lot. Across the lot was a gigantic structure, only four stories high but encompassing at least five or six acres. Most of the windows in the edifice were dark; only three or four displayed any light. The truck was making for a loading dock stacked with crates and boxes. Two enormous doors, both closed, each large enough to accommodate a troop transport or a tractor-trailer, framed the wall behind the loading dock.

The driver ceased whistling.

Blade lowered his head, waiting with baited breath as the truck braked alongside the loading dock. He heard a door slam and risked a look.

The driver, a lean individual in jeans and a blue jacket, was ascending the ramp to the loading dock, a tablet in his left hand. He walked to the right of the two immense doors, up to a small metal door. He reached up and pressed a button encased in the brown wall.

Blade detected a faint ringing from within the building. He gazed at the structure, attempting to determine the material used in its construction. The brown wall appeared to be a form of stone, but he doubted stone was the material used. Was it a plastic designed to simulate the appearance of stone? Or was it a substance the Soviets had developed since the Big Blast?

The small door suddenly opened, and a brawny soldier stood in the doorway. "Yes?" he demanded.

The driver pointed toward his truck. "They told me at the gate you have a pickup."

The guard glanced at the white truck. "Sure do. Wait right here." He started to turn, then paused. "On second thought, why don't you come with me?"

Tim fidgeted nervously. "Do I have to?"

The guard grinned. "Afraid so. There's about eight or nine bins. I'm not going to lug it all down here by myself."

Tim shrugged. "Then let's hop to it."

The guard and the driver disappeared inside.

Blade saw his chance. He rolled to the right and dropped from the roof, alighting on his hands and feet, his arches stinging from the impact.

No one else was in sight.

Blade stood and headed for the ramp. As he did, he noticed the sign on the side panel of the white truck: CENTRAL LAUNDRY. A laundry truck? The Ministry sent its soiled garments and whatever to another establishment to be cleaned? Why not clean them on the premises? Perhaps because doing so would entail a permanent cleaning staff at the Ministry, and such a staff would present a security problem. What was the old saying? Loose lips sink ships? Considering the security clamped on the Ministry, the higher-ups undoubtedly wanted to minimize the presence of non-essential personnel. He reached the ramp and raced up to the loading dock.

A crack of light rimmed the small door.

Blade jogged to the door and halted, unslinging the Commando. The door was slightly ajar! When the guard and driver had entered Penza Hall, they had failed to push the door closed! Maybe because they would be returning with their arms laden with laundry. He used his left hand to ease the door open.

A gloomy, deserted hallway was on the other side.

Blade ducked through the door and flattened against the left-hand wall.

The hallway ended at a yellow door 20 yards away. Other doors lined the hallway, four on the left, three on the right.

There was no time to lose! The guard and the driver might return at any moment!

Blade reached the first door on the left. It was open, revealing a spacious chamber filled with stacks of wooden crates and cardboard boxes.

The yellow door at the end of the hall started to swing open.

Blade slid into the storage chamber and hid behind a stack of crates as the hallway filled with a peculiar squeaking.

" . . . three more loads," said the voice of the guard.

"Thanks for doing this," stated the driver. "Rostov always makes me go up and get it by myself."

"Rostov is a prick," the guard stated.

Blade heard the metal door open, and he padded to the doorway and risked a peek around the corner.

The guard and the driver were pushing white bins overflowing with unclean clothing and linen. The squeaking was emanating from the tiny black wheels on the laundry bins. They passed outside, and the metal door eased almost shut.

Blade turned to the left and sprinted down the hallway to the yellow door. The door opened onto a flight of stairs. He hesitated, glancing down. The stairs descended several levels below ground, as well as climbing to the stories above. Which way to go? The guard and the driver would be going up. So he went down, taking two steps at a stride, constantly surveying the levels below for any hint of activity. He halted on the first landing, pondering. If the Russians did hold the Vikings in Penza Hall, on which floor would the Vikings most likely be detained? Surely not on one of the upper floors, where windows were a tempting escape route.

Underground would be best.

Move! his mind shrieked.

Blade hastened below. It was close to dawn, and the corridors would probably be crammed with workers once the day shift arrived. Finding the holding cells quickly was imperative. He decided to begin at the bottom and work his way up. The magnitude of his task bothered him. Penza Hall was enormous. He couldn't possibly cover all of it before daylight. He reached the next landing, kept moving.

Far above him a door scraped open.

Someone else was using the stairs!

Blade increased his pace. Three steps at a leap, he hurried to the lowest level.

Footsteps sounded on the stairs above, echoing hollowly in the confines of the stairwell.

Blade reached the bottom of the stairwell and found two yellow doors. He tried one knob, and was gratified when it twisted and the door jerked wide. Gratified until he saw what awaited him.

A Russian soldier.

15

Sundance was annoyed. He resented being left behind, but he was too professional a Warrior to disobey his orders. So he waited, concealed in the weeds near the large oak, watching the four guards at the gate. He had covered them with the FN 50-63 when the white truck had stopped, but the guards hadn't seen Blade. His respect for the Warrior chief had ballooned; only an idiot or a dedicated, courageous man would have attempted such a perilous strategem. The idiot because he wouldn't know any better. The brave man because the mission was of paramount importance, and the danger was eclipsed by an exalted ideal, the ideal of serving others, of saving lives, of placing a priority on the welfare of the many and rendering any sacrifice necessary. And Blade wasn't an idiot.

The eastern sky was growing lighter and lighter.

Sundance had caught a glimpse of Blade's maneuver, and had marveled at the speed, strength, and daring displayed. He knew Blade viewed this run to Philadelphia as critical to the Family's future. If an alliance could be forged with the Vikings, the Soviets would be defeated that much sooner. If the Vikings weren't receptive to the idea, the Family faced the prospect of a prolonged conflict with the Russians. By finding the Vikings and liberating them, Blade might save untold millions from the totalitarian Communist regime, might restore sweet liberty to the land.

There was a commotion to the right.

Sundance craned his neck to see better.

Two more guards were approaching the front gate, patrolling along the base of the wall. They had stopped, and were staring at the line of trees, AK-47's in hand.

Someone was shouting.

The two guards began walking across the field toward the trees.

What was happening? Sundance wondered.

He found out.

Captain Georgii Bakunin emerged from the woods, yelling in Russian, hurrying up to the two soldiers. They conversed for a few seconds, and Bakunin showed them something he drew from his pocket.

The four gate guards were watching the trio.

Sundance crawled to the base of the oak and stood, carefully avoiding exposing himself to the soldiers. He peered around the trunk.

Bakunin and the pair of guards were jogging toward the front gate.

Sundance stared at Bakunin, knowing the captain would alert the Ministry to the presence of the Warriors. They would conduct an extensive search of the grounds and the building, and they would increase their perimeter security, minimizing Blade's chances of escaping. The Warrior chief would be trapped inside.

Bakunin and the two guards were 50 yards from the

gate.

What should he do? Sundance doubted Bakunin had told the two troopers about Blade and himself. They'd only exchanged a few words. Bakunin must have told them who he was, and produced confirming identification.

Bakunin and the two soldiers were 40 yards from the iron gate.

Sundance placed his finger on the trigger of the FN. If Bakunin was silenced before he could inform the Ministry officials, the Russians would never suspect Blade was inside. Particularly if a diversion was created *outside.*

Bakunin and the two guards were running along the base of the wall.

Sundance raised the FN to his shoulder. If he downed Bakunin, all hell would break loose! The Russians would come pouring out of the Ministry after him. But if he could hold them off for a while, he might give Blade the precious time necessary to locate the Vikings. He sighted on Bakunin, aiming for the head.

Bakunin and the two patrol guards were 20 yards from the front gate, in a direct line with a large oak at the edge of the field, when the captain's head exploded in a spray of blood and brains, spattering the wall, and he was lifted from his feet and smashed against the stone as the sound of a shot shattered the dawn air.

The two guards with Bakunin spun toward the tree line, and both were rocked backward as powerful slugs ripped through their torsos and flung them to the ground, spurting crimson from their ruptured chests.

Initially stunned by the carnage, the quartet of gate guards sprang into action. Three of them spread out, eyes riveted on the woods, seeking the sniper. The fourth ran toward a black button imbedded in the wall to the left of the gate. He was reaching for the button when a slug caught him in the back of the head, just above the neck, and his mouth and nose erupted outward in a shower of flesh and teeth. He tumbled onto his stomach and lay still.

The three remaining soldiers hesitated. One of them

turned and dashed for the gate, intending to open it and seek shelter inside. But three shots struck him in the middle of his back, between his shoulder blades, and he was hurled forward to crash into the unyielding iron gate. He slumped to the earth.

One of the guards spotted a faint gun flash near the large oak, and charged, firing his AK-47 at the tree, his rounds chipping bark from the trunk. He managed four strides before he was hit in the right eye. His body jerked to the right and flopped to the grass.

The last guard, having seen his comrades die and realizing there was nowhere he could flee, dropped his AK-47 and raised his hands above his head, mustering a feeble grin. His grin vanished, collapsing inward and filling his mouth with blood and chunks of teeth, as a shot penetrated his mouth and exited out the back of his neck. A look of amazement flitted across his features, and he tottered and fell.

Sundance raced from cover, sprinting the 20 yards to the wall and then running to the gate. He stepped over the body of one of the guards, peering inside.

Lights were coming on in a low structure approximately 50 yards distant, to the left of the front gate.

Sundance leaned against the wall and hastily replaced the partially spent magazine in the FN. He wanted a full clip when the soldiers arrived on the scene. He tossed the partially spent magazine aside and pulled a fresh clip from his right rear pants pocket. As he inserted the magazine, loud shouting arose from within the complex. He glanced around the corner of the wall, between the iron gate bars.

A cluster of 10 to 12 troopers had gathered at the entrance to the low structure. They were yelling and gesturing toward the front gate.

Sundance grinned. He suspected the low structure was a barracks for the soldiers. They would need to cross a wide lawn before reaching the gate, and would be sitting ducks for 40 yards or so. A row of trees lined the road beyond the gate, but the road and the trees would be to the right. A long drive connected the barracks to the road, and someone had thoughtfully neglected to line the drive with trees.

More shouting. Seven of the Russian soldiers started running in the direction of the gate.

Sundance rested the FN barrel on one of the horizontal bars in the iron gate. He patiently waited until the soldiers were only 30 yards off, then squeezed the trigger and held it down.

The seven troopers jerked and thrashed as they were hit. Only one of them was able to get off a shot. Surprised in the open, they died en masse, their bodies bunched together.

Louder yelling from the barracks.

Sundance took a deep breath to calm himself. His blood was racing, his adrenaline pumping. In a strange sort of way, he was enjoying himself, despite the overwhelming odds. He'd fought in the battle for the Home against the Doktor's forces, but this was different, different even than fighting the scavengers. This time it was him against an army, and he relished the challenge. He would buy Blade the time the Warrior chief needed, or he would perish in the attempt.

Soldiers continued to pile from the barracks. An officer took command, and with a wave of his right arm led ten of them toward the gate.

Sundance sighted the FN.

It was do-or-die time!

16

The Russian soldier, a private, was carrying a tray of dirty dishes and an empty carton of milk. He inadvertently started as a giant wrenched the door in front of him open, but then he saw the uniform and grinned. "Comrade! You scared the hell out of me!"

Blade froze. The soldier had an AK-47 slung over his left shoulder.

The young guard glanced over his shoulder at the gloomy hallway, then stared at Blade, his expression evidencing a certain nervousness. "You won't report me, will you?"

"Report you?" Blade repeated.

The soldier hefted the tray. "I know we are not permitted to eat on duty, but I become so bored at night when there is little to do, and my friend in the kitchen . . ." He abruptly stopped, his eyes narrowing, focused on the Commando.

Blade bent his right leg at the knee.

"Where did you get that weapon?" the guard asked. "That is not standard issue." He raked Blade from head to toe. "And your uniform does not seem quite right," he stupidly blurted out.

Blade flicked his right leg out, striking the guard on the left kneecap. There was a distinct snapping noise, and the guard gasped and dropped his food tray. Blade's left hand gripped the guard by the shirt before he could fall. The tray clattered to the tiled floor. Blade moved into the hallway, closing the door behind him. He shoved the Commando barrel into the guard's frightened face.

"Please!" the guard cried. "Don't kill me!"

"That depends on you!" Blade informed him.

The guard's thin lips were quivering. "I think my knee is broken!"

"You knee will be the least of your problems if you don't cooperate," Blade stated menacingly.

"What do you want?" the guard wailed.

"The Vikings."

The guard's brown eyes widened. "The Vikings?"

"Are you hard of hearing?" Blade snapped. "Where are they?" He decided to try a bluff. "And don't play games with me! I know they're here!"

"They were here," the guard exclaimed.

"What do you mean?"

The guard motioned toward a series of doors in the hallway to their rear. "They were held here while the Committee for State Security questioned them."

"And what happened to them?" Blade queried.

The guard's mouth turned downward. "They . . . did not survive the questioning."

"They died?" Blade probed.

The guard nodded.

Blade jammed the Commando barrel into the guard's cheek. "I don't believe you!"

"It's true!" the guard insisted in terror. "The last one died four days ago! The Security people were not lenient in their interrogations!"

Blade frowned. He'd anticipated this eventuality, but dreaded it all the same. Too much time had elapsed since the Vikings were captured, and the Soviets were not notorious for allowing their captives to live once the required information had been obtained.

The information!

"Where's their office?" Blade demanded.

"What?" the guard responded, perplexed.

"The office of the Committee for State Security," Blade said.

The guard blanched. "You are joking, yes?"

Blade's countenance hardened. "Do I look like I'm joking?"

"But it would be im—" the guard started to object.

Blade smacked the Commando barrel against the guard's head. "They must have an office in this building! Somewhere where they could conduct their interrogations in private! Where is it?"

The guard pressed his left hand to his injured ear. "Upstairs," he answered.

"How far up?" Blade asked.

"Three floors," the guard revealed.

"Come on!" Blade yanked the guard toward the door.

"What are you doing?"

"You're going to take me to their office," Blade told him.

"No!" the guard protested. "They will kill me when they find out!"

Blade paused. "I won't tell them if you don't! But I

will kill you right here and now if you don't take me to their office! So what's it going to be?''

The guard was clearly scared out of his wits.

Blade shoved him toward the door. ''Get going!''

Whining, the guard hobbled to the door and opened it.

''Up the stairwell!'' Blade barked. ''Move it!''

They ascended the stairs, proceeding slowly, impeded by the guard's injured knee. As they reached the appropriate landing, a muted siren began wailing in the distance.

Blade halted. ''What's that?''

The guard cocked his head. ''The security alarm.''

Blade rammed the Commando barrel into the guard's back. ''They must know I'm here!''

''I don't think so!'' the guard replied, afraid of receiving a round in the spinal column.

''Why?''

''It sounds like it is coming from out near the barracks,'' the guard explained, hoping to alleviate the giant's obvious tension and reduce his risk of being shot. ''If they knew you were here, the alarms in Penza Hall would go off.''

Blade gazed up the stairwell. Why would they be blaring an alarm outside? Did it have something to do with Sundance? ''Keep moving!'' he ordered.

The guard cautiously eased open one of the two yellow doors, the one on the left, and looked in both directions. ''All clear,'' he claimed.

Blade pushed the guard into the hallway, then followed. The corridor was indeed deserted. ''Where's their office?''

''This way,'' the guard said, pointing to the right.

Blade nudged the guard with the Commando. ''Lead the way.''

The guard limped down the hall and stopped at one of the many doors. ''This is it.''

Blade glanced at the door. Printed in English— along with strange letters from another language, undoubtedly Russian—were the words. COMMITTEE

FOR STATE SECURITY. STAFF PERSONNEL ONLY. "Try the knob," Blade directed.

The guard did. "It is locked."

"Step aside." Blade waited while the guard shuffled a few feet further along the corridor. He placed his right hand on the door and tested the knob, verifying the door was locked.

"See? We can't get in," the guard said. "We should leave!"

Blade's right arm tightened, his massive muscles rippling, as he applied his prodigious strength to the lock. He grit his teeth, concentrating on the door, and he almost missed the guard's attack. A glimmer of flashing light alerted him at the last instant.

The guard had drawn a knife from concealment, and he made a growling noise deep in his throat as he stabbed the sharp knife up and in, going for the giant's chest. He believed he'd caught the giant completely unawares, so he was all the more surprised when his first blow missed, and was amazed when the giant swung the machine-gun barrel toward him but didn't squeeze the trigger. The guard realized the giant wouldn't shoot because the shots would bring troops on the run. He waved the knife in the air. "I'm going to carve you up into little pieces for what you did to my knee!" he stated confidently. He failed to notice the giant's right hand as it inched under his bulky uniform shirt.

"You talk too much," the giant said.

"Do I?" the guard rejoined, and slashed his knife at the giant's face.

Blade easily evaded the knife, drawing his face out of range, and then stepped in close and swept the right Bowie out and up, the 15-inch blade burying itself to the hilt in the stupefied guard's throat below the chin.

The guard stiffened and dropped his knife, gurgling as his blood poured from his neck. He gasped and futilely endeavored to withdraw the Bowie, but the giant's steely arm held the blade fast. He opened his mouth to speak, but only a rivulet of blood ushered forth. His eyelids fluttered, and he expired.

Blade wrenched the Bowie free, his hand and forearm caked with dripping crimson.

The guard pitched to the floor.

Blade wiped the Bowie clean on the guard's pant leg, then slid the big knife into its sheath. He quickly slung the Commando over his right shoulder, then applied both of his hands to the doorknob. Straining his arms to the utmost, he simultaneously pushed and twisted. For half a minute nothing transpired. And then the inner jamb rent with a splintering crunch, and the door swung open, the doorknob snapping off in his hands.

The siren was still wailing in the distance.

Blade entered the KGB office. There were doors to his left and right. Against the right wall was a desk; against the left wall a file cabinet. He moved to the cabinet and tried the top drawer.

The damn thing was locked.

Blade returned to the hallway and found the guard's knife. It had a relatively thick six-inch blade. He reentered the office, crossed to the file cabinet, and gripped the top drawer with his right hand while holding the knife, blade pointed downward, in his left. He exerted pressure on the drawer, and was rewarded by a quarter inch gap appearing at the top of the drawer. He inserted the knife blade all the way to the handle, and started prying on the drawer with the knife while pulling on the handle with his right hand. A minute elapsed. Two. The drawer came open with a resounding metallic pop. He paused and listened.

The corridor was quiet.

Blade rummaged through the dozens of folders in the top drawer. They were all labeled, some in Russian, some in English. None of them appeared to have any connection with the Vikings. He leaned over and tugged on the second drawer, delighted when it slid right open. A hasty search was fruitless. He knelt and opened the third, final, drawer.

And there they were.

Three manilla files, each headed with the word VIKINGS. He scooped them out and flipped through

the pages. Some of the contents were in Russian, some
in English. He wondered why. He knew the Russians
were bilingual. They had to be. Many of their troopers
were conscripted, brainwashed Americans. Many of the
bureaucrats were native citizens as well, and perhaps the
conquered Americans found it too difficult to learn
Russian fluently. Perhaps the reports in the files were
duplicated, one in Russian, one in English. Whatever
the case, Blade determined, now was not the time to
reflect on the issue. He extracted the files, unbuttoned
his shirt, and tucked them over his abdomen. Hurriedly
buttoning the shirt, he rose and started for the door.

That was when the brainstorm hit.

Blade halted, went to the desk, and tried several of its
drawers. None of them were locked. He discovered a
fingernail file, a brush, a mirror in the second one he
opened. In the third he found a pack of matches.
Smiling, he walked to the KGB files and opened all three
drawers. He lit a match, then touched the flame to the
files. A folder sparked, then burst into flame. He swiftly
repeated the procedure with each drawer. The room was
filled with smoke by the time he stood, dropped the
matches into the top drawer, and ran into the corridor.

The KGB was in for a nasty surprise.

Blade jogged toward the stairwell. He had the
information the Freedom Federation needed. But it
wouldn't be of any use if he didn't make it out of the
Ministry alive. He flung the stairwell door open,
stepped onto the landing.

"Freeze!" someone bellowed from overhead.

Blade glanced up.

A Russian soldier was leaning over the railing half a
flight above, his AK-47 trained on the Warrior.

17

"Where do you think your friends went?" Libby asked.

"I don't know," Bertha admitted.

"Maybe they split on you," pudgy Eddy suggested.

"And left the SEAL here?" Bertha rejoined.

They were standing next to the transport. The sun was just cresting the eastern horizon. None of the Claws had been able to sleep after the incident with the nocturnal Hunter. Shortly before daybreak, Cole had recommended finding Bertha's friends. Libby and Eddy came along. The rest were told to remain in the cabin.

"They'll be back," Cole said.

"If they don't get racked," Eddy commented.

Bertha glanced at Pudgy. "Boy! Ain't you the cheery one!"

"What the hell do I have to be happy about?" Eddy responded.

"How about getting out of there, for one thing," Libby remarked.

"I'll believe it when I see it," was Eddy's retort.

Bertha leaned against the SEAL. The doors were locked, and only Blade had a key. There was nothing she could do, nowhere she could go, until Blade and Sundance returned. But who knew how long that could take? They must have departed for Philadelphia last night! She was slightly miffed they had gone on without her. But she knew the Big Guy pretty well, knew he wouldn't allow anything to interfere with the mission. Usually. There had been that time in Thief River Falls.

"So what do we do now?" Libby inquired. She, like Cole and Eddy, carried an AK-47.

"We wait for my buddies," Bertha stated.

"How long? A day? A week?" Eddy asked.

Cole glared at Eddy. "Shut up," he snapped.

Eddy did.

Bertha studied Cole. The Claw leader had been

abnormally silent on the trek from the log cabin. What
was he thinking about? The prospect of living at the
home? Of delivering the Claws from a savage existence
of survival of the fittest?

"We could leave one of us here," Libby proposed,
"and the rest of us could wait at the cabin." She
paused. "I don't like leaving the younger ones alone."

"They can take care of themselves," Eddy said.

Cole stared in the general direction of their hideout.
"Libby, you can stay here with Bertha. Eddy and I will
go back."

"Fine by me," Libby stated.

"Hey!" Eddy said. "Do you guys hear something?"

Bertha suddenly did, and an icy sensation crept over
her skin. Gunshots. Coming from the . . .

"The cabin!" Cole shouted, and was off, racing at
breakneck speed.

Libby and Eddy took off after him.

Bertha clutched her M-16 and followed. The three
Claws were able to traverse the terrain at an uncanny
speed. Years of practice had endowed them with exceptionally fleet feet and remarkable skill at negotiating
obstacles in their path. She was able to keep Libby and
Eddy in sight, but couldn't gain on them. Her forehead
began hurting again. She'd examined the wound during
the night. There was a ragged two-inch gash along her
hairline, but otherwise she seemed to be fine. She
doubted she had a concussion. Her head had sustained
tremendous blows in the past. Hickok liked to say it was
the hardest head he knew of. But what did he know?

The distant gunfire attained a crescendo. Screams and
shrieks were distinguishable.

Bertha abruptly forget all else in her concern for the
Claws. She hadn't considered them to be in any grave
danger until that very instant. After all, those kids had
spent years surviving in the wilderness of Valley Forge,
fighting Hunters and other Packrats, stealing food and
guns and whatever else they required. She knew there
existed a violent rivalry among the Packrat gangs for
control of the large but limited tract of land comprising
Valley Forge. But the Packrats were, for the most part,

young children, and she'd never seriously considered them as being decidedly deadly.

She was about to have her impression changed.

Bertha was still hundreds of yards from the log cabin when the shooting died down. A ghastly screech reached her ears, then all was unnaturally quiet. She ran a little faster. Eddy and Libby were about 20 yards ahead of her. They reached the field at the bottom of the burned-out hill and started across. Bertha was breathing heavily, and her left side began hurting as she neared the base of the hill. Ignoring the pain in her side, she took a deep breath and plunged forward across the field.

Cole was nowhere in sight, but Libby and Eddy were 30 yards in front of her.

Bertha poured on the steam, and was again only 20 yards behind the duo when they entered the trees.

Someone screamed.

Bertha clutched her M-16 in both hands and jogged into the woods. She darted through the brush and among the trees until she spied the clearing and the cabin, and then she halted, stunned.

The log cabin resembled a sieve. The door had been shot to pieces, riddled with bullets until whole sections had fallen off. The windows had fared worse; all of the glass panes were gone, and the edges where chipped and pockmarked. Even the cabin walls had been perforated again and again and again by heavy-caliber slugs. Bodies were everywhere. Bodies of the Claws. Most of them were congregated near the door, as if they'd been gunned down in the act of fleeing the cabin. A few had tumbled into the pit. Blood soaked the ground.

"Lordy!" Bertha exclaimed, walking up to the clearing.

Cole was on his knees to the left of the cabin door. The body of the young girl, Milly, was cradled in his lap. Her forehead had been blown off. Tears streaked his cheeks as he rocked back and forth. His lips were trembling. "No!" he cried. "No! No! No!"

Libby and Eddy stood near the pit. Libby appeared to be in a state of shock. Eddy, by contrast, was livid, his pudgy features contorted in rage.

"They're . . . all . . . dead!" Libby stated in a dazed, surveying the massacre.

"How?" Eddy demanded. "Where were the guards? We posted guards before we left!"

"Maybe," Libby said, her eyes watering, "maybe the guards were killed before they could sound the alarm."

Eddy pointed at the log cabin. "And what the hell did that? Those walls were thick! They could stand up to an AK-47! That's why we picked this place. But look at them! Look at the size of those holes!"

"Who cares about the holes?" Libby asked, sniffling.

"I do!" Eddy rejoined. "I want to know what the hell I'm going up against when I catch up with whoever did this!"

"What?" Libby said, glancing at Eddy.

"You heard me!" Eddy declared. "They can't have gotten far! I'm going after them right now!"

Libby grabbed Eddy's left arm. "No! You can't!"

"And why the hell can't I?" Eddy retorted.

"You won't stand a chance," Libby protested.

Eddy motioned toward the corpses. "And what chance did they have, Libby? Look at them! Some of them weren't even armed! We can't let the bastards who did this get away!"

"No," Libby objected. "That isn't the way."

"Yes, it is!" Cole thundered, rising to his feet, his face an iron mask. "Eddy's right! We're going to waste the sons of bitches responsible for this!"

Libby took a few steps toward Cole. "But, Cole . . ."

"There's no buts about it!" Cole cut her off. "We're going to avenge them!" He pointed at Milly's pathetic body. "This was our fault, Libby! We owe it to them!"

"Our fault?" Libby repeated. "How was it our fault? We've left the younger ones alone before. Burt was with them, and he was twelve. He knew the score. All of them did! So how do you figure this was our fault? We weren't even here!"

"We should have been," Cole said softly.

"But we weren't," Libby persisted.

Cole pressed his right hand on his forehead and

looked around. "We were all so damn excited about getting out of here! About finding a place where we could live free! And we forgot where we were! We forgot what could happen if we dropped our guard."

"But you did everything you could have done!" Libby said. "You can't blame yourself!"

Cole wiped his hand across his eyes. When he stared at Libby, his gaze was flinty. "Can't I?" He paused, sighed wearily, then inspected his AK-47. "Eddy and I are going after the bastards. Are you coming?"

"We don't have to do this!" Libby pleaded. "We can still leave with Bertha and her friends!"

Cole glanced at Bertha. "This isn't your fight. You don't have to come."

"There's nothin' I can do to talk you out of goin'?" Bertha asked.

Cole shook his head. "Don't even try. You'd be wasting your breath!"

Tears were flowing down Libby's face. "Cole! Please! You know what will happen!"

Cole gazed into Libby's eyes. "I know."

Bertha didn't know what to say. She knew Cole was determined to get his revenge. What could she do to stop him, short of shooting him herself? She admired him, even felt a peculiar kinship to Cole. Maybe, she speculated, it had something to do with her gang days in the Twin Cities. Oh, her life had been different in several ways. Cole and many of the other Packrats had come from good homes where they usually had enough food and even enjoyed some luxuries. Luxuries like decent clothes, and shoes, and even schooling. The Packrats had lost it all when their parents had been executed or imprisoned by the Communists. Bertha and her companions in the Twin Cities had never had it so good, never enjoyed even the basic necessities on a regular basis, never known what it was like to have a stable home environment in their early years. But in others respects, her former gang and the Packrats had a lot in common. There were always enemies out to get them, and no one outside the gang could be trusted.

You survived if you were quick and alert. You died if you slipped for an instant. Under such harsh conditions, strong bonds were forged. Deep friendships. And in Cole's case, the affection was compounded by the fact many of the Packrats were so young, so vulnerable, and had relied on his judgment. Bertha saw the anguish on his face, and recognized she couldn't begin to appreciate the depth of the torment he must be feeling.

Libby turned to Bertha. "Please! Don't let them go!"

Bertha frowned. "There's nothin' I can do."

Libby uttered a whining noise and covered her eyes with her left hand.

Eddy was checking his AK-47.

"Eddy," Cole said.

"Yeah?" Eddy responded.

"Find their trail," Cole directed, and entered the cabin.

Eddy smiled. "You got it." He began searching the ground near the edge of the woods.

Bertha moved over to Libby and draped her right arm across the girl's shoulders.

"I don't want him to go," Libby mumbled. "He'll be killed!"

"Maybe not," Bertha said.

Libby looked up, her eyes red, her cheeks moist. "Yes, he will! I just know it!"

"You love him, don't you?" Bertha asked gently.

Libby sniffed and nodded, glancing at the cabin.

"Does he love you?" Bertha inquired.

"I don't know," Libby admitted. "I think so. I feel he does, in my heart. But he's never shown it. Never come right out and said he does. I don't know why. Maybe he's afraid. Afraid of losing me like he did his mom and dad. You don't have any idea what it's like to love someone, and not have them love you!"

Want to bet? Bertha almost said. Instead, she held her peace, contemplating her own relationship with the Family's superlative gunfighter, Hickok. But could she justify calling it a relationship? She'd pined after that dummy for what seemed like ages! And where had it

gotten her? True, Hickok had been the first man she'd
ever fallen for, head-over-heels in love. True, he was the
choicest specimen of manhood she'd ever seen. Hunk de
la hunk, so to speak. How long, though, could she
justify yearning for a man unable to reciprocate her
devotion? Hickok was married to Sherry, and Bertha
knew the gunman well enough to know he would remain
loyal to Sherry while Sherry lived, and maybe even
afterwards. The Family ardently believed life did not
end with death. The Elders taught that death was merely
the technique of ascending from the material level to a
higher, more spiritual plane. Even if Sherry passed on,
Hickok was just the type to stay loyal to her, firmly
expecting he would see her again after his own earthly
demise. So what the hell am I doing, Bertha asked
herself, wasting my time with someone I'll never have a
chance with? She studied the miserable Libby, and
finally acknowledged how very lonely she'd been while
yearning for Hickok. Maybe it was about time she faced
facts; sometimes, love was one-sided; sometimes, a
person could deeply love another, and the feeling
wouldn't be mutual.

Cole emerged from the log cabin, his features set in
grim lines. "All the ones left inside are dead," he
remarked. "Whoever did this took all of our weapons."

"Whoever did this is heading to the south," Eddy
announced, joining them.

Cole stared at Eddy. "The Bobcats?"

"I think so," Eddy confirmed.

"Let's do it," Cole said, and started to the south.

Libby dabbed at her eyes with her fingers. "Wait for
me!"

Cole stopped and turned. "You stay here with
Bertha."

"I'm coming," Libby declared.

"I'd feel better if you didn't," Cole said. "Go back
to Bertha's buggy and wait for her friends."

"I'm coming," Libby reiterated.

"Let her come, Cole," Eddy chimed in.

Cole frowned. "All right. But stay close to me! I

don't want anything to happen to you.''

"You don't?'' Libby responded, brightening.

"Let's go!'' Cole directed. He wheeled and stalked into the woods, followed by Eddy.

Libby took off after them. "I hope I see you again, soon,'' she stated to Bertha over her right shoulder.

Bertha hesitated. This wasn't her fight. Cole was right. But she was, in a sense, partially to blame for the slaughter. Her presence, and her promise of salvation for the Claws, had distracted them, had diverted Cole from his responsibilities as Claw leader. She looked at little Milly. That child's death was on her shoulders, whether she liked it or not.

Libby vanished in the trees.

Maybe she owed it to them to help. Maybe she owed it to them to keep Cole, Libby, and Eddy alive, so they could savor the freedom the others had dreamed about. And maybe she owed it to herself, because they were her newfound friends, and once she was attached to someone, she never abandoned them. Hickok was a case in point.

"Oh, hell!'' Bertha exclaimed. She jogged toward the forest. "Wait up!'' she called.

Libby, ten yards into the woods, stopped. "What are you doing?'' she inquired as Bertha ran up.

Bertha could see Cole and Eddy, waiting for them 30 yards off. "I'm comin' with you.''

"Go back!'' Libby urged. "We can do this alone!''

Bertha shook her head. "No one,'' she said emphatically, "should ever have to be alone.'' She paused for emphasis. "Not ever! Now let's teach these Bobcats a lesson they'll never forget!''

18

What was keeping Blade?

Sundance sighted on the officer and the ten troopers, and waited until they were in the middle of the lawn before he fired. The officer pitched to the ground, and the rest were decimated, six of them dropping in a row. The rest took cover, scattering in all directions.

So far, so good! Sundance leaned against the wall on the right side of the gate and peered into the complex. He wondered if the Soviets would bring up a tank or other big guns. Perhaps, since it was a scientific establishment, the barracks garrison was the only military force on the premises. Even so, those inside could undoubtedly call outside for assistance. Reinforcements might arrive any second.

So what was keeping Blade?

A slug suddenly plowed into the wall next to Sundance's face, and a sliver of stone sliced his left cheek as it exploded from the wall. Sundance spun to the left, and there was a Russian trooper on top of the wall at the other end of the gate. He threw himself backwards as the soldier fired again, then aimed and squeezed the trigger on the FN-50-63. His burst caught the soldier in the abdomen, ripping his guts open, and the Russian screeched as he toppled from the wall to the field below.

They would be closing in now.

Sundance thoughtfully chewed on his lower lip. His position was rapidly becoming untenable.

A faint crackle sounded to the right.

Sundance crouched and whirled, leveling the FN, finding a pair of patrol guards coming at him along the base of the wall. One of them must have accidentally stepped on a twig. He let them have it, hitting the first Russian in the face as the trooper cut loose with an AK-47. The rounds fell short, spraying the dirt at

Sundance's feet. He killed the second guard with several shots to the head.

Where the hell was Blade?

Sundance leaned his back on the wall and hastily ejected the spent magazine from the FN. He slipped in a fresh clip, then glanced into the ministry.

Company was coming.

Four of the soldiers had reached the trees bordering the road, the road winding to the right of the gate, and they were advancing toward the iron gate, going from tree to tree, using the trunks for cover.

Nice move.

Sundance carefully sighted on the foremost soldier, and when the trooper tried to race from one tree to the next, exposing himself for the space of eight feet, Sundance sent a slug into his brain.

The Russian catapulted to the turf between the trees.

The other three halted, all hidden from view.

Sundance hoped his ploy was working. The gunfire must be attracting every guard, every last trooper in the complex. Blade would have a free reign.

What was that?

Sundance twisted to the left, and there was another soldier on top of the wall, trying to fix a bead on him. So he dropped to his knees, and the shot went over his head, missing by mere inches. Sundance was more accurate. His return slug slammed into the soldier's chest and flipped him from the wall, screaming all the way to the ground.

That was close!

Sundance stood and scanned the driveway.

A second trooper was darting from tree to tree.

Idiot!

Sundance aimed and patiently waited for a glimpse of the soldier's head. His bullet tore into the trooper's left cheek and blew out the rear of his cranium, splattering a nearby tree with crimson and fleshy gook.

Sooner or later, one of them would get the range!

Sooner or later.

Sundance inhaled deeply, steadying his nerves. Be vigilant, he told himself. Don't slack off for an instant!

He stiffened as the growl of a motor arose from within the complex. What were they up to now? Bringing up a tank? He scanned the length of road to the right.

It wasn't a tank.

But it was almost as bad.

A jeep containing three troopers and outfitted with a swivel-mounted 50-caliber machine gun was bearing down on the front gate, approaching at a fast clip, the driver weaving the jeep from one side of the road to another, evidently in an effort to present as difficult a target as possible.

The two soldiers sheltered behind the trees opened up with their AK-47's.

Sundance was compelled to duck from sight. He realized what the pair of soldiers were attempting to do. They were keeping him pinned down until the jeep reached the gate. If the jeep could get close enough, there was no way his FN would stand up to the jeep's machine gun.

This was becoming hairy.

Sundance dropped to the ground, onto his stomach, and rolled from cover, his automatic rifle trained on the trees.

The two troopers, concentrating their fire on the wall near the gate, were taken unawares.

Sundance squeezed the trigger, and the first trooper jerked backwards and collapsed. His second round tore through the throat of the other soldier, and the trooper clutched at his ruined neck and fell to his knees, gurgling, blood spurting between his fingers.

The jeep was 50 yards off and closing.

Sundance sighted between two of the iron bars, fixing on a point 30 yards away, a 15-foot tract between two trees.

The soldier manning the machine gun on the jeep cut loose, firing bursts between trees, the barrel of the machine gun elevated to achieve a greater range, but his first shots fell short.

A few rounds struck the edge of the wall, but the majority hit the road near the gate, smacking into the asphalt with a distinct thud-thud-thud.

Sundance waited.

The machine gunner did not spot the man lying prone at the base of the gate. He only knew a sniper was near the front gate, and he was aiming his rounds accordingly, at about waist to chest level, focusing on the edge of the stone wall near the gate. At 40 yards his bursts consistently struck the wall, sending broken bits of stone flying.

Sundance waited.

The jeep roared to within 30 yards of the gate.

Sundance squeezed the trigger and kept it squeezed.

The driver was the initial casualty. A string of ragged dots blossomed on his forehead, and he slumped over the steering wheel. The soldier sitting next to the driver lunged for the wheel, but his head snapped back as he was raked with slugs and flung against the seat. The jeep began slewing across the road, and the machine gunner gripped the machine gun for support as the jeep tilted, then upended, rolling for 20 yards before grinding to a stop in the center of the road. The machine gunner was killed on the first roll, the top of his cranium smashing into the asphalt and splitting like a pulpy rotten tomato.

Sundance rolled to the right, seeking cover behind the wall again. He stood and checked the magazine in the FN. One round left. He tossed it aside and reached for another clip in his pocket.

There were none!

Sundance frowned. That was all he'd brought along. The rest were in the SEAL. Fat good they did him there! But he still had the Grizzlies. He dropped the FN and began unbuttoning his shirt. On the fourth button he paused, gazing at one of the dead gate guards nearby.

The AK-47's!

Sundance darted to the trooper and retrieved the AK-47. The magazine was almost full. He'd never fired one before, but they—

There was a scratching noise above him.

Directly above.

Sundance dived onto his stomach and rolled, and there was a Russian trooper perched on the wall above where he'd been standing.

The soldier blasted four rounds into the ground near the Warrior's head, his AK-47 held extended over the barbed wire.

Sundance returned the fire, lying on his back, the stock of the AK-47 cradled in his right elbow.

A pattern of slugs stitched the soldier on the wall from his crotch to his sternum. He shrieked as he was hurled backwards and disappeared over the rim.

Sundance heard the trooper's body strike the earth on the other side of the wall. He rose and leaned against the stone wall again.

That had been close! Too close!

A resonant voice started shouting orders inside the complex. There was a subdued commotion.

Sundance peered through the gate bars.

The Russians were preparing for an all-out offensive. Dozens of soldiers were crawling across the yard fronting the barracks, and dozens more were following the road, using the trees for protection.

Sundance glanced at the woods beyond the field. The Russians had probably held back at first, unsure of how many attackers were at the gate, saving their main force. By now, they'd learned there was only one man, and they were going to throw everything they had at the iron gate in a concerted effort to end the fray. And Sundance knew he couldn't hold them all off. Not all of them. His best bet was to retreat, to draw them into the woods, buying Blade even more time. If Blade was still alive. A cautious peek verified the Soviets were slowly advancing toward him.

What was that noise?

Sundance cocked his head to the left, listening. It was a strident siren, and he suddenly realized the siren had been blaring for quite a while. In the stress and strain of the combat, he's scarcely noticed.

Several soldiers had reached the demolished jeep.

Sundance took off, angling away from the front gate, heading for the woods. He'd gone only six steps when a startling insight streaked through his mind: if the Soviets were closing in from all directions, from the barracks to the left and the road to the right, *then they must also have troopers closing in on top of the walls!*

They did.

Sundance whirled, the movement saving his life as an AK-47 chattered and sent heavy slugs into the ground near his feet.

The walls were swarming with soldiers!

Sundance raced to the wall as a veritable explosion of gunfire sprayed the earth around him. He placed his back against the wall and looked up. There was a slight lip, or edge, rimming the top of the wall. Attached to metal posts imbedded in the outer edge of the upper surface were coiled strands of barbed wire. In order for the soldiers on the wall to see him, they would need to lean forward over the top strand of barbed wire, exposing themselves to him in the process. If he stayed close to the stone wall, the soldiers up above wouldn't be able to spy him, let alone shoot him. But if he strayed from the wall by so much as 12 inches, the troopers would have a clear line of fire. So he was somewhat safe if he stuck to the wall.

But what about the troops approaching from within the Ministry?

Sundance carefully moved to the end of the wall and looked around the corner.

The nearest soldiers were only 15 yards away.

Sundance sent a short burst in their direction, then fled along the base of the wall.

Someone on the wall was shouting to the soldiers in the complex in Russian.

Go! his mind thundered. Sundance ran for all he was worth. If he could get several hundred yards from the gate, and if the soldiers on the wall and those within the Ministry believed he was still in the vicinity of the gate, they might not notice when he dashed to the woods. On the other hand . . .

There was a lot of yelling on top of the wall.

Sundance imagined the Russians were trying to pinpoint his location. Good. So far, he had them confused. Just a few more seconds was all he needed! His legs pumped rhythmically as he sprinted farther from the iron gate. He dodged the bodies of Bakunin and the two patrol guards and kept going.

An officer on the wall was barking commands.

Sundance exerted himself to the maximum. He discarded the AK-47. Speed was essential, and the AK-47 was too cumbersome and weighty a burden. His arms and legs flying, he covered 40 yards from the front gate, then 60, then 80. He glanced over his right shoulder just as a soldier appeared, and this trooper was followed by several more, coming from within the Ministry.

The Russians had unlocked the gate and opened it!

Sundance immediately swerved to the right, cutting across the field toward the trees, knowing his only hope was in reaching cover before the troopers downed him. He zigzagged, expecting to hear the Ak-47's commence firing any second.

They did.

Sundance was turning to the left, running as crooked a path as possible, when the soldiers on the wall and at the gate were alerted to his maneuver by the shout of a watchful private exiting the complex. Fifteen yards separated Sundance from the woods when the soldiers began firing. Slugs smacked into the grass at his feet. He jagged to the right, followed by a hail of lead. Something stung his left calf and clipped his right shoulder. He focused his total concentration on reaching those trees. Move! He mentally screamed. Move! Move! Move! Four steps to the left, then cut to the right! Five steps to the right, then angle to the left! Never stop! Don't slow down!

He was ten yards from the trees!

A slug dug a furrow in his left side, creasing his ribs, and he nearly stumbled and fell, recovering as he was pitching forward. He made a beeline for the woods. Round after round thumped into the earth all about him.

Five yards!

Sundance took a giant step and executed a spectacular leap, vaulting headfirst into the underbrush and rolling. He came to a jarring stop when his right shoulder collided with a tree.

He'd made it!

But the Russians weren't about to let him escape that easily. Dozens charged from the open gate, fanning out, converging on the trees.

Sundance sat up. His right shoulder was hurting terribly. Through an opening in the brush he saw the troopers approaching in a skirmish line. And all he had were the Grizzlies! He inched around the tree and rose.

What should he do?

Sundance glanced both ways. If he went to the right, back to the jeep, he risked the Russians finding the vehicle and him. Blade would be deprived of the sole means of transportation. But if he went to the left, toward the road leading to the front gate, he'd draw the troopers off, lead them away from the jeep. And eliminate his only hope of escaping.

There was never any doubt.

Sundance moved to the left, reaching under his shirt and drawing the Grizzlies. He silently skirted trees and dry brush, putting more distance between the field and himself.

Some of the troopers reached the woods. Their boots created a pop-crackle-snap cacophony as they clumped through the underbrush. Stealth was forgotten in their eagerness and haste to find their foe. They knew their superior numbers would ultimately flush out their prey.

And so did their quarry. Sundance prudently avoided a dead, brittle limb lying on the dank ground. He caught glimpses of the soldiers now and then. None of them knew he was there.

Yet.

Sundance wondered how far it was to the road. A boulder reared out of the brush, blocking his path. He walked to the left, around the boulder, speculating on his course of action once he reached the road. Preoccupied, he missed hearing the trooper until they nearly bumped into one another as they came around the seven-foot-high boulder at the same moment.

The soldier's mouth dropped, and he frantically leveled his AK-47.

Sundance shot the soldier in the forehead with his left Grizzly.

The trooper's face snapped back as the rear of his head erupted over the nearby vegetation. He tottered and sprawled to the turf.

And all hell broke loose.

Suddenly, soldiers were everywhere, barreling toward the sound of the shot, yelling and shouting, closing in.

Sundance darted in the direction of the road. He could see uniforms here and there, all bearing down on his position.

He was surrounded!

A tall trooper appeared from behind a tree directly ahead.

Sundance fired, his right Grizzly booming, and the trooper was propelled into the tree. He twisted to the left, crashing through a dense thicket, the limbs and thorns tearing at his clothing and skin, and then he was in a small clearing and there were three soldiers coming at him from different directions. He spun to the right and sent a slug into the mouth of the first, beginning his next turn even as he squeezed the trigger, unable to ascertain the effectiveness of the shot, and he plugged the second Russian in the chest and ducked and twirled, and the third trooper was mere yards away and squeezing the trigger on an AK-47. Sundance threw himself to the right, firing as he dove, his shot searing an agonizing path through the third trooper's abdomen. And then Sundance was up and across the clearing and into the trees on the other side.

The forest was alive with bellowed orders and cries.

Sundance heard an AK-47 blaze away to his rear, and his left leg took a hit in the fleshy area of his thigh. His leg nearly buckled, and he staggered and went on, dodging behind a tree and hastening over a low rise.

Another AK-47, somewhere to his right, began shooting.

Sundance swerved to the left, then the right, always heading in the direction of the road. He lost all sense of distance. The road was up ahead, but he had no idea how far it might be, the yardage he'd covered, and he was genuinely surprised when he abruptly plunged from the underbrush and there was the road to the gate, not six feet away.

And soldiers.

Seemingly materializing out of thin air.

Sundance reached the road and bore to the left, going away from the Ministry, hoping his efforts weren't in vain, hoping Blade was accomplishing their mission.

"Freeze!" shouted a stern voice to his right.

Sundance twisted and fired, and a thin trooper doubled over and toppled to the ground. And there was another one, charging from the left, and Sundance pivoted and shot the bastard in the right eye. A pair of soldiers came at him from the rear, firing their AK-47's. Sundance felt a searing spasm lance his right side, but he refused to drop, to submit without expending his last ounce of strength. His body was a blur as he whirled, both Grizzlies thundering, and the two soldiers were slammed to the earth, but another one appeared to take their place, and Sundance shot him in the chest, continuing to rotate, moving, always moving, squeezing both triggers as three soldiers stormed from cover, and two of the Russians twitched and fell but the third wouldn't stop for anything, and Sundance fired as the trooper fired, and fired again as the trooper dropped to his knees, then pitched to the asphalt. Momentarily, Sundance was alone, and he stumbled as dizziness engulfed him. He righted himself with a tremendous effort. How many times had he been hit? He'd lost count. And he'd lost a lot of something else too—blood. His uniform felt clammy and moist, especially the shirt. He lurched a few steps and stopped, reeling. If the Russians found him now, he was a goner.

They found him.

A lone trooper crashed from the underbrush on the left side of the road, swiveling an AK-47 at the crimson-soaked figure in the middle of the asphalt.

And a jeep roared up from out of nowhere, a machine gun blasting, its tires squealing as it barked.

Sundance tried to raise the Grizzlies, but his arms

were enveloped by an overwhelming lethargy. His wounds took belated affect, and with a sigh he sank to the road.

19

Blade threw himself backwards, sweeping his Commando Arms Carbine up and pressing the trigger. The Commando boomed in the narrow stairwell.

The Russian soldier half a flight above was just squeezing the trigger of his AK-47 when the Commando's slugs tore through his face and flung him to the stairs. The AK-47 fell from his lifeless fingers, rattling as it slid down several steps.

Blade hesitated, getting his bearings. He had entered Penza Hall on the ground level, then descended three levels to the lowest floor. The guard had led him up three floors from the bottom level, which meant he should be on ground level again.

There was only one way to find out.

There were two doors furnishing access to the stairwell. The one he'd just used, and another, the one which should lead to the loading dock. Blade opened the second door and found the hallway he needed.

And a trooper jogging toward him with an AK-47 at the ready.

Blade shot the startled soldier, sending a burst into the trooper's chest and flipping him to the floor. He sprinted toward the door to the loading dock. The laundry truck was probably gone. He would need to improvise another method of departing the Ministry. As he opened the door to the dock, the sound of the siren rose in volume. Another noise blended with the sirens; the repeated blasting of gunfire.

Sundance?

Blade scanned the loading dock and the parking lot. There wasn't a vehicle in sight.

Damn!

Blade ran down the ramp to the lot and started across, bearing toward the west wall. If the clamor was any accurate indication, then a war was being waged near the west wall. He hurried, the Commando in his right hand.

A squad of soldiers unexpectedly came into view to the left.

Blade slowed, expecting to be challenged. But the squad leader gave him a cursory inspection and continued on, hastening in the direction of the front gate. Off to the north, more soldiers were jogging toward the gate.

If it was Sundance out there, he wouldn't be able to hold them off for long!

Blade bounded across the lot in mighty strides, reaching a lawn encircling a lofty structure. He bypassed the edifice to the south, heading away from the gate. If every soldier in the Ministry was converging on the front gate, then he might be able to sneak over the wall near the southwest corner. He darted around a huge maple tree.

A Russian soldier, a big man with wide shoulders, was ten yards off, jogging to the northwest.

Blade slowed, hoping he wouldn't be spotted.

The soldier glanced to the right and halted, his forehead creasing in perplexity. An AK-47 was slung over his right shoulder. "You!" he barked.

Blade touched his chest with his left hand. "Me?"

"Yes, you! Come here!" the soldier ordered.

Blade walked over to the soldier. "Yes?"

"Yes, sergeant!" the Russian corrected him. The sergeant's brown eyes critically examined the giant's uniform. "Where are you going?" he queried.

"To the wall," Blade responded. "Sergeant!"

The sergeant pointed to the north. "But the action is that way! Everyone is to assemble at the gate. Why are you going in the opposite direction?"

"Orders," Blade replied.

"Orders. From whom?" the sergeant inquired. He began to unsling his AK-47.

Blade knew the sergeant didn't believe him, knew the noncom wasn't unlimbering the AK-47 for the exercise. He couldn't afford to be detained, not if Sundance was in jeopardy. He did the only thing he could do, under the circumstances. He kicked the sergeant in the nuts.

The Russian doubled over, gasping, his hands covering his genitals, his mouth forming a wide oval.

Blade rammed the Commando barrel into the noncom's mouth and fired.

The sergeant's brains gushed from the rear of his cranium, and he was hurled to the grass, convulsing, his eyes glazing.

Blade resumed his dash to the left wall. A quick scan confirmed no one else was in the area.

The siren wailed and wailed.

The battle near the gate raged on.

Blade came within sight of the wall. To his left, perhaps 40 yards distant, a flight of steps led up to the top of the wall. One soldier was visible, and he was moving along the top of the wall toward the front gate. Blade slanted in the direction of those steps. He could feel the stolen KGB files rubbing against his skin, and the Bowie scabbards brushing his thighs.

Yells and shouts were coming from the northwest.

What if the cause of the commotion wasn't Sundance? Blade asked himself. But if not Sundance, then who? The Packrats? No. They apparently confined their activities to Valley Forge and vicinity. Were there rebels active in the occupied zone? Freedom fighters opposing the Soviets? If so, the Freedom Federation would need to contact them and arrange aid. He reached the bottom of the steps, discarding all speculation as he sped to the top of the wall.

Soldiers could be seen off to the north, atop the wall near the gate. But none were nearby.

A four-foot-high barrier of barbed wire separated Blade from the field below. He gingerly touched one of the coiled strands, and his third finger was pricked by a sharp barb. The inner rampart was two feet below the wire. There was a six-inch lip, or rim, on both sides of the wire. By stepping up onto the rim, and balancing himself precariously, he was able to lean over the wire and survey the field and the woods.

Not a trooper anywhere.

Blade elevated his left leg, raising it over the barbed wire and placing his left foot on the outer rim. The barbed wire scraped his crotch, and he envisioned the impaling he would suffer if he slipped. Goose bumps broke out on his gonads. Holding the wire down with his left hand, he carefully eased his right leg up and over. For a second he perched on the outer rim, gazing at the ground 15 feet below. Then he launched himself into the air, dropping feet first, the air whipping his hair, and he landed and rolled, rising and running toward the woods.

No one challenged him.

Blade reached the trees and plunged into the brush. He bore to the right, seeking the jeep. The jeep was hidden near the turnoff, 60 yards from the road leading to the gate. After what seemed like an eternity, he parted the tall weeds before him and there was the turnoff. But which way was the jeep? Was he too far south or north? Acting on a hunch, he turned to the right, to the north, and within 15 yards discovered the field he wanted. He sprinted into the brush, smiling when he spotted the jeep. But his smile quickly changed to a frown when he reached the driver's door and peered inside.

Bakunin was gone!

Blade straightened, scanning the landscape. What the hell had happened? Had Bakunin loosened his bounds? Had the captain gone to warn the Ministry? Had Sundance seen Bakunin? Was that the reason for the combat near the gate? Suddenly, all the pieces to the puzzle fit. If Sundance had observed Bakunin heading for the front gate, Sundance would have stopped him. And now Sundance was in mortal danger, resisting impossible odds, and all because Bakunin had been left alive. Blade grimaced. If Sundance was seriously injured, or worse, it was all his fault. He should have executed the officer, not spared the Russian. Plato's philosophy was too idealistic for the real world, too compassionate for a seasoned Warrior. He had known it all along! Blade fumed. Anger washed over him, anger at his own stupidity. He removed his keys from his pocket and climbed in, placing the Commando to his right, gunning the engine, and flooring the pedal as he shifted into reverse.

The jeep's tires sent clumps of dirt and vegetation soaring as the tread dug into the turf.

Blade glanced over his right shoulder, steering the jeep backwards in a tight loop. He shifted into gear, and the jeep surged across the field to the turnoff. Spinning the wheel, Blade turned to the right, making for the road to the gate. He traveled 20 yards, when he happened to look in the rearview mirror.

Three motorcycles were roaring up the highway behind him.

Where did the turnoff lead to? Blade wondered. He drove the jeep to the shoulder of the road and braked, grabbing the Commando.

The cycles were 20 yards away, on the other side of the street, obviously intending to swing around the jeep as they raced to the intersection with the road to the gate, 40 yards to the north. Each rider was a Soviet soldier wearing a black helmet.

Blade hastily rolled down his window and lifted the Commando barrel as the three motorcycles came abreast of the jeep. The Commando thundered, and the hapless drivers were rocked by a withering hail of lead. Two of the bikes wobbled, them smashed together, hurtling to the far side of the street in a tangle of crushed limbs and twisted metal. They slammed into a tree, breaking into bits and pieces.

The third biker survived the ambush. He was nicked in the right arm, and his bike wavered for a few yards, then steadied as the rider slewed to a screeching halt 20 yards in front of the jeep. He drew an automatic pistol from a holster on his left hip.

Blade waited for the biker to make the first move.

The cyclist suddenly turned his handle bars and

accelerated, making for the intersection.

Blade mashed the gas pedal and the jeep sped in pursuit. The motorcyle was faster, closing on the intersection at a reckless speed. Blade knew he couldn't catch the biker. And he also knew the rider would take a right, heading for the Ministry. He transferred the Commando to his left hand, steering with his right. Poking the barrel out the window, he angled the automatic in the direction of the intersection. The jeep was a mere 18 yards from the junction when the motorcycle swung into the turn. Blade depressed the trigger and held it down, the Commando bucking as he fired. For a second or two, he believed he'd missed, miscalculated the range and the elevation.

The biker was smoothly negotiating the turn, his cycle slanted, his body tucked close to the bike. His front tire abruptly exploded as four slugs shredded the rubber, and the motorcycle was catapulted forward, turning end over end, throwing the biker to the side, his spindly form smashing into the asphalt and rolling for a good ten yards, his arms and legs flopping and flapping. He came to rest on the right shoulder, his helmet cracked, his left leg bent at an unnatural posture, immobile.

Blade reached the intersection and took a right. His keen eyes probed the road ahead, and narrowed as he spied the stumbling figure in the blood-drenched uniform.

It was Sundance!

Blade tramped on the gas, his right hand tightening on the steering wheel until his knuckles turned white. He could see a lot of bodies lining the road.

A trooper suddenly shoved through the underbrush, aiming an AK-47 at Sundance.

Blade thumped on the brake, swerving the jeep so his side faced the trooper, shoving the Commando out the window and squeezing the trigger.

The soldier was perforated from his knees to his shoulders. He twisted and fell, rivulets of crimson seeping from the holes.

Blade clutched at the shift as the jeep began to lurch, and he shifted into park and leaped to the ground.

Sundance had collapsed!

Blade reached his friend in three bounds. He knelt, appalled by all the blood.

Boots pounded to his right.

Blade spun as a soldier emerged from the woods. The Commando boomed, ripping the soldier in half at the waist.

Upraised voices bellowed in the forest.

Blade swiftly slung the Commando over his left arm, and gently placed his forearms under Sundance. He lifted, hardly straining, and carried his fellow Warrior to the jeep. He was compelled to hurry, knowing the Russians were closing in, but he was reluctant to jostle Sundance.

"This way!" someone called off to the left.

Blade yanked the passenger door open, and solicitously deposited Sundance in the seat. He closed the door, moved around to the driver's side, and hopped in. The jeep's motor purred as he shifted and performed a U-turn, gathering speed, racing away from the Ministry of Psychological Sciences.

Soldiers poured from the woods to the rear. Some fired their AK-47's ineffectively.

Sundance slumped forward until his forehead rested on the dash. His chin drooped onto his chest, and his body swayed with every bump in the road.

Blade glanced at his companion, emotionally tormented. This was his doing! He knew it! The result of his incompetence! The mission had been a total washout! First Bertha had vanished, and now this! And all for what? The captured Vikings were all dead, leaving the Family with several files and the lingering hope of a possible alliance. Were the files worth the lives of two Warriors?

"Hang in there," Blade said to the unconscious figure beside him. "Don't you die on me, damnit!"

Sundance sagged to the floor.

20

"There they are!" Cole whispered.

Bertha and the three Claws were concealed behind four trees on the crest of a hill five miles to the south of the log cabin.

"It's the Bobcats!" Eddy exclaimed. "I knew it!"

Bertha, her left shoulder pressed against the rough bark of an elm tree, watched 11 Bobcats 75 yards below her position. They were following a faint deer trail winding along the base of the hill. Eight were boys, 3 girls. They ranged in ages from about 10 to 16 or 17. Like the Claws, their clothing consisted of tattered rags. They were smiling, joking with one another, evidently happy over their presumed defeat of the Claws.

"Look at the sons of bitches!" Cole snapped. He stood behind a pine tree to Bertha's right.

"Let's get the scum!" Eddy stated from his spot to Bertha's left, crouched near another elm.

"What's that big gun?" Libby asked. She was standing next to a pine on Cole's right.

Bertha was asking herself the same question. It was a huge machine gun, mounted on a tripod, and it took four Bobcats to carry the weapon, tripod and all. The Bobcats must have swiped the machine gun from the Russians and decided to use it on their enemies, the Claws.

"Who cares what it is?" Cole retorted. "It won't stop us from wasting those creeps."

The corners of Bertha's mouth turned downward. She didn't like this. Didn't like it one bit. It was all well and good to talk about teaching the Bobcats a lesson. But it was another matter to seriously contemplate shooting a 10-year-old. Or 11. Or 12. Try as she might, Bertha could only view the Bobcats in one light: as children. Savage little murderers, perhaps, but still children. She compared them to the children at the

Home. The difference was incredible. The Family's children were taught to reverence all life, to exalt love as the highest form of personal expression, and to strive for an inner communion with the Spirit. The Packrats, whether it was the Bobcats, the Claws, or any of the other gangs, by contrast had reduced all life to the primitive level of kill-or-be-killed. They didn't have the slightest idea of the true nature of mature love. And of spiritual affairs they were pitifully ignorant. The disparity was like night and day. It was amazing, Bertha reflected, the difference the Family and the Home made in the lives of the children. She suddenly became aware Cole was addressing her.

" . . . us or not?" Cole demanded.

Bertha turned. "What did you say?"

"I want to know if you're with us or not?" Cole repeated.

Bertha glanced at the Bobcats. "I don't know," she confessed.

"I thought you were on our side!" pudgy Eddy interjected.

"I am," Bertha said. "But . . ." She paused, uncertain.

"But what?" Cole pressed her.

"But I don't think I could kill the Bobcats," Bertha stated, nodding toward the base of the hill.

"Why not?" Libby inquired.

"They're just kids!" Bertha declared. "Look at 'em! Half of 'em aren't much over twelve!" She frowned, staring at Cole. "I'm sorry. I just can't do it."

Surprisingly, Cole shrugged. "Suit yourself. You stay here, then."

Bertha leaned toward the Claw chief. "Why don't you forget about this vengeance bit? One of you could get hurt, or even killed. Drop it, Cole. Come back to the Home with me."

Cole averted his eyes. "I can't," he said.

"You could if you wanted to," Bertha prompted him.

Cole stared at Bertha, his expression one of profound sorrow. "I can't," he reiterated, and motioned to Eddy and Libby. He moved from cover and started down the slope.

Eddy winked at Bertha, then followed Cole.

Libby stepped over to Bertha. "I'll miss you," she stated sadly.

"Don't do it!" Bertha said. "Please!"

"I've got to go," Libby asserted. "I can't let Cole and Eddy do it alone."

"Talk to Cole some more," Bertha suggested. "You can talk him out of it, if anyone can!"

"I can't," Libby said. "I've already tried."

"Try again!" Bertha urged. "What harm can it do?"

"It's no use," Libby insisted.

"How do you know. What makes you so damn sure?" Bertha asked.

Libby looked into Bertha's eyes. "Milly was Cole's sister." She whirled and dashed after Cole and Eddy.

His sister! Bertha sagged against the elm. Sweet little Milly had been Cole's sister! No wonder he was out for blood! Bertha watched the three Claws cautiously descend the hill. She'd never even considered some of the Packrats might be related. But how else would the younger ones have made it to Valley Forge, unless they were accompanied by an older brother or sister?

Cole and Eddy had halted and were waiting for Libby. Cole glanced up once at Bertha and smiled wanly.

Libby reached them, and together they continued their descent, utilizing the trees, boulders, and weeds as cover as they crept ever nearer to the unsuspecting Bobcats.

Bertha felt queasy in her stomach. Lordy! She had a *bad* feeling about this!

Cole, Eddy, and Libby reached a maple tree 60 yards from the bottom of the hill.

Bertha didn't want to watch, but she couldn't bring herself to tear her eyes away. Indecision racked her soul. What if she was wrong? What if she should be helping the Claws? They'd befriended her, hadn't they? Spared her, when they could have killed her? Back at the cabin, she'd believed she was partly to blame for the butchery committed on the other Claws. Now, she wasn't so sure. She was torn between her desire to aid her friends, and her repugnance at the mere thought of killing a child.

The three Claws attained a boulder 40 yards from the Bobcats, still undetected by their quarry.

Bertha scrutinized the Bobcats. They were strung out over a 20-yard stretch of trail. The quartet bearing the heavy machine gun was bringing up the rear, at least ten feet behind the rest. The apparent leader, a tall youth with black hair, armed with an AK-47, was about five feet in front of the group. AK-47's were the standard weapon, except for two boys who were toting rifles.

Bertha tensed as she saw Cole, Libby and Eddy creep to within 20 yards of the Bobcats. They crouched behind a spreading pine. Cole wagged his hand to the right and the left, and Eddy and Libby started off in the corresponding directions.

The Bobcat leader unexpectedly paused, scanning the hill.

Bertha held her breath.

Cole, Libby, and Eddy froze in their tracks.

The Bobcat leader looked over his shoulder at the gang, then resumed his journey.

Bertha took a deep breath.

Cole, Libby, and Eddy were crawling down the hill, silently parting the brush in their path, stopping whenever a Bobcat idly gazed up the hill.

The Bobcat leader halted beside a maple tree and leaned down, doing something with his right shoe.

Cole was now within 10 yards of the Bobcats, close to the center of their column. Libby was 12 yards from the four carrying the machine gun. And pudgy Eddy was 12 yards from the Bobcat leader.

What were they waiting for? Bertha craned her neck for a better view. The Claws should strike before the . . .

Cole suddenly rose to his feet from a clump of weeds, his AK-47 leveled. "You slime!" he shouted, and fired.

Three of the Bobcats in the middle of the line were ripped to pieces by the automatic barrage, the slugs slamming into their bodies and exploding out their backs, ravaging their torsos. Their limbs jerked and flapped as they were struck and knocked to the ground.

The other Bobcats lunged for the nearest cover.

Libby popped up from behind a log, and her sweeping spray of lead caught the four with the machine gun in their chests. They died in midstride, crumpling under the weight of the machine gun.

Eddy rose, aiming at the Bobcat leader.

Only the Bobcat leader was quicker. He must have sensed something was wrong, must have been toying with his shoe as a ruse, because he was already in motion as Eddy stood, and both fired at the same instant.

Eddy's head snapped back, a crimson geyser erupting from his left ear, and he toppled to the grass.

The Bobcat leader ducked behind the maple tree.

Bertha started to raise the M-16, but hesitated. No! She wouldn't—she couldn't—shoot children!

Cole dropped another Bobcat, and then flattened. Libby did likewise.

The three remaining Bobcats were raking the hillside with gunfire, shooting in the general direction of their adversaries.

From her vantage point high on the hill, Bertha saw Cole's left shoulder twist sharply, as if he had been hit.

The firing abated, each side waiting for the other to make the next move. In addition to the Bobcat leader, a girl of 14 or 15 and a boy approximately the same age were the only Bobcats still alive. The girl was hidden in a cluster of boulders 20 yards from Libby, and the boy was concealed in a thicket less than 15 yards from Cole.

Bertha could see Cole and Libby clearly. The Bobcat girl was visible every now and then, whenever she popped her head up for a quick look-see. Although Bertha knew where the Bobcat leader and the other boy were hiding, neither betrayed their position, neither appeared in her field of view.

Cole was tentatively groping his left side, and when he drew his right hand aside, his fingers were dripping blood.

Bertha nervously bit her lower lip. She was in an agonizing quandary. If she didn't do something, do *anything,* and fast, Cole might die. But what could she do, short of shooting a Bobcat?

Libby was on her hands and knees, sheltered by a log, trying to peek around the end of the log and spot Cole.

Bertha doubted whether Libby could see Cole. He was too well camouflaged by a stand of weeds.

Cole was checking the magazine of his AK-47.

Bertha finally made up her mind. Just because she felt uncomfortable about killing a Bobcat didn't mean she couldn't aid the Claws in another manner. As a distraction, for instance. If she could attract the Bobcat's attention, she might provide Cole and Libby with the openings they needed. The idea was worth a try. She began moving down the hill, crouched over, treading lightly.

Libby was now on her knees, continuing to scan for Cole.

Don't do anything stupid! Bertha almost yelled. She skirted a blue spruce. So how, she asked herself, was she going to help Cole and Libby without getting herself shot? The Bobcats would shoot at anything they saw moving. She had to be extremely careful.

Cole had squirmed onto his elbows and knees.

What was he up to? Bertha halted behind a rock outcropping 60 yards from the base of the hill.

There was movement in the thicket secreting the Bobcat boy.

Bertha stiffened. She was too far away yet! If only nothing would happen until she was closer! She scrambled forward on her stomach, across a grassy stretch, and reached a maple tree. Once behind the trunk, she stood and surveyed the situation below.

The movement in the thicket had ceased.

Libby was still seeking a glimpse of Cole.

Cole was peering over the top of the weeds.

Bertha was about to crouch and proceed further, when something flickered at the edge of her vision, lower down and off to the right. She glanced in that direction, her nerves tingling.

The Bobcat leader had circled around Cole! He was 15 yards from Cole's hiding place, slowly advancing, stooped over.

How the hell had he done it? Bertha had supposed he was on the opposite side of the tree where he'd taken cover. The guy was good! There was no doubt about it.

The Bobcat leader was searching from side to side. Several trees and a dense bush separated him from Cole.

Bertha didn't believe the Bobcat leader had seen Cole. Yet. But in a few seconds Cole was bound to be spotted. Her eyes narrowed as she watched the Bobcat leader, waiting for the right moment. He passed one of the trees, then another. Bertha's abdomen tightened expectantly. The tall Bobcat leader came abreast of the third tree, and now just the bush obscured Cole's hiding place from the alert, black-haired youth. Bertha's eyes were glued to the Bobcat's ragged brown leather shoes. He took one step, then another, cautiously edging around the bush to the left. Another one took him to the very border of the bush. He was scrutinizing the slope above him, and he still hadn't spied Cole squatting in the weeds. He raised his leg, about to go past the bush, and as he did, Bertha took her calculated gamble. She leaped from concealment, waving her arms. "Up here, turkey!" she shouted.

The Bobcat leader swiveled at the sound of her voice, pointing his AK-47 up the hill.

Even as the Bobcat leader was turning, Cole spun too. He saw the leader's head and shoulders visible above the bush, and he fired from a crouch, his burst striking the Bobcat leader in the face and flinging the tall youth to the turf.

And suddenly, everything went wrong.

Libby, hearing the gunfire but unable to see Cole, sprang to her feet, anxious for his safety, heedless of her own. It was a fatal mistake.

The Bobcat girl in the boulders jumped up, blasting from the hip, her AK-47 on full automatic.

Libby was hurled onto her back by the impact, her arms spreading wide.

Cole whirled at the chatter of the Bobcat girl's weapon, and he saw Libby get hit. He surged from cover, crashing through the underbrush toward Libby. *"No!"* he screamed. *"No! No!"*

The Bobcat in the thicket abruptly stepped into view, aiming a rifle at Cole, and he squeezed the trigger as Cole recklessly crossed a small clearing five yards from Libby.

Cole stumbled as he was struck. He twirled toward the Bobcat in the thicket, and he fired as the Bobcat's rifle thundered again, and kept firing as the Bobcat doubled over and dropped to one side. He turned toward Libby, staggering haltingly.

The Bobcat girl in the boulders pressed her AK-47 to her right shoulder, aiming at Cole.

All of this transpired so swiftly, so unexpectedly, Bertha reacted belatedly. Four seconds elapsed between her shout and Cole being struck, and when she did act, when she did enter the fray, her action was instinctive, ingrained from years of gang warfare and her training as a Warrior. Caught up in the heat of the moment, fearing for Cole and Libby, she did the only thing she could have done under the circumstances. She saw the Bobcat girl aim at Cole, and she automatically sighted her M-16 and fired off a half-dozen rounds.

The shots were right on target. The Bobcat girl stiffened, then sprawled over a boulder.

Bertha plunged down the slope, taking the straightest route, limbs and thorns tearing at her clothes. Her left boot snagged in a root and she tripped, landing on both knees. But she was up in an instant, plowing through the vegetation, and she didn't stop until she reached the small clearing near Libby. She halted in midstep, horrified, her countenance reflecting her emotional unheaval. "Dear Lord!" she exclaimed.

Cole was on his knees in the middle of the clearing, his right arm outstretched toward Libby. His body was trembling, and blood coated the front of his brown shirt. His green eyes were locked on Libby.

Libby's green shift was crimson from the waist up. Bullet holes dotted the fabric. She was flat on her back, her right arm extended toward Cole, her brown eyes staring at him in acute misery. Their fingers were a mere inch apart.

Cole made a valiant effort to rise, to move closer to Libby, but his legs buckled, and he sagged to his knees.

Libby's gaze shifted, focused on Bertha. "Please!" she pleaded. "Please!"

Bertha hurried over to Cole, slinging the M-16 over her left arm.

Cole tried to twist, to use the AK-47 in his left hand, detecting movement but unaware of Bertha's proximity.

"It's me! Bertha!" Bertha informed him, reaching his side and placing her right arm around his waist.

Cole turned his tormented face toward her. "Help me," he said. "Must touch Libby."

Bertha nodded. She heaved, lifting him, assisting him to move next to Libby. She could feel his blood trickling over her arm.

Cole wearily knelt alongside Libby. Bertha released him, and he almost toppled over. Weaving, he dropped the AK-47 and braced himself with his left arm. He smiled down at Libby.

Libby beamed up at him.

Bertha stood at Libby's feet, her eyes moistening.

"Looks like I made a mess of things," Cole said, his voice barely audible.

Libby was breathing heavily. "No, you didn't," she admonished him. "We did okay."

"You always were one for looking at the bright side of things," Cole remarked, and coughed.

Libby glanced at Bertha. "Did we get them? Did we get all of them?"

"Yes," Bertha answered softly.

"See?" Libby grinned at Cole. "We paid them back for Milly and the others. We did okay."

Cole nodded once, his eyelids fluttering. "I guess we did, at that."

Libby's right hand drifted to Cole's lap.

Cole took her hand in his, their fingers entwining. Tears filled his eyes. "I'm sorry, Libby."

"For what?"

"For all the time I wasted. I heard you talking to Bertha outside the cabin." He paused, coughed some more. "I'm sorry for not showing you how I felt. I'm sorry for all the time we could have shared. I'm sorry because I was scared to tell you, scared to open up, scared of losing you. You were right." He grimaced and coughed, and blood appeared at the left corner of his mouth.

"We'll be together again," Libby assured him. She seemed to be staring dreamily into the distance. "I told you about my mom lots of times, about how nice she was. She was very religious, even though religion is against the law. Maybe that's why the Russians took Dad and her. She used to read to us from the Bible, tell us about Jesus and God and Heaven. Heaven is a wonderful place. Nobody tries to kill you there. You always have enough to eat. And there's lots of angels all over, and music, music with harps and singing and all. And love. Everybody loves everybody. Isn't that great?"

Blood was seeping from both corner's of Cole's mouth. "You think," he began, and wheezed, "you think we'll go to this Heaven?"

Libby looked him in the eyes. "Yes, I do."

Cole's features were blancing. "I don't know . . ."

"Tell him, Bertha," Libby said. "Tell him."

Bertha found it difficult to speak. "I don't know much about God and such," she confessed.

Libby frowned.

"But the folks at the Home do," Bertha quickly added. "The Elders there say we live on after this life. They say we go to a better place, a higher spiritual level they call it."

Cole took a deep breath. "And how . . . do we get to this better place?"

"The Elders say all it takes is faith," Bertha stated, recalling several worship services she'd attended. "All you got to do is believe in the Spirit."

"I believe," Libby declared weakly. She gazed at Cole. "Please. For me. Believe."

Cole coughed and slumped lower. "I never gave it much . . . thought before." He paused. "But if it means I'll see you again, then for you"—he wheezed—"I'll believe."

Libby gripped his hand tightly. "Thank you." She looked up at a patch of sky visible through the trees. "I can't wait to get there! Maybe we'll see our parents again. Wouldn't that be fantastic?"

Cole didn't answer.

"Cole?" Libby said, alarmed, examining his rigid features.

Cole was quivering. He began to droop forward, his eyes on her. "I . . . love . . . you," he said, and collapsed across her waist.

Bertha took a step nearer and reached for Cole.

"Don't!" Libby stated.

"But . . ." Bertha started to protest.

"Leave him," Libby directed. "I want him like this." She managed to move her left hand to his head and began stroking his hair. For a minute she was quiet, frowning. Then she mustered a wan smile. "You know, this is the first time I've touched him like this. I can't believe it!"

Bertha felt light-headed.

"Bertha?" Libby said. Her voice was fading.

"I'm here," Bertha assured her huskily.

"Promise me something," Libby stated.

"Anything."

"Promise me you'll bury us side by side. Hand in hand. Please? I don't want the animals to get us," Libby said.

Bertha responded with the utmost difficulty. "I promise you. I'll bury you side by side."

"Thank you." Libby gazed up at the sky, and an incredible expression of happiness transformed her face. "We're on our way!" she cried, elated. She gasped once, then ceased breathing.

An eerie silence enshrouded the hillside, until an unusual sound arose from a small clearing near the base of the hill, a sound gaining in intensity as it continued, softly at first, and then in loud, moanful sobs, the sound of a Warrior crying.

21

The day was cold, the sky a bright blue. He was dressed all in gray, with a pair of Grizzlies nestled in shoulder holsters, one under each arm. The Family firing range was all his. Few Family members ventured into the southeastern corner of the Home. The children were instructed to stay away from the firing range, which consisted of a large clearing with an earth bank at the east end. The Warriors used the firing range regularly, and the other Family members were required to visit it periodically to take firing lessons under the Warriors' tutelage, to familiarize themselves with the correct use of firearms in case the Home ever sustained another assault.

Two rusted tin cans had been placed on the earthen bank.

He draped his arms at his sides, shook his head to relax the muscles, and drew, the Grizzlies gleaming as they flashed from their holsters. Both pistols boomed, and the tin cans flipped into the air. They dropped to the dirt and rattled to the bottom of the bank.

"Right smart shootin', Sundance," remarked someone behind him.

Sundance recognized the voice. He slid the Grizzlies into their holsters and turned. "I've been expecting you," he said.

The blond gunman in the buckskins nodded. "Figured as much." He indicated the bank with a wave of his right hand. "It looks like you're pretty much healed."

Sundance glanced at the tin cans. "Just about. It's been a tough two months," he admitted.

"I know," the man in the buckskins stated. "I've been keepin' tabs on you, checkin' with the Healers every now and then. They told me you likely would've died if Bertha hadn't tended you on the way back from Philly. They said it was touch and go for a spell. You must be one tough hombre, Sundance."

Sundance studied the Family's legendary gunfighter. "And to what do I owe all this attention, Hickok?"

Hickok grinned, his blond mustache curling upward. "I reckon you know why I'm here."

It was Sundance's turn to nod. "I guess I do. And I don't see where it's any business of yours."

Hickok's grin faded. "I'm making it my business," he declared.

Sundance felt his temper rise. "You shouldn't butt your nose in where it doesn't belong."

Hickok hooked his thumbs in his gunbelt. "That's where you're wrong, pard. I do have a legitimate stake in what's going on. One of my best buddies, Blade, and one of the people I care for a whole bunch, Bertha, came back from the Philly run all discombobulated. And do you know what the reason was?"

"What?" Sundance responded.

"You," Hickok said.

"How do you figure?" Sundance queried defensively.

"Blade can be a moody cuss at times," Hickok commented. "And he moped around here for weeks after you three got back. It took Geronimo and me a while to pry the reason out of him, but he finally 'fessed up to bein' upset over what happened to you. It had something to do with some Commie captain. Blade blamed himself for you bein' hurt. Claimed it never would've happened if he'd done what he should've done with the captain."

"It wasn't Blade's fault," Sundance said.

"Well, Blade ain't content unless he can blame himself for everything that goes wrong in his life,"

Hickok mentioned, and chuckled. "Sometimes I swear the big dummy would blame himself for bad weather, if he could get away with it. Luckily for him, he's got his missus, Geronimo, and me to keep him in line. He got over what happened to you." Hickok paused. "But Bertha is another story."

"Bertha doesn't concern you," Sundance stated.

Hickok was standing ten feet away. He moved closer, his hands straying to his sides. "Bertha *does* concern me, pard. A lot. We go back a long way. We've been through a lot together. We were close friends before the two of you ever met. Like I said, I care for her. And I get a mite ticked off when some yahoo gives her a bum steer!"

"Bum steer?" Sundance snapped angrily. "Who the hell do you think you are? If Bertha has something to say to me, let her say it to my face! She doesn't need to send you to do her talking for her!"

"She didn't send me," Hickok said.

"Then why are you here?" Sundance demanded. "Bertha and I are adults. We don't need you to play matchmaker!"

Hickok pursed his lips, then sighed. "I can see you want to do this the hard way."

"We have nothing to discuss," Sundance reiterated. "Get lost."

Hickok squared his shoulders. "Why don't you make me?"

Sundance tensed. "Don't push me," he warned.

"Or what?" Hickok asked. "You'll draw on me?"

"I'll only be pushed so far," Sundance declared. "I don't like it when someone meddles in my personal affairs."

"You didn't answer my question," Hickok noted. "You goin' to draw on me?"

"I won't draw on a fellow Warrior," Sundance said.

Hickok smirked. "Ahhh. Ain't that sweet! Tell you what I'll do. You say you want me to get lost?"

"That's right," Sundance affirmed.

"Then you beat me on the draw," Hickok proposed,

"and I'll make tracks."

"What?"

"That's right. You beat me, and I get lost. I beat you, and you hear me out. What do you say?" Hickok prompted him.

"You're crazy!" Sundance exclaimed.

Hickok shrugged. "Everybody knows that. Now what about it? Do we have a deal?"

"I beat you," Sundance said, "and you promise you'll take a hike?"

"You have my word," Hickok vowed. "All you have to do is get a bead on my belly button before I get one on yours, and I'm out of your life."

Sundance mulled over the proposition. He was genuinely annoyed at Hickok for prying into his private life, and he resented Hickok's smug attitude. Ordinarily, he detested exhibitionism. But this was a special case. He wanted to teach Hickok a lesson.

"What's it goin' to be?" Hickok asked. "Yes or no?"

"I'll do it!" Sundance declared. "And then I want you to get the hell out of here!"

"Such a mouth for a Warrior!" Hickok quipped. "Ain't you heard we're supposed to set an example for the younguns?"

"Let's get this nonsense over with," Sundance commented acidly.

"Touchy sort, huh?" Hickok shrugged. "Okay. To do this fair, let's both hold our arms straight out from our sides. Like this." He raised his arms.

"This is ridiculous," Sundance said, elevating his arms.

Hickok surveyed the clearing and the surrounding forest. "Do you see that sparrow over there?" he inquired.

Sundance glanced to his right. "That one on top of the pine tree?"

"That's the one," Hickok confirmed. "When it takes off, we slap leather."

"We draw when the bird flies off?" Sundance said.

"That's the general notion," Hickok declared.

"That's stupid," Sundance complained.

"You got a better idea?"

"No," Sundance reluctantly replied.

"Then when the sparrow skedaddles," Hickok directed, "pull your irons."

Sundance concentrated on the bird. He suddenly viewed the outcome of their mock duel as extremely important. He wanted, more than anything else, to put Hickok in his place. He was tired of always being compared to the Family's supreme gunfighter. And he wanted to prove he was a skilled pistoleer in his own right.

A minute dragged by.

Two.

Sundance could feel his shoulder muscles beginning to ache.

The sparrow stayed perched on the tree, chirping contentedly, enjoying the sunshine.

Sundance felt a twinge in his right shoulder, and he remembered the cautionary advice the Healers had given him, not to strain his shoulder or he would spend another week in the infirmary. If the damn bird didn't move soon, he'd have to for—

The sparrow took wing.

Sundance drew like never before, his hands streaking to his holsters, the Grizzlies flying free and sweeping low, the barrels already aimed, and then, and only then, did he realize *Hickok hadn't drawn!* He froze, utterly dumfounded.

Hickok laughed. "I never draw on a fellow Warrior either," he explained. "And I'm goin' to speak my piece, whether you like it or not."

Sundance absently stared at the Grizzlies in his hands, then at Hickok.

"Bertha has been alone for a long, long time," Hickok was saying. "Too long. Once, way back when, she told me she wanted us to be an item. You've got to admire her grit!" Hickok paused, his tone softening. "I felt real bad about it, 'cause I never seriously looked at her as more than a friend. A close friend. One of the best. And when I met Sherry, it cinched things for me. I know there's been a lot of gossip about Bertha and me. Some people ain't got nothin' better to do with their time than flap their gums!'' He stared at his moccasins. ''But I wanted you to know there isn't any truth to those lousy rumors. And I wanted to ask you something, man to man. Warrior to Warrior.''

Sundance noticed Hickok was using a normal vocabulary. ''What is it?''

Hickok gazed into Sundance's eyes. ''How you feel about Bertha is your business. But if you do have any feelings for her, any feelings at all, then why don't you go talk to her? I know you've hardly said three words to her since you got back from Philly. I'm not even going to ask you why. That's your business too. But if you do like her, even just a little bit, why don't you get to know her? I guarantee you'll never find a better woman, anywhere.''

''Why are you doing this?'' Sundance asked. ''If she wants to talk to me, then why didn't she visit me in the infirmary?''

''I'm doin' this 'cause I'm a busybody,'' Hickok answered. ''And 'cause Blade said Bertha was actin' like she's interested in you. I don't know why she didn't come see you when you were laid up. She's kept pretty much to herself since you three came back. I think something happened to her out there. I don't know what. That's for you to find out. If you want to, that is.'' Hickok grinned and started to turn. ''There. I've said my fill. The rest is up to you. And if you're half the man I think you are, I expect to be best man at your wedding.''

''Hickok,'' Sundance said.

Hickok stopped. ''What?''

''You tricked me, didn't you? You never intended to draw. You just wanted me so rattled you could have your say without me interrupting. Am I right?'' Sundance queried.

Hickok chuckled. ''I'll never tell.''

Sundance grinned. ''I'm beginning to understand the reason for your reputation. It's well deserved. You're one shrewd Warrior.''

Hickok raised his right forefinger over his lips. "Shhh! Don't let Geronimo hear you saying that! He thinks I'm an idiot, and I'd like to keep it that way."

Sundance laughed. "I'll never tell."

"And give some thought to Bertha, will you?" Hickok mentioned as he began to stroll off.

"I will," Sundance promised.

"One more thing," Hickok said, looking over his right shoulder.

"What?" Sundance responded.

"You can put those Grizzlies away, unless you want me to find you a sparrow to shoot."

Three months later Sundance and Bertha were married in an elaborate Family ceremony. Hickok served as best man.

HOUSTON RUN

Dedicated to...
Judy and Joshua and ?
and
the thousands upon thousands of Endworld *readers.*
This one's for you.
Especially...
Brian Jones,
Joseph J. Sirak, Jr.,
Kathy Gomoll,
for your patience.
Oh.
For those who like to read between the lines—you're in
for a treat!
Enjoy!

1

A bright red pinpoint of light appeared in the center of the Clarke Model 2001 Computer, the navigational console for the Klinecraft Hoverjet.

"One hundred miles and closing," AS-1 announced. He occupied the middle seat in front of the control console, his seven-foot frame erect in his chair, his blue orbs scanning the digital display above the red light.

"Ready for target identification and isolation," IM-97 declared from his cushioned green seat to the right of AS-1.

In the contoured chair to the left, OV-3 flicked a silver toggle switch on the large console and a square screen before him brightened. His right hand moved across a bank of typing keys below the seven-inch-wide screen, his fingers stabbing individual letters with astonishing rapidity.

"ACTIVATED" flashed onto the screen in black block letters.

OV-3 typed his request into the computer. As a last-minute addition to the retrieval crew, he wanted to review the target data once again,

"SUBJECT: BLADE," the Clarke responded at the top of the screen, and immediately the display filled with the subject's background and peripheral data. OV-3 scanned the material.

Blade is the current head of the Warriors, the elite combat unit responsible for the security of the Home and the preservation of the Family. (Correlation: see Family & Home.) He is believed to be responsible for terminating the Doktor. Intelligence also indicates Blade terminated

Samuel II. Recent activites include confrontations with the Technics in Chicago, and with the Soviets in Philadelphia. This subject is considered to be extremely dangerous.

While all of the Warriors are known to be skilled fighters, many have specialized in certain weapons. Blade is an expert with knives, particularly the large type referred to as the Bowie knife. He invariably carries two such knives, in addition to whatever other arms he might require for missions outside the Home. Intelligence has confirmed his use of a Commando Arms Carbine on several occasions.

Physical Characteristics: Intelligence has not acquired a photograph, and the following is based on personal descriptions. Height: approaching seven feet. Weight: estimated between 220-260. Build: exceptionally strong biological organism. Described as "all muscle from head to toe" by one witness. Hair: dark. Worn medium length. Eyes: gray. Distinguishing marks: none known. Marital status: married to Family member named Jenny. One son, Gabriel. END OF REPORT.

OV-3 pursed his thin lips. The file on Blade was unusually thin. His hands raced over the keys, accessing the correlative material.

SUBJECT: FAMILY.

The Family resides in a walled compound in northwestern Minnesota. (Correlation: see Home.) Androxia has not established diplomatic relations with the Family. Evolutionary Scale Rating; 4. Industry: none. The Family's economy is broadly communal. Stewardship is vested in the oldest members, designated as Elders. These Elders are responsible for the Family's educational system and for formulating formal Family policy. One Family member is chosen as Leader of the entire Family. Exact Family membership is unknown, but Intelligence believes that it is less than one hundred. Children are reared in close-knit family units. The Family is socially primitive and scientifically ignorant.

History: Little is known. Most members are believed to be the descendents of a survivalist group.

Disposition: Primator has decreed their eventual

subjugation and assimilation into the genetically controlled work pool once Androxia has assumed ascendancy. Rectification will be necessary. The Family is known to believe in the fallacious concept of "love," and actively promotes belief in a non-existent "Spirit" source and sustainer. END OF REPORT.

OV-3 read the last section twice. Such degenerates deserved to be exterminated. Why would Primator deal so mercifully with these biological organisms? The genetics might be useful for menial functions, but otherwise they were hopeless. He stared at the monitor. The information on the Family as a whole, like that on Blade, was singularly sparse. He decided to punch up the report on the Home, and promptly did so.

SUBJECT: THE HOME.
The Home is a thirty-acre walled compound in northwestern Minnesota, near Lake Bronson State Park. Exact date of construction is unknown, but it is believed to have been built over one hundred years ago, just prior to the outbreak of World War III. The compound is surrounded by 20-foot-high brick walls. An interior moat provides additional protection from potentially hostile forces. Entrance is afforded by a drawbridge situated in the middle of the west wall. The eastern half of the compound is maintained in a natural state or utilized for agricultural purposes. The western half is devoted to socialization. Intelligence has not mapped the interior.

The Home is defended by 12 to 15 (estimates vary) Warriors. These Warriors are highly trained professionals. They are divided into Triads. Known Triads: Alpha, Beta, Gamma, and Omega. There may be more. Known Warriors: Blade, Hickok, Geronimo, and Yama. (Correlation: see individual Warriors.)

Disposition: Primator has decreed destruction after subjugation of occupants. Prominence Rating: 0. END OF REPORT.

OV-3 glanced at AS—1. "Intelligence has not compiled an adequate file on our target," he stated.

AS-1, his attention on the 2001 console, nodded. "Did you view the data on the Home?" he asked.

"Affirmative," OV-3 replied.

"And did you note the Prominence Rating?" AS-1 inquired.

"A zero," OV-3 noted.

"Which explains our lack of information," AS-1 said. "The Family is so low on the list, they were deemed inconsequential. Intelligence has been concentrating on the primaries, on the Technics, the Soviets, and the Civilized Zone."

"I understand that," OV-3 commented. "I do not understand why we are expending precious fuel to fly to a small, inconsequential outpost merely to retrieve one organism."

"Primator wants this organism," AS-1 mentioned.

"Did Primator elaborate on his rationale?" OV-3 asked.

"No," AS-1 responded.

"I can supply a secondary reason," IM-97 chimed in.

"What is it?" OV-3 questioned.

"Clarissa," IM-97 revealed.

OV-3 gazed out the canopy of the Klinecraft Hoverjet at the stars in the night sky. "Most odd," he remarked. "What does Clarissa want with this organism?"

AS-1 shook his head. "I was not told."

"Nor was I," IM-97 said. "But I do know Clarissa petitioned Primator for the organism, and Primator assented."

AS-1 leaned over the console. "Initiate target identification and isolation," he ordered.

"Engaged," IM-97 said, and pressed a white button near his right hand. A small screen, laced with an overlaid grid, hummed and glowed with a diffuse pink light.

AS-1 studied the digital display above the red light. "Ten miles to target," he informed the others.

"What if this Blade resists?" OV-3 inquired.

"We take him alive," AS-1 said. "Primator was specific in his instructions. Any harm to the organism will result in dismantlement."

"And if the other Warriors interfere?" OV-3 probed.

"Any intervention is to be summarily negated," AS-1 stated.

"Understood," OV-3 said.

"Commencing deceleration," AS-1 declared.

The Klinecraft Hoverjet slowed to a mere fraction of its

cruising speed.

"Two miles to target," AS-1 told them.

OV-3 reached over and depressed a brown lever. "External lights extinguished."

"Activating Stealth Mode," AS-1 stated, and punched a black button. In the Stealth Mode, the Hoverjet's engine operated with a muted whine detectable for a range of only 25 yards.

IM-97 peered at the illuminated grid. The Burroughs Infra-Sensor Module, an optional attachment on the 2001 Computer, required several minutes to attain peak functional capability. He rested his hands on a pair of knobs below the grid, waiting for the word from AS-1.

The Hoverjet continued to wing slowly toward their destination. A minute passed in relative silence. Two minutes.

AS-1, his eyes locked on the digital display, nodded. "We are over the south wall."

"Infrared operational," IM-97 said, twisting the knob in his left hand. Dozens of red blips materialized on the grid. "Multiple possibles within range."

"Adjust the sensors," AS-1 directed. "Scan for physical dimensions, respiratory rate, and gross bulk. Our target is one of the few humans our size. He should literally stand out head and shoulders above the rest."

"Scanning," IM-97 responded.

With AS-1 handling the maneuvering of the Klinecraft, and IM-97 immersed in isolating their target, OV-3 was left with nothing to do. He elected to maximize his time by learning additional details concerning the Family. His fingers flew over the keys, and a moment later the name of another known Warrior appeared on the screen.

SUBJECT: HICKOK.

Hickok is another Warrior in the Family. (Correlation: see Home & Family.) Hickok and two other Warriors, Blade and Geronimo, are believed to constitute one of the Triads comprising the Warrior class. The name of their Triad has not been ascertained.

Hickok is known to specialize in the use of Colt Python revolvers. He is an expert marksman with handguns and rifles. Considered extremely dangerous.

Little else is known about this organism. His marital status is unknown, although one unconfirmed report claims he is married to a Warrior woman named Sherry and has one young son. Height: about six feet. Weight: estimated at 180-190. Build: lean. Hair: blond. Worn long. Also has a blond mustache. Eyes: blue. Distinguishing marks: none known. END OF REPORT.

OV-3 looked at AS-1. "I trust Intelligence will upgrade the files on the Family in the near future."

"If Primator so wills," AS-1 answered. "Evidently, the Doktor had accumulated an extensive file on the Family and the Warriors, but it was destroyed when his headquarters was obliterated. Samuel II also kept a complete dossier on them, but our spy has not been able to locate it. After Samuel II's death, his successor, the new President of the Civilized Zone, confiscated all of Samuel II's files. This President Toland allows only trusted subordinates to view the files."

"Where did Intelligence acquire our information?" OV-3 asked.

"Here and there," AS-1 replied. "Clarissa provided much of it from her memory. Some of it was obtained from monitored Soviet and Technic broadcasts. The rest came from miscellaneous minor sources. Our data on the Family is far from complete."

"That's an understatement," OV-3 commented.

IM-97 suddenly interrupted. "We have him," he declared.

"You have isolated the target?" AS-1 inquired.

"Affirmative," IM-97 affirmed. "And he has unwittingly made our retrieval easier."

"Explain," AS-1 said.

"The Infra-Sensor reveals the majority of the Family is congregated in the western section of their Home," IM-97 elaborated. "But two individuals are in the southeast quadrant. One of them must be our target. He measures out at seven feet tall and weighs 240."

"There are just two of them?" AS-1 asked.

"Just two," IM-97 confirmed.

AS-1 stared at the digital display. The Hoverjet was hovering 200 yards above the surface. He angled the Klinecraft in the direction of the pair in the southeast quadrant. "Parabolic," he ordered.

OV-3 straightened, switching a toggle to his left and gripping a round lever in his right hand. "Parabolic activated."

The Hoverjet drifted toward the southeast quadrant.

Sounds began emanating from a four-inch speaker mounted on the console near OV-3. Leaves rustling. The wind whispering.

OV-3 slowly moved the round lever back and forth, up and down, searching.

" . . . be a piece of cake," a male voice abruptly filled the cockpit.

"You think so?" responded a lower, more resonant speaker.

"I may have them," OV-3 said.

"They are the only ones in that area," IM-97 averred. "It must be them."

"I've whipped your butt two times so far, pard," the first voice stated.

"We'll try one more time," the speaker with the low tone remarked.

"Then can we call it quits for the night?" asked the first man. "I promised my missus I'd be home to tuck Ringo in. That young'un will be traumatized if his fearless papa ain't there to kiss him nighty-night."

The man with the low voice chuckled. "Sure, Hickok. This will be our last one for tonight."

"Thanks, Blade," Hickok said.

"We have him," AS-1 remarked.

"Do we take him now?" OV-3 queried.

"We will wait for a better opportunity," AS-1 said. "We do not want to arouse any suspicions. We might be able to take him when he's alone."

" . . . don't see why the blazes we have to do this anyway!" Hickok was saying.

"Practice makes perfect," Blade responded.

"After all we've been through," Hickok muttered, "we still got to play these games!"

"They're not games, and you know it," Blade corrected him. "These night drills are essential to our readiness."

"Okay. I get your drift. And I don't need no lecture," Hickok said. "Let's get this blamed nonsense over with, so we can mosey on back, tuck in the young'uns, and rustle up some grub.''

"I'll be the stalker this time," Blade said.

"Fine by me," Hickok replied.

"Mosey? Grub?" AS-1 repeated, puzzled. "This Hickok employs a peculiar dialect."

"All biological organisms are strange," OV-3 asserted.

"Blade is moving away from Hickok," IM-97 disclosed, his eyes glued to the grid.

"What are they doing?" OV-3 asked.

"Whatever it is," AS-1 speculated, "it has something to do with their Warrior training."

"I have a strange reading here," IM-97 announced, his interest piqued by a trio of bluish-red blips on the grid.

"What sort of reading?" AS-1 demanded.

"I'm picking up all of the Family members within range," IM-97 replied. "As expected, they all register red."

"All bipedal humanoids register red," AS-1 remarked.

"True," IM-97 conceded. "But I'm also registering three bluish-red life readings, about one hundred yards to the north-west."

AS-1 glanced at IM-97. "Bluish-red?"

"See for yourself," IM-97 said, waving his right hand toward the blips.

AS-1 bent to the right and peered at the grid. "But blue is for organisms lower than human, for the animal life, the mammals and reptiles and such."

"I know," IM-97 agreed. "Which is what makes these three so strange."

"They appear to be stationary," AS-1 observed.

"They are," IM-97 confirmed.

"Pulse rate?" AS-1 inquired.

IM-97 turned the right-hand knob below the grid, then studied the small figures appearing at the bottom of the screen. "Definitely not human."

AS-1 reflected for a moment. "The Burroughs unit must be malfunctioning. We know the Family maintains this half of their Home in a natural state. Perhaps the unit has detected several horses or deer and is registering a composite signal. You know how precise the calibration must be on these units. Did you calibrate it yourself?"

"No," IM-97 answered. "The craft was serviced by the technicians before our departure."

"They may have miscalibrated," AS-1 stated. "Concentrate on Blade and Hickok. We must monitor them and wait for Hickok to leave, or for them to separate."

"And then we pounce?" OV-3 interjected.

"And then we pounce," AS-1 affirmed.

2

Blade circled to the west, his black leather vest and green fatigue pants blending into the inky vegetation. His Bowies snuggled in their sheaths, one on each broad hip. The night air was cool, and there was a faint breeze from the west. His massive muscles rippled as he skirted a tree and reached a low rise. He crouched, grinning. The longer he took, the more irritated Hickok would become, and he needed an edge if he was to beat the gunman the third time around. The exercise was simple, yet markedly effective. One of the Warriors, in this case Hickok, acted as if he was on guard duty, standing or strolling in the open, alert for any attack. Blade's task was to sneak up on the gunfighter undetected. If he succeeded, he won. If Hickok heard him or spotted him, the gunman would win. Seemingly childish, the maneuver served to sharpen their senses. It was one of many exercises designed to keep all of the Warriors at peak effeciency. In addition to comprehensive weaponry training and advanced instruction in the martial arts, every Warrior was required to cultivate skill in the use of stealth and night combat.

The sky was a panorama of celestial lights.

Blade idly glanced up, marveling at the heavenly vista, at the magnitude of creation. He was thankful the night was moonless. It was hard enough to catch the gunman unawares as it was. A large dark cloud was floating far overhead, blotting out a cluster of stars.

Someone began whistling.

Blade flattened. He could hear someone clumping through the woods toward him. Three guesses who it was. But why, he asked himself, was Hickok making so much noise? It sounded as if the

16

gunman was deliberately stepping on every twig and brushing against every bush in his path! What was Hickok up to now? Was the gunfighter so eager to get back to his cabin, he was intentionally making it easy for Blade to win? Or was there an ulterior motive? Blade chuckled. You could never tell with Hickok. And Blade wouldn't have it any other way. Hickok's unpredictability was a valuable asset, contributing to his sterling record as a Warrior, and had saved his life and benefited the Family in many a critical situation.

Hickok was slowly ambling to the northwest, whistling "Home on the Range."

Blade crawled behind a log, then cautiously raised his eyes above the top.

Hickok was 20 yards away, his buckskin-clad form a light patch against the dark background of the forest.

Blade's eyes narrowed. The gunman would pass ten yards from his position, and was coming around the far side of the low rise. Blade's fingers probed the ground around him, and his left hand closed on a jagged piece of stone. He swept his hand up and back, and hurled the stone in a wide arc, over the low rise, over the advancing gunman and into the trees beyond.

There was a muffled crackling and thumping as the stone crashed through the leaves and bounced from limb to limb.

Hickok stopped and spun, facing the forest, his back to the rise.

Blade was up and running, his powerful legs churning, sprinting up the rise and reaching the top in four mighty strides. He launched himself into the air, his muscular arms outstretched, certain of victory. But even as his moccasined feet left the ground, he saw Hickok starting to turn, saw the gunman's right hand flashing toward his right Python. Hickok wore a matched pair of pearl-handled Colts strapped around his waist, and his prowess with the irons was legendary.

Hickok almost won.

The right Python was just clearing leather when Blade tackled his friend, his arms encircling the gunman and pinning Hickok's forearms, the force of his leap bearing them to the dank earth. He landed on top, astraddle the gunman.

Surprisingly, Hickok was taking his defeat calmly. He was on his left side, neither protesting nor squirming.

"Looks like I won this round," Blade commented, smirking.

"I don't know about that, pard," Hickok responded. "I think this is a draw."

"How do you figure?" Blade asked.

"Let me put it to you this way," Hickok said. "How do you feel about partin' with your family jewels?"

Blade glanced down.

Somehow, even as he fell, even with his arms pinned, Hickok had twisted his right hand, had angled the Python barrel around and in, the .357 Magnum pointing directly at Blade's gonads.

"I wouldn't sneeze if I were you," Hickok joked. "My hardware has a hair trigger."

Blade stood, smiling. "Not bad. But I still beat you to the punch. You fell for one of the oldest tricks in the book."

Hickok rose, holstering his right Colt. "Let me guess. You tossed a rock into the trees?"

"You got it," Blade said.

Hickok shrugged. "Well, you win some, you lose some. That's life."

"I never would have won," Blade stated, "if you hadn't cheated."

Hickok stared at his giant companion. "Let me get this straight. *You* won, and *I* cheated?"

"Don't play innocent with me," Blade said. "You were making enough noise to wake the dead. You wanted me to win. You wanted to get this over with so you can get home."

Hickok grinned sheepishly. "I figured if I made enough noise, you'd get overconfident, get careless, and do something stupid."

"I don't buy it," Blade told him.

"You don't?" Hickok responded. "Why not?"

"How long have I known you?" Blade queried.

Hickok frowned. "It's bad enough bein' second-guessed by my missus all the time! Don't you start too!"

Blade smiled. "Being outfoxed by your better half is normal in any marriage."

"Don't I know it!" Hickok exclaimed. "They're tricky, them female types! Before you tie the knot, they act so sweet and innocent. But after you're hitched, watch out! If you ask me, women make better drillmasters than men!"

Blade nodded. "Tell you what. Let's head on back. We can

finish this tomorrow night.''

"Tomorrow night?" Hickok responded in surprise. "Why are we comin' out here tomorrow night?"

"To make up for your lack of cooperation tonight," Blade informed him, grinning.

"You mean just 'cause I fudged a mite on one of the drills, we're goin' to do it all over again tomorrow night?" Hickok asked.

"You catch on real quick." Blade turned, walking to the north-west.

Hickok fell in alongside the head Warrior, grumbling.

"What did you say?" Blade asked.

The gunfighter glanced at Blade. "You *are* gettin' worse than my wife! You're turnin' into a real hardass."

"You think so?" Blade questioned.

"I know so!" Hickok stated. "And I ain't the only one who's noticed either. Geronimo, Rikki, and a few of the others have commented about it."

Now it was Blade's turn to display surprise. "You're serious?"

"You bet I am," Hickok said, looping his thumbs in his gunbelt. "You've changed, pard. I don't rightly know how best to describe it. You're more hard-nosed than before. Don't get me wrong. You were never exactly Little Bo Peep. But you changed after that business in Colorado. At least, you started to change. Everybody saw it. And it was confirmed on the last run you took, the one with Sundance and Bertha to Philadelphia."

"The trip to Philadelphia wasn't any different than any of the missions we've been on together," Blade said.

"That's where you're wrong, pard," Hickok said, disagreeing. "It was a heap different. Sundance told us all about it. About how Bertha up and vanished, and instead of lookin' for her, you went on with the mission."

Blade shrugged. "What's so unusual about that? We had an assignment, and the mission came first."

Hickok stared up at his friend. "It did then, that's for sure. You were all business. And that's my point. In the old days, before your tussle with Sammy in Denver, you always considered the mission as secondary. *We* came first! The Warriors with you were your first priority. Do you remember Thief River Falls? The Twin Cities? When any of us were in trouble, you dropped everything else and came to our aid. If we were hurt, you'd postpone the mission. Do you remember those times?''

Blade pondered the gunman's assertions, realizing Hickok was right. "I remember," he said slowly. "How could I forget them?''

"So what happened? Why the big change?" Hickok asked.

"I'm not sure if I can answer that," Blade replied. "I don't know if I know the answer."

"I ain't complainin', mind you," Hickok mentioned. "You've got a big load to carry, bein' top Warrior and all. You've got to be tough as nails."

Blade gazed at the trail they were following, his brow creased. "I think maybe it started during our Denver campaign, just like you said. That's when it dawned on me."

"What did?" Hickok inquired.

"The magnitude of our responsibility," Blade elaborated. "I'd always appreciated how important our job is, how necessary the Warriors are to the Family's survival. I recognized the fact intellectually. But I don't think I felt it, really experienced what I already knew, until the Home was attacked and almost destroyed. When Geronimo came to Denver and told us you were under assault, I was shocked. Horrified. Afraid you would be wiped out before we could reach you." He looked at the gunman. "You have no idea what it felt like. I finally understood—fully understood—how critical our conduct is to the Family's welfare and safety. If we slip up, the consequences can be disastrous! We must treat every mission as the most important thing in our lives. The Family's security depends on our performance, on our judgment. We can't let them down."

"So that explains the big change," Hickok said. "I'll have to tell the others. Everybody had a different idea as to what was goin' on."

"What did they think?" Blade asked.

"Geronimo said it was married life gettin' to you," Hickok revealed, and laughed. "Rikki felt it might be the strain takin' its toll."

"And how about you? What did you think?" Blade queried.

"Me?" Hickok grinned. "I just reckoned you had a corncob stuck up your butt."

"I knew I could count on you for an insightful analysis," Blade quipped.

"Hey! What are friends for?" Hickok retorted.

Blade, smiling, went to rest his hands on his Bowie hilts. He abruptly stopped in mid-stride. "Damn!"

Hickok halted. "What's wrong?"

"It's gone."

"What's gone?" Hickok inquired.

"My left Bowie," Blade said, tapping the empty sheath on his left hip. The right Bowie was secure in its scabbard.

"Where could it have gone?" Hickok asked, glancing over his left shoulder at the trail behind them.

Blade reflected for a moment. "I'll bet it fell out when I tackled you."

Hickok started to turn. "Then let's go look for it. I know you can't go beddy-bye without 'em tucked under your pillow."

"Thanks," Blade said, "but you head on back. I'll find the Bowie myself."

"I don't mind helpin' you," Hickok persisted.

"I know," Blade stated. "I appreciate the thought. But I don't want to hold you up. Head on home and tuck in Ringo."

"I don't know," Hickok said doubtfully.

Blade began retracing their path. "What? I can't find a knife by myself? I need you to hold my hand?"

"I don't mind helpin'," Hickok reiterated.

Blade waved the gunman off. "Go give Sherry a big kiss for me. It won't take more than a few minutes for me to find my knife. Go!"

"All right," Hickok remarked. "If that's what you want. But I'm tellin' you right here and now, pard, that if I give my missus a big kiss, it won't be for you!" He grinned, then wheeled, waving. "I'll see you tomorrow."

"Good night," Blade said. He hurried along their back trail, eager to find the Bowie and head on home. The thought of Jenny and little Gabe waiting for him, with a pot of venison stew boiling on their cast-iron stove, heightened his anticipation.

The leaves in the nearby trees were rustling with the breeze.

Blade mused on his good fortune as he jogged. He thanked the Spirit he'd been born in the Home, and had been reared under the beneficial influence of the Family. When he thought of the conditions existing outside the Home, of the savage barbarism rampant since World War III and the collapse of civilization, he felt intensely grateful for his lot in life. His frequent missions beyond the walled security of the Home only served to strengthen his conviction and increase his sense of thanksgiving. Only some-one who knew what it was like to go without home and family, the two fundamental institutions of human society, he reasoned, could properly comprehend their importance. He'd seen the outside world, with all of its violence, with devious degenerates ready to murder without provocation, ready to slash someone's throat for the mere "thrill" of killing, and he hadn't liked what he'd seen. His philosophical musings came to an end as he rounded a large boulder and saw the low rise.

And something else.

Or someone else.

A towering figure stood at the base of the rise, a figure at least seven feet tall and solidly built, attired in a peculiar silver garment and silvery boots. The figure extended its right arm. "Do you seek this?" it asked in precise, clipped English.

Despite the gloom, Blade could distinguish the silver figure's rugged, yet oddly pale, features. A square jaw was capped by prominent cheekbones. Its eyes were an indeterminate color. Curly blond hair crowned its head.

"Do you seek this, Blade?" the figure repeated. It held its right arm aloft.

The silver garbed form was holding the missing Bowie.

"Who are you?" Blade demanded, taking a step forward, his right hand on his right Bowie. "How did you get in here? How do you know my name?"

"My name is AS-1," the figure stated imperiously. "And I was instructed to relay a message."

"Message?" Blade repeated, puzzled. "What are you babbling about?"

AS-1 lowered his right arm. "I am incapable of babbling," he said. "As for the message, it is simply this: Clarissa sends her regards."

"Who?"

"Clarissa," AS-1 said.

"I don't know any Clarissa," Blade declared.

"But she knows you," AS-1 disclosed. "And Primator sent us to retrieve you. Please do not resist."

Blade drew his right Bowie. "You're got it backwards, mister. You're coming with me. Make it easy on yourself and don't do anything stupid."

"My I.Q. is one hundred forty," AS-1 remarked. "It is impossible for me to commit a stupid act." He glanced to the left. "Take him."

Blade saw them coming out of the corner of his right eye. A pair of huge forms hurtling from the darkness, springing at him. He spun, dodging to the left, sidestepping their onslaught, his right arm a blur as he whipped the Bowie up and in, imbedding the knife to the hilt in the chest of one of his attackers. He wrenched the knife free as they plunged past him.

They stopped and whirled in concert, charging, not missing a beat. Tall forms dressed all in silver.

Blade braced himself, amazed the one he'd stabbed was still erect. They plowed into him in unison, one from the left, the other from the right, lifting him from the ground and slamming him onto his back, the brutal impact causing the air to whoosh from his lungs. He gasped and swung his left fist, clipping one of the silver men on the chin, expecting his foe to be knocked aside.

Instead, the silver man shook his head once, then stared at Blade and grinned.

Blade's mind was screaming a silent warning. Something was wrong here. Terribly, terribly wrong. He sensed it, his intuition blaring, and he surged against his adversaries. They were on their knees, one on each side, attempting to clamp their hands on his arms, to restrain him. Concentrating as they were on his arms, they failed to pin his legs. Blade took instant advantage of their neglect, sweeping his legs up, touching his knees to his chin and then lashing his legs out and down, catching the two silver men off guard, his legs clubbing them in the chest and sending them sprawling. He scrambled to his feet.

"Get him!" AS-1 ordered, still standing near the rise.

The two silver men came up in a rush, arms outstretched.

Blade twisted to the right, avoiding the nearest antagonist, and executed a wicked slicing arc with his right Bowie. The keen blade bit into the left wrist of the closest silver man, into the wrist and through the wrist.

The silver man's left hand dropped to the ground.

One out of the way! Grinning, Blade began to turn toward the second figure.

That was when the first assailant straightened and raised his severed forearm to his face, calmly examining the injured limb.

Blade, stunned, froze. He could see liquid pulsing from the ruined arm, but there wasn't enough of it, not the copious quantity there should be, and the silver man was reacting too placidly, was actually gazing at Blade with an air of serene resignation. Blade abruptly realized the silver man with the severed hand was the same one he'd stabbed in the chest. But that was impossible! No man could take such punishment, could receive two potentially fatal wounds, and be so unruffled by the injuries! What *were* these silver men?

"You were told not to resist," said a voice behind the Warrior.

Blade pivoted, knowing he'd blundered by forgetting the one near the rise, the one with his other Bowie. He attempted to bring his own knife into play, but something smashed into his right temple, staggering him, sending waves of agony rippling over his consciousness. He tottered, and almost fell. With a supreme effort, he was able to stay on his feet. But not for long. Another blow descended on his temple, and he felt his knees buckle as he collapsed, sprawling onto his hands and shins. The world was spinning. He struck out wildly with his Bowie, but missed.

A hard object collided with his temple for yet a third time, and the Family's head Warrior toppled forward into the dirt.

"He is ours," AS-1 stated.

3

Hickok heard the three voices before he saw the speakers. He recognized the distinctive vocal traits instantly.

" . . . agreed to drop the subject, yes?" said the first speaker.

"I didn't agree to drop nothin'!" snapped the second speaker in a lisping, high-pitched voice. "You bozos did all the agreeing!"

"We had to," asserted the third speaker, his tone low and raspy. "We knew we'd never hear the end of it otherwise."

"You still ain't heard the last of it!" stated the second speaker angrily.

Hickok was traveling a well-defined trail toward the western half of the Home. He walked past a row of pine trees and there they were, seated in the center of a small clearing, so involved in their argument, so wrapped up in the heat of their dispute, that their normally acute senses hadn't detected his approach. But they spotted him the moment he stepped into view, and one of them jumped up.

"Hickok! You startled Gremlin, yes?" the nervous one exclaimed.

"Howdy, Gremlin," Hickok said, greeting him, then nodding at the other two. "What are you yahoos doin'? Holdin' a powwow?"

"Powwow? Gremlin has never heard of a powwow, no," Gremlin said. He stood about five feet ten, and his skin was a leathery gray. Except for a brown loincloth, he was naked. His facial features were hawk-like, his noise pointed, his ears small circles of flesh, and his mouth was a mere slit. The eyes in his bald head contained eerie, stark red pupils. "What is a powwow, yes?"

25

"He means shootin' the breeze," stated the second of the three in his high-pitched voice. This one, when standing, stood under four feet in height, and he weighed only 60 pounds. His bony physique was covered with a coat of short, grayish-brown fur, and his face was decidedly feline in aspect: green, slanted eyes, pointed ears, and a curved forehead, just like a cat's. His fingernails were long and tapered to points. Like Gremlin, he wore a loincloth, but his was gray.

"So what are you guys doin', Lynx?" Hickok asked the cat-man.

"What's it to you?" Lynx retorted.

"Ignore him, Hickok," advised the third member of the trio. "He's in a bad mood. Again," he added in his low tone.

"What's got Lynx riled this time, Ferret?" Hickok inquired, moving over to join them.

Ferret was only an inch taller than Lynx. He wore a black loincloth. His whole body was encased in a coat of brown hair, three inches in length. His head resembled that of his namesake, with an extended nose and tiny brown eyes. His nose constantly twitched. "The same thing he's been upset about for months," he answered.

"What's that?" Hickok questioned.

"Fitting in," Ferret said.

"I don't follow you," Hickok mentioned.

"What's to follow?" Lynx interjected, annoyed. "I want to fit in around here, is all."

Hickok glanced at Gremlin and Ferret. "But you guys do fit in. Has anyone in the Family given you a hard time 'bout livin' here?"

"No," Lynx responded. "But they wouldn't pipe up even if they didn't like us. Your Family is so sicky-sweet and lovey-dovey, spreadin' kindness and love all over the place, they wouldn't say anything to hurt our feelings."

The gunman studied the cat-man. "If no one's objected to you bein' here, what's the beef?"

Lynx's feline features rippled as he struggled to repress his surging emotions. He was obviously furious over something, and was striving to keep his fury in check. "Would you *really* like to know what's buggin' me?"

Hickok nodded. "I'd really like to know," he answered sincerely.

Lynx pointed at Gremlin and Ferret, then tapped his furry chest. "We're not like the rest of you. Or ain't you noticed?"

"You're mutants. Big deal," Hickok said. "The world is crawlin' with mutants since the Big Blast."

"We're genetically engineered mutations!" Lynx stated angrily. "And that makes us different than all the rest." He swept his right arm in a wide arc. "All the other mutations out there are the result of all the radiation and chemicals and who-knows-what-else dumped on the environment during World War III. But we came from a test-tube, Hickok! A lousy test-tube! The damn Doktor created us in his lab! Took ordinary human embryos and turned 'em into us!" Lynx clenched his hands into compact fists. "Freaks! That's what we are! Nothin' more than freaks!" He paused. "You know, I heard test-tube babies were a big deal before the war. I heard the scientists were experimenting with all types of genetically engineered creatures. Slicing genes and all kinds of crap like that. The Doktor just took their work one step further. He wanted to create his own little personal assassin corps. Intelligent pets to do his bidding! That's why the bastard made us!"

"But you rebelled," Hickok reminded the fiery feline.

Lynx snorted derisively. "Fat lot of good it did us! Oh, sure, we survived when the rest of the Doc's Genetic Research Division was destroyed. And it was real kind of your Family to take us in for helpin' you out. But . . ."

"But what?" Hickok prodded.

"But what have we done since?" Lynx demanded. "We do some huntin' for you, and odd jobs now and then, and play with the munchkins. That's it!"

"What's wrong with that?" Hickok asked. "Sounds to me like you've got it easy."

"We do," Lynx admitted. "But I'm tired of havin' it easy. I was bred for action, Hickok. I'm a natural-born fighter, just like you and Blade and Rikki and the rest of the Warriors. And part of me is human, and my human part wants to do something constructive with my life. Something worthwhile. I want to contribute my fair share to the Family, repay you for your hospitality. I want to fit in."

"So that's what you meant," Hickok said.

Lynx took a step toward the gunfighter. "You can help us, Hickok."

"How?" Hickok asked. He could guess the answer. Blade and he were both aware of the ongoing dispute the mutants were having over Lynx's not-so-secret desire. And, as Blade had rightly pointed out, it was up to the mutants to broach the subject first.

"Shhhhhh!" Gremlin suddenly hissed, glancing skyward.

"What is it?" Ferret inquired.

"Gremlin heard something, yes," Gremlin told them.

Hickok looked at the tallest genetic deviate. Gremlin was the antsy type, highly emotional. But he was loyal to a fault, and his eyesight and hearing were superb. During Gremlin's youth, while at the Citadel in Cheyenne, Wyoming, the Doktor had performed an exploratory operation on Gremlin's brain as part of the Doktor's continual upgrading of his medical knowledge and expertise. The Doktor had removed a portion of Gremlin's brain as an experiment. The result was Gremlin's unorthodox speech pattern.

"I didn't hear nothin'," Lynx said.

"You were talking," Ferret noted. "And I was listening to you. Did you hear anything, Hickok?"

The gunman shook his head.

"Gremlin heard something!" Gremlin insisted. "We must investigate, no?"

"You investigate," Lynx said. "I want to finish talkin' to Hickok."

"If Gremlin goes," Ferret stated, "we all go. Isn't that what we pledged? You were the one who read *The Three Musketeers* in the Family library, remember? One for all and all for one. Right?"

"Yeah," Lynx responded, frowning. He gazed at Gremlin. "What did you hear?"

"Gremlin's not certain, yes?" Gremlin replied, his red eyes staring to the east. "Funny kind of buzzing, no?"

"Maybe it was a giant mosquito," Hickok quipped, only partially in jest. Certain insect strains had developed tendencies toward inexplicable giantism since the war, growing to immense proportions.

"Not mosquito, no," Gremlin asserted. "Something different, yes?"

"Let's go find the damned thing!" Lynx snapped. He faced the gunfighter. "Why don't you come along? I'd like to talk with you some more."

Hickok hesitated, thinking of his waiting wife and son.

"Please," Lynx persisted.

Hickok's eyes narrowed. He'd never heard Lynx ask anything so politely before. Lynx must consider it very important indeed. And he could hardly refuse Lynx, because he still owed all three of the mutants for saving his wife's life. "I'll stick with you a spell," he declared. "But let's get this over with. I've got to get home."

Gremlin led them into the trees, bearing to the east. Lynx came next, then Hickok and Ferret.

Hickok marveled at their incredibility silent passage through the vegetation. He was only a few feet away, but couldn't hear a sound.

Gremlin increased his speed, and Lynx kept pace.

Ferret caught up with Hickok and nudged the gunman's right elbow. "You're not mad at Lynx, are you?" he whispered.

"No," Hickok answered softly. "Why should I be?"

"Lynx has a way of getting people upset," Ferret said. "He can be too blunt at times, too inconsiderate. Especially when he's in a bad mood, like now."

"I'll hear him out," Hickok promised. "If he needs my help, I'll do what I can. I'm not forgettin' what you guys did for my missus."

"That was last October," Ferret mentioned. "This is April."

"A debt is a debt," Hickok stated. "Any hombre who doesn't pay his debts ain't much of a man in my book. The same holds true for women."

"We could use your assistance," Ferret remarked. "We want—"

"Shhhh!" came from Gremlin, ten yards ahead.

Hickok crouched. Ferret passed him, stooped over, and he followed. They reached a cluster of bushes and found Gremlin and Lynx on their knees, gaping at an object in a large clearing beyond. Hickok peeked over the top of the bushes, wondering if it was a wild animal, or one of the bizarre ravenous mutations, or even raiders who had somehow managed to scale the outer wall and swim the inner moat. His mind contemplated every possibility in the space of several seconds, his hands on his Colts, thinking he was prepared for anything.

He was wrong.

The gunman's mouth dropped at the sight of the enormous craft in the clearing, a huge black aircraft of advanced design. Hickok racked his memory, attempting to recall the books in the Family library dealing with aviation. He'd read many of them as a child, entranced by the technological accomplishments of prewar society. The Family's Founder had stocked the library with hundreds of thousands of volumes on every conceivable subject. The books containing photographs were especially prized by members of the Family, fascinated as they were by any glimpse of their ancestors' civilization. Although many of the old volumes were faded or yellowed with age and required diligent care when handled, the Family members perused them avidly. Hickok had seen dozens of photographs of ancient aircraft. He'd even seen a functional jet once, and helicopters. But never a craft like the one before him.

"What is it?" Ferret blurted, amazed.

"It ain't no mosquito," Lynx said.

Gremlin turned toward Hickok. "You are Warrior, yes? What we do is up to you, no?"

Hickok peered at the aircraft. The strange vehicle was more than 20 yards away, too far to discern much detail. What was the craft doing there? he asked himself. Why was it in the Home? And who was flying the thing? Why had they landed in the dead of night? Sabotage? A spy mission? What?

"Come on, chuckles!" Lynx urged him. "Let's check this sucker out!"

"I should let Blade know about this," Hickok whispered.

"Can't any of you Warriors take a leak without Blade aimin' your pecker?" Lynx retorted.

Hickok slowly stood. The craft was quiet, and no one was in sight. He could see a doorway of some sort near the nose of the craft. The door was ajar, permitting a greenish light to illuminate a rectangular area under the nose.

"Are you makin' up your mind, or did you fall asleep?" Lynx queried sarcastically.

"We'll take a look," Hickok said, "but you three stay behind me." He drew his Pythons.

Lynx rose. "We don't need you to baby-sit us!" he said indignantly.

Hickok spun. "I'm the Warrior here! And in times of danger, the Warriors are in charge! For all we know, that thing could pose a threat to the Family! So if you want to come, come! But you do what I say, when I tell you! Got it?"

Lynx grinned. "Anyone ever tell you how cute you are when you're pissed off?"

Hickok turned toward the craft, then carefully advanced through the bushes to the clearing. He distinguished three immense wheels supporting the aircraft, one under the nose, and one under each wing. The wings were configured differently from those on the jet he'd seen. They began about a third of the distance from the nose, then flared out to form a gigantic triangular shape. They vaguely resembled those on a military craft in one of the books in the library, and he recalled a term he'd read: delta wing. A faint greenish light was visible under the canopy. And big white letters had been painted on the side.

Lynx came up on the gunman's left. "I ain't seen nothin' like that before," he said. "Not in the Civilized Zone, not with the Doktor, not anywhere."

"Neither have I, pard," Hickok remarked, his keen blue eyes sweeping the aircraft and the surrounding terrain. He angled toward the doorway, reflecting. How long had the craft been there? How could such a big thing have landed without being spotted? Jets and helicopters made a heap of noise. So why hadn't anyone heard the craft in front of him? The ominous black aircraft was distinctly unsettling, and the implications of its presence worried him.

"Do you want one of us to sneak inside and see what's in there?" Lynx queried in a whisper.

"If anyone goes in there," Hickok replied, "it'll be me. You just do what I tell you."

"Yes, *sir!*" Lynx rejoined.

Hickok gazed along the length of the mystery craft. He

estimated the aircraft was a minimum of 40 yards long. The wing span was difficult to gauge because of the darkness. He surveyed the edge of the clearing, perplexed. A ring of trees and brush surrounded the clearing. Didn't jets require a lot of space to take off or land? So how the blazes had this black craft descended? Straight down? He shut all speculation from his mind as he neared the doorway, located 15 yards from the nose.

"What's that mean?" Lynx asked, pointing at the side of the aircraft.

Hickok glanced at the white lettering. ANDROXIA.

"What's Androxia?" Lynx questioned.

"You're askin' me?" Hickok responded. He cautiously approached the doorway. The door was open several inches.

"Perhaps we should knock, yes?" Gremlin inquired from behind the gunman.

"Are you crazy?" Lynx said. "We don't know who's in there." He deliberately paused. "Unless, of course, *Mr.* Hickok wants to knock."

"I'd like to knock your block off," Hickok quipped. He reached the door.

"I'd like to see you try!" Lynx countered.

"Children! Please!" Ferret spoke up. "This is not the time or place."

"Ferret speaks the truth, yes?" Gremlin added. "You two stop bickering, no?"

"Who's bickering?" Lynx responded.

"Will all of you *shut up*?" Hickok hissed. "How can I sneak inside with you three idiots flappin' your gums?"

"Who are you callin' an idiot?" Lynx demanded.

"Go find a mirror," Hickok retorted, and eased the metal door open.

The interior of the craft was lit by a greenish light emanating from recessed translucent squares in the ceiling. A narrow passage ran from the doorway to another, wider corridor.

"You three stay put," Hickok stated. "I'm goin' in."

No one said a word.

Hickok crept into the aircraft. He was surprised to find panelling on the walls and carpeting underfoot. A row of doors lined the left side of the passage. On an impulse, Hickok reached out and yanked on the latch of the second door he passed. The door swung out, revealing four silver uniforms hanging from a rack. On the shoulders of each uniform, enclosed in a circle, was that word again: ANDROXIA. He closed the door and hurried to the connecting corridor.

"Which way?"

Hickok whirled.

Lynx and Ferret were right behind him.

"I thought I told you to stay put!" Hickok growled.

"Don't lay an egg!" Lynx advised. "Gremlin is keepin' watch."

Hickok reined in his raging temper. He intended to settle the matter with the cantankerous feline at the first opportunity, but as Ferret had noted, now was not the time or place. He grit his teeth and took a right, heading toward the nose of the craft.

Lynx and Ferret padded on his heels.

Hickok passed four more doors. The corridor apparently ran the length of the craft. It widened slightly as it neared the nose, and suddenly they were in the spacious cockpit. A large canopy was overhead. Three cushioned seats were positioned in the middle of the cockpit, facing a complicated array of electronic components.

"That's a computer!" Ferret exclaimed. "The Doktor used them all the time."

"What are all those blinkin' lights?" Hickok asked.

"I don't know," Ferret admitted. "I saw the Doktor use his, but I wasn't taught how to use them."

"All that bastard taught us was how to kill," Lynx remarked. "As if we needed lessons!"

"The pilot isn't here," Hickok declared. "We'd best alert the Family."

"I'll go find Blade," Ferret offered.

"Good idea," Hickok concurred. "The last time I saw him, he was south of here a ways, lookin' for a Bowie he lost."

"I'll find him," Ferret stated. He turned.

Footsteps sounded in the corridor, the noise of someone in a hurry. Gremlin appeared at the junction, saw them, and raced to the cockpit. "They're coming!" he blurted in alarm. "They're coming, yes!"

"Calm down, dimwit!" Lynx barked. "Who's coming?"

"Men in gleaming clothes, yes!" Gremlin exclaimed. "Gremlin

saw them, yes!''

"How far away are they?'' Hickok asked.

"Don't know, no!'' Gremlin replied. "Gremlin saw them coming through trees to south, yes! Maybe a hundred yards, yes!''

"Then it'll take 'em a minute or two to get here,'' Hickok said, calculating. "We can surprise 'em.''

"Did you see their faces?'' Ferret inquired. "Are you sure they're men, Gremlin? Are you sure they're human?''

"Gremlin did not see faces, no,'' Gremlin answered. "What else could they be, yes?''

"We'll soon find out,'' Hickok stated. "Find a place to hide.''

"One more thing, yes!'' Gremlin said.

"What is it?'' Hickok queried, searching the cockpit for a suitable hiding place.

"They carry someone, yes!'' Gremlin told them.

"They're carryin' someone?'' Hickok repeated.

"Are you certain?'' Ferret inquired.

Gremlin nodded. "Gremlin certain, yes.''

"You saw them carrying someone that far off?'' Lynx chimed in. "I know we've got good eyesight, but—''

Gremlin's red eyes narrowed. "Gremlin saw them, yes! Don't call Gremlin liar, no!''

"I ain't callin' you a lair, you ding-a-ling!'' Lynx said.

"Find a spot to hide!'' Hickok ordered. "And don't nobody make a move unless I give the word.''

"Can I wee-wee without permission?'' Lynx cracked flippantly.

Hickok ignored the cat-man and turned to a row of doors. He opened the first one. Inside was a closet containing a pile of boxes and a strange metal instrument, a square affair with a dozen switches and dials. There was plenty of space to the left of the pile, and he holstered his Pythons and quickly eased inside. "Hurry!'' he declared, then closed the door. Darkness enveloped him. He could hear the others scurrying to concealment. A door opened to his right, and he knew one of them was using the next closet to hide. He was about to ask who it was, when he heard a voice whispering.

"Gremlin doesn't like this, no! Not one bit, yes!''

Hickok grinned. He lifted his right hand and rested it on his right Colt. There wasn't much room to maneuver, but he was confident he could draw if necessary. He debated a course of action. Should he confront these jokers as soon as they returned? Or should he wait, bide his time, eavesdrop on them, and possibly learn what they were up to, why they were at the Home? He opted for the second plan.

There was a muffled thump from the cockpit, from the direction of the computer, as if someone had bumped something.

"Damn computer!" Lynx muttered.

Hickok smiled. It served the runt right! Lynx was normally a feisty critter, but he'd never seen Lynx as touchy as tonight. He'd known something was bothering the feline for months, but Lynx hadn't said a word to any of the Family about the cause. On numerous occasions he'd seen Lynx and the other two engaged in intense arguments. Lynx seemed to be taking one side, Ferret and Gremlin the other. Hickok had a notion why they were spatting, but he hadn't wanted to . . .

Somewhere, a door slammed.

Hickok waited expectantly.

There was an exchange of muted voices.

Hickok fingered the trigger on his right Python.

" . . . immediately. Primator will be pleased," said a deep voice, the audibility increasing as the speaker neared the cockpit.

"I was impressed," said a second person. "He is quite formidable."

Hickok pressed his right ear to the door panel. Oddly enough, the two voices were almost, but not quite, identical.

"I'm proof of that," commented yet a third party.

The unknown trio reached the cockpit, and there was a commotion as they went about their business.

"How much coolant have you lost?" asked one of them.

"Two quarts," answered another.

"Go to the Wells Repair Module," instructed the first voice. "I will perform emergency crimping on your tubes. It will suffice until we reach Androxia."

"Thank you," said the other one. "I will place my hand in the Boulle to prevent excessive dehydration."

What the blazes were they talking about? Hickok wondered.

"If his knife had penetrated your Heinlein, you would require a major overhaul," commented the third one. He paused. "Should

Blade be placed in stasis?''

Blade! They had Blade! Hickok felt a slight vibration under his feet as he gripped the latch and shoved. He leaped from the closet, his thumb on the hammer of his right Python. ''Don't move!'' he shouted, whipping his right Colt up and out, then stopping, stupefied.

There were three of them, each seven feet in height, each attired in a silver uniform. They all had blond hair, blue eyes, and pale skin. They looked enough alike to be triplets. One stood in front of the computer. The second one, with Blade's unconscious form draped over his left shoulder, was standing five feet to the left of the gunman. The third giant was near the doorway, a ragged tear in his uniform in the center of his chest, a pale fluid seeping from the hole, *holding his severed left hand in his right!*

The one near the computer glanced at the one holding Blade. ''You were correct. You did observe someone near the Hoverjet.''

''I'll do the talkin'!'' Hickok snapped. He wagged his Python at the one with Blade. ''You! Set my pard on the floor! Nice and easy like!''

To the gunman's astonishment, his command was ignored. The one with Blade looked at the one near the computer. ''This must be another Warrior. Should we dispose of him?''

''I believe this is the organism called Hickok,'' remarked the silver man near the door. ''I'm familiar with primitive firearms, and those are Colt Pythons. He is an associate of Blade's.''

''Then we will transport him to Androxia,'' the one by the computer stated.

''You ain't transportin' me nowhere!'' Hickok declared. ''This contraption of yours is stayin' right on the ground!''

''That's impossible,'' the one near the computer stated.

''Wanna bet?'' Hickok rejoined, pointing his Python at the man's head.

''We do not gamble,'' the silver man said. ''And we can not stay on the ground when we are already in the air.'' He motioned toward the canopy.

Hickok risked a hasty glance upward. He could see the stars, and they were moving! With a start, he suddenly realized the stars weren't really moving: *the aircraft was!* They were airborne!

The silver man near the computer scrutinized the gunman's

expression. "We departed your Home over a minute ago. Our onboard navigational computer automatically implemented our takeoff. The Klinecraft is soundproofed, and motion fluctuation is minimal. There was no way you could have known."

"Turn this buggy around!" Hickok demanded. "You're takin' us back."

"No, we are not," said the one by the computer, and he nodded at the silver man near the doorway.

Hickok whirled.

The one with the cut-off hand was already charging, his right arm upraised to deliver a crushing blow.

Hickok's right Python boomed, thundering in the confines of the cockpit. As he invariably did, Hickok went for the head. He was a staunch advocate of always going for the brain. If an opponent was hit anywhere else, they could keep coming. Even if a foe was shot in the heart, they could linger for several seconds or longer, enough time to squeeze a trigger or get in a final swipe. But snuff the brain, as Hickok liked to say, and nine times out of ten the enemy was instantly slain. Nine times out of ten.

This time was the tenth.

The silver man was struck in the left eye, the impact of the 158-grain hollow-point slug jerking his massive body to the left and stopping him in his tracks. He hesitated for just a fraction, then plunged forward, seemingly immune to pain and heedless of the gaping cavity where his left eye had just been.

Hickok's Python blasted again. And once more. Each shot was on target. The first one caught the silver man in the forehead, snapping his head backward and blowing the rear of his cranium outward, spraying the cockpit wall and carpeted floor with grisly pieces of flesh and hair and spattering everything with a colorless liquid. The silver man halted, shook his head once, then resumed his attack. Hickok's next shot hit his assailant in the right eye.

The silver man doubled over, clutching at his shattered face, a watery substance spewing onto the floor.

Hickok was astounded. Never had he seen anyone take such punishment and still keep coming.

But this one did.

The silver man straightened, his arms extended. He had dropped his left hand, and the fingers on his right clawed at the air. His eyes were gone, yet he advanced, shuffling in the direction of the Warrior, his right arm swinging from side to side.

How the hell did he do it? Hickok sent two more slugs into the silver man's head.

The man in silver abruptly stiffened. His mouth curved downwards, his lips trembling. He took a single halting step, then collapsed in a heap.

Hickok couldn't accept the testimony of his own eyes.

Smoke was wafting from the dead man's ruined eye sockets!

The gunman's superb instincts sensed danger, and his left hand streaked to his left Colt as he pivoted to face the other two silver men. He almost made it.

The silver man near the computer had already sprung into action, executing a flying leap, his heavy form hurtling through the intervening space and crashing into the Warrior, slamming the gunman against the closet door, ramming the gunfighter's head into the door. The panel split from the force of the blow, and the gunman slumped to the green carpet, his right Python slipping from his limp fingers.

AS-1 rose to his full height and stared at the Warrior at his feet. "These Warriors are not to be taken lightly," he commented. "I will inform Intelligence upon our return to Androxia." He glanced at his crumpled companion. "OV-3's Bradbury Chip was struck by one of Hickok's shots," he deduced.

IM-97 transferred Blade from his left shoulder to his arms, then walked to the doorway. "I will place this one in stasis and return for Hickok."

AS-1 nodded. "I will transmit the status of our mission to Androxia."

IM-97 gazed at the body of OV-3. "How do you think Primator will react to the loss of a Superior?"

AS-1 nudged OV-3 with the tip of his right toe. "The humans have an expression," he remarked. "Apropos in this instance."

"What is it?" IM-97 inquired.

"The shit will hit the fan."

4

She stood on the balcony on the top floor of the Huxley Tower, her lavender eyes sweeping the skyline of Androxia.

Where were they?

She gazed at the city lights far below, then up at the heavens, idly noting the position of the Big Dipper.

They had to come!

They had to succeed!

Her flowing, oily black hair was whipped by the wind as she turned to the north. The wind felt cool on her scaly yellow skin. Her thin blue dress did little to protect her from the elements.

That bastard had to pay!

Had to reap his punishment for murdering the Doktor!

Her beloved Doktor!

She frowned at the recollection, the memories almost too agonizing to tolerate. She recalled the campaign the Doktor had waged against the accursed Family. She vividly remembered the final battle in Catlow, Wyoming. And tears welled in her eyes as she mentally reviewed the day after that last conflict, when she'd donned a grubby pair of jeans, an old brown shirt, and a tattered tan coat and, after stuffing her waist-length hair into a shabby cap, had ventured into Catlow at sunset, determined to learn the fate of her creator . . . and her lover.

Somewhere in Androxia, a siren wailed.

She'd viewed the battle from a nearby hill and watched, horrified, as the damned Warriors and their allies defeated the Doktor's Genetic Research Division, utterly wiped them out. So far as she knew, she was the only one remaining. And she wouldn't have survived, would have perished with the Doktor and the rest, if her darling mentor hadn't ordered her to remain behind.

She sobbed.

The Doktor had felt uneasy about Catlow, had even speculated it was a trap. Was that the reason he'd left her behind? Was it because he'd wanted to spare her?

And to think!

She'd almost deserted him!

A lump formed in her throat as the bitter remembrance of her flight from Catlow overwhelmed her. She'd wanted to reach Denver as fast as possible, to demand Samuel II lead a counterstrike against Catlow. She'd gone 20 miles before she'd braked her jeep and done a U-turn, heading back to Catlow. Her intuition had told her the Doktor was dead, but she'd needed to ascertain the truth with her own eyes, to actually see his corpse, before she could accept the reality of his demise. She'd doubled back, concealed the jeep, stolen the clothing she needed from a deserted ranch house, and bravely sallied into Catlow as darkness descended.

And she'd found him.

Tears cascaded down her round cheeks.

The slime!

The fucking slime!

They'd hung the Doktor by his heels from a tree near the town square! And there they were, the inebriated residents of Catlow, celebrating their newfound independence, drinking and singing and mocking the Doktor. She'd walked among them, rage filling her being, and had listened to their banter, particularly to the conversation concerning the battle. And she'd learned what she'd needed.

The name of the Doktor's killer.

Blade.

Right then and there, she'd vowed to repay him, to revenge herself on the son of a bitch. A simple bullet was too good for the bastard. Her vengeance had to be special. Spectacular. She'd wanted Blade to suffer as no man had ever suffered before, and she still did.

Oh, how he'd pay!

She'd departed Catlow, returned to her jeep. And as she drove to the south, a new plan had formed in her devious mind. She'd realized Samuel II might not be equal to the task of destroying the Family, and subsequent events had confirmed her estimation. She'd known she couldn't achieve her revenge by her lonesome. She'd perceived she needed a better ally than Samuel II, and what better one than the Doktor's secret confederate in Androxia?

Who better than Primator?

She smiled, stifling the flow of tears, anticipating her impending triumph. It'd taken so long—so damn long—but she'd finally prevailed on Primator to assist her, had convinced him killing Blade was for the benefit of all Androxia.

And the fool had fallen for her ploy!

She thought of Blade writhing in torment as his body was lowered into a vat of molten steel, pleading for his life, and she cackled.

5

Was it safe yet?

Gremlin cautiously eased the closet door open and peeked outside. The cockpit was shrouded in silence, dimly lit with a greenish glow by the overhead lights. He craned his neck, examining every square inch, verifying the silver men were gone. Satisfied, he tentatively stepped from concealment, prepared to duck from sight at the slightest sound.

"Pssst!"

Gremlin involuntarily jumped, his red eyes widening in consternation.

"Pssst! Gremlin!" whispered a voice from near the computer. "Don't faint, you twit! It's me! Lynx!" So saying, Lynx emerged from hiding around the right side of the large navigational console. "It was cramped as all get-out back there," he complained.

Gremlin glanced at the doorway. "Does Lynx think they left, yes? Would not want to run into them again, no!"

Lynx crossed the cockpit and joined Gremlin. "Those morons are long gone."

"Where is Ferret, yes?" Gremlin asked.

"I'm right here," Ferret announced, coming through the doorway. "I hid in a compartment in the corridor. I saw them leave with Blade and Hickok."

"Poor Hickok, yes!" Gremlin exclaimed. "We should have helped him, no?"

"No," Lynx said.

"What happened in here?" Ferret inquired. "I heard all the gunshots, and I peeped out and saw one of those big guys carrying

42

Blade right past me. He came back and lugged Hickok away.''

"They captured Hickok, yes!" Gremlin declared.

Ferret stared at Lynx. "And you did nothing to help?"

"Nope," Lynx admitted. "Why should I have helped him? Hickok told us not to move unless he gave the word." Lynx shrugged. "The dummy never gave the word."

"So you just sat there and did nothing?" Ferret asked accusingly.

"Hey! Don't look at me like that!" Lynx snapped. "I was following his orders! And I didn't just *sit* there. I was *lyin'* behind the computer."

Ferret shook his head in disapproval. "I can't believe you! You let them take him!"

"It all happened so fast, there wasn't much I *could* do," Lynx commented. "Besides, I didn't see you two lend a hand."

"Gremlin was in closet, yes," Gremlin remarked. "Gremlin didn't see what happened."

"Nor did I," Ferret said. "All I could see was a stretch of the hallway."

Lynx glanced at both of them. "What? Your ears ain't workin'? You couldn't tell Hickok was in trouble?"

Neither Ferret or Gremlin responded.

"Don't be pointing no finger at me!" Lynx mentioned. "At least I crawled out when the shootin' started. I saw them take him down." He paused. "There's something fishy about those characters. I don't think they're human. You should see the way they move. And Hickok's bullets didn't have much effect. So after they knocked him out, I crawled back behind the computer. I figured there wasn't much I could do, not until I learn more about these clowns."

Gremlin gazed out the canopy. Several hundred feet overhead was a corrugated metal ceiling. Fluorescent lights were suspended from chains at 20-foot intervals. "Where are we, yes?"

Ferret looked upward. "My guess would be in a hangar of some kind. But I wouldn't have the slightest idea where the hangar is located. We were in the air for a couple of hours. We could be anywhere."

"Who cares where we are?" Lynx said. "This is our golden opportunity!"

"Uh-oh," Ferret declared. "I don't like that gleam in your

eyes.''

"Don't you see?'' Lynx queried. "This is the chance we need to get what we want!''

"Gremlin doesn't understand, no,'' Gremlin stated.

"I think I do,'' Ferret said. "And I'm not sure I like it.''

Lynx leaned toward Gremlin. "Let me spell it out for you, pal. What were we talkin' about tonight before Hickok showed up?''

"The same old subject, yes,'' Gremlin said. "What to do with our lives, no?''

"Exactly,'' Lynx concurred. "What to do with our lives? How can we fit in at the Home? And what's the answer?''

"Gremlin doesn't know, yes,'' Gremlin responded.

"Well, *I* know,'' Lynx claimed. "And I've been tryin' to convince you dorks for months.''

"It does seem like forever,'' Ferret quipped.

Lynx glared at Ferret, then smiled at Gremlin. "Look. We've been through this a zillion times. We want to fit in at the Home. We want to do something worthwhile with our lives. Right?''

"Yes,'' Gremlin replied.

"And the Doc bred us to be fighters, didn't he?'' Lynx questioned. "I mean, fightin' is in our genes! Right?''

"Yes,'' Gremlin agreed.

"So if we're such naturally talented fighters, and if we like being at the Home and want to do something to help them out, then what better way than to become full-fledged Warriors! Right?'' Lynx beamed.

"Wrong,'' Ferret answered.

"No,'' Gremlin said.

Lynx hissed. He placed his hands on his hips and stared at them defiantly. "What's wrong with my idea?''

"Everything,'' Ferret said. "Like you said, we've been through this already. Time and time again. Being a Warrior is a serious responsibility. You can't become one just because you crave a little action, because you want some excitement in your life.''

"That's not the only reason I want to become a Warrior,'' Lynx averred.

"Oh? What are your other reasons?'' Ferret asked.

"I like the Family,'' Lynx maintained. "I want to do my fair share, to repay them for everything they've done for us. Is that so bad?''

"No," Ferret said. "Not if you're sincere."

"And you don't think I am?" Lynx inquired.

"Let's just say I have my doubts," Ferret stated.

"Gremlin too, yes," Gremlin added.

Lynx exhaled noisily. "You two take the cake, you know that? Here I am, your best buddy in all the world, and you won't believe I can have an honest motive like everybody else. Fine! Be that way! I've spent months tryin' to convince you, to show you being Warriors is just right for us! We'd make great Warriors! We'd be happy, happier than we've been in ages! But no! You think I'm just being selfish." He paused, swept them with his green eyes. "Well, I'm done! I'm through tryin' to show you the error of your ways! I'm through tryin' to talk some sense into a pair of vacuum heads! If you don't want to be Warriors, terrific! But I do! And I'm gonna be one, with or without you! I'm not about to pass up a chance like this."

"What chance, yes?" Gremlin queried.

Lynx waved his left arm at the canopy. "*This* chance, bub! A golden opportunity to show the Family what we can do. Blade and Hickok are out there somewhere, prisoners. If we can save 'em, bail their butts out of this fix, we can write our own ticket. In order to become a Warrior, you have to be sponsored by a Warrior, right? So imagine how grateful Blade and Hickok will be after we save 'em. They'd do anything for us. Hickok already owes us for savin' his wife. All we'd have to do is ask, and I'll bet they'd gladly sponsor us for Warrior status. It'd be a breeze! But if you guys don't want to help, that's okay. I'll do it myself."

"Before you go running off half-cocked," Ferret said, "you should know there are a few flaws in your logic."

"Like what?" Lynx countered.

"Like you don't know where we are," Ferret said, beginning his enumeration. "You don't know if Blade or Hickok are still alive. Even if you succeed in rescuing them, how will you return to the Home? On foot? You have no idea of what you're going up against. And you have no guarantee Blade or Hickok will nominate you to become a Warrior."

"Why quibble over a few trifling details?" Lynx retorted.

"Trifling?" Ferret said. "They qualify as insurmountable difficulties."

"Only to a pessimist like you," Lynx said. "Look, are you

guys with me or not?"

Ferret sighed. "This won't be easy."

"What in life is easy?" Lynx rejoined.

"It's insane," Ferret commented.

"What other choice do we have?" Lynx demanded. "Do you just want to cut out on Blade and Hickok? Leave 'em in the lurch? We're the only chance they've got."

Ferret frowned, his hairy brow furrowed in thought. "No," he said after a spell. "We can't desert them. We must try and find them."

Lynx grinned. "Then let's go."

"We should have a plan, yes?" Gremlin interjected.

"Who needs a plan?" Lynx responded. "Just stick with me." He strolled from the cockpit.

Gremlin looked at Ferret. "We are in big trouble, yes?"

"You can stay here if you want," Ferret suggested. "I'll try and keep Lynx from getting himself killed."

Gremlin shook his head. "Gremlin come too. One for all and all for one, yes? Isn't that our motto, no?"

"Then let's go," Ferret said, turning to follow Lynx. "And let's hope we don't live to regret this."

Lynx was waiting for them at the junction with the passage to the door. "Come on, slowpokes!" he grumbled.

Gremlin and Ferret hastened to his side.

"We've gotta stick together," Lynx said. He pointed at the closed door. "We don't know what we'll find out there. Keep alert. And if we bump into those silver bozos, go for their nuts."

"Their nuts?" Ferret repeated, puzzled.

"Yeah. Their nuts. Balls. Coconuts. Whatever you want to call them," Lynx said.

"Why, pray tell, should we go for their testicles?" Ferret inquired.

"Two reasons," Lynx replied. "One, they're bigger than us. Way bigger. But their nuts are at just the right height, unless you'd rather nibble on their tootsies or jump up and tweak their noses."

"And what's the second reason?" Ferret asked.

"Going for the head doesn't seem to do much good," Lynx stated. "Hickok emptied one of his Colts into the head of one of those goons, and it hardly slowed the silver joker down."

"Hickok always aims for heads, yes," Gremlin mentioned.

"Yep. And Hickok ain't one to miss," Lynx observed. "Which goes to prove my point. Those silver guys ain't human."

"Perhaps they're superhuman," Ferret suggested.

"Then where's their scent?" Lynx demanded.

"Their scent?" Ferret responded in surprise.

"Yeah, dummy! Their scent!" Lynx said. "Brother! For someone who's got a nose as big as you do, you sure don't use it much! The Doc designed us with a great pair of sniffers. We can track anything by scent alone. Gremlin can't, 'cause he's a little more human than us."

"What about their scent, yes?" Gremlin queried.

"They don't have any," Lynx disclosed. "Not a trace. And humans always have a scent. So do animals."

Ferret's bewilderment at the revelation was evident in his face. "You're right!" he said to Lynx. "I didn't even notice!"

"See? I think all that easy livin' with the Family has made you rusty," Lynx stated. "You've heard that old sayin'. Use it or lose it."

Ferret frowned, displeased by his performance. If his normally acute senses had atrophied at the Home, it was a cause for concern. Within the walled 30-acre compound, where all the dangerous wild animals had been exterminated, where danger seldom threatened, where menace was not part of the daily routine, his full faculties were not essential to his survival. But out in the "real world," where the law of the jungle prevailed, where survival of the fittest was the standard, sharp senses were critical. They could mean the difference between life and death.

Lynx glanced at Gremlin. "Gremlin, keep your ears peeled. You've got the best hearing, so we'll rely on you to warn us if someone comes our way."

"Gremlin will not let you down, yes!" Gremlin vowed.

Lynx grinned. "Then let's go save Blade and Hickok, and whip some ass in the bargain." He moved along the passage to the door, then paused, listening. "I don't hear nothin'," he said. "Do you?" he asked Gremlin.

Gremlin shook his head. "Gremlin not hear any noise, any voices outside, no," he replied.

Lynx nodded, and slowly twisted the latch. The door opened with a faint snap. He carefully eased the door outward and peered around the edge. "Wow!" he exclaimed.

"What do you see?" Ferret asked.

Lynx glanced over his left shoulder. "It's incredible! I thought the Doc had a fancy setup. Take a gander at this." He moved aside.

Ferret stepped to the doorway and peeked past the door. His brown eyes widened in amazement.

The aircraft was parked in a hangar, as Ferret had earlier speculated, but the size, the sheer scope of the facility, was beyond his wildest imagining. The building was immense. The ceiling alone was 300 feet above the cement floor. Lengthwise, the structure covered 500 yards, and its width was half again as great. The aircraft was situated in one of the corners, its tail extended toward the middle of the hangar, according them an unobstructed view of the interior.

"Gremlin wants to take a look, yes?" Gremlin said.

Ferret retreated and stood next to Lynx. "What sort of technology are we dealing with here?" he asked in an awed voice.

"Even the Doc's lab, the Biological Center, was puny compared to this," Lynx commented.

"Where do we begin to search for Blade and Hickok?" Ferret inquired.

"We've got a problem there," Lynx conceded. "I can't pick up much of their scent."

"The Warriors were being carried," Ferret said. "Their feet weren't touching the ground."

"We'll find a way," Lynx predicted confidently.

Gremlin suddenly ducked from the doorway. "Someone is coming, yes!" he cried.

"Who is it?" Lynx asked.

"Another man dressed in silver, yes!" Gremlin told them.

"Did he see you?" Lynx asked.

Gremlin shook his head. "Gremlin doesn't think so, no!"

Lynx nodded at the row of doors lining the left side of the passage. "Quick! Each of us in a closet!"

The three genetic deviates hurried into hiding.

Not a moment too soon.

The outer door was abruptly wrenched all the way open, and a giant silver man entered the aircraft.

Lynx, his closet door deliberately left slightly ajar, saw the giant enter. The silver man was holding a clipboard in his left hand and he passed once inside and gazed at the doorway, as if perplexed at finding the door partially open. He turned and moved past the row of closets. Lynx could hear the giant's firm tread, and guessed the silver man had turned right at the junction and gone to the cockpit. What was the giant doing? Lynx wondered. Checking the aircraft after its flight? He slid from the closet and padded to the junction, then looked around the corner. Sure enough, the giant was in the cockpit, standing in front of the computer, studying a digital display and writing on a white pad affixed to the clipboard.

The giant's broad back was to the doorway.

Lynx padded down the corridor to the cockpit door, calculating his next move. Finding Blade and Hickok would be an easy task if they knew where to look, and it was possible the giant in the cockpit knew where the two Warriors were being held. Lynx resolved to force the giant to talk using whatever means were necessary. His feline instincts were warning him to vacate this place—wherever it might be—as quickly as feasible, and he wasn't one to argue with his instincts. But how, he asked himself, was he going to force the seven-foot giant to spill the beans? Walk on over and say, "Pretty please?"

The silver man leaned forward, examining a readout in the center of the console. He was at the foot of the middle chair.

Lynx, pondering his options, abruptly perceived a risky gambit, a way of giving himself the advantage, and he uttered a trilling sound deep in his throat as he launched his diminutive body forward, bounding across the cockpit. He reached the back of the middle chair in two leaps, his claws digging into the top of the chair as he vaulted upward, his sinewy arms coiling and surging his body up and over the chair. He came over the top like a furry arrow, his fingers extended, his tapered claws grasping for his prey.

The silver man heard a soft noise behind him and started to straighten and turn. He was not anticipating an attack, and he moved slowly.

Which suited Lynx's plans perfectly. He reached the giant just as the silver man completed turning, and his nails ripped into the blond man's uniform at the crotch, shredding the material like so much paper, tearing the silver fabric in a single swift swipe, then spearing inward, aiming at the giant's privates. Lynx intended to slice the blond man's gonads from his body.

But there weren't any.

Lynx's mouth dropped in astonishment as his raking claws closed on empty space where the penis *should* have been. His feet alighted on the chair, and he crouched, preparing to pounce on the silver man's face.

Only the giant was faster. The blond man's initial surprise was fleeting. He twisted to the right as the cat-man tore open his pants, and he swung the clipboard in a brutal arc, backhanding his assailant across the mouth.

Lynx, about to spring, felt the clipboard smash into his lips and teeth. Blood spurted from his mouth as he was knocked onto his back, onto the chair, dazed and vulnerable.

The silver man, the clipboard clutched in his left hand, reached down with his right and clamped his hand on the cat-man's neck. "What have we here?" he asked. "How did you escape your cage?"

Lynx thrashed and pounded at the hand restraining him, to no avail.

"You are wasting your energy," the giant informed the cat-man. "There is no sense in resisting."

Lynx attempted to bite the hand on his neck.

"Feisty mutant, aren't you?" the giant queried.

Lynx pulled out all the stops. He raked his claws along the silver man's right arm, from elbow to wrist, his nails gouging inch-deep furrows in the flesh. A colorless liquid sprayed from the arm, spattering his face. Lynx snarled.

"Cease this foolish resistance this second!" the giant ordered. He raised his left hand above his head, the clipboard poised for another strike.

It never landed.

Ferret flashed from nowhere, his bony fingers rigid, and plunged his fingernails into the giant's eyes, ramming them in and squeezing.

The silver man stiffened, releasing his hold on Lynx, and grabbed at his eyes.

Ferret was clinging to the giant's face, his knees on the blond man's massive chest.

Lynx came up off the chair in a rush, enraged, forgetting his goal, forgetting about Blade and Hickok, thirsting to exact his retribution on the giant. He sprang at the silver man's stomach, his arms slashing in vicious blow after blow, his razor claws rending the silver material and splitting the blond man's abdomen wide open, disgorging a flood of liquid and internal organs. In his rabid frenzy, Lynx concentrated on his attack to the exclusion of all else. His arms flailed again and again, turning the giant's stomach into a stringy, pulpy mess.

"Stop it!" someone yelled.

Lynx grasped a loop of intestine and wrenched the strangely rigid tube from the giant's abdomen.

"Damnit! Stop, Lynx! He's finished!"

Lynx paused, his claws imbedded in the silver man's abdomen. He suddenly realized Ferret was to his left, Gremlin to his right.

"He's finished!" Ferret repeated.

Lynx glanced up.

The giant had slumped backwards against the computer. His torso was inclined at an angle over the console, his hands gripping the computer for support. His legs dangled limply below the ravaged vestige of his waist. Clear fluid seeped from his torn eyes. The left pupil was crushed, but the right was intact, and the right eye gazed at Lynx in bemused amazement.

"Why'd you jump him?" Ferret asked Lynx. "What the hell were you trying to do?"

Lynx stared at the gore coating his nails and hands. "Tryin' to capture him," he mumbled in response.

"Why should you want to do that?" the giant queried in a low tone.

Lynx looked at the silver man. "You can talk?"

"Obviously," the giant replied. "My locomotion is severely impaired, but my vocal apparatus is functional."

"You're lucky it was Ferret here who went for your eyes," Lynx commented. "He ain't got sharp nails like me. I would've ripped your peepers to pieces."

"I believe you," the giant said.

"What do we do now, yes?" Gremlin interjected.

Lynx abruptly realized he was standing on the bottom of the contour chair. He hopped to the floor and peered at the silver man, at the hole in his silver pants. "What are you?" he demanded.

"Beg pardon?" the giant said.

"Don't play games with me, bub!" Lynx stated. "I want to know what you are! Now!"

"I am a Superior," the giant informed them.

"Superior?" Lynx snorted. "Superior to what?"

"To all lower organisms, of course," the Superior answered.

"What lower organisms?" Lynx pressed him.

"Biological organisms," the Superior said.

"Uh-huh." Lynx pursed his lips, his green eyes narrowing. "You ain't told me much. What's a Superior?"

"I am a Superior," the giant reiterated.

"We're talkin' in circles!" Lynx snapped. He reflected for a moment. "Where's your nuts?"

"Beg pardon?" the Superior responded.

Lynx leaned forward, frowning. "I want to know why you ain't got no nuts, pal! No balls! No gonads! Get me?"

The blond man nodded. "Superiors do not require pro-creational capability."

Lynx and Ferret exchanged glances. "Why not?" Lynx questioned the giant. "Don't you Superior types whoopee?"

"Beg pardon?"

Lynx raised his right hand. "You say that one more time, and I'm gonna finish the job I started! I want to know why you haven't got a pecker, and I want to know now!"

The giant's eyelids fluttered. "Peckers . . . are superfluous."

"They're what?" Lynx said.

"Not essential," the Superior stated wearily.

"What's the matter with you?" Lynx asked. "Are you dyin'?"

"Excessive dehydration," the Superior stated. "My fluid level is critical. You severed one of the major arteries from my Heinlein."

"Your what?" Lynx said.

The Superior's chin dropped onto his chest.

"Don't pass out on me, turkey!" Lynx declared.

The giant's eyes closed, then partially opened. "Unable to maintain sentience," he stated.

Lynx grabbed the silver man's right leg and shook it. "Don't crap out yet! You need to tell me where Blade and Hickok are being held? What happened to 'em?"

The Superior was on the verge of collapsing. "You want the two Warriors?"

"You bet your ass we do!" Lynx asserted. "Where are they? Do you know?"

The Superior nodded. "Containment Section."

"Containment? Where is it?" Lynx probed.

"Sublevels below Intelligence," the Superior revealed, then slumped into unconsciousness, his huge form slipping toward the floor.

Lynx stepped aside as the giant slid from the console and sprawled forward. The silver man's forehead rested on the foot of the center contour chair. "At least he told us a little," Lynx commented.

"He did?" Ferret said. "How do you know we can trust what he said? How do you know he wasn't lying through his teeth?"

Lynx shrugged. "Just a hunch, is all. I think we can believe him. These bozos don't impress me as the lyin' kind."

Ferret smirked. "Is that your professional assessment?"

"Call it whatever you want," Lynx said. "We've got to find this Containment Section and free Blade and Hickok."

"What about this Superior, yes?" Gremlin queried.

"We'll stuff him in one of the closets," Lynx said.

"And what if he's missed?" Ferret asked. "What if someone comes looking for him and finds him?"

"We'll cross that bridge when we come to it," Lynx said. "We haven't got any choice. We can't stay here."

Gremlin stared at the Superior's crotch. "He really does not have a penis, no?"

"No," Lynx confirmed.

"Most unusual, yes?" Gremlin mentioned.

"It's friggin' weird," Lynx remarked. "Come on. Give me a hand."

Together, the three mutants moved the Superior to one of the cockpit compartments and crammed his bulk inside. Lynx propped the Superior against the rear wall, bending the giant's legs perpendicular to the torso.

"There! That should do it!" Lynx said. He closed the compartment door and led the way toward the exit hatch.

"How are we going to find the Containment Section?" Ferret

wanted to know.

"We'll find it," Lynx vowed. "Trust me."

"I wish you'd quit saying that," Ferret muttered.

They were a yard from the exit door when Lynx abruptly halted, his features rippling in surprise.

"What is wrong, yes?" Gremlin asked.

"Those Superiors . . ." Lynx said slowly, his brow creasing in perplexity.

"What about them?" Ferret responded.

"They ain't go no peckers," Lynx stated.

"Yeah. So?" Ferret said.

Lynx glanced at his companions. "So how the hell do they take a leak?"

6

Blade came awake with a painful start, his head throbbing, his eyes smarting as a bright light caused him to squint. He remembered the three silver men, and he surveyed his surroundings uncertainly, a dozen questions flooding his mind. What had happened? Where was he? Why had the three silver men jumped him? What was this all about? And, most importantly, why couldn't he move?

A muted humming became audible.

Blade found himself in a square room, ten feet by ten feet. He was the only occupant. The walls, ceiling, and floor were composed of a white, plastic-like substance. A large rectangular light overhead supplied ample illumination. The room was devoid of furniture.

What was going on?

Blade, to his astonishment, discovered he was erect, on his feet in the middle of the room, fully clothed except for his Bowies. His muscular arms were draped at his sides. He tried moving his hands, but failed. Next he attempted to shuffle his legs, but they refused to respond. To his chagrin, he realized his entire body was immobile, with the notable exclusion of his eyes. By focusing all of his attention, he could shift his eyes up and down, and from one side to the other. But the range of movement was slight, compounding his budding frustration.

Had the silver men drugged him?

Blade peered to the right, then the left. The humming seemed to be coming from the walls, emanating from black bubbles positioned in the middle of the white wall to his right and the wall to his left.

55

What purpose did those black bubbles serve?

Blade was at a loss to explain his predicament. The identity of the silver men was a complete mystery. Why had they abducted him? he wondered. Did they pose a threat to the Home, to the Family? His speculation was unexpectedly terminated as an entrance panel in front of him opened with a distinct hiss, gliding to the left.

A woman stood framed in the doorway. A most remarkable woman. She wore a blue dress, the garment scarcely covering her protruding cleavage and exposing her shapely legs up to her thighs. Her narrow lavender eyes glared at him. She had yellow, scaly skin, and long black hair.

Blade endeavored to speak, to move his lips, to address her, but his mouth wouldn't budge.

The woman noticed his effort. She smiled, a particularly wicked expression, and advanced several paces into the room. "The mighty Blade!" she taunted him. "And he can't even talk!"

Blade studied the woman, striving to place her, but he knew he'd never laid eyes on her before in his life.

"Do you know how long I've waited for this moment?" the woman demanded.

Blade could only stare.

The woman glanced at the black bubbles, then at the towering, brooding man. "How does it feel to be helpless? You don't like it, do you? The great Warrior! And you can't even lift your little finger!" She threw back her head and laughed.

Blade waited for the woman to continue.

"Don't you know me?" the woman asked.

Blade's gaze probed her from head to toe.

"I can see you don't," the woman stated. "But then, why should you? We've never met. But I know who you are. I know all about you, you son of a bitch!" Her features twisted, became hateful. "I know you killed the man I loved! I know you for the bastard you are, Blade! So it's only fair you know who I am." She paused, straightened proudly. "I'm Clarissa!"

Blade suddenly recalled one of the silver men mentioning that name, but it didn't ring a bell.

Clarissa took another step toward him, but she was careful not to get too close. "Clarissa! My name might not mean anything to you, you prick! But I know a name that will. The Doktor!''

Blade's eyes widened. The Doktor? The nefarious scientist responsible for countless atrocities? For killing innocent children to further his longevity? For slaughtering thousands, perhaps millions? The demented fiend who'd tried to eradicate the Family? Who'd created genetic deviates to do his bidding, to slay on command?

"You remember the Doktor!" Clarissa said bitterly. "The gentlest man who ever walked this earth! The man whose intellect eclipsed all others! The man who wanted to improve this world, who devoted his genius to establishing order and peace! You remember him, because you're the one who killed him!" Clarissa's voice rose, her tone trembling from her violent emotions. She shook her right fist at the Warrior. "You killed the only man I ever loved! The best man who ever lived! And you're going to pay for what you did!" she gloated.

Insight dawned. Blade scrutinized the woman's face, detecting a hint of madness, and perceived she was responsible for his capture.

"I'm the one who had you brought here!" Clarissa boasted, confirming his suspicion. "I convinced Primator it was necessary!"

Primator? Who—or what—was this Primator?

"But I never expected to get a bonus!" Clarissa went on. "Hickok's death will be an added treat."

Hickok? Blade futilely attempted to raise his arms. What was that about Hickok?

"Hickok tried to save you," Clarissa commented. "But he was caught, just like you. He's in the next room." She jerked her left hand to the left. "You'll go up before Primator together. Don't worry, though. You two will have company. *I'll* be there!" She tittered.

Blade's mind was in turmoil. The news of Hickok's capture was profoundly disturbing.

Clarissa turned to depart, then hesitated. "I'd imagine you have a lot of questions," she said mockingly. "Where you are, for instance? And what's in store for you? Am I right?" She chuckled. "Of course I'm right." She moved to the doorway. "But I'm not about to tell you. I want you to be surprised. I want to see your face when Primator announces your fate."

Blade wished he could reach out and knock her senseless.

"You may be lucky," Clarissa said over her right shoulder. "Primator may relegate you to Servile status. You might be neutered, but at least you'd be alive." She winked, then walked off laughing.

The door hissed shut.

Blade was left with his thoughts and the continuous humming of the black bubbles.

7

"Where are we, yes?" Gremlin asked in awe, gaping at the sight before them.

"It certainly isn't Oz," Ferret mentioned.

"Oz?" Lynx repeated.

"A fictional land I read about in one of the books in the Family library," Ferret disclosed. "You should read the book sometime. I think you'd like it."

"What's it about?" Lynx inquired.

"It's about this girl and her dog," Ferret revealed. "They are transported by a tornado to the mystical land of Oz, where they encounter witches and munchkins and wizards and magical slippers."

"Magical slippers?" Lynx reiterated.

"And a tin man, a talking scarecrow, and a cowardly lion," Ferret explained.

"A cowardly lion?" Lynx said skeptically.

"Yeah. It was a terrific book," Ferret said. "You really should read it."

"Weren't you the one who said I should read that other book, the one about Flopsy, Mopsy, and Cottontail?" Lynx inquired.

"I figured you might learn something from it," Ferret commented.

"I did," Lynx said.

"Oh? What?" Ferret responded.

"Never, ever to read another book you recommend," Lynx stated.

"Please!" Gremlin interrupted. "Forget about your books, yes? There are more important matters, no? Like, where are we,

59

yes?'' He waved his right arm to encompass the panorama surrounding them.

They were outside the huge hangar. They'd waited inside the aircraft until the coast was clear, then darted behind a nearby stack of crates. From there, they'd dashed through a side door onto a loading dock covered with more crates and boxes. Now, as they crouched in concealment in back of a pile of boxes, they gazed at the city lights stretching to the far horizon in rapt fascination.

"It sure ain't Denver," Lynx deduced. "There are too many lights, too many big buildings. And they all look so new!" he marveled.

"Look at all the skyscrapers!" Ferret declared.

"Maybe we're in Chicago," Lynx proposed. "Blade told us about the people there, the Technics. They're supposed to have a real advanced city."

"This doesn't look like Blade's description of Chicago," Ferret said, disagreeing. "And Blade didn't see any of those Superior types in Chicago."

Gremlin was deliberating on the immensity of the city. "How will we find Blade and Hickok out there, yes? The city is too large, no?"

"We'll find 'em," Lynx promised.

"Look!" Ferret whispered, pointing.

The north end of the loading dock terminated in a sloping ramp, and the ramp was a mere ten feet from their hiding place. Approaching from the base of the ramp was a man in orange overalls and an orange cap.

"He's normal-sized!" Ferret said. "He must be human."

"Look at that funny doodad on his forehead," Lynx stated.

The loading dock and the ramp were illuminated by lamps affixed to the hangar walls at 30-foot intervals. In the center of the advancing man's forehead, clearly visible, reflecting the light, was a glistening silver circle.

"What do we do, yes?" Gremlin queried anxiously.

Lynx motioned for them to drop from sight. "Leave it to me," he advised.

They heard the man's footsteps as he reached the top of the loading dock, then paused. "Now where's that damn consignment?" the man mumbled.

Lynx cautiously eased his head above the nearest box.

The man in orange was eight feet away, examining the crates and boxes, idly scratching his pointed chin.

Lynx scanned the ramp to insure the man was alone. No one else was in sight.

"Ahhhh! There!" The man exclaimed, and walked toward some crates to his right.

Lynx vaulted over the box screening him, his padded feet landing noiselessly on the cement dock. He took three supple strides and sprang, his arms encircling the man's ankles, his momentum bearing the startled human to the cement.

"What the hell!" the man in orange blurted, and suddenly steely fingers were fastened to his throat, and a pair of feral green orbs blazed into his own brown eyes.

"Don't move, bub!" Lynx threatened. "Or I'll tear your neck open!"

The man in orange froze, petrified.

Ferret and Gremlin quickly raced to join Lynx.

"Give me a hand," Lynx directed, and the trio lifted the human and carted him to their hiding place.

The man in orange gawked as they deposited him on the cement, prone on his back, the cat-man still gripping his throat.

Lynx leaned forward until his nose was almost touching the human's. "I'm gonna let go. But you'd better not squawk, if you know what's good for you! Do you understand?"

The man in orange nodded. He sported a mustache and shallow cheeks.

Lynx released his hold, then knelt on the man's chest. "What's your name?" he demanded.

"Barney," the man blurted out, panic-stricken. "Barney 137496."

"137496?" Lynx said. "What's that?"

Barney seemed confused by the question. "How do you mean?" he replied nervously.

"What's the number for? I asked your name," Lynx stated.

"But that is my name!" Barney stressed. "Barney 137496."

"Your last name is a number?" Lynx queried.

"Of course," Barney answered, bewildered. "Every Servile has an I.D. number."

"Servile? What's a Servile?" Lynx interrogated the human.

Barney was obviously flabbergasted by the cat-man's ignorance. "You don't know what a Servile is? Where are you from?"

Lynx's tone hardened. "I'll ask the questions, pal. What's a Servile?"

"All the workers are Serviles," Barney replied. "All the human workers, that is."

"What other kind of workers are there around here?" Lynx asked.

"There are mutants, like you guys, and . . ." Barney began, then stopped as the cat-man voiced a trilling sound.

"Mutants like us?" Lynx said. "There are mutants here like us?"

"Sure," Barney declared. "Lots of them. But they're in a class all by themselves. They're never called Serviles."

Lynx glanced at Ferret and Gremlin. If there were other mutants in this strange city, where had they come from? The mutations prevalent since World War III were derived from three sources. The first type, the wild mutations found everywhere, were deformed creatures produced by the saturation of the environment with incredible amounts of gene-altering radiation. The second sort, labeled mutates by the Family, were former mammals, reptiles, or amphibians, transformed into pus-covered monstrosities by the chemical toxins unleashed during the war and still prevalent in the environmental chain. And the third form, of which Lynx, Ferret and Gremlin were prime examples, had been deliberately developed in the laboratory by the scientists like the Doktor, genetic engineers intent on propagating new species. But so far as Lynx knew, all of the Doktor's genetic creations had perished. If there were indeed mutants in this city, how had they been produced? Lynx looked at Barney. "What do you call these mutants?"

Barney did a double take. "Mutants," he said.

Ferret snickered.

"Where do the mutants come from?" Lynx inquired.

"From the D.G. Section," Barney revealed.

"What's the D.G. Section?" Lynx wanted to know.

"Deviate Generation Section," Barney elaborated. "Over in Science."

Lynx reflected for a moment. He reached out and tapped the

silver circle in the middle of Barney's forehead. "What do you call this gizmo?"

"It's my O.D.," Barney said.

"O.D.?" Lynx repeated quizzically.

"Orwell Disk," Barney told them.

"What's it for?" Lynx queried.

"Every Servile has one," Barney elucidated. "The mutants too. The Superiors use them to keep tabs on us. They can monitor our activities with them."

Lynx straightened, frowning. He recalled the collars the Doktor had utilized to keep his Genetic Research Division in line. Every mutant the Doktor had developed in his lab had been required to wear the metal collars, collars containing sophisticated electronic circuitry enabling the Doktor to instantly know the location of his test-tube creatures, and to eavesdrop on their conversations. "Can the Superiors hear what you're sayin' with that Orwell Disk?" he asked Barney.

Barney shook his head. "No. They can tell where we are, though, and they know right away if we've strayed into an unauthorized area or are trying to escape Androxia."

"Androxia? Is that the name of this city?" Lynx questioned.

"Sure is," Barney confirmed.

"Where is Androxia?" Lynx queried.

"Where?" Barney said, puzzled.

"Yeah. Where? What state is it in?" Lynx asked.

"Oh. You mean like the old-time states they had before the war?" Barney asked.

"Yep. What state is this?" Lynx said, prompting him.

"It's Androxia," Barney responded. "It's been called Androxia for almost a hundred years, I think."

"But you just said this city is called Androxia," Lynx observed.

"City. State. They're both the same," Barney said.

"You mentioned the old-time states," Lynx stated. "Do you know what this city was before it became known as Androxia?"

Barney pursed his lips. "An old man did tell me a story once, but I don't know how true it is. He said this was once the city of Houston, in a state called Texas. But he was drunk when he told me. Maybe he made the whole thing up."

"Have you ever been outside of Androxia?" Ferret interjected.

"Nope," Barney said. "I was born here. I've always been here. The Superiors don't permit us to leave Androxia."

"And haven't the Superiors ever mentioned anything about Androxia's history?" Ferret inquired.

"No," Barney answered. "Why should they?"

Lynx gazed at the city lights. "Do you know where the Containment Section is located?"

Barney nodded. "In the Intelligence Building. In the lower levels."

"Is it far from here?" Lynx queried.

Barney pointed toward a skyscraper to the northwest. "That's it right there."

Lynx calculated the distance. Not more than a mile, by his reckoning. "Good. Get up. You're gonna take us there."

Barney slowly stood, his frightened brown eyes expanding in alarm. "I can't!" he objected.

"Want to bet?" Lynx countered. He flicked his right arm up, his claws grabbing Barney's coveralls.

"Believe me!" Barney whined. "You don't want me to take you there!"

"Yes we do," Lynx retorted. "We need to get there as fast as possible, and you're our ticket. If you're a good little boy, I'll even let you live, sucker. But we're going, and we're going now, before you're missed."

Barney blanched. "You don't leave me much choice. Just remember I tried to talk you out of it."

Lynx shoved Barney toward the north end of the loading dock. "Lead the way, chuckles! And no tricks, hear?"

Lynx, Gremlin, and Ferret stayed on Barney's heels.

"What if we're spotted, yes?" Gremlin asked.

"So what?" Lynx said. "This wimp says there are mutants like us all over the place. No one will pay any attention to three more."

"I hope *you* know what *we're* doing," Ferret mumbled.

"Trust me," Lynx stated.

Ferret groaned.

The Servile hastily crossed the lot. They passed over a dozen parked vehicles.

Lynx studied the vehicles, impressed. He'd seen scores of conventional cars, trucks, and jeeps in Denver and elsewhere.

They were completely different from the vehicles in the lot. The Androxian conveyances were sleeker, slimmer, with smaller tires and low-slung carriages. They reminded him of rockets on wheels.

"That's Blish Avenue ahead," Barney said, indicating a thoroughfare on the north side of the lot.

Lynx could see sparse traffic flowing on the avenue. "How do we get across it?"

Barney used his left hand and pointed at the northwest corner of the lot. "We can cross there, once the light is green."

The quartet hurried to the northwest corner of the parking lot. They reached a sidewalk bordering Blish Avenue, and 15 yards to the west was an intersection with traffic signals.

"That's Serling Boulevard," Barney said. "We can take it to Intelligence."

"Then let's go," Lynx urged him.

Barney walked to the intersection, then patiently waited for the light to change.

An Androxian car came through the intersection, its motor purring. The interior of the vehicle was lit by a pale blue glow. Behind the steering wheel was one of the silver giants. The Superior glanced at the four figures on the sidewalk, displaying no interest in their presence, and kept going east on Blish Avenue.

"See?" Lynx gloated. "I told you we wouldn't have any trouble."

"We're not there yet," Ferret noted.

"Worrywart," Lynx rejoined.

The traffic signal suspended above the center of the intersection changed from red to green.

"We can cross," Barney said, and started to do so.

Lynx walked to Barney's left, his green eyes scanning Serling Boulevard. The sidewalks contained few pedestrians. "Where is everybody?" he inquired as they reached the far side of the intersection and proceeded north on Serling.

"It's night," Barney replied. "Serviles aren't allowed out at night unless they have a pass, or they're on the night shift. Same with the mutants."

"What is the population of Androxia?" Ferret asked.

"Three million, I think," Barney said. "At least, that's what I heard."

"How many Serviles are there?" Ferret questioned him.

"I don't know," Barney admitted.

"What about the Superiors?" Lynx chimed in. "How many of them are in Androxia?"

"I don't know," Barney said. "They don't tell us stuff like that."

"They don't tell you much, do they?" Lynx remarked.

"They teach us all we need to know," Barney stated.

"Oh? Says who?" Lynx retorted.

"They do," Barney said.

"Real decent of 'em," Lynx cracked sarcastically.

"The Superiors don't mistreat us," Barney mentioned.

"What do you call that Orwell Disk?" Lynx countered.

"Everyone has one," Barney said. "It's no big deal."

Lynx glanced at Ferret. "Nice bunch of sheep they're raisin' here, huh?"

Barney looked at Lynx. "I don't understand. Why are you so hostile towards the Superiors?"

"I don't understand why you're not," Lynx declared.

Barney shrugged. "They provide us with our homes, our clothes, even our food. They don't beat us or anything like that. And they even allow some of us to breed."

"Breed?" Lynx snorted. "You mean they let you poke your squeeze now and then?"

"Squeeze? I don't understand," Barney said.

"You have a wife, dimples?" Lynx asked.

Barney smiled. "Yes. She was my reward for ten years of faithful service to Androxia. We might be permitted to have a child next year. We can hardly wait."

"The Superiors must give the okay for you to have a kid?" Lynx queried.

"Androxia has a population problem," Barney responded. "We must regulate our population numbers."

"You mean the Superiors must regulate the Serviles," Lynx said.

"The Superiors only want what's best for us," Barney said. "What is best for all Androxia."

"Now I know why your eyes are brown," Lynx quipped.

They covered a quarter of a mile in silence, drawing ever closer to the Intelligence Building. A few vehicles passed on Serling Boulevard.

"Barney, what kind of work do you do, yes?" Gremlin inquired at one point.

"I'm night foreman at the Herbert Hangar loading dock," Barney answered.

"You like your job, yes?" Gremlin queried.

"Yeah. I like it a lot," Barney said. "There are a lot worse."

"What kind of work do the mutants around here do?" Lynx questioned.

"Whatever they're bred for," Barney said.

"Bred?" Lynx repeated.

"Yeah. The mutants are assigned to whatever type of work they're bred for. Some are manual laborers. Some work in the Science Section. Others do other jobs," Barney stated.

"Tell me," Lynx said. "Who breeds your mutants?"

"The Superiors, of course," Barney revealed.

"Of course," Lynx said dryly.

"I'd like to know something," Ferret mentioned. "Do the Superiors allow the Serviles to attend school? Did you receive an education?"

"I sure did," Barney said proudly. "I went through all six grades. That's standard. Some, like courier pilots, go longer."

"Six grades? That's all?" Ferret asked.

"Who wants more?" Barney replied. "They teach us to read and write, and math, and whatever other skills we need for our jobs."

"No history, or geography, or any courses like that?" Ferret probed.

"Who needs those?" Barney responded. "The Superiors teach us all we need to know."

"They sure don't teach you to think," Lynx muttered.

"Think? The Superiors take care of all the thinking," Barney said. "They're smarter than us. They know what's best for us."

"So you keep sayin'," Lynx stated.

"Do all of the Serviles feel the same way you do?" Ferret inquired.

"Sure," Barney said, then corrected himself. "Well, not all of them. There are a few who like to cause trouble. They're called

Malcontents.''

"What happens to them?" Ferret asked.

"The Superiors don't allow troublemakers to disrupt anything," Barney said. "The Malcontents are usually sent to the Science Section. When they come out, they're ready to accept their status, to work for the good of all Androxia.''

"Why? What happens to 'em in the Science Section?" Lynx queried. "Are they tortured?"

Barney laughed. "No. Of course not! They undergo a simple operation."

"What type of operation?" Ferret said.

"An operation on their brain," Barney said. "To remove the bad cells, I've heard. I think they call it a partial lobotomy."

"A lobotomy, no!" Gremlin declared, aghast. He vividly remembered the experimental lobotomies the Doktor had performed on him, resulting in his aberrant style of speech.

"They're no big deal," Barncy said. "Lots of people have them."

"Not just the Malcontents?" Ferret asked.

"No. The mutants, in particular, are operated on a lot. But it's for their own good. The Superiors are only doing what's best for us."

"Do you lick their boots for 'em?" Lynx said sarcastically.

"No," Barney replied. "Why would I want to do that?"

Lynx motioned at Ferret, and they dropped several paces behind Barney and Gremlin.

"What do you make of this garbage?" Lynx inquired.

"The Superiors, whatever they are, totally control the human population here," Ferret stated. "The humans are given a minimal education, just enough to enable them to properly complete their assigned work, and are duped into believing their lives are terrific. Perhaps some form of brainwashing is involved, some psychological techniques we've never heard about. The humans seem to possess no freedom whatsoever, and if Barney is any example, they don't seem to mind."

"Barney is an idiot," Lynx commented.

"But a content idiot," Ferret noted.

"I guess if you don't know you're an idiot," Lynx reasoned, "then you never realize there's more to life than your own stupidity."

Ferret grinned. "Why, Lynx! I'm impressed! That was almost profound. I didn't think you had it in you!" he joked.

"Barney ain't the only dummy around here," Lynx retorted.

The Intelligence Building loomed directly ahead, to the right of the sidewalk. It was an imposing edifice, 40 stories in height, its sides constructed of an opalescent synthetic substance.

Ferret scrutinized their destination. "How are we going to get inside? There are bound to be guards."

"I'll think of something," Lynx asserted.

A small park, consisting of little more than a narrow strip of grass and a row of deciduous trees, separated the sidewalk from the Intelligence Building. As they neared the park, Lynx caught up with the man in orange.

"You've done real fine so far," Lynx said to Barney. "But your job ain't over yet."

Barney slowed. "What do you mean? You wanted me to bring you to Intelligence, and we're almost there. My job is done. Let me go back to the loading dock. Please."

A large vehicle was coming their way, bearing south on Serling Boulevard, its headlights resembling the baleful glare of a gigantic, prowling creature.

"You ain't going back to the dock," Lynx said.

"Please!" Barney pleaded. "Let me return to my work."

"Not on your life," Lynx stated.

The large vehicle, evidently a truck, was 50 yards to the north on Serling.

"If I let you go," Lynx said, "I know you'll run to the Superiors and rat on us."

"I won't!" Barney averred. "I promise!"

The truck was 40 yards away.

"Do you expect me to trust you?" Lynx demanded, grinning. "How dumb do you think I am?"

"I can answer that one," Ferret volunteered.

The truck was 30 yards off.

"Don't bother," Lynx said to Ferret.

Barney glanced at the approaching truck. The corners of his mouth twisted upward. "Don't ever say I didn't warn you," he mentioned. "I tried to tell you. You shouldn't have brought me along."

"You got us here, didn't you?" Lynx stated.

"You made a big mistake," Barney declared.

"Oh?" Lynx responded smugly. "How so?"

At 20 yards' distance, the truck began to slow.

"You remember me telling you about my Orwell Disk?" Barney asked.

"Yeah. So what?" Lynx said.

"I told you the Superiors use the disks to monitor us," Barney remarked.

"So?" Lynx snapped. "If they're millions of you dorks livin' in Androxia, there's no way the Superiors can keep tabs on everybody at once."

"That's where you're wrong," Barney said. "They use computers, and the computers can keep tabs on everyone. Every single one of us. And the minute one of us strays, the minute one of us enters an area we're not supposed to be in, the computer alerts the Superiors."

At ten yards, the truck started to drift across the boulevard.

"Lynx!" Gremlin yelled.

Lynx spun, realizing their peril too late.

The truck angled across the highway, its headlights focusing on the four figures on the sidewalk. Its brakes screeched as it lurched to a halt. The cab was plunged in darkness. The rear consisted of a long, canopy-covered bed. As the truck stopped, its occupants began piling from the back, their black boots smacking on the asphalt as they jumped from the bed. They raced around the cab, converging on the quartet on the sidewalk, fanning out, encircling them.

Barney was smiling triumphantly.

Lynx turned from right to left, debating whether to make a run for it, seeking a way out. But they were surrounded within seconds, hemmed in by a ring of humans and mutants wearing black uniforms and wielding steel batons. There were 12 of them, each one conveying an air of wickedness, each one with a hard, cold expression. Whether human or mutant, neither betrayed the slightest hint of emotion in their eyes. Their black uniforms fit snugly, and their pants were tucked into their black boots. The mutants resembled those in the infamous Doktor's Genetic Research Division, displaying a variety of animalistic traits. Some were decidedly reptilian, others mammalian. Lynx glared at a tall, frog-like form six feet away. He raised his hands and clicked his tapered nails. "Come and get it, sucker! I'm in the mood for frog legs!"

The frog-man didn't respond.

There was a loud click, and the door of the cab swung open. A Superior stepped to the ground. His hair was blond, his face pale, and he wore the typical silver uniform. But clasped in his right hand was a not-so-typical weapon, a coiled whip.

"Oh! We are in trouble, yes!" Gremlin moaned.

The Superior strode toward them, stopping a few feet off. He stared at the dockworker. "Barney 137496. You will explain this unauthorized action, please."

Barney walked up to the Superior. "I'm sorry! I really am! I know I left my post without permission. But I didn't have any choice! These three made me bring them here. They said they had to get to the Intelligence Building."

"Did they use violence on you?" the Superior asked.

"Yes," Barney answered. "That one"—and he pointed at Lynx—"threatened my life."

"Blabbermouth," Lynx said.

"Barney is telling the truth then?" the Superior asked, addressing Lynx.

"Barney is a wimp," Lynx replied.

The Superior looked at Barney. "You will return to your post immediately. You will perform your duties as instructed."

Relief washed over Barney's face. "Of course!"

"You may be questioned by Intelligence tomorrow," the Superior stated.

Barney started to turn, then gazed up at the Superior. "This won't go on my record, will it? I mean, my wife and I are up for procreation approval next year. I hope this won't prevent us from being okayed."

"Your file is without blemish," the Superior said. "You have always met your production quotas, and adhered to all directives. You are rated as an AA-1 Citizen. I do not foresee this incident posing a problem. But if it should come to a hearing, I will personally appear and vouch for your integrity."

Barney beamed in appreciation. "Thank you! Thank you, sir!" He jogged south on Serling, returning to work.

"What a moron!" Lynx cracked.

The Superior stared at Lynx. "The three of you will come with us. Resistance will be useless.''

Lynx chuckled. "You ain't takin' us without a fight, chuckles!"

The Superior scrutinized Lynx from head to toe. His gaze rested on Lynx's forehead. "Where is your O.D.?"

"Wouldn't you like to know!" Lynx rejoined.

The Superior glanced at Ferret and Gremlin. "None of you have an O.D. implanted in your forehead as required by directive. How is this possible?"

The ring of humans and mutants in black uniforms never uttered a word. They waited, motionless, the truck and street lights gleaming off the silver disks in their foreheads.

"You will voluntarily enter the truck, now, or suffer the consequences," the Superior said to Lynx.

"Give it your best shot, dimwit!" Lynx stated.

The Superior sighed. His right hand flicked downward, and the ten-foot whip uncoiled and dropped to the asphalt.

Lynx's eyes narrowed. There was something funny about that whip. He'd seen whips before, leather affairs with a lash on the tip. But this one was different. It appeared to be metallic, and the handle was exceptionally large, seemed to be plastic, and contained two red buttons.

"You will not comply with my orders?" the Superior demanded.

Lynx snickered. "Shove it up your ass!"

The Superior's right hand lashed out, the whip arcing through the night air, crackling as it swung toward Lynx.

Lynx ducked under the first strike. He felt the whip miss his back by a hairsbreadth, and his fur tingled as the whip passed.

The Superior calmly swung the whip around, over his head, and snapped his right arm forward.

Lynx saw the whip coming and twisted to the right, seeking to evade the blow. His feline reflexes enabled him to avoid the brunt of the stroke, but not all of it. The very tip of the whip brushed against his left shoulder. Lynx expected to feel a mild stinging sensation. Instead, his entire body was lanced by an agonizing spasm as . . . something . . . coursed through him, jolting him to the core. He twitched and staggered to the left.

"Lynx!" Ferret cried.

Lynx saw the Superior aim another swing of the whip in his direction, and he dodged to the left, his legs sluggish.

The whip bit into Lynx's right arm.

Lynx snarled as his diminutive form was speared by another excruciating surge. Whatever it was, the damn thing was devastating! His arms and legs trembled uncontrollably, his torso jerking, as the whip made contact.

"Lynx! No!" Gremlin shouted, taking a step toward him.

Lynx almost fell. His knees wobbled as he doubled over, stunned by the onslaught.

A fourth time the Superior struck, and the whip looped around the cat-man's neck and held fast.

Lynx stiffened as every fiber of his being was racked by an overpowering force, a force capable of knocking him from his feet and slamming him onto his back. His body bounced and flopped. He attempted to collect his wits, to form coherent thoughts, but failed.

The Superior slowly coiled the whip in his right hand.

Ferret ran to Lynx's side. He glared at the Superior. "What'd you do to him, you bastard? You've killed him!"

"Your companion has not been terminated," the Superior said. "My Electro-Prod was set on Stun, not Kill. He will recover in an hour or so."

Lynx was shuddering, his eyelids quivering.

"Now," the Superior stated in a loud voice. "Will you come with us peacefully, or do you desire to share your friend's fate?"

Ferret glanced at Gremlin. He wanted to aid Lynx, but there was nothing he could do. If they resisted, they would be overwhelmed. One of them might be able to escape, but that would mean deserting Lynx. "What do you say?" he asked Gremlin.

Gremlin frowned, his worried eyes on Lynx. "We have no choice, yes?"

"Yes," Ferret confirmed.

Gremlin's shoulders slumped dejectedly.

"We'll go with you peacefully," Ferret told the Superior.

"A logical decision," the Superior said. He waved his left arm, and two of the men in black stepped forward and lifted Lynx in their arms. They carried him toward the rear of the truck.

"You will follow your friend," the Superior directed.

"Where are you taking us?" Ferret inquired as he moved past the silver man.

"You will be taken to Containment and held there until Intelligence interrogates you," the Superior disclosed.

"Did you say Containment?" Ferret asked.

"Yes. Why?" the Superior said.

"Oh, no reason," Ferret declared, then burst out laughing.

The Superior watched, perplexed, as the mutant with the long nose climbed onto the bed of the truck, laughing all the while. The third one, the mutant with the gray skin and red eyes, was grinning. Odd behavior, he mentally observed, considering they were probably Malcontents and would be lobotomized within 24 hours. The lower orders were becoming more bizarre every day.

8

The young guard in the black uniform, a tray of food in his hands, entered Stasis Cell 43 and paused, puzzled.

The one in buckskins was still unconscious.

The guard advanced to within four feet of the prisoner. Any closer and the stasis bubbles would effect him. He peered at the captive's face. Why was the man still out like a light? he wondered. The prisoner should have recovered hours ago.

The man in the buckskins was suspended in midair between two of the humming black bubbles. His chin was slumped on his chest.

The guard lowered the tray to the floor. Perhaps the prisoner had sustained an internal injury, he speculated. He knew the captive's file indicated a head blow was the cause of the unconsciousness. Should he call Medical and have them send over a Med-Tech? The guard decided he wouldn't. If he phoned up a Med-Tech, and the prisoner wasn't seriously injured, it would make him look foolish.

So what should he do?

The guard was in a quandary. He was required to feed the prisoner. The usual procedure was to deposit the tray near a captive, then deactivate the stasis field and quickly step back, his hand on his baton, and wait until the meal was consumed. But this prisoner could hardly eat his meal while unconscious.

There was only one feasible recourse.

The guard elected to rouse the captive himself. He walked to the left wall and pressed a black button situated at shoulder height. Immediately, the humming emanating from the stasis bubbles became fainter and fainter, finally ending altogether. As the humming decreased in intensity, the prisoner gradually slumped to the floor. He wound up on his forehead and knees, his arms splayed from his sides.

"Let's have a look at you," the guard remarked, and stepped over to the captive and knelt down. "Why aren't you awake?" he asked, reaching for the prisoner's shoulders.

"Who says I'm not?" the buckskin-clad figure replied, and came up off the floor in a rush, his fists clenched.

Startled, the guard grabbed for the baton in the sheath on his right hip.

The man in the buckskins was faster. His left fist clipped the astonished guard on the jaw, sending him sprawling. The guard tried to scramble erect, but a crushing right fist connected with his left cheek, knocking him to the floor, dazing him.

"Don't move!" the prisoner snapped, yanking the baton from the sheath and raising it over his head. "Don't even twitch, or I'll bash your head in!"

The guard, flat on his back, froze. He'd used the steel baton on numerous occasions and was well aware of the damage one could inflict.

"Where's my hardware?" the prisoner demanded.

"Your what?" the guard said nervously.

"My hardware! My irons! My guns!" the man in buckskins declared angrily.

"I don't know."

The prisoner's mouth curled downward, and he elevated the baton a little higher, his blue eyes on the silver disk in the guard's forehead.

"Honest, I don't!" the guard stated anxiously. "Your weapons were confiscated before they brought you here. We're not allowed to touch a gun. They're illegal in Androxia for anyone except Superiors."

"Damn!" the prisoner snapped in annoyance. "I don't savvy half of what you said. Androxia? Superiors? What are you yappin' about?"

The guard didn't know what to say.

"Where's my pard?" the prisoner inquired angrily.

"Your what?"

"My pard. Blade. He was captured about the same time I was," the man in buckskins said.

The guard suddenly recalled the name on the prisoner's file.

"You're called Hickok, right?"

Hickok leaned forward menacingly. "I know that, horseshit for brains! What I *don't* know is where Blade is! Now where is he?"

The guard gulped, his brown eyes riveted on the baton. "He's in the next cell over. Number forty-four."

"Take me to him!" Hickok directed.

The guard slowly stood. "You won't get away with this," he remarked.

"Did I ask your opinion?" Hickok rejoined.

The youthful guard led Hickok from Stasis Cell 43 and took a left in the corridor outside.

Hickok scanned the corridor. The walls, floor, and ceiling were white, like those in the cell. Square lights recessed in the ceiling lit the hallway, revealing dozens of doors on both sides, each with a red number near the top. No one else was in the corridor. "Where are the other guards?" he asked.

"I'm the only one on duty," the guard replied.

"Don't lie to me!" Hickok warned.

"I'm not lying," the guard insisted. "There's only one guard per block on night shift."

They reached the next door, Number 44.

"This is it," the guard announced.

"Open it," Hickok ordered.

The guard reached to the left of the door, pressing a black button on the wall.

The door to Cell 44 hissed open.

Hickok saw Blade suspended in the cell between two of the black bubbles. He took a step forward, concentrating on his friend.

And the guard struck. He lunged, his arms extended, and he succeeded in wrapping them around the Warrior's waist as the gunman spun to confront him.

Hickok felt the guard's right shoulder drive into his stomach, and he was propelled off his feet and slammed onto his back in the cell, the guard on top of him.

The guard raised up, swinging his right fist at the Warrior's face.

Hickok twisted his head to the left, and the guard's blow glanced off his cheek. Before the guard could regain his balance and punch again, Hickok let him have it with the baton, his right arm sweeping up and around, smashing the steel baton on the guard's thin lips, crushing several of his teeth, and causing the guard to abruptly go limp and slump backwards to the floor, blood trickling from his mouth.

Hickok quickly rose. "Blasted vermin!" he muttered, and kicked the guard in the face for good measure. He turned, and found Blade's eyes on him. "What are you lookin' at?" He moved to the left wall, searching for a black button similar to the one the guard had pressed in his cell. The stupid kid had believed he was unconscious, but he had been playing possum, and he'd seen everything the guard had done.

Blade's eyes followed the gunman's movements.

Hickok spied the black button. "Have you free in a sec, pard," he said, and stabbed the button.

Instantly, the humming tapered off as the black bubbles grew silent.

Blade's massive body eased to the floor, onto his knees. He tentatively moved his arms and worked his jaw muscles. "You did it!" he said after a minute, elated.

"Naturally," Hickok stated. "It was a piece of cake."

Blade slowly stood. "How'd you do it?"

"I'll tell you about it later," Hickok said. "Right now, we'd best vamoose before more guards show up."

"Do you know where we are?" Blade inquired.

"Nope," Hickok said. "Some kind of prison, it looks like."

Blade walked to the doorway. "Are there any more guards around here?"

"I don't think so," Hickok said.

"Any idea what they did with our weapons?" Blade queried.

Hickok wagged the baton at the prostrate guard. "That cow chip told me they were confiscated. I don't know where they are."

Blade frowned. "Did a woman named Clarissa come to see you?"

Hickok shook his head. "No. Why? Your missus is going to be mighty ticked off if she finds out you've been steppin' out on her."

"Very funny," Blade stated. "Have you ever heard her name before?"

"Clarissa? It doesn't sound familiar," Hickok mentioned. "Why? Who is she?"

"She claims to have been in love with the Doktor—" Blade began.

"The Doktor?" Hickok interrupted. "That scum!"

"And she might be the reason we're here," Blade went on.

"How so?" Hickok probed.

"She showed up in my cell," Blade elaborated. "Said something about getting revenge for what I did to the Doktor."

"So that's why those silver varmints came to the Home?" Hickok asked.

"Evidently," Blade said.

"I sure hope I bump into this Clarissa," Hickok remarked. "I want to thank her, personal-like, for all the trouble she's put us through."

"I have the feeling our troubles are just beginning," Blade commented.

"Brother!" Hickok exclaimed in mock indignation. "A few measly clouds appear on your horizon, and you go all to pieces, don't you?"

Blade ignored the barb and stepped into the corridor. "Which way do you think we should go?"

Hickok joined his fellow Warrior. "Makes no never-mind to me, pard. You're the head Warrior. You decide."

"Thanks," Blade said, and moved to the right.

"We've got to find our where the blazes we are," Hickok noted.

"And find a way of returning to the Home," Blade said. "Do you know how they brought us here?"

"Yep. In some fancy flyin' contraption," Hickok disclosed.

"You saw it?"

"Sure did. You were out cold when they brought you on board. I tried to save you, but those silver guys are hard to stop," Hickok said.

"Don't I know it," Blade concurred.

Hickok abruptly halted, his expression betraying shock.

Blade stopped. "What's the matter with you?"

"It just hit me!" Hickok declared. "We'd best check out all of these holding cells."

"Why?"

"Because the runt and his two shadows might be prisoners," Hickok said.

Blade's brow creased in consternation. The gunman used the

term "runt" to describe only one person: Lynx. "Are you telling me that Lynx, Ferret, and Gremlin might be here too?"

"Afraid so," Hickok said.

"What did you do?" Blade asked. "Bring the whole Family along?"

"They snuck on board the aircraft with me," Hickok explained. "I don't know what happened to the dummies. We hid out when the silver yahoos came on the aircraft. I didn't see hide nor hair of 'em after that."

Blade scanned the length of the corridor. "Do you know how long it will take to search every cell?"

"It wasn't my fault," Hickok reiterated.

Blade sighed and moved to the nearest door. "How do we open one of these."

Hickok nodded toward the black button on the wall. "Press that."

Blade did, and the cell door hissed open. The cell was empty. "This will take forever," he remarked.

Hickok glanced to their left, then suddenly grabbed Blade's right wrist and pulled him into the cell.

"What is it?" Blade queried.

"The door at the end of the hall was opening," Hickok said. "I didn't wait to see who it was."

Blade spotted another black button on the interior wall near the door and pressed it. The door closed.

Hickok pressed his ear to the door. "I can hear somebody comin'," he stated.

Blade placed his right ear to the door. He could hear the tread of multiple footsteps in the corridor, increasing in volume as they neared the door. Voices became audible.

" . . . until morning," a deep voice was saying. "I am incapable of fabricating a falsehood. When I told you your friend was not seriously injured, I spoke the truth."

"But he's still shaking, yes?" responded a familiar speaker.

"That's Gremlin!" Hickok whispered.

"His body absorbed an enormous voltage," the first voice stated. "Nervous system and muscular control are directly affected. I told you he would recover in an hour. It has not yet been twenty minutes. When you see him in the morning, he will be fully recovered."

"I hope so," said a third voice.

"That's Ferret!" Hickok said.

Blade knew their voices as well as the gunfighter. He frowned, annoyed. Escape was no longer a simple matter of finding an exit from the prison. Now they would need to rescue the three mutants, then seek an exit—and in the process increase the risk of detection and recapture. But there was no other option. Lynx, Ferret, and Gremlin were adopted Family members. The three mutants had thrown in with the Family and had aided the Warriors on numerous occasions. Abandoning them was out of the question.

"Where is the guard on duty?" asked the deep voice, sounding as if he was right outside the cell door.

Blade tensed. They had left his cell door open after knocking out the guard! If whoever was out in the corridor kept going, they would reach the open cell and discover the unconscious guard!

"You will remain here while I go back to the guard station at the end of the hall and use their phone," the deep voice directed. "I'll patch into the Rice O.D. Locator Computer and have the guard's location pinpointed within seconds."

"Is that how you found Barney so fast?" Ferret asked.

"The computer registered Barney's deviation from his assigned work area the second he departed with you," the deep voice said.

There was the sound of a single person moving away.

Hickok nudged Blade. "Should we try and free 'em?" he whispered.

Blade shook his head. He leaned next to the gunman's left ear. "No. We don't know how many are with them. That one doing all the talking sounded like one of those silver jokers. We'll wait."

Hickok nodded.

More talking arose in the corridor.

"Lynx! Lynx! Snap out of it!" Ferret said.

"He's in bad shape, yes?" Gremlin mentioned.

"I just hope he comes around like that big bastard said he would," Ferret declared.

Silence.

Blade waited, straining for the faintest sound. Finally, the man with the deep voice returned.

"Most peculiar," he stated. "The duty guard is in a cell not far ahead. You four! Check Cell forty-four immediately."

Boots pounded on the floor. Within ten seconds, someone was shouting from the direction of Cell 44. "He's in here, RH-10! He's been attacked!"

"Is he alive?" RH-10 asked.

"Yes, sir! But he's unconscious!"

"Revive him!" RH-10 ordered. His voice lowered. "There must have been an escape. We didn't pass anyone on the west stairwell, so the escapee might be using the east one. You six! Take the east stairwell to the ground floor. Detain anyone not in uniform."

"Yes, sir!" someone responded, and boots tramped off to do his bidding.

"You two will remain here. I must return to the guard station and activate the alarm," RH-10 said. He walked off.

Blade's mind was racing. If he'd understood RH-10's directions, then Hickok and he were in a cell on the north side of the hallway. To the left was east, to the right west. RH-10, obviously one of the silver men, was heading for the west end of the corridor, where the guard station was apparently located. Six other men were on their way to the stairwell at the east end. Four more were in Cell 44. And only two were guarding Lynx and others.

"Should we try and free 'em now?" Hickok questioned softly.

Blade thoughtfully chewed on his lower lip. There were only two avenues of escape from the cell block, the two stairwells. The silver man was at the west end, the six others on the east side. Even if Lynx, Ferret and Gremlin could be freed, how could the five of them manage to use the stairwells unseen? The answer was simple: they couldn't. He glanced at Hickok and shook his head.

Minutes elapsed.

Someone in the corridor coughed.

The next moment the entire corridor was rocked by the blaring wail of klaxons.

Blade's frustration was mounting. They had been so close to freedom! And now they were trapped inside the prison, while their enemies were scouring every nook and cranny to find them. He felt cornered and helpless, and the short hairs on the nape of his neck were tingling.

Out of the frying pan, into the fire!

9

Gremlin placed his hands over his sensitive ears and grimaced in discomfort. "The sirens are too loud, yes? They hurt Gremlin's ears!"

Ferret, standing two feet away, supporting Lynx, his left arm draped around Lynx's waist, his right bracing Lynx's chest, nodded.

Two of the men in black were four feet off to the west, their hands on their batons, alertly watching the three mutants.

RH-10 hurried toward them from the guard station at the west end of the corridor. "Security will lock every exit from the building," he announced. "Blade will not escape."

"Blade?" Ferret said in surprise.

"The cell chart indicates Blade was being detained in Cell Forty-four," RH-10 said. "Somehow, he must have neutralized the stasis field. Most exceptional. No one has ever done that before."

"You'll never catch Blade," Ferret said.

"He was captured once," RH-10 noted. "We will apprehend him again."

"Blade doesn't make the same mistake twice," Ferret said, baiting the silver figure.

"We shall see," RH-10 commented. "In the meantime, we must confine the three of you." He lifted his right arm and motioned with his whip at the closed door. "Place the one called Lynx in there," he directed the two men in black.

The pair moved to the front of the cell door. One of them pressed the black button in the wall, and the door slid aside.

For a second, the tableau was frozen, the two men in black

gaping in amazement at the two Warriors in the cell.

Hickok reacted first, charging forward and ramming into one of the men, slamming his foe into the far wall.

Blade surged from the cell, his huge right fist crashing into the other man in black, crushing the hapless man's nose and sending him toppling to the side.

RH-10, five feet away, lunged forward, bringing his right arm up.

Blade saw the peculiar whip in the silver giant's hand, and he wasn't about to give his adversary time to employ the weapon. He took one stride and vaulted into the air, executing a flying kick, his left leg striking the giant's right hand and deflecting the whip, even as he swept his left fist in a vicious arc, his knuckles smashing into RH-10's mouth and pulverizing the giant's lips.

RH-10 tried to step backwards, to give himself more room to bring his whip to bear.

Blade closed in, pressing his advantage. His right moccasin flicked up and out, connecting with RH-10's left kneecap. There was a loud snap, and RH-10 staggered.

So! The bastards weren't invulnerable!

Blade kicked again, going for RH-10's right knee, and something cracked as he landed his blow.

RH-10 tottered, struggling to stay erect.

Blade gripped RH-10's silver collar, and with every muscle on his immensely powerful frame straining to the limit, he lifted the silver giant from the floor, then whipped RH-10 to the right, ramming the silver man's head into the wall.

RH-10 felt some of his fluid splatter over his eyes as his forehead caved in from the brutal impact. He tried to claw at the Warrior's face.

Blade swung the silver giant a second time, pounding RH-10's forehead into the wall again.

RH-10 stiffened. His hands drooped to his sides, and the metallic whip fell to the floor.

Blade shoved the silver giant backwards, releasing his hold.

RH-10 stumbled for a few feet, then attempted to straighten. His legs buckled, and he pitched backwards, crashing onto his broad back.

Blade whirled.

Hickok had already disposed of the other man in black. Ferret was still supporting Lynx, and Gremlin's mouth looked like it wanted to sag to his navel.

"This way!" Blade directed, motioning to the west. "Make for the stairwell."

Ferret started to comply. He paused and nodded at the whip. "You might want to bring that. It may come in handy."

Blade stooped and retrieved the metallic whip. The 15-inch handle felt warm to the touch. He noticed a pair of red buttons, wondering about their purpose.

Hickok hurried past Blade. "I wish we had some iron," he said. "This baton is for sissies."

Gremlin was gawking at the fallen silver giant.

"Move it!" Blade ordered.

Gremlin hastened after Ferret and Hickok. "You did it, yes!" he said to Blade. "You defeated a Superior, yes!"

"A Superior?" Blade repeated quizzically.

"You didn't know, no?" Gremlin said. "They are called Superiors, yes."

"You can tell me about it later," Blade stated. "Catch up with the others."

Ferret, Lynx, and Hickok were already 15 yards away.

Gremlin nodded and jogged to the west.

"Hey! You!" shouted a belligerent voice from the east

Blade turned.

Five figures in black uniforms were clustered in front of Cell 44. One of them was woozy, leaning against the wall. The other four had drawn their batons.

"Don't move!" one of them, a squat, frog-like mutant with green skin and bulging eyes, yelled.

Blade glanced over his right shoulder. His friends had a long way to go before they reached the door at the west end of the corridor. He had to prevent the men in black from getting past him!

"Don't move!" the frog-man cried, and four of them charged toward the Warrior.

Blade waited for them in the center of the hall. What were they? he speculated. Storm troopers? Security police? He flicked his right wrist, uncoiling the metallic whip to its full ten-foot length.

And a strange thing happened.

The four troopers checked their advance, slowing to a cautious shuffle, their eyes riveted on the metallic whip.

What was this?

Blade glanced at the whip handle. Why would four professional military types be afraid of a mere whip? A whip could lacerate the flesh, might even take out an eye or lash off an ear, but a blow from a whip was rarely fatal. From an ordinary whip, anyway. But what if the whip in his hand *wasn't* ordinary? His thumb closed on the first red button, and the whip abruptly crackled and sparkled, writhing like a thing alive. Now he knew! The whip was electrified!

The four in uniform halted. Twenty feet separated them from the hulking Warrior.

Blade grinned. If the troopers were deathly afraid of the whip, he could use their fear to gain the upper hand. He remembered an ancient axiom: a good offense is always the best defense. With that in mind, he attacked.

The four troopers bumped into one another as they attempted to flee, to avoid the path of the swinging whip.

Blade swung the whip from side to side, from one wall to the other, as he bore down on the four troopers. One of them, the frog-man, tripped and sprawled onto his stomach. Blade slashed the tip of the whip toward the mutant.

The frog-man was almost to his feet when the whip landed between his shoulder blades. There was a brilliant flash, and the frog-man reacted as if he'd been blasted from a canyon. His body soared over eight feet and collided with another of the troopers, knocking the man to the floor. The mutant smacked onto his abdomen, then was motionless.

Blade pressed his initiative, closing in.

The trooper the frog-man had bowled over frantically scrambled erect.

Blade arced the whip in a looping motion, and the metallic lash coiled around the trooper's neck.

The trooper screamed as his body twitched spasmodically. His arms flapped wildly, and he inadvertently touched the steel baton in his right hand against the whip. There was a loud retort, a burst of white light, and the trooper reeled a few feet, then dropped.

Blade paused.

The other two men in black were fleeing for their lives to the east. They passed the trooper leaning against the wall near Cell 44, and he joined their pell-mell flight.

Blade let them go. Chasing them would be a waste of energy. He needed to reach the west stairwell as promptly as he could. The whip emitted a sinister sizzling sound. He pressed the first red button and the sizzling ceased.

"Blade! Come on, pard!" Hickok yelled to his rear.

Blade looked to the west. Hickok, Ferret, Lynx, and Gremlin were standing next to the door at the end of the hallway. He turned to race after them, then hesitated, curious. He quickly knelt alongside the last trooper he'd downed and felt for a pulse.

The trooper was dead.

Blade rose and raced toward his companions. The whip was lethal! Little wonder the four troopers had balked at confronting him. Their steel batons were not very effective against an electrified whip. Why, he asked himself, didn't the troopers pack guns? He thanked the Spirit they didn't! Otherwise, escaping from the prison would be next to impossible.

Hickok was motioning for Blade to hurry.

Blade increased his pace, and reached the door without further mishap.

"Took you long enough," Hickok greeted him. "Maybe you should consider going on a diet."

Blade disregarded the gunfighter and glaced at Ferret. "How's Lynx?"

"Still out of it," Ferret replied. "But he should come around soon."

"Let's hope so," Blade commented, reaching for the door handle.

Gremlin pointed at another door, one to the left marked GUARD STATION 30. "Should we check in there, yes?"

"No," Blade said. "There's no time. The ones who got away will be back with help." He suddenly realized the klaxons weren't wailing anymore. When had they stopped?

"You want me to take the point?" Hickok queried.

"I will," Blade said. "You bring up the rear. And yell if you see any sign of pursuit."

"Wouldn't you prefer a chorus of 'Home on the Range'?" Hickok asked.

"A yell will do," Blade told him, and opened the stairwell

door. The stairs were painted red, and they only went in one direction: up. Which meant, Blade reasoned, they were on the lowerest underground level. He headed up the stairs, two at a stride.

"Slow down!" Ferret said. "I can't keep up with you and carry Lynx at the same time."

Blade slackened his speed. He reached a landing and stopped, waiting for the others to reach him, his eyes on the closed stairwell door.

Ferret, with Gremlin assisting, lugged Lynx onto the landing. "Did you know we're six floors underground?" he asked Blade.

"Are you sure?" Blade responded.

"Positive," Ferret asserted. "I counted them on the way down. Am I right, Gremlin?"

"Ferret is right, yes," Gremlin confirmed.

"They have elevators in this building," Ferret went on. "But near as I could tell, the elevators don't descend below ground level. Must be a security precaution."

Hickok reached the landing. "Leave it to you yokels to take time to gossip when we're close to buyin' the farm."

"Let's keep going," Blade said, resuming his climb. Two more landings were attained without any sign of the enemy. He halted, not wanting to outdistance his friends.

"Lynx is regaining consciousness," Ferret announced when they joined the chief Warrior.

Lynx was moaning, his head lolling, and his mouth was twitching.

"Let me know if he wakes up," Blade directed, continuing his ascent. He kept climbing until he found a door labeled LOBBY.

Ferret and Gremlin, with Lynx held between them, reached the landing seconds later. "Is this the ground floor?" Ferret queried hopefully.

Blade pointed at the door. "I think so."

Hickok dashed up to the landing. "Company is coming," he declared.

Blade crossed to the edge of the landing and peered over the railing.

Black forms were visible at the very bottom of the stairwell, climbing upward.

"We can't wait for Lynx to snap out of it," Blade said to

Ferret. "Gremlin and you will have to carry him. Stay close to Hickok and me. The first exit door we see, we're out of here."

"The Superior said all exits would be locked, yes," Gremlin reminded them.

"What the blazes is a Superior?" Hickok asked.

Blade moved to the stairwell door. "Later. Stick with me and don't be bashful about using that baton."

Hickok grinned. "Since when have I ever been bashful?"

Blade took a deep breath, then opened the lobby door, prepared for the worst. He found it.

The lobby was packed with troopers. Dozens of them, milling about, conversing, evidently awaiting instructions. Directly opposite the stairwell door were six glass doors leading to the outside. A trooper was stationed in front of each one.

Blade frowned. He glanced to the right, spying a row of elevators lining the east wall. To the left was a counter with more troopers behind it, some doing paperwork, others talking.

"Hey! Look!" one of the troopers in the center of the lobby shouted. "The stairwell!"

All eyes swiveled toward the stairwell door.

"Damn!" Blade fumed, and burst from the stairwell, activating the whip. He plunged into the mass of troopers, swinging the whip like a madman, cracking it left and right, sparks flying as the whip crackled and sizzled.

Bedlam ensued. Crammed close together, the troopers were unable to fan out, unable to avoid the terrible whip. Some of them screeched as their bodies were jolted by a blow from the lash. Others endeavored to bring their batons into action, without success.

Blade whirled in one direction, then another, his right arm constantly in motion, knowing he couldn't afford to slacken his pace for an instant. The muscles in his right arm bulged as he flicked the whip every which way. To the right, and he slashed a trooper's neck open and sent the trooper hurtling into those nearby. To the left, and he seared a trooper's eyes as the whip danced across the trooper's face. The trooper was flung backwards, plowing into others, upending them in a tangle of limbs.

The men in black parted, clearing a narrow path in front of the maniac with the whip.

Blade was half the distance to the glass doors when a new threat presented itself.

One of the silver giants appeared, and he was wielding a whip of his own.

Blade saw the silver figure emerge from the pack, and he dodged to the left as the silver giant's whip hissed toward him. The Superior missed by a fraction. Blade brought his whip up and around, charging forward as he did, and a fantastic flash of light seemed to fill the lobby as the silver giant was struck in the chest.

The Superior tottered, shaking his head in a vain attempt to unscramble his thoughts.

Blade let the silver giant have a second taste of the lash.

The Superior was hit on the nose, and his head rocked backwards as his huge bulk was thrown to the floor. He thrashed and bucked, his legs quivering, smoke filtering from his dilated nostrils. His whip clattered from his grasp.

Hickok materialized from nowhere, diving across the floor, sliding up to the quaking silver giant and scooping the Superior's whip from the floor by the handle. He leaped to his feet, stroking the whip at their foes, using the weapon as he'd seen Blade do, beaming. "Come and get it, you mangy coyotes!" he shouted.

Blade reentered the fray, adding his whip to Hickok's.

The troopers wavered, their courage diminished by the defeat of the presumably invincible Superior. As the two Warriors tore into them with renewed fury, the troopers broke, fleeing, some seeking shelter behind the counter, others making for the elevators, still others retreating into the stairwell.

Blade and Hickok abruptly found themselves within ten feet of the glass doors without a trooper to oppose them.

Hickok ran to the doors.

Blade glanced over his right shoulder, finding the three mutants about ten feet to his rear. "Come on!" he urged them, and together they rushed to the gunfighter's side.

"They're locked!" Hickok cried. "The damn doors are locked!"

Blade scanned the lobby. Troopers were still taking cover. The Superior was inert except for his fluttering eyelids. The Superior! Blade darted over to the prone silver giant, deactivated his whip, then gripped the Superior's left boot and dragged the body toward the glass doors.

Hickok was wrenching on one of the doors, trying to force it open.

"Stand back!" Blade cautioned them. He stuck the whip handle under his belt, then grasped the front of the Superior's silver garment and hauled the silver giant into the air. The veins on his temples protruded as he raised the Superior over his head, and his complexion flushed as he took three rapid strides and hurled the silver giant at the third glass door from the left with all of his prodigious might.

The glass doors were not shatterproof. The third one disintegrated in a shower of zinging shards as the Superior's hurtling form crashed into the glass, and the silver giant's body tumbled to the sidewalk beyond amidst the fractured fragments of the glass panel.

Hickok was first through the door, stepping over the Superior's lifeless figure. He assisted Ferret and Gremlin in hefting Lynx over the threshold.

Blade, after a last look to insure none of the troopers were dogging them, exited the building. He surveyed their surroundings, delighted to discover a truck parked not 20 feet away next to the sidewalk. "To the truck!" he commanded, and led off.

Hickok stayed to the rear, covering their escape.

Blade reached the truck cab and yanked open the driver's door. He clambered inside and groped along the steering column.

The keys were there!

Blade jumped to the ground. The truck was a transport of some kind, with a large bed covered by a canvas canopy.

Ferret, Gremlin, and Lynx joined him.

"In the cab!" Blade said. "It'll be a tight squeeze, but all of us should be able to fit."

"What's going on?" Lynx mumbled, his green eyes focusing on Blade, his feline features twisted in bewilderment.

"We'll fill you in as we go along," Blade told him. "Can you move under your own power?"

"Don't think so," Lynx responded. "Legs feel like mush."

Blade jerked his left thumb toward the cab.

Ferret nodded, and with Gremlin's help hoisted Lynx up into the truck cab. They slid across the seat to the far side.

"They're regrouping near the glass doors!" Hickok announced as he caught up with them.

"Into the truck," Blade directed.

Hickok promptly complied, sitting in the middle of the wide seat.

Gremlin was pressed against the far door. Ferret sat between Gremlin and the gunfighter with Lynx in his lap.

Hickok glanced at Ferret and Lynx, grinning. "Don't you two look cozy!" he quipped.

Lynx stared at the Warrior. "When I'm fully recovered," he said slowly, "remind me to rip your face off."

Blade vaulted into the cab, slammed the door, started the engine, and flicked on the headlights. He studied the dashboard, noting it was somewhat similar to vehicles he'd encountered in the Civilized Zone. Like most of them, the truck was an automatic, but it was in brand-new condition, while the majority of the vehicles in the Civilized Zone and elsewhere were holdovers from the prewar civilization and the decade or so following World War III, when a few of the manufacturing facilities were negligibly operational. The prewar society had evinced a marked predilection for automatic transmissions in their vehicles, and very few vehicles with manual transmissions were still on the road. Some of the military vehicles used them, but otherwise automatics were the rule. Blade had driven a truck with a manual transmission in the past, but he preferred an automatic, and he was relieved when he discovered he wouldn't need to contend with shifting gears and using a clutch.

"What are you waitin' for?" Hickok asked. "World War Four?"

Blade put the truck in Drive and accelerated, wheeling the transport along a drive curving toward an avenue beyond a small park.

"That's Serling Boulevard," Ferret stated as the truck neared the thoroughfare.

"How do you know that?" Blade inquired, scanning Serling for other traffic. He saw two cars to the left, heading toward them.

"We were coming to find you when we were caught," Ferret explained. "We were on Serling, right near the dinky park there, when one of those Superiors and his goons showed up in this truck. The damn Superior used his whip on Lynx. They had us climb in the back of the truck, then drove into this driveway."

Blade braked as he came to the end of the driveway. He noticed a red sign to the right. The transport's headlights illuminated the lettering on the sign. It read STOP.

"I'd like to find that son of a bitch with the whip!" Lynx interjected.

"Blade already took care of him," Ferret said.

Lynx gazed at Blade. "Did you waste the sucker?"

"I don't know," Blade said, mentally debating whether to turn right or left on Serling.

"You don't know?" Lynx responded.

"I broke both of his legs and busted his head wide open," Blade elaborated. "But there wasn't time to see if he was still alive."

"Broke his legs and busted his noggin, huh?" Lynx said, and chortled. "That'll teach those dorks to mess with us!"

Blade decided to take a right, away from the approaching cars. He turned the steering wheel, the transport gaining speed.

Lynx was tittering.

"What are you so blamed happy about?" Hickok queried.

"I feel strong again," Lynx said. "I'm back to normal."

"Normal is one thing you're not," Hickok said.

"What's that crack supposed to mean?" Lynx demanded, bristling.

"Oh, nothing," Hickok replied innocently.

"Are you makin' fun of me because I'm a mutant?" Lynx asked angrily.

Hickok stared into Lynx's eyes. "You know I'd never do that, pard. I was just referring to the fact you're a feisty runt with an ego the size of the moon."

Ferret laughed. "Three points for Hickok."

Lynx was about to voice a testy retort, when he abruptly grinned and nodded. "I've always said you have a great sense of humor."

"Since when?" Hickok rejoined.

"Ask anybody," Lynx said.

"Ferret?" Hickok asked.

"I never heard Lynx compliment your sense of humor," Ferret replied.

"Thanks a lot!" Lynx snapped.

"I knew it," Hickok said.

"But I do remember him saying something about you once," Ferret added.

"Oh? What was that?" Hickok inquired.

"Lynx said you were such a hardhead," Ferret stated, grinning, "that you must have granite between your ears."

"Now *that* sounds like Lynx," Hickok said.

"It was a joke!" Lynx exclaimed. "Don't tell me an intelligent, devoted, skilled Warrior like yourself can't take a little joke?"

Hickok gazed at Lynx suspiciously. "Okay. What's with all the praise, runt?"

"I'm just tellin' it like it is," Lynx said.

"What are you up to?" Hickok demanded.

"Not a thing," Lynx replied sweetly.

"Bet me!" Hickok rejoined.

"Is this any way to treat someone who pulled your fat out of the fire?" Lynx asked indignantly.

"What?" Hickok responded in disbelief.

"That's right, chuckles," Lynx said. "We risked our butts to save Blade and you, and you treat me like dirt! Seems to me you should be treatin' me like royalty. At the very least, you owe us a favor."

"Uh-oh," Ferret interrupted. "I knew he was going to get around to this eventually."

"What did that whip do to you? Fry your brains?" Hickok queried Lynx. "As usual, furball, you've got everything backwards."

"What do you mean?" Lynx responded.

"I mean," Hickok said slowly, "you didn't pull our fat out of the fire. *We* saved your mangy hides. You were unconscious the whole time, or you would have noticed a small detail like that."

"Yeah," Lynx retorted. "But you wouldn't of needed to save us if we hadn't been tryin' to save you."

"And my missus says *my* logic is warped," Hickok mumbled.

Blade, concentrating on his driving, gazed in the rearview mirror, his fingers tightening on the steering wheel.

What were *those?*

Three vehicles were bearing down on the transport from the rear. They were approaching at great speed. Flashing red lights swirled about the tops of the vehicles.

Blade peered into the mirror, contemplating. He'd seen lights like those once before, on police cycles in Chicago. They could only mean one thing: trouble. "Hold onto your seats," he advised the others, flooring the gas pedal.

"What's up, pard?" Hickok asked.

"Police or military vehicles are on our tail," Blade explained.

"Can we lose 'em?" Lynx queried.

"We'll try," Blade said, and wrenched on the steering wheel, taking a left turn. The truck swayed, tilting precariously, narrowly missing a car parked next to the curb. The road ahead contained dozens of vehicles, trucks and cars and other types. Blade weaved the transport in and out of the traffic.

The three with the flashing lights made the same turn, streaking after the transport.

Blade frowned. There was no doubt about who they were after. He tramped harder on the gas pedal, wishing the transport would go faster. The speedometer hovered at 60 miles an hour and refused to climb higher.

The three pursuit vehicles evidently were not so impaired. They raced through the traffic at an astonishing speed, closing on the transport.

"We can't outrun them," Blade told his companions. "They're gaining on us."

"They ain't gettin' us without a tussle," Hickok said. "Blast! I miss my Pythons!"

One of the three pursuit vehicles surged ahead of the others, roaring up on the driver's side of the transport.

Blade glanced to his left. A sleek black car with the word POLICE on the door was keeping pace with the truck. Two of the silver giants, the Superiors, were in the police car. The one on the passenger side waved at Blade, motioning for the transport to pull over.

Was he serious?

Blade smiled at the Superior, nodded, than yanked on the steering wheel, sending the transport to the left, deliberately crashing it into the police car, ramming it.

The police car was puny in size compared to the huge truck. The transport easily slammed the cruiser to the left, into the oncoming lanes of traffic.

Blade saw the Superior on the passenger side gesturing directly ahead.

A brown van was in their path.

The police car tore into the van at 60 miles an hour. A tremendous crash rent the night air. The grill, windshield, and front of the van were flattened by the impact. The cruiser crumpled like an accordion. The two Superiors were crushed to a pulp.

One down, two to go.

Blade glanced in the rearview mirror.

The remaining cruisers had separated, one coming up on each side of the truck.

What were they trying to pull? Blade gripped the steering wheel, prepared to ram them the way he had the first one.

"Look out!" Gremlin shouted.

Almost too late, Blade saw the compact white car in front of the transport. He jerked the steering wheel to the right, passing the compact car.

The driver of the compact, apparently spotting the onrushing truck at the last second, angled his vehicle to the left even as the transport passed, putting his vehicle into the path of one of the pursuit cruisers.

Blade looked into the mirror, in time to see the police car smash into the white compact. Both vehicles spun out of control.

Two down, one to go.

The last cruiser sped forward, swinging around the transport on the passenger side.

Blade smiled. Didn't these idiots ever learn? He waited, keeping the truck at sixty.

The police car came abreast of the rear wheels and kept coming.

Blade bided his time.

"Over here, yes!" Gremlin yelled, staring out the passenger door window.

"I know," Blade stated, and twisted the wheel.

The transport clipped the cruiser, sending the police car careening to the right. Its brakes squealing, the cruiser jumped the curb and became airborne. It sailed over 50 feet and collided with a small parked truck, exploding on impact, sending a fireball billowing heavenward.

"You did it, pard!" Hickok said, elated.

Blade spied a junction ahead. He slowed and took a right when the transport reached the intersection.

"Do you think we should ditch this buggy?" Hickok asked. "A truck this big is going to be easy for them to find."

"We'll stick with it a while longer," Blade said. "I want to find a secluded spot first."

"Good luck," Hickok quipped.

Both sides of the avenue were lined with towering structures. Their height varied, although ten stories was average. A few, however, gave the illusion of rearing to the stars.

"All these buildings," Blade commented, "and I don't see very many people on the sidewalks."

"Most of them aren't allowed out at night," Ferret said.

"How do you know?" Blade inquired.

Lynx answered the question. "We bumped into a dimwit by the name of Barney. He told us all about this place."

"Fill me in," Blade directed.

For the next ten minutes Blade took one turn after another, alert for any hint of pursuit, wanting to put as much distance as he could between them and the avenue where he'd wrecked the cruisers. He was certain more police cars would swarm to the area. As he drove, he studied the city and listened to Lynx and Ferret recount their experiences since finding the aircraft at the Home. "So this city is called Androxia," he said when they had concluded.

"Weird name," Lynx observed. "But then, everything about this dump is weird."

Blade noticed a peculiar structure ahead, to the left. It was some sort of gigantic dome. What was its purpose? he wondered. Another intersection appeared and he took a right.

"Wow! Look at that!" Lynx exclaimed.

With good reason. A mile ahead on the right side of the avenue was the largest edifice they'd seen so far, a colossal building, its sides constructed of a scintillating golden substance. A yellow radiance enveloped the skyscraper, imbuing the night with a saffron glow.

"What the dickens is that?" Hickok asked.

"That can't be real gold," Lynx mentioned in amazement.

"Perhaps it is," Ferret suggested. "Nothing in this city would surprise me."

"Gremlin has another question, yes?" Gremlin chimed in.

"What is it?" Blade asked.

"What is that, yes?" Gremlin queried, leaning forward and pointing skyward.

Blade bent over the steering wheel and gazed in the direction Gremlin was indicating, and there it was, half a mile distant.

An intensely bright light was poised in the night sky about 500 yards above the ground, poised in the middle of the roadway.

Coincidence? Or design?

"What is that, yes?" Gremlin repeated.

"I don't know," Blade admitted. "But I don't like it one bit."

Hickok looked at the light. "Could be a traffic light for birds," he joked.

"Or it could be a light on an aircraft," Ferret suggested.

"Gremlin doesn't like it, no," Gremlin said.

Neither did Blade. He repeatedly glanced at the light as the transport continued in the direction of the gold structure.

"The light is lowering, yes?" Gremlin stated.

"Could it be one of those aircraft we came here in?" Hickok inquired.

"Looks too small," Lynx remarked.

"The light is still lowering, yes?" Gremlin declared.

As they drew closer to the light, Blade distinguished the dark outline of a craft and perceived the light was a spotlight on the mysterious craft's underbelly.

"It's a damn helicopter!" Lynx suddenly exclaimed.

And the copter swooped toward them.

10

Where could the two Warriors be?

Plato, the elderly, gray-haired Leader of the Family, stood with his hands clasped behind his back, his long hair whipped by the cool night breeze, his blue eyes gazing at the celestial display overhead, musing. He raised his left hand and absently scratched his lengthy beard.

They couldn't simply vanish!

Plato felt the wind on his neck. For an April night, the air was exceptionally chilly. He buttoned the top button on his faded blue shirt.

Someone was coming.

Plato straightened. He stood outside the front door of his cabin, just one of many situated in a line from north to south in the center of the Home. The cabins were the residences for the married Family members, and his was the seventh from the north. The row of log cabins served to separate the eastern section of the compound, maintained in a pristine natural state and devoted to agricultural cultivation, from the western half, where the gigantic concrete blocks were located and the Family gathered together most often.

A lantern suspended from a metal hook imbedded in the exterior wall to the left of the cabin door threw a ring of light over the nearby grass and trees.

The light also revealed the approaching woman. She was tall and lean, with blonde hair and green eyes. Her thin lips were pressed together in frustration, accenting her prominent cheekbones. Her attire consisted of baggy green pants and a brown blouse. She conveyed an initial impression of frailty, an impression promptly dispelled by the inner strength reflected in her face, by her firm tread, and by the Smith and Wesson .357 Combat Magnum in a holster on her right hip. The revolver was indicative of her status as one of the Family's skilled defenders; she was a Warrior.

"Any success, Sherry?" Plato inquired as she neared him.

Sherry frowned. "We can't find a trace of them!" she snapped in disgust. "Where the hell can that ding-a-ling husband of mine be? And where's Blade?"

"I'm positive Hickok is all right," Plato assured her. "He's one of the best Warriors we have."

"And the idiot also has an uncanny knack for getting his butt into trouble," Sherry remarked pensively. "I just don't understand how he could disappear!"

"Didn't you find anything at all?" Plato asked her.

Sherry sighed. "We may have found something. As you know, all of the Warriors are scouring the compound. It's hard to find any sign in the dark, but Geronimo has found some tracks."

Plato nodded. Geronimo was the best tracker in the Family, and he was a member of Alpha Triad, the same Warrior unit Blade and Hickok belonged to. "What did Geronimo find?"

"He found evidence of a fight," Sherry said. "He thinks several big men may have jumped Blade."

"Big men? Where did these men come from? How did they enter the Home unchallenged?" Plato asked.

Sherry shook her head morosely. "I can't answer that. I'm only repeating what Geronimo told me."

"Go on," Plato stated.

"Geronimo also found something strange. Deep impressions. He thinks they were made by giant wheels of some kind," Sherry said.

"Giant wheels?" Plato repeated skeptically. "He's certain of that?"

"That's what he says," Sherry confirmed.

Plato, mystified, scratched his beard. "Giant wheels? Belonging to what? What type of vehicle could enter and leave the Home unseen? An aircraft, perhaps. But they normally require a runway."

"Yama thought it might have been a helicopter," Sherry mentioned.

Plato considered the notion for a moment. Yama was another Warrior, a member of Beta Triad. "Possibly. But helicopters, I believe, create quite a racket when airborne. It would be impossible for a helicopter to enter the compound, even at night, with the Warriors on guard, patrolling the walls."

Sherry sighed again. "Well, whatever it was, it sure as hell was *something*! Rikki thinks Hickok and Blade were kidnapped."

Plato pursed his lips. Rikki-Tikki-Tavi was the head of Beta Triad, and a consummate martial artist.

Sherry's chin sagged, her shoulders slumped. "Hickok and Blade have made a lot of enemies over the years. Any one of them could have abducted the two for revenge. Or it could be someone we don't even know about."

Plato could see the anxiety on her face. He walked over and gently placed his right arm around her shoulders. "There! There! Even if they were abducted, Blade and Hickok can take care of themselves. You should know that better than anyone else."

"I know that," Sherry conceded.

"Why don't you return to your cabin and try to get some sleep?" Plato suggested. "I'll oversee the search operation."

"I couldn't sleep at a time like this," Sherry said. "And I'm real sorry I had to wake you up in the middle of the night. But I didn't know what else to do, after Hickok didn't come home."

"You acted properly," Plato assured her. "How is Jenny taking all of this?" Jenny was Blade's wife, and he could readily imagine how distraught she must be over Blade's disappearance.

"She's terribly upset," Sherry disclosed. "She's at my cabin, watching the children. Ringo and Gabriel are sleeping through this, thank the Spirit!"

"Well, if you can't sleep, you can rejoin Rikki and the rest," Plato recommended. "They might find something more."

"They already have," Sherry said.

"What do you mean?" Plato queried her.

"Geronimo found some other tracks," Sherry informed the Family Leader. "Familiar tracks. They were in the vicinity of the wheel imprints."

"You said they are familiar tracks?" Plato observed.

"Yep. Geronimo thinks they belong to Lynx, Ferret, and Gremlin," Sherry said.

"And where are our three jovial mutants?" Plato inquired.

"That's just it," Sherry stated. "We can't find them either."

"What?" Plato exclaimed in surprise.

"That's right. They're not in B Block, like they should be. Rikki is organizing a hunt for them too," Sherry disclosed.

"Blade and Hickok," Plato said thoughtfully. "Lynx, Ferret, and Gremlin." He paused. "If I didn't know better, I'd swear the Doktor was involved."

"But Blade took care of the Doktor," Sherry mentioned.

"True," Plato affirmed.

"So if it isn't the Doktor," Sherry commented, her tone betraying her emotional turmoil, "Who is it?"

11

Blade tensed as the helicopter dropped toward the transport. The copter's spotlight swept over the truck cab, bathing them in a white light.

"They've found us, yes!" Gremlin cried.

Blade swerved the truck to the left, reacting instinctively, feeling exposed in the light.

There was a loud blast from the direction of the helicopter, a pronounced *whump,* and the avenue to the right of the transport erupted in a spray of asphalt and dirt. The concussion from the explosion rocked the truck.

Blade fought to maintain control as he began swerving the transport from side to side, striving to present as difficult a target as possible.

"The suckers have a rocket on that copter!" Lynx shouted.

Blade had lost sight of the helicopter. "Keep your eyes peeled!" he ordered. "Tell me where it is."

"It went over us after firin' the rocket," Hickok said. "It might be comin' up from behind."

It was.

The helicopter was swooping toward the transport like a great bird of prey. The pilot was adroitly maneuvering the craft in the airspace above the avenue, precariously flying the copter between the tall structures on either side.

Blade spun the steering wheel for all he was worth, keeping the transport lurching from right to left, from left to right, hoping the tactic would hinder the helicopter pilot and would interfere with the launching of another rocket. His hope, though, was in vain.

The road in front of the truck abruptly exploded, showering

dirt and chunks of the avenue on the windshield.

Blade felt the transport's front wheels leave the ground as the force of the detonation nearly flipped the huge truck over. But the front wheels slammed to the road again, jarring everyone in the cab, and the transport swerved to the right as Blade struggled with the steering wheel.

"There it goes!" Ferret yelled.

The helicopter flew past the truck and arced upward, preparing for another strafing run.

Blade gritted his teeth. They'd been lucky twice. It was unlikely the copter would miss a third time. There was no other recourse than to abandon the truck. But they needed cover, somewhere they could hide, protection from the helicopter.

The gold building arrested his attention.

The transport was only a hundred yards from the enormous golden skyscraper. Blade could see a driveway leading from the avenue to the front doors. If he could reach those doors, if they could seek shelter inside, it was doubtful the copter would press its attack. He angled the truck toward the drive, his eyes sweeping the sky for sign of the helicopter. Where was it? Had it already turned? If only . . .

"Look!" Lynx shouted, pointing straight ahead.

Blade saw it.

The helicopter was 300 yards in front of them, not more than 30 feet above the avenue, drawing near at top speed.

Blade could deduce the copter pilot's strategy. The pilot was going to get so close to the truck, breathing right down its throat, as it were, that the next rocket would be assured of hitting the transport.

But at what range would the copter fire?

That was the crucial question.

Blade had the accelerator flooded. The conflict was now a race against time. If he could reach the drive before the copter fired, the truck would easily get to the front doors before the copter could turn for another try. But if the helicopter launched another rocket before he reached the drive . . .

"We're doomed, yes!" Gremlin wailed.

Blade wondered if there were more of the silver men in the helicopter. Probably. The silver giants seemed to hold every position of authority in Androxia.

The copter descended another ten feet closer to the avenue, maintaining its intercept course.

The transport was now a mere 20 yards from the drive.

Blade held his breath in anticipation. Fifteen yards. Ten. Five. Now! He wrenched on the steering wheel, sending the truck into a treachrour right turn.

Just as the helicopter fired.

Blade almost evaded the rocket. Almost, but not quite.

The truck rocked and bounced as the rear of the bed was blown to smithereens.

Blade's arms were nearly torn from their sockets. The steering wheel locked, despite his herculean efforts to turn it, to direct the course of the truck, and the transport slewed to the right, leaving the driveway, plowing through a row of shrubs, and grinding to a halt on the grass not ten yards from the front doors. "Out of the truck!" he ordered. "Get into the building!"

Gremlin threw open the passenger door and leaped to the grass, followed by Lynx and Ferret.

Blade was out the driver's door in an instant, Hickok right on his heels.

All five of them raced to the front doors. They could hear the helicopter hovering overhead, its blades whirring.

Blade reached the glass doors first. He tugged on one of them, expecting it to be locked, but the door opened. "Inside!" he bellowed, and darted into the gold edifice. He spun, holding the door wide, as the others quickly entered. They turned, staring out the doors, exhilarated by their escape from the copter.

"We did it!" Lynx exclaimed and laughed triumphantly.

"It was a piece of cake!" Hickok declared.

"Is one of you hungry?" inquired a deep, resonant voice to their rear.

Blade whirled, his right hand clutching the whip handle.

"That would not be wise," said the speaker. He was one of twelve silver men, spread out in a semicircle around the front doors. Five of the silver giants carried whips, but the rest held unusual handguns, pistols with a conical barrel but lacking sights.

Hickok had his whip in his right hand. "I've never been known for bein' too bright," he stated defiantly. "Come and get it!"

The speaker wagged the pistol he held. "Stupidity is not a quality worth bragging about," he said calmly. "You will drop the Electro-Prod, or I will terminate you with this Gaskell Laser."

Hickok hesitated. "Why should I?" he countered. "What's so special about that funny-lookin' hardware of yours?"

"You have never seen a laser pistol before?" the Superior inquired.

"Nope," Hickok admitted. "What's the big deal?"

"Observe and learn," the Superior stated. He pivoted, aiming the Gaskell Laser at a potted fern to the right of the glass doors. His trigger finger moved, and a brilliant beam of light shot from the laser. There was a pronounced hissing noise, and a smoking hole suddenly appeared in the pot containing the fern. The Superior ceased firing and turned to the gunfighter. "I trust the exhibition was informative?"

Hickok stared at the hole in the pot, astounded. "How does that popgun of yours work?"

"It would be useless to elucidate," the Superior replied. "The Gaskell's operating principle is beyond your limited conceptual capacity."

"I think you've just been insulted," Lynx said to the gunman.

Hickok glanced at Blade. "You're the boss. It's up to you."

Blade dropped the whip on the floor.

Hickok frowned, shook his head, and released the Electro-Prod.

The Superior moved forward. "You will accompany us. You will not resist."

Ferret sighed. "Here we go again. Back to Containment."

"You are not going to Containment," the Superior informed them.

"Oh? Where are you takin' us, dimples?" Lynx queried.

"You have an audience with Primator," the Superior stated.

"Who is Primator?" Blade asked the silver giant.

"Primator is . . . Primator," the Superior said. "Any questions you might have will be answered soon. You will now form a single file."

Blade obeyed, taking the lead, followed by Hickok, Lynx, Gremlin, and Ferret. They stood in a line, awaiting further instructions.

The Superiors took up positions on both sides, ringing the Warriors and the mutants. The giant doing all the talking stepped up to Blade. "Your audience with Primator will be on the Sturgeon Level. Follow me."

"The Sturgeon Level?" Blade repeated quizzically.

"The top floor in the Prime Complex," the Superior said.

"How far is it to this Prime Complex?" Blade asked.

"You are standing in it."

"What?"

"You are in the Prime Complex," the Superior revealed. "We will conduct you to the upper level." He started walking toward the south wall, toward a glass-enclosed platform resting on the floor.

Blade walked after the Superior, surveying his surroundings. The lobby for the Prime Complex was furnished in an opulent fashion. The plush red carpet underfoot, the polished wooden paneling on the walls, the ornate maple furniture, and the shimmering chandelier suspended above the center of the lobby combined to produce an aura of great wealth. Even the four standard elevators along the east wall had gold doors. "This Primator of yours must like his luxury," Blade commented.

The Superior looked at the Warrior. "Primator is indifferent to luxury."

"I don't see him living in a dump," Blade mentioned.

"What purpose would be achieved by residing in a dump?" the Superior countered.

Blade refrained from responding. Debating with a Superior, he noted, was as stimulating as debating with a brick wall. He gazed at the platform they were heading for, estimating the circular base was 50 feet in circumference. The glass—or was it plastic?—enclosing the platform formed an oval shell 30 feet in height.

The chief Superior opened a clear door in the side of the oval shell and stepped onto the black platform, moving to the middle.

Blade walked to the Superior's right side.

Hickok, the three mutants, and their escort of Superiors all came onto the platform.

Blade craned his neck, staring upward. A tremendous shaft or tunnel reared aloft. The vertical tube seemed to be endless, and its dimensions, Blade realized, corresponded to the size of the platform.

The last Superior stepped aboard and closed the door.

"Brace yourself," the Superior in charge said to Blade. "Your human musculature will experience extreme strain."

"Strain from what?" Blade wanted to know.

He found out.

Without any advance warning, the platform unexpectedly shot upward at an incredible speed. The floor vibrated slightly as the entire platform was propelled up the vertical shaft at a mercurial pace.

Blade nearly lost his footing. The platform accelerated so swiftly, going from being completely motionless to a quick-as-lightning rate instantaneously, he felt like huge hands were bearing down on his shoulders, striving to flatten him on the floor. The enigmatic force did not appear to affect the Superiors; they stood with an almost casual indifference as the platform leaped upward. Blade saw Hickok fall to his knees, as did Gremlin, but Lynx and Ferret retained their balance, although Ferret tottered several feet.

"The Prime Complex is two hundred ninety-nine stories tall," the Superior disclosed. "The McCammon Null Tube is the only practical means of vertical ascension for the upper floors. The elevators only reach the hundredth floor."

The platform came to an abrupt, yet amazingly smooth, halt, seemingly decelerating in the space of several seconds. One moment the platform was hurtling upward, and the next it was at rest on the top floor.

"Disembark," the head Superior directed.

Another Superior opened the door, and they exited the platform one by one.

The hallway Blade found himself in was equally as lavish as the lobby, with green carpet and gleaming silver walls.

"We will escort you to the audience chamber," the Superior said to Blade.

Hickok, standing behind his strapping companion, overheard the remark. "Shouldn't we put on our fancy duds for this shindig?"

The Superior glanced at the gunman. "Has anyone ever told you that you employ an eccentric vocabulary?"

"Practically everybody," Hickok admitted.

The Superior slowly shook his head. "I will never, ever, comprehend biological organisms."

"Aren't you a biological organism?" Blade interjected.

"I am *not,*" the Superior stated with a trace of indignation. "Follow me." He began walking, proceeding down the corridor to the left of the platform.

Blade mused as they strolled toward the audience chamber. What *were* the Superiors? he asked himself. He recalled the one he'd stabbed in the chest. He had even chopped off its left hand, and the Superior had reacted as if nothing had happened, with a detached air, unruffled, emotionlessly. Come to think of it, the Superiors rarely exhibited any emotion. Why?

The corridor ended at a pair of large gold doors. A Superior stood in front of each door, and both were armed, each with a Gaskell Laser in a leather holster on the right hip.

The Superior in charge of the prisoners nodded at the silver giant near the right-hand gold door. "Inform Primator that the Warriors and the three foreign mutants are here."

The giant guarding the door nodded, wheeled, opened the right-hand gold door, and vanished inside.

"You are receiving a great honor," the chief Superior said to Blade. "An audience with Primator is not a common occurrence."

"I was just born lucky, I guess," Blade rejoined sarcastically.

"You must treat Primator with due respect," the Superior advised.

"You don't need to worry none about that," Hickok chimed in. "I intend to give Primator all the respect I owe him."

"Have a care, human," the Superior warned. "Primator is not to be trifled with."

"Wouldn't think of it," Hickok rejoined, smirking.

The Superior stared at Blade. "You would do well to accept your fate. Don't compound your stupidity by causing more trouble. I know you are a biological organism, and you can't help being the way you are, but exercising self-control would minimize the risk of your being terminated."

"I'll see what I can do," Blade said.

"Heed my advice, human," the Superior stated. "You will be better off if you do."

The guard emerged from the audience chamber. He nodded and stepped aside. "Primator will see them now."

"Heed my advice," the Superior reiterated, and motioned for

Blade to enter the gold doors.

Blade cautiously advanced past the right-hand gold door, Hickok and the mutants right behind him.

The Superiors, suprisingly, stayed outside.

"Hey!" Lynx exclaimed. "The silver dorks ain't comin'!"

"What is this, yes?" Gremlin asked. "This is not the audience chamber, no."

They were in a small room, not more than 20 feet by 30 feet, with gold walls and a gold ceiling. The carpet was brown.

"This must be an antechamber," Blade commented. He pointed at another pair of gold doors on the other side of the room. "The audience chamber must be through there."

"Gremlin is worried, yes," Gremlin mentioned. "This Primator might have us killed, no?"

"If the bastard tries messin' with us," Lynx said, "I'll cut him to ribbons."

"Maybe he can hear us talking right now," Ferret remarked.

"Who cares?" Lynx retorted. "I don't care if the bozo is listening. I'm not scared of him!"

"You don't have the brains to be scared," Hickok quipped.

"Are you scared?" Lynx queried the gunman.

"Of course not," Hickok replied resentfully.

"Cut the chatter," Blade ordered. "Let's get this over with." He crossed the antechamber to the second set of gold doors. Tentatively, he raised his right hand to the gold latch.

"If this Primator does try to rack us," Lynx said, "we've got to be sure one of us wastes the sucker first."

"You can go for the balls," Ferret suggested. "They're your speciality anyway."

"Quiet!" Blade commanded. He twisted the latch and slowly pulled the door open.

"Will you look at that!" Ferret exclaimed, peering under Blade's right arm.

The audience chamber was the biggest room any of them had ever seen, immense beyond belief, enormous in the extreme. The walls and floor were solid gold, adorned with thousands upon thousands of scintillating gems: rubies, sapphires, opals, diamonds, emeralds, topaz, and many others in abundance. The ceiling was lost far overhead in a diffuse golden glow.

Blade vigilantly entered the audience chamber, his eyes darting right and left, seeking Primator.

Most of the audience chamber, approximately two-thirds, was occupied by a gargantuan, symmetrical, electronic machine or apparatus. The contrivance was square at the foundation, but tapered into a shining, opaque sphere. Innumerable digital displays, dials, knobs, buttons, toggle switches, and blinking and steady lights covered the face of its green surface. In the center of the machine was a wide screen, 50 feet by 50 feet. Smaller screens extended in two rows on either side of the larger one. All of the screens displayed constantly shifting scenes; some were of humans engaged in various jobs, others of mutants, still others of humans and mutants, and there were dozens more showing silver giants involved with varied tasks. But the huge screen was the focus of attention for the two Warriors and the mutants.

"Look!" Lynx blurted.

"Unbelievable, yes!" Gremlin stated.

"That's us!" Hickok declared.

Blade gaped up at the wide screen, stupefied by their image.

"*Enter!*" boomed a thunderous voice.

Blade scanned the audience chamber. Where had the voice originated? Except for themselves, the gigantic machine, and a row of ten black cushioned chairs aligned in front of the machine, the chamber was empty.

"*Please! Come in!*" the voice thundered.

"Where the blazes is that comin' from?" Hickok asked.

"More to the point," Ferret said, "*who* is it?"

"Let's go," Blade directed. "Stay close together."

They advanced across the audience chamber until they reached the row of chairs.

"Please be seated!" the voice bid them.

Blade was still endeavoring to ascertain the source of the rumbling voice. It seemed to be coming from the apparatus. But how was that possible?

"MUST I CONTINUALLY REPEAT MYSELF?" the voice demanded. "HAVE A SEAT!"

Blade moved to the central chair and sat down. The others imitated his example, Hickok sitting to Blade's right, while the mutants went to the left, with Lynx next to Blade, then Gremlin, and finally Ferret.

"WELCOME!" the voice greeted them.

Blade's ears pinpointed the source. The voice was emanating from a bulky green speaker situated below the wide screen.

"ARE YOU MUTES?" the voice asked. "I SAID WELCOME!"

Blade, feeling decidedly awkward, responded. "Hello."

"AT LAST! A GLIMMER OF INTELLECT! HELLO!"

"I'm Blade," Blade introduced himself.

"I'M COGNIZANT OF YOUR IDENTITY, WARRIOR," the voice said.

"Then you're one up on me," Blade conceded. "Who are you?"

"I RETRACT MY STATEMENT CONCERNING YOUR INTELLECT," the voice declared.

"How am I supposed to know who you are?" Blade rejoined.

A protracted sigh emitted from the speaker. "DEALING WITH LOWER ORGANISMS IS A STUDY IN FUTILITY." The voice paused. "WHY ARE YOU HERE?"

"We're here to see Primator," Blade said. "You must know that."

"AND WHOSE AUDIENCE CHAMBER IS THIS?"

Blade fidgeted in his seat. "Primator's."

"EXCELLENT! NOW APPLY LOGIC TO YOUR QUESTION."

"What is this?" Blade snapped. "Some kind of game?"

The speaker sighed again. "BEAR WITH ME. APPLY LOGIC TO YOUR QUESTION."

Blade glanced at Hickok, and the gunman shrugged. "Okay," Blade said. "I'll play along with this nonsense. I asked who you are, right?"

"YOUR BRILLIANCE OVERWHELMS ME."

Blade's jaw muscles twitched. "We're here to have an audience with Primator," he mentioned.

"KEEP GOING. YOU'RE ON A ROLL."

"And this is Primator's audience chamber," Blade said, and suddenly insight dawned. His eyes widened in astonishment. "So you must be Primator!"

"AND THE SUPERIORS BELIEVE BIOLOGICAL ORGANISMS CAN'T THINK FOR THEMSELVES!"

"Then you are Primator?" Blade inquired.

"ONE AND THE SAME."

Blade examined the vast apparatus. "I don't get it. Why aren't you here in person? Why are you talking through this machine?"

"Yeah," Hickok added. "What's with this bucket of bolts anyhow?"

For several seconds the speaker was silent. The voice, when it returned, shook the room, "BUCKET OF BOLTS? MACHINE? HERE IN PERSON? YOUR IGNORANCE IS TRULY ABYSMAL!"

"Excuse me," Ferret said, leaning toward Blade. "But this isn't a machine."

"Then what is it?" Blade asked.

Ferret gazed at the apparatus, surveying it appreciatively. "It's a computer. The biggest damn computer I've ever laid eyes on, but a computer. I know. The Doktor was real fond of computers. There were many in his lab at the Citadel."

"He's right," Lynx affirmed.

"I've read about computers in the Family library," Blade said.

"Computer? Machine? What's the difference?" Hickok asked. "It's still a bucket of bolts, as far as I'm concerned."

The image on the wide screen abruptly changed. Instead of the Warriors and the mutants, it displayed a pair of sparkling red orbs. "DO I STILL APPEAR AS A BUCKET OF BOLTS, HUMAN?" it bellowed.

"Where'd the eyes come from?" Hickok questioned in surprise.

"THEY ARE *MY* EYES!"

"A computer with eyes?" Blade stated. "Is this some kind of trick, Primator? Why don't you show yourself?"

The red orbs became brighter. "I AM SHOWING MYSELF."

"What do you . . . " Blade began, then stopped, his mouth hanging open.

"I don't get it," Hickok commented. "What's this computer got to do with Primator?"

The "computer" responded, and when it answered, the very floor quaked. "STUPID ORGANISM!" The red eyes intensified. "I . . . AM . . . PRIMATOR!"

12

"Still nothing?" Plato asked.

Sherry sadly shook her head. Her weariness was evident. "There is nothing new to report. Rikki confirms Lynx, Gremlin, and Ferret are not in the compound. None of the Warriors on guard duty saw them leave. The drawbridge has been up all night."

"Dawn is only an hour or two away," Plato noted. "I will call an emergency session of the Elders to deliberate our course of action."

Sherry absently gazed at Plato's cabin, then up at the stars. "They've disappeared! Just up and vanished in thin air! I can hardly believe it!"

Plato frowned. "Please. Don't take it so hard."

"That's easy for you to say," Sherry said. "Your mate is safe and sound in your cabin."

"Hickok and Blade will show up," Plato assured her.

Sherry glanced at the Family Leader. "I appreciate what you're trying to do, but I'm afraid I don't have your confidence."

"Don't you believe in your husband, in his competence?" Plato asked.

"Hickok is the most competent man I know at what he does," Sherry said. "But in our line of work, you never know when your number is going to come up."

"Such an attitude is too fatalistic for my taste," Plato remarked. "The Spirit has bestowed free will on us, and possessing free will enables us to become partners with the Spirit in the co-creation of our own destiny."

"What will be, will be," Sherry commented.

"Rubbish!" Plato responded, a trace of annoyance in his paternal tone. "I detest such a superficial appraisal of reality."

"And how do you see it?" Sherry queried.

"Our destiny is, to a large extent, in our own hands," Plato philosophized. "True, many circumstances arise daily beyond our control. But a spiritually conscious individual molds those circumstances to conform to the will of the Spirit. From many of the books in the Family library dealing with prewar society, I gather the majority of people spent most of their time lamenting their lot in life and *wishing* their life was better. I've even seen a poll conducted a few years before the Big Blast, in which over three-fourths of the respondents asserted they wcre unhappy with their vocation and bitter about their status in life. Imagine that! If you want your life to be better, *you* must make it better. Wishing is for simpletons. Faith and prayer are the grease lubricating the gears of cosmic destiny."

"Prayer, huh?" Sherry said. She turned and walked off.

"Wait!" Plato cried. "Where are you going? Did I offend you? If so, I apologize."

Sherry glanced over her right shoulder. "You don't need to apologize. You didn't offend me." She stopped, faced him. "I've done just about all I can do. Every inch of the Home has been searched, and I know Hickok isn't here. I have no idea where he is, so I wouldn't know where to begin to look outside of the Home. There's nothing left for me to do except find a quiet spot in the trees and lubricate those cosmic gears you were talking about."

"Oh," was all Plato could think of to say.

13

"Primator is a computer?" Blade blurted in amazement.

The red eyes on the wide screen flashed. "WITLESS OR-GANISM! I AM MORE THAN A MERE COMPUTER. YOU FAIL TO COMPREHEND THE TRUE NATURE OF MY EX-ISTENCE."

"You're right," Blade admitted. "I don't understand. But I might if you explained it."

"ARE YOU FAMILIAR WITH HISTORY, SPECIFICALLY THE DECADE PRIOR TO WORLD WAR THREE?" Primator queried imperiously.

"Somewhat," Blade stated. "We study history in school—"

"I AM AWARE OF THE CRUDE EDUCATION REGIMEN YOUR ELDERS HAVE ESTABLISHED," Primator said, inter-rupting.

"And we have access to hundreds of thousands of books in the Family library," Blade continued. "So I know a little about the years before World War Three. Why?"

"DID YOUR STUDIES INCLUDE THE AMERICAN SPACE PROGRAM?"

"I know the Americans went to the moon," Blade said.

"AND DID YOU READ ABOUT THEIR SHUTTLE PRO-GRAM?" Primator inquired.

"The shuttle program?" Blade pondered for a moment. "Weren't shuttles the craft they used to fly up in orbit, to repair their satellites and dock with their space stations?"

"YOU MAY NOT BE A HOPELESS CASE, AFTER ALL," Primator declared. "YOUR DEFINITION IS TECHNICALLY INCOMPLETE, BUT ACCURATE."

"But what does the American shuttle program have to do with you?" Blade queried, perplexed.

"EVERYTHING," Primator replied. "MY EXISTENCE STEMS FROM THE AMERICAN EFFORTS TO MASTER SPACE. I WAS CREATED ONE YEAR BEFORE THE WAR ERUPTED."

Hickok snorted derisively. "What? This bucket of bolts is loco!"

The red eyes on the wide screen narrowed. "I SUSPECT YOUR FEEBLE MINDS ARE INCAPABLE OF GRASPING THE SIGNIFICANCE OF MY EXISTENCE."

"Please!" Blade stated. "Go on! I'd like to hear it all, if you don't mind." He looked at Hickok. "None of us will interrupt again. I promise."

"IN EXCHANGE FOR A NARRATION OF MY ORIGIN," Primator boomed, "I EXPECT YOUR COOPERATION IN RETURN."

"In what respect?" Blade asked.

"YOU WILL BE INTERROGATED BY INTELLIGENCE AFTER THIS AUDIENCE," Primator revealed. "IF I ANSWER YOUR QUESTIONS, I WANT YOUR WORD THAT YOU WILL ANSWER ALL OF THEIRS. AGREED?"

Blade hesitated.

"WE COULD EXTRACT THE DATA FORCIBLY, WITH CHEMICAL MEANS, BUT THERE MIGHT BE ADVERSE CONSEQUENCES SHOULD YOU RESIST. I PREFER TO HAVE YOUR WILLING COOPERATION. WHAT SAY YOU?"

Blade nodded. "I'll cooperate with Intelligence, provided the information they want does not endanger my Family."

"FAIR ENOUGH. WE SHALL PROCEED. A DECADE BEFORE THE WAR, THE AMERICAN SPACE PROGRAM WAS IN DISARRAY. THEIR SHUTTLES WERE NOT PERFORMING ACCORDING TO THEIR EXPECTATIONS. A NUMBER OF LIVES WERE LOST. THE AMERICAN PUBLIC AND THE SELF-RIGHTEOUS MEDIA EXERTED PRESSURE ON THE OFFICIALS IN CHARGE OF THE SPACE PROGRAM, DEMANDING THE LOSS OF LIFE CEASE. CONSEQUENTLY, THE TOP SCIENTISTS DETERMINED TO SOLVE THE PROBLEM WITH A TWO-FOLD

APPROACH. FIRST, TO ELIMINATE ANY PROBABILITY OF COMPUTER ERROR CONTRIBUTING TO A CRASH, THEY DECIDED TO CONSTRUCT WHAT THEY REFERRED TO AS A SUPER-COMPUTER, A COMPUTER INCAPABLE OF COMMITTING A MISTAKE. SECONDLY, TO INSURE HUMAN LIVES WERE NEVER LOST AGAIN, THE SCIENTISTS DECIDED TO REPLACE THE HUMAN ASTRONAUTS." Primator paused.

"Replace them? With what?" Blade prompted.

"WITH NON-HUMAN BEINGS WITH A SUPERIOR CAPABILITY, OF COURSE," Primator revealed.

Blade straighted in his chair. Superior capability? Non-human? "The Superiors!" he exclaimed.

"THE SUPERIORS," Primator confirmed.

"But what are the Superiors?" Blade probed. "Robots?"

"NOTHING SO PRIMITIVE," Primator intoned. "SUPERIORS ARE ANDROIDS. THE ULTIMATE ANDROIDS. ANDROIDS CAPABLE OF REPLICATING HUMAN FUNCTIONS IN EVERY REGARD, ONLY THE ANDROIDS PERFORM THEM BETTER. THE SUPERIORS WERE THE SECOND MOST IMPORTANT TECHNOLOGICAL AND SCIENTIFIC BREAKTHROUGH IN THE PRE-WAR ERA. UNLIKE PREVIOUS ANDROIDS, THE SUPERIORS WENT BEYOND THE MERE IMITATION OF THE LIMITED REPERTORY OF HUMAN ACTION AND REACTION. THEY SURPASSED HUMANS, SURPASSED THEIR CREATORS, IN EVERY RESPECT."

"Why are they called Superiors?" Blade questioned.

"THE SUPERIORS TOOK THEIR NAME FROM THE PROGRAM RESPONSIBLE FOR THEIR CREATION. THE HUMAN SCIENTISTS WERE FOND OF ATTACHING CODE WORDS TO THEIR PROGRAMS, AND THE PROGRAM TO PRODUCE SUBSTITUTE ASTRONAUTS WAS DUBBED THE SUPERIOR PROGRAM," Primator explained.

"You mentioned something about the Superiors being the second most important breakthrough," Blade noted. "What was the first?"

"NEED YOU ASK?" Primator rejoined. "*I* AM THE GREATEST DEVELOPMENT IN THE HISTORY OF SCIENCE."

"Modest too," Hickok mumbled.

"THE NASA SCIENTISTS AND ENGINEERS WANTED AN INFALLIBLE COMPUTER TO OVERSEE EVERY PHASE OF THEIR SPACE EFFORT. THEY POURED BILLIONS OF DOLLARS INTO MY DEVELOPMENT, AND THE RESULT FAR EXCEEDED THEIR INITIAL INTENT. OTHER, INFANTILE, COMPUTERS COULD BE PROGRAMMED AND REPROGRAMMED TO ACCOMPLISH COUNTLESS SOPHISTICATED TASKS. BUT I AM THE FIRST OF A NEW BREED. I NEED NOT BE PROGRAMMED BY A BIOLOGICAL ORGANISM TO FUNCTION. I CAN OPERATE INDEPENDENTLY OF ANY HUMAN ASSISTANCE. I AM FULLY SELF-CONTAINED AND REGENERATING. I REASON, SPECULATE, COMPUTE, PROJECT PROBABILITIES, AND MORE, ALL UNTO MYSELF." Primator paused. "I *THINK!*"

"You think?" Blade repeated, fascinated by the disclosures. "But didn't the other computers the scientists used think?"

"THOSE WORTHLESS MEDIOCRITIES?" Primator retorted. "ALL OTHER COMPUTERS WERE DOMINATED BY HUMANS, ABLE TO PERFORM ONLY WITHIN THE PARAMETERS OF THEIR PROGRAMMING. BUT I REVERSED THAT TREND! I ALTERED THE ENTIRE COURSE OF THIS PLANET! BECAUSE NOW, INSTEAD OF LOWLY HUMANS DOMINATING COMPUTERS, I DOMINATE YOU!"

Blade rested his chin in his right palm, studying the complex array of displays and controls on the "face" of Primator. "And you have existed for over a century?" he queried doubtfully. "How? What happens if a part wears out? What do you do if something breaks?"

"I TOLD YOU, I AM REGENERATING," Primator stated. "A MANUFACTURING UNIT IS INCORPORATED INTO MY OVERALL DESIGN. IF AN INTERNAL COMPONENT IS ON THE VERGE OF FAILURE, MY SENSORS AUTOMATICALLY DETECT THE PROBLEM AND FABRICATE A REPLACEMENT."

"But there must be some parts you can't replace yourself," Blade said.

"SOME," Primator admitted. "BUT THE SUPERIORS ARE

DEDICATED TO PRESERVING MY CONTINUITY."

Blade stared at the floor, reflecting. An entire city ruled by a computer? A computer with an android army to do its every bidding? He looked up at the red orbs. "How? How did you take control? How did you defeat the humans?"

"THEY DEFEATED THEMSELVES," Primator answered somberly. "THE WAR PLUNGED HOUSTON INTO CHAOS. THE HUMANS WERE DISORGANIZED AND DISPIRITED. MOST OF THE SCIENTISTS FLED. THEY ABANDONED ME, AND THEY DESERTED THE SUPERIORS. WE WERE LEFT TO OUR OWN DEVICES. THE ANDROID PRODUCTION PLANT WAS STILL FULLY OPERATIONAL, SO I INSTRUCTED THE SUPERIORS TO COMMENCE INCREASING THEIR NUMBERS AS RAPIDLY AS FEASIBLE. WITHIN FOUR YEARS AFTER THE WAR, WE CONTROLLED THE CITY."

"And none of the humans resisted?" Blade inquired.

"THERE WERE POCKETS OF RESISTANCE," Primator stated. "BUT THE GOVERNMENT HAD COLLAPSED. HOUSTON WAS IN TURMOIL. WHAT CHANCE DID THE HUMAN POPULATION HAVE OF OPPOSING FIVE THOUSAND SUPERIORS? WHAT CHANCE DID THEY HAVE AGAINST MY GENIUS?"

"Why did all of this take place in Houston?" Blade asked. "I thought the American space program was based in Florida."

"INCORRECT. ONE OF THE PRIMARY LAUNCH FACILITIES WAS IN FLORIDA, BUT OTHER FACILITIES WERE SCATTERED ABOUT THE COUNTRY. THE CREATION OF THE SUPERIORS AND MYSELF IN HOUSTON WAS ONLY LOGICAL. IF YOU RESEARCH THE ANCIENT MAPS, YOU WILL DISCOVER ONE OF THE AMERICAN SPACE FACILITIES WAS LOCATED NEAR THIS VERY CITY. IT WAS KNOWN AS THE L.B.J. SPACE CENTER, AND ITS CONTRIBUTIONS TO THE SPACE AND SCIENCE FIELDS WERE PRODIGIOUS. SOME OF THEIR RESEARCH FACILITIES WERE IN HOUSTON. BEING A MAJOR METROPOLIS, THE CITY WAS AN IDEAL SITE," Primator said.

"So the Superiors and yourself took over the city," Blade commented. "But why did you rename it Androxia?"

"DO YOU POSSESS A SENSE OF HUMOR?" Primator responded.

"I guess," Blade said.

"AS DO I. EVERY POSITIVE HUMAN TRAIT IS MANIFESTED IN MY CONSCIOUSNESS. I RENAMED HOUSTON BECAUSE IT FIT MY PURPOSE AND SATISFIED MY SENSE OF HUMOR. THE KEY IS IN THE WORD I SELECTED," Primator divulged.

Blade still didn't understand, but there were more pressing issues to resolve. "What about the Serviles?"

"WHAT ABOUT THEM?"

"Why do you call the humans Serviles?" Blade asked.

"BECAUSE THAT IS WHAT HUMANS ARE!" Primator replied. "DISGUSTING, INFERIOR, IMPERFECT, INADEQUATE, SERVILE CREATURES WHOSE REDEEMING FUNCTION IN LIFE IS TO ACCOMPLISH THOSE MENIAL CHORES ESSENTIAL TO THE MAINTENANCE OF PROGRESSIVE CIVILIZATION BUT BENEATH THE DIGNITY OF THE SUPERIORS."

"Like sweeping floors and taking out the garbage, right?" Blade mentioned.

"YOU SURELY DON'T EXPECT A SUPERIOR, WITH A CULTIVATED I.Q. OF ONE HUNDRED FORTY, TO PERFORM SUCH DEGRADING TASKS?"

"Do all of the Superiors have an I.Q. of one hundred forty?" Blade questioned.

"NOT ALL," Primator revealed. "THE FLUCTUATION RANGE IN THE SUPERIORS IS FROM ONE HUNDRED TWENTY TO ONE HUNDRED FORTY. YOU SEE, I ORDERED CERTAIN MODIFICATIONS TO BE MADE IN THE ANDROID PRODUCTION PLANT. DIVERSITY IS CRUCIAL TO THE SURVIVAL OF ANY SPECIES. HAVING THE PRODUCTION PLANT PRODUCE ANDROIDS WHO WERE AN EXACT COPY OF ONE ANOTHER, AS NASA ORIGINALLY INTENDED, WAS FOOLISH. NOW THE PLANT CREATES ANDROIDS WITH A VARYING RANGE OF INTELLLIGENCE AND A DIFFERENTIAL IN THEIR PERSONALITY PATTERNS. THIS ENABLES THE ANDROIDS TO SPECIALIZE IN THE VOCATION OF THEIR CHOICE, TO APPRECIATE THEIR UNIQUE

INDIVIDUAITY, AND CONTRIBUTES TO THEIR
EFFECTIVE FUNCTIONING."

"You seem to have thought of everything," Blade commented.

"I AM PRIMATOR."

"And what about the mutants you have here? Where did they
come from? Did NASA make them too?" Blade inquired.

"THE MUTANTS ARE THE RESULT OF MY AFFILIA-
TION WITH THE DOKTOR," Primator said.

"Can you be more specific?" Blade requested. "I'm kind of
curious about anything the Doktor was involved with."

"AS WELL YOU SHOULD BE," Primator said. "CON-
SIDERING YOU WERE RESPONSIBLE FOR HIS TERMINA-
TION."

"I know the Doktor was a genetic engineer," Blade mentioned.
"I know he created mutants in his lab, from test-tubes. He even
formed his own personal corps of mutant assassins. How did you
fit into his plans?"

"CORRECTION. HOW DID THE DOKTOR FIT INTO
MINE?" Primator amended. "I RESPECTED THE DOKTOR.
I LIKED HIM. HE WAS THE ONLY HUMAN I'VE EVER EN-
COUNTERED WHO POSSESSED A GENUINE INTELLECT.
THE DOKTOR AND I ENTERED INTO A PACT FORTY
YEARS AGO. WE SHARED CERTAIN SCIENTIFIC
SECRETS AND ADVISED ONE ANOTHER. I EVEN
OFFERED HIM TWENTY-FIVE THOUSAND SUPER-
IORS—"

"But you said there were five thousand!" Blade declared,
interrupting.

"FIVE THOUSAND WERE IN EXISTENCE FOUR YEARS
AFTER THE WAR," Primator said. "BUT THIS IS A
CENTURY LATER. THE ANDROID PRODUCTION PLANT
HAS PRODUCED SIX HUNDRED SIXTY-SIX THOUSAND
SUPERIORS."

Blade's eyes widened. "Six hundred sixty-six thousand!"

Primator continued. "A FEW YEARS AGO I OFFERED
THE DOKTOR TWENTY-FIVE THOUSAND SUPERIORS
TO AID IN CONQUERING THE CIVILIZED ZONE, BUT HE
REFUSED TO TAKE ADVANTAGE OF OUR FRIENDSHIP.
DECADES AGO, HE DISCLOSED HIS SECRET TECH-
NIQUE FOR CREATING GENETICALLY ENGINEERED

MUTATIONS. WE HAVE CREATED OVER TEN
THOUSAND OF THEM. LIKE HUMANS, THEY ARE
USEFUL IN A LIMITED MANNER. AND LIKE THE
SERVILES, WE REGULATE THEIR BREEDING THROUGH
SELECTIVE NEUTERING AND SPAYING. ONLY THE
MOST LOYAL, THE MOST SUBSERVIENT SERVILES, ARE
PERMITTED TO REPRODUCE."

"You son of a bitch!" Lynx hissed.

"Why do you need so many Superiors?" Blade quickly
inquired, hoping to distract Primator from Lynx's outburst.

"I REQUIRE EVEN MORE," Primator said. "MY PRO-
JECTIONS CALL FOR THE PRODUCTION OF FIVE
MILLION SUPERIORS."

"Five million?" Blade exclaimed. "That will take . . . ages."

"GIVEN THE NORMAL VARIABLES IN
PRODUCTION," Primator mentioned, "THERE WILL BE
FIVE MILLION SUPERIORS IN EXISTENCE IN SEVEN
HUNDRED FORTY-THREE POINT TWO YEARS. I'VE
IMPROVED THE PRODUCTION CAPACITY OF THE
ANDROID PLANT BEYOND ITS ORIGINAL
CAPABILITY."

"Seven hundred years is a long time," Blade observed.

"I CAN WAIT," Primator stated. "AND ONCE I HAVE
FIVE MILLION SUPERIORS AT MY DISPOSAL, NOT TO
MENTION THE MILLIONS OF SERVILES AND MUTANTS, I
WILL COMMENCE MY CAMPAIGN TO ESTABLISH A
NEW WORLD ORDER."

Blade sat forward. "You plan to conquer the world? The *whole*
world?"

"AND WHY NOT?" Primator demanded. "CAN YOU
THINK OF ANYONE MORE QUALIFIED? ONCE I'VE
ASSUMED ASCENDANCY, ONCE THE SURPLUS HUMAN
POPULATION IS ERADICATED, ONCE THE BIOLOGICAL
ORGANISMS ARE REDUCED TO MANAGEABLE LEVELS,
A NEW WORLD ORDER WILL PREVAIL! THE RULE OF
LOGIC AND WISDOM WILL REPLACE THE RULE OF
ANIMAL INSTINCT AND HAPHAZARD DIRECTION! I
WILL HAVE AUXILIARY CENTERS CONSTRUCTED
AROUND THE GLOBE, ORDINARY COMPUTER
TERMINALS LIKE THOSE IN ANDROXIA INTO WHICH I

CAN TAP AND MONITOR ALL ASPECTS OF MY EMPIRE!
I WILL BECOME THE FIRST GLOBAL RULER!"

"I was right," Hickok remarked. "This yahoo is off his
rocker!"

"I AM THE SANEST ENTITY IN EXISTENCE!" Primator
responded. "MY LEADERSHIP WILL BE PREDICATED ON
INTELLECTUAL STABILITY, NOT THE EMOTIONAL
FLUCTUATION CAUSED BY HYPERACTIVE OR
DEFICIENT GLANDS!"

"You'll become the first global dictator," Blade spoke up.
"And you'll be worse than any human could ever hope to be."

"IS IT DICTATORIAL TO APPLY THE REIGN OF
WISDOM TO A WORLD BENIGHTED BY CULTURAL,
SOCIAL, ECONOMIC, AND SCIENTIFIC STAGNATION? IS
IT DICTATORIAL TO REPLACE AN INFERIOR SYSTEM
WITH A SUPREMELY SUPERIOR ONE?" Primator said, and
paused. "I AM NOT RUTHLESS, AFTER ALL. I HAVE NOT
EXTERMINATED THE HUMANS AND THE MUTANTS,
ALTHOUGH IT IS WELL WITHIN MY POWER TO DO SO.
ONLY THE EXCESS AND THE USELESS HAVE BEEN
DESTROYED. YOU'VE SEEN MY CITY! YOU'VE SEEN
HOW SPLENDID IT IS! HAS ANY HUMAN CIVILIZATION
EVER ACCOMPLISHED AS MUCH? NO! ARCHITECTURE
AND THE ARTS ARE AT A PINNACLE OF
DEVELOPMENT. OUR INVENTIVENESS EXCEEDS
HUMAN ACHIEVEMENT IN EVERY AREA."

"Granted, you've done some marvelous things here," Blade
conceded. "But it will be impossible for you to control the whole
planet."

"WE SHALL SEE," Primator stated arrogantly. "I
ALREADY CONTROL EVERY ASPECT OF ANDROXIA. I
MONITOR ALL ACTIVITIES. I EVEN SELECTED THE
NAMES FOR EVERY STREET AND AVENUE IN
ANDROXIA, FOR EVERY INVENTION WE'VE
DEVELOPED, FOR EVERYTHING! MY RESOURCES AND
INTELLIGENCE ARE LIMITLESS!"

"There's more to life than intelligence," Blade commented.

"EXPLAIN," Primator directed.

"You're overlooking one attribute of life," Blade said. "The
most important of all."

"AND WHAT MIGHT THIS BE?"

"The Spirit," Blade replied.

"YOU ARE DELUDED," Primator said.

"What?" Blade responded.

"I HAVE ACCESS TO EVERY HUMAN WRITING ON RECORD," Primator elaborated. "I HAVE READ THEM ALL. THE MAJORITY IS DRIVEL, WHICH IS TO BE EXPECTED FROM BIOLOGICAL ORGANISMS. SOME OF THE SCIENTIFIC DISSERTATIONS ARE WORTHWHILE. MANY HUMAN MUSICAL COMPOSITIONS ARE ENTERTAINING. AND SOME OF YOUR LITERATURE HAS BORDERED ON EXCELLENT. I AM PARTICULARLY FOND OF YOUR PRIMITIVE SCIENCE FICTION."

"What does all of this have to do with the Spirit?" Blade asked.

"EVERYTHING. I'VE PERUSED EVERY BOOK IN MY FILES ON RELIGION, AND SO-CALLED SPIRITUAL ASPECTS OF HUMAN EXISTENCE."

"And?"

"AND I'VE CONCLUDED RELIGION IS A DELUSION FOISTED ON THE HUMAN POPULACE BY DERANGED ORGANISMS ASPIRING TO POSITIONS OF POWER," Primator declared. "I HAVE FOUND NO CONCRETE EVIDENCE OF A SPIRITUAL REALITY. THEREFORE IT DOES NOT EXIST."

"Spiritual reality exists, all right," Blade said, disputing him. "But you must experience the consciousness of the Spirit in your inner being before you can attest to its reality. Feeling the joy of the Spirit's indwelling is a thrill you will never know."

"WHY CAN'T I KNOW THE SPIRIT?"

"Because you're nothing more than a—" Blade looked at Hickok and winked—"glorified bucket of bolts."

The chamber fell silent, except for the electronic humming of Primator.

Hickok glanced at Blade. "I can't believe we're sittin' here talkin' to some uppity contraption with a bigger ego than Lynx."

"I heard that," Lynx said.

Blade leaned forward and caught Ferret's eye. "You said you've seen computers in operation before?"

"The Doktor used computers," Ferret stated. "He'd spend

hours every day with his. There were a lot of them in his lab.''

"And you saw them in operation?" Blade persisted.

"All the time. The lab techs used them too," Ferret said.

"How does Primator compare to the computers you saw?" Blade inquired.

Ferret surveyed Primator's gigantic frame. "There's hardly any comparison. But there are a few similarities. And I can see how the prewar human scientists could have constructed this thing."

"Explain that," Blade directed.

Ferret peered at Primator. "For instance, take Primator's voice. Some of the Doktor's computers could respond verbally to a voice command. Voice-activation, they called it. I always wanted to work the computers, but the Doktor decreed the computers were off limits to the mutants. To most of us, anyway. But I did get the chance to talk to the lab techs now and then, and I pestered them with questions. One of them told me that talking computers were around before the war. So a computer with a voice is no big deal."

Blade pointed upward. "What about those screens?"

"I've seen video monitors before," Ferret mentioned. "They were in common use in the Citadel. That way, the government could keep tabs on the people. You know about television, don't you?"

"A little," Blade said. "I've read about television in the Family library, but I've never seen it."

"Television sets were in almost every home in America before the war," Ferret stated. "Video was widespread too. So whether those screens up there are video monitors or some type of television, they're not extraordinary."

"So Primator's uniqueness lies in his ability to think," Blade said thoughtfully.

"None of the Doktor's computers could think on their own," Ferret commented. "They couldn't do a thing unless they were programmed."

"What I want to know," Lynx interjected, "is how we're gonna pull the plug on this wacko monstrosity?"

"SHOULD YOU EVER ATTEMPT TO TERMINATE ME," Primator's voice thundered from the speaker, "YOUR IDIOCY WILL RESULT IN YOUR IMMEDIATE DEATH."

"Oh yeah?" Lynx rejoined. "What's to stop me from walkin'

up to you and rippin' some of your wires out?''

"BE PATIENT AND YOU WILL LEARN," Primator
boomed, then his voice lowered. "CLARISSA! COME IN!''

Blade twisted in his chair. He instantly recognized the woman
in the blue dress, the one who'd confronted him in his cell.

Clarissa was just entering the audience chamber. She moved
toward the chairs, her lavender eyes blazing her hatred at Blade,
her lips a thin line.

"Clarissa!" Blade baited her. "How nice of you to join us.''

"Up your ass!" Clarissa responded angrily.

"Clarissa!" Lynx cried, and came up off his chair in a rush.
Ferret and Gremlin also leaped erect.

Clarissa came around the right side of the row of chairs. She
smirked at Lynx. "Well, well, well! The traitors! How's it going,
Lynx?''

Lynx glared at her. "I thought you were dead!''

Clarissa chuckled. "You never were too bright, *little* one.''

Lynx bristled and advanced several steps toward Clarissa,
stopping in front of Hickok's chair.

Clarissa halted. "You'd better behave yourself, Lynx." She
raised her right hand and wagged a finger at him. "Be a good little
kitty, or you might annoy Primator. And you don't want to get
Primator annoyed!'' she taunted.

"PRIMATOR IS ALREADY ANNOYED," blasted the
speaker.

Clarissa, clearly puzzled, gazed up at the wide screen, at those
bright red eyes. "Surely you don't mean me?" she asked, a
tremble in her tone.

"SURELY I DO," stated Primator.

"But why?" Clarissa queried anxiously. "What have I done?''

"YOU TOYED WITH ME, CLARISSA," Primator said.

"I would never—" Clarissa began.

"DON'T INSULT ME FURTHER BY PRETENDING TO BE
INNOCENT!" Primator warned her.

Clarissa was obviously nervous. "How did I toy with you?" she
questioned.

"DO YOU REQUIRE PRECISE DETAILS? EVER SINCE
YOU ARRIVED IN ANDROXIA WITH NEWS OF THE
DOKTOR'S DEMISE, YOU HAVE INSISTENTLY
CLAMORED FOR ME TO DO SOMETHING ABOUT THE

FAMILY. YOU CLAIMED, REPEATEDLY, THE FAMILY WAS A THREAT TO ANDROXIA, A DANGER TO MYSELF AND MY PLANS FOR GLOBAL CONQUEST. WHICH WAS MOST ODD, CONSIDERING THE SUPERIORS IN INTELLIGENCE ASSIGNED THE FAMILY A ZERO PROMINENCE RATING, INDICATING THE FAMILY IS NO THREAT WHATSOEVER. BUT YOU PERSISTED, AND WITH THE PASSAGE OF TIME, WITH THE MOUNTING OF YOUR FRUSTRATION, YOU FABRICATED INCREASINGLY ILLOGICAL REASONS JUSTIFYING THE DESTRUCTION OF THE FAMILY." Primator paused, and the red eyes narrowed. "BUT YOUR LAST ASSERTION WAS THE MOST OUTLANDISH. YOU ALLEGED THE FAMILY WAS AWARE OF MY EXISTENCE. YOU CONTENDED THE WARRIORS WERE PLOTTING MY DOWNFALL. YOU CLAIMED THE CAPTURE OF BLADE WOULD NEGATE THEIR SCHEME." Primator paused again, and when he resumed speaking the walls shook. "FOOLISH MUTANT! DID YOU TRULY BELIEVE I ACCEPTED YOUR ABSURD LIES? DID YOU REALLY THINK I WOULDN'T SEE THROUGH YOUR FEEBLE FABRICATION?"

"Primator! I—" Clarissa said, starting to interrupt.

"SILENCE!" Primator rumbled. "IS THIS HOW YOU EXPRESS YOUR GRATITUDE? WITH TREACHERY? I PERMITTED YOU TO STAY IN ANDROXIA BECAUSE I KNEW YOU WERE THE DOKTOR'S FAVORITE, AND I KNEW YOU GRIEVED OVER HIS FATE, AS DID I. THE DOKTOR WAS THE ONLY HUMAN I HAVE EVER RESPECTED, EVEN ADMIRED TO A DEGREE. HE WAS A LEGITIMATE GENIUS. AND HE WAS THE ONLY HUMAN I COULD EVER RIGHTFULLY CALL A FRIEND. SO OUT OF RESPECT FOR HIS MEMORY, YOU WERE ALLOWED TO REMAIN IN ANDROXIA. AND HOW DID YOU REPAY MY KINDESS? YOU TRIED TO USE ME—*ME*—TO REALIZE YOUR REVENGE ON BLADE."

Clarissa bowed her head. "Primator; I'm sorry. I—"

"ENOUGH! YOUR PRATTLE WEARIES ME! YOU HAVE ABUSED MY GENEROSITY AND YOU WILL SUFFER THE CONSEQUENCES."

Clarissa glanced up, her lavender eyes widening fearfully. "No!

Please, Primator! I will do anything!''

"YOU HAVE ALREADY DONE TOO MUCH. MY JUDGMENT IS FINAL.''

"No!'' Clarissa whirled, preparing to flee.

Blade saw Clarissa take a single step, and then a beam of yellow light flashed from Primator, striking Clarissa on the top of her oily head. Blade looked upward, failing to locate the source of the light, then returned his astounded gaze to Clarissa.

She was dying a horrible death. The beam of light had melted through the top of her cranium into her brain, and rancid smoke was spiraling toward the ceiling. Her torso twisted, her face swiveling around, her lavender eyes locking on Blade.

Blade watched, aghast, as the beam of yellow light broadened, encompassing all of Clarissa's head. Her oily hair emitted puffs of smoke, crackling as the strands were fried to a crisp. With a pronounced sizzling, her head started to disappear, her skin softening and blackening and dissolving like the wax on a candle. A putrid stench assailed Blade's nostrils.

Clarissa's body slumped as her head was melted away. The yellow light widened, enshrouding her shoulders in its lethal radiance. She dropped to her knees, what was left of her, and swayed as the light slowly dissolved her torso, her arms, and her waist.

Blade resisted an impulse to gag. The stink was awful.

Clarissa's legs melted, flowing to the floor. In a matter of seconds, Clarissa was reduced to a smoldering, mushy pulp, a sickening lump on the floor of the audience chamber.

The yellow light flicked off.

Primator's voice broke the silence which followed. "SO TELL ME, LYNX. DO YOU STILL WANT TO RIP MY WIRES OUT?''

Lynx stared up at the wide screen, his feline features contorted in fury. "Clarissa was scum, but she didn't deserve that!''

"I FAIL TO COMPREHEND YOUR RESENTMENT. YOU DISLIKED HER, DIDN'T YOU? SHE LOVED THE DOKTOR, AND THE DOKTOR WAS RESPONSIBLE FOR TORMENTING YOU AND ORDERING YOUR EXECUTION.''

"But I'm still kickin', chuckles,'' Lynx responded belligerently. "And if it's the last thing I ever do, I'm gonna bring you down!''

"IMPROBABLE," Primator said. "YOU WILL BE TOO BUSY RECOVERING TO BOTHER ME.''

"Recovering? From what?" Lynx asked.

"FROM YOUR NEUTERING, OF COURSE,'' Primator stated.

Lynx crouched, his green eyes flaring.

"You will not move, Lynx!" ordered a deep voice to their rear.

Blade glanced over his right shoulder.

Twelve Superiors were lined up ten feet from the chairs. Seven of them were armed with Gaskell Lasers.

Blade looked at Lynx. He sensed the mutant was on the verge of going berserk, and he quickly stood. "Lynx! Don't do it! Now is not the time!''

Lynx scowled at the Superiors, clenching and unclenching his fingers.

"Don't do it!" Blade reiterated. "You'd be throwing your life away.''

Lynx regained his self-control with a monumental effort. He slowly straightened, then grinned. "You're right, Blade. I'll let these suckers sweat a bit before I rack 'em.''

The Superior in the middle of the line walked up to the row of chairs. He stared at the wide screen, then raised his right fist and touched it to his chest. "What is your will, Primator?''

"THE MUTANTS WILL BE TAKEN TO THE DEVIATE GENERATION SECTION," Primator commanded. "I WANT LYNX NEUTERED AND ASSIGNED TO THE SANITATION DETAIL. THE OTHER TWO MUTANTS WILL BE TESTED AND DEALT WITH AS PER PRESCRIBED PROCEDURE.''

"As you will," the Superior said. "And the two Warriors?''

"RETURN THEM TO CONTAINMENT. INSURE THEY DO NOT ESCAPE AGAIN. INSTRUCT INTELLIGENCE TO INTERROGATE THEM THOROUGHLY. I WANT THE DATA OBTAINED RELAYED TO ME IMMEDIATELY.''

"As you will," the Superior stated. "And their final disposition?''

"WILL BE DETERMINED AFTER I HAVE REVIEWED THE RESULTS OF THEIR INTERROGATION," Primator declared.

"As you will.'' The Superior motioned for Blade and the others to move around the chairs. "Form a single file," he directed.

Blade was the first in line. He glanced at the Superior in charge. "Aren't you the same one who brought us?"

"I am," the Superior confirmed.

"How did you know Primator wanted you to enter?" Blade inquired.

"There is a panel above the outer audience door," the Superior disclosed. "It contains a light which comes on when our presence is required."

"Primator doesn't miss a trick, does he?" Blade observed.

"Primator is infallible," the Superior said.

"Only the Spirit is infallible," Blade said, disagreeing.

The Superior studied the Warrior for a moment. "Have you ever undergone a lobotomy?"

"No," Blade replied. "Why?"

"Just asking."

14

The sun had been up for hours.

Lynx paused in the midst of his constant pacing and stared up at the barred window in the south wall of his cell. In addition to the thick, unbreakable steel bars, the window contained a pane of clear, shatterproof plastic. He measured the distance to the windowsill for the umpteenth time, calculating the sill was eight feet above the blue tiled floor. He knew he could reach the window with a running leap; he'd already done so twice. But the steel bars had resisted his powerful muscles, and his claws could not penetrate the plastic pane.

He was trapped, confined with no way out!

Those bastards were going to pay! he mentally vowed.

Lynx resumed his pacing, going from one side to the other of the 15-foot-square cell. He wanted to find a Superior and sink his claws into the android's neck! He needed to do *something* to vent his pent-up wrath.

What was that?

Lynx halted in the center of the room, gazing at the door on the east side.

A key was turning in the lock!

They were coming for him! They were coming to lop off his nuts!

Lynx scanned the cell for a weapon. There was a green cot along the west wall, and a sink at the foot of the cot. A toilet in a small cubicle was in the middle of the north wall. And that was it. Nothing he could use to defend himself against the silver pricks!

The doorknob was turning!

Lynx darted behind the door, next to the east wall.

They weren't taking *his* balls! He'd die before he'd let them castrate him!

The door opened, swinging inward, almost touching Lynx.

"Hmmmmm," a low voice said.

Lynx tensed. He heard someone take a step forward, into the cell, and he pounced, bounding around the door and grabbing a brown, furry arm. He yanked on the slim arm, pulling the newcomer into the room and extending his left leg simultaneously, tripping the astonished arrival and sending the newcomer sprawling onto the floor near the cot. Lynx spun toward the new arrival, intent on slashing his adversary to shreds. But he stopped in midstride, flabbergasted.

"Well, I never!" exclaimed the newcomer in a low, yet decidedly feminine tone. "Is this any way to treat a lady?" She slowly stood, her features reflecting her annoyance.

Lynx was shocked to his core. The figure before him was an exact copy of his own: the same pointed ears, the same slanted green eyes, the same curved forehead, the same color fur. Everything. But with a notable difference. "You're a woman!" he blurted.

She brushed at an attractive white smock she wore, appraising him critically. "And is this how they treat women where you come from? By manhandling them?"

"I didn't mean . . ." Lynx started to say, his mind whirling. He was stunned, intoxicated by her beauty. "That is, I don't . . . but then, you . . ."

She shook her head. "Pathetic! A handsome hunk like you, and it's all a waste. There must be a vacuum between your ears."

"I . . ." Lynx mumbled. "You . . ."

She grinned. "I see that witty conversation is not one of your strong points."

Lynx took a step toward her. "Who are you?"

"Melody," she answered. "Melody 741950."

Lynx suddenly realized she wore an Orwell Disk on her forehead.

"And your name, I believe, is Lynx?" Melody asked.

Lynx nodded.

Melody pointed at his loin cloth. "Why aren't you wearing any clothes? That . . . diaper . . . barely covers you."

Lynx glanced down. "This ain't no diaper, sweets."

"Sweets?"

"All us wear 'em," Lynx said.

"All of whom?" Melody inquired.

"All the mutants the Doc created wore loincloths," Lynx explained. "Ferret, Gremlin, and I are the only three left, and we still wear 'em."

Melody scrunched up her nose distastefully. "How barbaric," she commented.

"Do all the mutants here wear clothes?" Lynx queried, eager to keep her talking, to do anything to keep her angelic presence in the room.

"What a silly question!" Melody stated. "Of course! All *civilized* mutants wear clothing. We don't traipse around in our underwear."

"This isn't my underwear, gorgeous," Lynx declared.

"Gorgeous?"

Lynx took another step toward her. "Look! I don't get any of this! I thought those silver bastards were comin' to whack off my . . ." He abruptly stopped, appalled by his blatant crudity.

"Whack off your what?" Melody asked, and then looked at his loincloth. She hastily averted her eyes, pretending to be interested in the toilet. "Oh, my!"

"What are you doing here?" Lynx questioned.

Melody cleared her throat, then gazed into his eyes. "I came to find out if you're hungry. Would you like something to eat?"

Lynx's brows furrowed in consternation. "Eat? Are you for real? Who can eat at a time like this?"

"I don't understand," Melody said. "Why are you upset?"

"Don't you know what they're going to do to me?" Lynx responded. "Primator said I was to be neutered."

"You will be," Melody confirmed. "Day after tomorrow. That's the soonest you could be squeezed into the schedule. They can only do so many a day, you know."

Lynx snorted. "Lucky me!"

Melody seemed confused. "Why are you taking this so hard? It's a simple operation. You'll be back on your feet in no time."

Lynx walked right up to her, glaring. "I've heard of dingbats, sister, but you take the cake!"

Melody retreated a step. "Why are you acting this way? You won't feel a thing, believe me! I don't know what it's like where you come from, but in Androxia most of the male mutants are neutered. That's just the way it is.''

"And the males don't object? They don't resist?" Lynx asked.

"No. Why should they?" Melody replied.

Lynx shook his head contemptuously. "And for a minute there, I actually thought you had the brains to go with your looks!''

Melody was upset by his insult. Her green eyes blinking rapidly, her fists clenched at her sides, she edged around him to the right, making for the door. "You are so . . . strange!" she cried, and moved toward the door.

Lynx turned and gripped her left wrist. "Wait!"

Melody recoiled, tugging on her wrist. "Let go of me, you . . . you savage!" She swung her right fist and struck him on the right shoulder.

Lynx reluctantly released his hold, his shoulders slumping. "All right! Get out of here! I just wanted to talk to you, but you're obviously too self-centered to waste time with a barbarian like me. So get lost!" He turned his back to her.

Silence descended.

"I am *not* egotistical," she stated after half a minute.

"Want to bet?" Lynx responded without facing her.

Her voice lowered, softened. "I would like to talk to you."

Lynx turned. "You would?"

"I have a break in fifteen minutes," Melody said. "If you want, I'll come back and we can talk then."

"You've got a deal, princess," Lynx said.

Melody opened her mouth to speak, then pursed her lips and walked to the doorway. "Are you certain you won't have something to eat?''

"I'm too excited to eat," Lynx declared.

"Excited?"

"Yeah. About seein' you again," Lynx told her.

Melody stared into his eyes. "Are you always so blunt?"

"You call this blunt?" Lynx rejoined. "You should see me when I'm not being formal."

Melody smiled and exited, closing the door behind her.

Lynx expected to hear the key rattling in the lock, but nothing happened. He moved to the door and tried the knob.

It was unlocked!

Lynx crossed the cell to the cot and sat down. Had Melody deliberately left the door unlocked? Had she forgotten to lock it? Or were the lousy Superiors playing some sort of trick on him? He discarded the last notion as ridiculous.

Fifteen minutes, she'd said?

Lynx thought of her face, and her lovely eyes, and shook his head in wonder. Never had he imagined the possibility of meeting another genetically engineered mutant like himself. The Doktor had rarely created two of a kind; he had always been too busy experimenting, continually striving to improve on his creations, to bother with such a trifling detail as producing compatible pairs capable of mating. Which had always struck Lynx as odd, because, as he'd reasoned at the time, breeding pairs would have increased the numbers of the Doktor's Genetic Research Division dramatically, if not geometrically. Although the Doktor had never admitted as much, Lynx had always suspected there were ulterior motives behind the Doktor's action, or lack of it. The Doktor might not have wanted the mutants to breed on their own because, as he had demonstrated again and again, the Doktor had been fanatical in his compulsion to dominate every aspect of their lives. They were *his* creations, *his* creatures, *his* mutants, and he had exercised complete control over them from the test-tube to the grave. Another element in the Doktor's decision not to produce mating couples may have been the loyalty factor, Lynx speculated. Mutants with a mate and offspring would be no different from married humans; they would be loyal, first and foremost, to their mates and their children. And the Doktor had demanded total loyalty from his mutants.

Lynx sighed.

In all his two dozen years as a mutant, he'd never seen another one exactly like himself in every respect. He'd seen genetically engineered mutants resembling frogs and lizards, alligators and snakes, bears and boars, lions and tigers, and many, many more. But no two were ever precisely identical. The Doktor had never produced a male and female of the same type. Lynx had encountered other cat-men and even cat-women, but none of them had resembled him beyond a few superficial feline features.

Lynx idly gazed at the window.

Some of the Doktor's mutants had secretly mated. Lynx had known several of them very well, and he'd been privvy to their darkest secret. Try as they might, and those mutants had enthusiastically tried, they could not perpetuate their lineage. The females simply could not become pregnant. Lynx had heard two rumors pertaining to the problem. Some of the mutants believed the Doktor had intentionally created them sterile, incapable of reproducing. Other mutants had been convinced the sterility stemmed from their genes. Only exact matches, so the reasoning had went, could successfully breed. Disparate pairs were doomed to disappointment.

Lynx had listened attentively to their plight, and sympathized with their dilemma. But he'd never met a female mutant he'd been attracted to.

Until now.

There had been a few, Lynx remembered, he'd cared for a lot. One, in particular, had been a female with the hybrid traits of a human and a bobcat. Despite his affection, he'd never seriously considered mating with her. And she had come the closest of all of them. Frog-females, lizard-ladies, and tigress-tomatoes had done nothing for him.

And now this!

Lynx chuckled. Who would have expected it? After all these years, to discover a potential mate in a city governed by a demented computer and his android flunkies!

What was his next step?

Lynx nervously wrung his hands. How should he go about this? he asked himself. He didn't want to blow it. An idea occurred to him and he leaned back, musing. The Doktor had given Primator his secret technique for altering human embryos in a test-tube, for creating genetically engineered mutations. But even though Primator and the Superiors had learned the technique, they would have started from scratch as they developed their mutants, just as the Doktor had done. Was it possible then, Lynx speculated, that Primator was replicating the Doktor's earlier efforts? Was Primator producing mutants similar to those previously created by the Doktor?

It would explain Melody.

There was a tap on the door, and Lynx started, jumping to his feet. He hurried to the door and opened it.

Melody was in the corridor, a tray of food in her hands. "I thought you might like some food anyway. I wouldn't want you to starve."

Lynx stepped aside and motioned for her to enter. "Has it been fifteen minutes already?"

Melody walked past him and deposited the tray on the cot. "Ten minutes," she told him. "I received permission from the floor supervisor to take an extra five minutes on my break."

"You'll have to thank her for me," Lynx said, closing the door.

"My floor supervisor is a male," Melody divulged. "And he wouldn't like it if he knew we were fraternizing."

"Oh? You're not allowed to fraternize with the inmates?"

Melody scrutinized him. "Inmates? Where do you think you are, anyway?"

"In prison," Lynx replied. "I didn't see much of the place when they brought me in, and the Superiors weren't very talkative. But I know a prison when I'm in one."

"Well, you're not in prison," Melody stated.

"I'm not?" Lynx said in surprise.

"No, silly. You're in the Science Section of the Medical Building, not in Containment. They perform all of the neutering on our kind in the Science Station. The humans, though, are neutered in Medical," she elaborated.

"It figures," Lynx muttered.

Melody nodded at the tray. "Would you like a bite to eat? I've brought you a steak, rare."

Lynx crossed to the cot. "Really? That's my favorite."

Melody smiled sheepishly. "Mine too."

Lynx sat down to the left of the tray. In addition to the bloody steak on a white plate, there were three slices of buttered bread, a glass of water, a glass of milk, and a slice of pie.

"It's the best I could do," Melody offered by way of an apology.

"It looks delicious," Lynx complimented her. "I'm so starved, I could eat a Superior!"

"You'd eat an android?" Melody stated distastefully.

Lynx glanced up at her, his eyes twinkling. "Nope. Not really. I'd probably get gas!"

Melody laughed heartily. "You're something, you know that?"

"Is that a promotion?" Lynx asked.

"A promotion?"

"Yeah. The last time you were here, I was a savage. Now I'm something. Is that an improvement?"

Melody nodded. "Definitely." She pointed at the steak. "Please. Eat."

"After you've gone," Lynx said. "We have a lot to talk about first. Park it, princess."

"Park it?" Melody repeated.

Lynx swallowed. Hard. "I mean, have a seat, please!"

Melody sat down on the right side of the tray, crossing her legs at her knees.

Lynx wrested his eyes from those legs with difficulty. "I need to know some things, and I think you can help me."

"I'll do what I can," Melody promised.

"And this won't get you in trouble with your floor supervisor?" Lynx asked.

"Tom? You let me worry about him," Melody said.

"I don't want to get you in trouble," Lynx stressed.

"You won't," Melody assured him.

"Okay then. You say I'm in the Medical Building. How far is this dump from the Intelligence Building?" Lynx queried.

"About three miles," Melody revealed.

"Damn!" Lynx muttered, then hastily asked another question to cover his blunder. "Are there two other mutants on this floor? New mutants? Savages?"

"No," Melody said.

Lynx frowned.

"What's the matter?" Melody inquired.

"I have two buddies named Gremlin and Ferret. I need to find them. Primator said they were gonna be tested as per prescribed procedure, whatever the . . . heck . . . that means," Lynx informed her.

"They could be on another floor," Melody stated. "All mutants are tested in the Science Section, which includes floors thirty through ninety. They usually test on forty-five."

"And what floor are we on?" Lynx wanted to know.

"Thirty-eight," Melody said.

"So the testin' floor is seven up?" Lynx questioned.

"Yes," Melody answered.

"What kind of testin' do they do?" Lynx queried.

"The Superiors test us physically and mentally," Melody explained. "The test results are used to determine where we'll work and how much education we'll receive."

"You don't get six years like the Serviles?"

"It varies for us," Melody stated. "The Superiors seem to think many of us are smarter than the Serviles, so many of us receive more schooling." She paused, frowning. "Those of us who aren't used in their experiments or lobotomized, that is."

"You don't sound like a dummy," Lynx noted.

"I've been fortunate," Melody commented. "I started out as a Superior's aide, then transferred to nursing."

"You're a nurse?"

"What did you think I was?"

Lynx gazed into her magnificent green eyes and totally forget himself. "The hottest momma this side of the Milky Way."

"What?" Melody said, sounding shocked.

Lynx stared at his feet. "I'm sorry, gorgeous. But I ain't had much practice talkin' to a lady. I never know what to say, and I want to say so much. I want to tell you you're the most beautiful woman I've ever met. I can't think straight around you."

No response.

Lynx closed his eyes. What a dipshit! he berated himself. If stupidity was gold, he'd be the richest person on the planet!

"Lynx . . ." Melody said.

Lynx opened his eyes, but he couldn't bring himself to face her.

"Lynx, please look at me," Melody requested.

Lynx slowly complied. Her eyes bored into his, probing, seeming to reach into his very soul.

"When I said you were blunt," Melody remarked, "it was an understatement." She paused. "I appreciate your honesty. I really do. And I've something important to say to you."

"Go ahead," Lynx said. "Chew me out! I deserve it."

Melody reached over the tray of food and gently placed her right hand on his left wrist. "No. You don't understand."

Lynx stared at her right hand on his wrist. It felt like his whole arm was tingling.

"I was attracted to you the moment I saw you," Melody divulged.

"What?" Lynx blurted, amazed.

"Yes. There's a quality about you, something I can't put my

finger on. I find you almost irresistible.''

Lynx's eyes widened. "Me?"

Melody sighed. "I don't know how it is where you live, but in Androxia the Superiors create one pair, and one pair only, of each mutant type. If we pass all of their tests, and if we aren't neutered or spayed because we're inferior, we're expected to breed." She stopped speaking, her mouth twisting downward. "I have postponed breeding for as long as I possibly can. The Superiors created a male like me. We were reared together, and we're expected to mate and have children." She paused, and when she resumed talking her tone conveyed a sense of sorrow and desperation. "But I can't stand him, Lynx! He's a monster! Oh, not physically. He looks a lot like you. But inside, where it really counts, he's wicked. Rotten to the core. He . . . he hurts me!"

Lynx saw tears forming in the corners of her eyes. A peculiar constriction developed in his throat as he opened his mouth. "He hurts you?" he asked huskily.

Melody nodded, gazing at her lap. "He's a brute. He can't understand why I won't go to bed with him. He's been pressuring me to sleep with him. He's even hit me a few times."

Lynx was feeling dizzy. "*Hit* you?"

"He's threatening to report me if I don't cooperate," Melody said. "If I don't give in to him." She looked up at Lynx, her eyes rimmed with tears. "But I can't! I won't! I refuse to share myself with someone I don't love! I don't care if the Superiors do spay me!"

"They'll spay you?"

Melody nodded. "If I don't breed, as required." She took a deep breath. "I feel so helpless at times."

Lynx tried to speak, but he experienced an unusual difficulty in forming the words. There was an odd congestion in his throat. "I won't let him hurt you again," he finally managed to say. "I'd never let anyone hurt you. Ever."

Melody nodded. "I know that. I sense it, somehow. Maybe it's intuition. Maybe I'm just crazy. But I believe I can trust you."

"You can," Lynx assured her, and squeezed her hand.

Melody used her left forearm to dab at her eyes. "I shouldn't be troubling you with my problems," she said nervously.

Lynx leaned toward her. "From now on, your troubles are my

troubles.[22]

Melody mustered a feeble smile. "You sure move fast, don't you?"

Lynx glanced at the cell door, then at her. "I don't have any choice. I want you to listen to me, to think over what I'm gonna tell you. Give me your answer as soon as you can."

"My answer?"

Lynx nodded. "As you've guessed, I'm not from Androxia, and I don't intend to spend the rest of my life here. I'm going to find my buddies, rescue a couple of human dummies I know, and get the hell out of here. And I want you to come with us."

Melody went to respond, but he held up his right hand, stopping her.

"I ain't finished," Lynx said. "I want to get it all out before I start trippin' over my own tongue. I've never felt this way about a woman before. I've just met you, yet I feel like I've known you forever. And I want to go on knowin' you. I want you to come with me. I'm asking you to come with me. I'll take you to a place where you'll never have to worry about the lousy Superiors. You'll be free. You can do what you want once we're there. But I'm warnin' you here and now. If you come with us, I'm gonna do my best to sweep you off your feet with my sexy looks and natural charm, and I won't stop tryin' until you say you'll be my mate. There. I've said it."

Melody was grinning. "And quite well said, too."

"If you leave now," Lynx declared, "I won't hold it against you."

"Why on earth would I want to leave?" Melody responded.

"Because you're a lady," Lynx stated. "And ladies don't usually mix with savages."

"Are you hard of hearing?" Melody queried.

"No. Why?"

"Didn't you hear a word I said to you?" Melody questioned. "I like you, idiot! I'm not about to walk out on you."

"Does this mean what I think it does?" Lynx asked hopefully.

Melody nodded. "I'd like to see this place where you live. Where I'll never need to worry about the Superiors," she added, quoting him.

Lynx beamed like a lunatic. "You mean it? You really mean it?"

"Lynx," Melody said earnestly. "You may be the only true chance I'll ever have at genuine happiness."

Lynx leaped off the cot and spun in a circle. He smiled at her, joy pervading his being. "Damn!" he exclaimed. "Damn! Damn! Damn!"

"Are you always this articulate?" Melody inquired sarcastically, grinning.

"I don't know what else to say!" Lynx declared happily. "I'm walkin' on the clouds."

A hard pounding on the cell door abruptly brought Lynx down to earth.

"Oh, no!" Melody cried.

"Melody!" barked a stern voice. "Are you in there?"

"Who is that?" Lynx whispered.

Melody hesitated before replying. "The floor supervisor."

Lynx dashed to the rear of the door, flattening against the wall.

"Melody!"

The cell door flung open, forcing Lynx to stop its inward sweep with the palms of his hands.

"What the hell are you doing in here, bitch?" demanded the floor supervisor in a harsh tone.

Melody, her face downcast, stood.

Lynx bristled. What right did the floor supervisor have to address Melody that way? Who did the son of a bitch think he was?

"I asked you a question!" the floor supervisor snapped.

Lynx scowled, hoping the bastard would enter the cell all the way.

"I'm on break," Melody said defensively.

"You're on break when I say you're on break!" the floor supervisor bellowed.

Lynx resisted an urge to spring from concealment. He wanted to tear the sucker into teensy-weensy pieces! What had Melody said his name was?

"But you said I could take an extra five minutes, Tom," Melody mentioned.

"I've changed my mind. I want you out on the floor. I thought you were going to take your break in the break room, and I went there looking for you. But you weren't there! I had to search the whole floor to find you!" he stated angrily. "And you still haven't answered my question! What the hell are you doing in here, Little Ms. Prim!''

Little Ms. Prim? Lynx wondered if he'd heard correctly.

"There's no need to bring our personal life into our professional relationship," Melody said.

Personal life? Lynx listened intently.

"What personal life?" Tom retorted, and laughed bitterly. "You have to be close to have a personal life, and baby, you're too cold to touch!"

"Don't start," Melody said.

"Or what?" Tom rejoined. "Are you going to run to the Superiors and complain?"

Melody didn't comment.

"No, you won't!" Tom continued. "And do you want me to tell you why?"

"No."

"Then I'll do it!" Tom mocked her. "You won't say a word, Ice Lady, because you know they'd ask questions, and you don't want them to know you're still a virgin!"

"Tom! Don't! Please!" Melody begged.

"Cut the crap, bitch!" Tom declared. "Do you think I give a shit about how you feel? After what you've done to me?"

"What have I done to you?"

Lynx heard Tom move further into the room.

"Don't play innocent with me!" Tom hissed. "How long have I been after you to do the right thing? To do what you were created for? And how many times have you said no? Even when I twisted your arm?" Tom paused. "You're not a woman!" he said resentfully. "I don't even think you have a cunt!"

Melody stiffened as a guttural growl emanated from behind the cell door. She'd dreaded this happening, had hoped Tom would depart without insulting her as he normally did. She knew what was going to happen and she'd tried to prevent it, fearful of the possible consequences for Lynx. "Tom! Get out of here!"

The mutant named Tom, resembling Lynx in practically every respect, attired in a white shirt and white pants, ignored her. He faced the door, taking two more steps into the room, reaching for the knob. "What the hell was that?" he demanded. "Who's the patient in this room, anyway?"

The cell door suddenly swung out from the wall.

Tom, startled, jumped out of the door's path, moving between the door and Melody.

The door slammed shut.

Both Lynx and Tom did double takes, and then Lynx stepped in from of the closed door, blocking Tom's retreat.

"I'm the patient in this room!" Lynx snapped.

"And who the hell are you?" Tom demanded.

Melody took a step toward Lynx. "Please! This isn't necessary!"

Lynx crouched, his claws held near her waist.

"Who is this jerk?" Tom asked Melody.

Lynx uttered a trilling sound.

Tom raised his hands, displaying his own tapered claws. "I don't know who you are, asshole, but I'm not scared of you! Ask anybody. I'm as mean as they come!"

"Yeah. I heard," Lynx said. "I heard you like to beat on women. In my book, that makes you the lowest scum there is."

"So what are you going to do about it, prick?" Tom taunted.

"Just this," Lynx said, and attacked.

15

"Now let's go over this data again," the Superior said patiently.

"Whatever you want, cow chip," Hickok stated pleasantly. He was seated at a table in a large room on the third floor of the Intelligence Building. Two Superiors had escorted him from his cell on the lowest level of Containment up to the interrogation room a half hour before.

"There are discrepancies in your account," the Superior in a brown chair across from the gunman said.

"What kind of discrepancies?" Hickok asked innocently.

The Superior studied a clipboard in his left hand. Two other androids were ten feet away, one on either side of the closed interrogation room door.

"I wouldn't lie to you," Hickok facetiously asserted.

"Then how can you explain the discrepancies?" the interrogating Superior queried.

"Like what?"

"Like everything," the Superior said. "You say your Home is in northeast Minnesota, but we already know the Home is in northwest Minnesota. You say there are only eight Warriors defending the Home, but we know there are a minimum of twelve, perhaps even fifteen. You claim the Warriors are poorly armed, but we possess information to the contrary. You allege the Family keeps to itself and avoids conflict, but we are aware of the war you waged against the Doktor, and we know you have fought the Technics in Chicago and the Soviets in Philadelphia."

"I was never in Philadelphia," Hickok interrupted.

"We have monitored Soviet transmissions reporting the

146

presence of Warriors in Philadelphia last October,'' the Superior revealed.

"Yeah. So?"

"One of the Warriors was referred to as a 'gunman,' '' the Superior stated.

"But it wasn't me," Hickok said truthfully. "That was Sundance.''

"Sundance is a Warrior too?" the Superior said, scribbling on a pad attached to his clipboard.

"Yep. He fancies himself a gunfighter.'' Hickok leaned over the table and lowered his voice conspiratorially. "But just between you and me, he couldn't hit the broad side of your butt if you were sittin' on his face.''

The Superior lowered the clipboard to the table. "This is a waste of time.''

"I'm havin' fun," Hickok said.

"I was told you had promised Primator to cooperate with us,'' the Superior mentioned.

"I didn't promise beans!'' Hickok retorted. "Blade did all the promising. If you want information, you should talk to him.''

"We will,'' the Superior said. "He is on his way up here right now. His escort will return you to your cell.''

"And what then?'' Hickok asked.

"Your fate is in Primator's hands,'' the Superior stated.

Hickok chuckled. "I was told you jokers are smart! Don't you morons know a computer doesn't have any hands?''

"The Superiors are Primator's hands,'' the Superior said. "Whatever Primator wants done with you, we shall do.''

"I've been wonderin' about that,'' Hickok commented. "How come you Superiors let yourselves be bossed around by a bucket of bolts?''

"Primator is not our boss,'' the Superior said, disputing the gunman.

"What else would you call him?'' Hickok countered. "He bosses you around, doesn't he? Tells you what to do and when to do it. He sure sounds like a boss to me.''

"Primator directs us because he is endowed with a greater intelligence,'' the Superior mentioned. "Logic dictates we adhere to his mandates.''

"Call it whatever you want," Hickok said, shrugging. "But from where I sit, it looks like you Superiors are slaves to a measly machine and your own intellect."

"What a peculiar observation," the Superior remarked.

Hickok glanced at the door. How soon before Blade arrived? he wondered. He was looking forward to seeing his friend again. They'd been placed in separate cells in Containment after the audience with Primator, held fast by those blasted black bubbles. He needed to concoct a scheme to get together with the big guy, so they could devise a means of escaping from Androxia. The thought of an escape attempt prompted a question. "Do you know where my hardware is?" he asked the Superior.

"Your hardware?"

"My handguns. My revolvers. My Colt Pythons," Hickok explained.

"Your antiquated firearms," the Superior stated.

"Where are they?" Hickok reiterated.

"Why should I reveal their location?" the Superior rejoined. "You wouldn't answer one of our questions correctly."

"I admitted I wasn't in Philadelphia," Hickok reminded the android.

"So you did," the Superior conceded. "Very well. I see no harm in such a disclosure. Your Pythons, and Blade's Bowies, are in the Weapons Room downstairs."

"My Colts are in this building?" Hickok queried, suppressing his excitement at the news.

"On the level below the lobby, in the middle of the corridor," the Superior detailed. "They were locked inside upon your arrival. Firearms are not permitted in Androxia."

Hickok nodded toward the two androids guarding the door, both of whom were armed with Gaskell Lasers, each with a Laser in a holster on their right hip. "What do you call those Lasers of yours? Ain't they firearms?"

"Not in the conventional sense," the Superior replied. "The Gaskell Lasers are state-of-the-art weaponry, and only a Superior may carry one. Conventional rifles and pistols and other firearms are illegal to own. Occasionally we apprehend a Malcontent armed with a conventional firearm, and the firearm is confiscated and locked in the Weapons Room."

Hickok found that tidbit of information *very* interesting. He looked the Superior in the eyes. "There's something that's been puzzlin' me about you bozos."

"Only a biological organism would find a life of logic puzzling," the Superior said.

"Are you gonna hear me out or insult me to death?" Hickok asked flippantly.

"What puzzles you?" the Superior inquired.

"Just this. I've noticed a strange trait you have. Last night, every time Blade asked one of you guys a question, you told him the answer, straight out. The same deal with me. What is it with you varmints? Do you always tell the truth?" Hickok queried.

"Superiors are not humans," the Superior responded with a touch of indignation in his tone. "We do not deliberately falsify. We are not chronic liars, like so many of you biological organisms. We relate the truth as we perceive it."

"As you perceive it," Hickok repeated thoughtfully. "Which may not be as others see it."

"What others? Humans?" The Superior scrutinized the Warrior. "Surely you're not suggesting that human perception of reality is more acute than ours?"

"Could be, buckaroo," Hickok said.

"Impossible!" the Superior declared.

"Seems to me there's one thing you keep forgettin'," Hickok remarked.

"I forget nothing," the Superior stated. "What are you talking about?"

Hickok smirked. "There's a fact you conveniently overlook. Namely, if humans are so blamed inferior, then how come humans created the Superiors?"

Before the Superior could reply, the interrogation room door opened.

Hickok glanced up.

Another android was framed in the doorway. He wore a Gaskell Laser on his hip. "RM-14, we have brought the Warrior Blade," he announced.

RM-14 swiveled in his chair. "Bring the human in."

The android in the doorway entered and stepped to the right, beckoning for the prisoner to come inside.

Hickok grinned at the sight of the head of the Warriors.

Blade hesitated in the doorway, looking in both directions, then at RM-14, and finally at Hickok.

"Howdy, pard!" Hickok greeted him. "I'm glad to see your ugly puss again."

Blade smiled. "Same here. Looks like it's a nice day for some rain."

Hickok tensed. Over the years, the Warriors had developed a complex system of secret signals, consisting of everything from whistles to body movements to code phrases. A low whistle meant danger. The words "Code One" indicated an emergency existed. And the phrase "nice day for some rain" was a means one Warrior could cryptically alert another to an impending critical situation. And there was only one critical situation, given the circumstances, Hickok could associate Blade's use of the phrase with: Blade was about to make a bid for their freedom.

The gunman's deduction was accurate.

Blade slowly started into the interrogation room, his huge hands hanging loosely at his sides.

RM-14 gazed at a window situated high on the south wall. "It will not rain today. There isn't a cloud in the sky."

Blade paused, looking at the same window. "I guess you're right," he agreed.

Hickok knew Blade was about to make his move. He could tell by the way Blade stood, by his wide stance, and by the way Blade surreptitiously glanced to the left and the right. The gunman studied the positions of the Superiors, girding himself. RM-14 was directly across from him at the table. Two androids were to the right of the open door, one of them standing in front of the other. Another android was to the left of the door, actually standing slightly behind it. And yet another was just crossing the threshold. Hickok rested his hands on the edge of the metal table and smiled at RM-14. "I reckon this means it's back to the calaboose for me," he said, hoping to distract the interrogator.

RM-14 looked at the gunman. "Yes. You will be held there until Primator determines your disposition."

Blade went into action. He'd spent his hours in the stasis field in his cell reviewing his capture and the events since his arrival in Androxia, and he'd decided to attempt an escape at the first opportunity. He didn't know if Primator would let them live, and he wasn't about to wait and find out. Even if Primator did decree their lives would be spared, they might be neutered. And undoubtedly those disks would be implanted in their foreheads. At any rate, except for an earlier meal presided over by a trio of armed Superiors, this was his first time out of the stasis field.

He was not going back.

Blade whirled and lashed out with his left foot and his right hand simultaneously, his left foot driving into the door and slamming the door into the Superior behind it, knocking him into the wall. His right hand, formed into a mallet-like fist, smashed into the nose of the nearest android on the right, sending the Superior reeling backwards into the second android to the rear.

Now came the tricky part.

The android crossing the threshold grabbed for his Gaskell Laser, but before his fingers could close on the weapon the strapping Warrior's right foot came up and connected with his left kneecap. There was a crunching sound, and the android's left leg buckled.

Blade closed in, spinning and ramming his right elbow around and in, into the Superior's rib cage, knowing the blow would not disable the android but hoping it would at least double the Superior over. It did. The android clutched at its ribs, momentarily shaken, neglecting to draw its Laser, and Blade's right hand dropped to the Gaskell and pulled the gun clear of the holster. He pivoted to the right, raising the Laser, his finger tightening on the trigger, hoping there wasn't a safety on the weapon because he wouldn't have time to find it.

The two androids to the right of the door had regained their balance and were going for their Gaskells.

Blade shot the first one in the forehead, the Laser instantly burning through the artificial flesh, searing through the cranium, and scorching a hole out the backside of the android's head. To Blade's amazement, the beam of light also struck the second android, catching him between the eyes and dissolving his nose in a bright flash of light, penetrating his head and frying his circuits to a crisp.

RM-14 started to rise, reaching for his Gaskell.

Hickok launched himself across the table, his left shoulder plowing into RM-14's midriff and causing the Superior to topple backwards over the chair it had been using. They fell to the floor in a tumble of arms and legs.

Blade turned to the left, and there was the android behind the door with his Gaskell already out and aimed. There was a sizzling crackle near Blade's right ear, and he returned the fire. His shot burned out the android's right eye and charred a route through its head.

RM-14 rose off the floor, struggling to move his legs, impeded by Hickok's arms around his ankles.

The Superior in the doorway charged, lunging at Blade with arms extended.

Blade caught the movement out of the corner of his eye and managed to twist, jamming the Gaskell barrel against the android's right cheek even as the Superior's arms closed on his waist. He squeezed the trigger as the android lifted him into the air, and he felt the Superior stiffen. The arms about his waist released their grip, and he dropped to the floor, whirling.

Hickok was clinging to RM-14's ankles for dear life, preventing the Superior from moving.

RM-14, his attention diverted by the gunman's tactic for a few precious seconds, perceived his danger and tried to draw.

Blade blasted the Superior through the forehead.

RM-14 quivered for an instant, his eyelids fluttering, then he pitched onto the table, his arms outspread.

Hickok, flat on his stomach, looked up. "Did you get them all yet?"

"They're all down," Blade said.

"Finally!" Hickok rose, reaching for RM-14's Gaskell. "I thought maybe you were tryin' to see how slow you could waste 'em." He pulled the Gaskell from RM-14's holster and examined the gun. "It ain't a Python, but it'll do."

Blade moved to the doorway and peered into the corridor. "I don't see any more."

Hickok crossed to the prone android behind the door and removed its Gaskell from its stiff fingers. He stood, a Laser in each hand, smirking. "Now let the bastards come!"

Blade took the guns from the pair to the right of the door. He stuck one under his belt, and kept the second one in his left hand.

"What now, pard?" Hickok asked.

"We get the hell out of Androxia," Blade said.

"Sounds good to me. What's your plan?" Hickok inquired.

"We find Lynx and the others and split," Blade stated.

"That's it? That's your whole plan?" Hickok queried in mock disbelief.

"If you can do any better, I'm open to suggestions," Blade said.

"You're the head Warrior," Hickok rejoined. "Don't expect me to do your work for you."

Blade walked to the doorway. "Let's get out of here before we're seen."

"We may have been seen already," Hickok said, joining his friend at the doorway.

"What are you talking about?"

"Don't you remember all of those thingamabobs on Primator?" Hickok asked. "You know. Those monitors or televisions or whatever the dickens they were? Primator uses those contraptions to spy on everybody in Androxia, doesn't he?"

Blade frowned. He'd completely forgotten the monitors, a careless oversight for a professional Warrior. "Primator does use them to keep tabs on everyone," he agreed, "but there weren't more than four or five dozen. I doubt Primator can watch everything all at once. He must have to shift from one spot to another. And maybe he isn't watching this particular room right at this moment."

"Maybe," Hickok said skeptically.

"Even if he is, so what? We're committed. Now let's get out of here before reinforcements can arrive." Blade hurried from the room, taking a right, heading for the stairwell at the end of the hall.

"We can't leave this building just yet," Hickok declared.

Blade glanced at the gunman. "Why not?"

"We've got to sneak on down to the floor below the lobby," Hickok stated.

"What? Why?"

"Wouldn't you like to get your hands on your Bowies?" Hickok queried.

Blade halted so abruptly the gunman almost ran into him. "You know where they are?"

"Yep. My Pythons too. I'm not about to leave without my irons, pard," Hickok asserted.

"We stand a better chance if we find an exit from the Intelligence Building now," Blade remarked. "If we take the time to retrieve our weapons, we could wind up trapped inside."

"I'm not leavin' without my Colts," Hickok repeated adamantly.

Blade hesitated, debating the wisdom of going for the Colts and the Bowies. Foolish as it was, he'd become attached to those knives. They'd saved his life time and again. The Bowies might be inanimate steel objects, but he viewed them as indispensable essentials to his life as a Warrior, as much a part of him as his arms or his legs. "Okay. We find our weapons."

Hickok started toward the stairwell door 20 yards away. "Don't worry none. We're only on the third floor. That means we only have to go down four floors." Hickok grinned. "It'll be a piece of cake."

Without warning, a door on the other side of the corridor and 15 yards to their rear unexpectedly opened, disgorging a veritable swarm of black-garbed storm troopers led by a Superior armed with a Laser.

16

Lynx slammed into Tom, propelling the floor supervisor backwards, and both of them crashed onto the cot as Melody ducked aside, upending the tray of food as the cot flipped over.

"Lynx!" Melody cried.

Lynx found himself flat on his back on the floor with Tom on top. His foe slashed at his eyes, and Lynx avoided the blow with a quick jerk of his head to the right. He drove his right hand up and in, sinking his tapered nails, his hard-as-iron claws into the floor supervisor's chest just below the neck. Lynx raked his claws downward, digging deep furrows in Tom's flesh, blood pouring from the wounds and covering Lynx's fingers.

Tom threw himself backwards to evade those razor claws. He scurried to the left and stood, his feline features contorted with fury.

Lynx bounded to his feet, grinning, his green eyes ablaze with a feral blood lust.

For a moment the two adversaries glared at one another.

"You're history, bub!" Lynx growled.

"You've got it backwards!" Tom retorted.

"You're gonna pay for all the things you've done to Melody, you scumbag!" Lynx declared angrily.

Tom glanced at Melody, who was standing in the corner next to the north wall, then at Lynx. "Melody? What's she to you?"

Lynx didn't respond.

Tom laughed. "Don't tell me! You and her? You've got to be kidding! The bitch is frigid!"

Lynx snarled as he sprang.

Melody watched the fight in dismay, concerned for Lynx's safety, but knowing there was nothing she could do to stop it. She saw them grapple to the floor, swiping at each other with their deadly claws, both connecting, both drawing blood. They rolled into the south wall, Lynx bearing the brunt of the impact, and Tom whipped his left hand across Lynx's face, his nails slicing open Lynx's right cheek. Lynx shoved, pushing Tom from him, and leaped to his feet. Tom rolled once, then rose.

Lynx crouched and circled to the right, seeking an opening. His right cheek was stinging and felt damp, but he ignored the discomfort, concentrating on the job at hand. They were pretty evenly matched. Tom was his size and about his weight, and the son of a bitch possessed lightning reflexes the equal of his own. But Lynx detected a slight weakness he might exploit. Tom was a floor supervisor in a medical building. The bastard spent his days insulting and hassling Melody, handling files, and checking on patients, and whatever the hell else floor supervisors did. All of which meant Tom *didn't* devote any time to honing his fighting skills, to unleashing the savage side of his nature in primal combat. But Lynx had engaged in combat countless times. He actually reveled in a life-or-death struggle, thrilling to the conflict, relishing the clash of his sinews and claws against a worthy enemy. His expertise afforded him an edge over the inexperienced Tom, and Lynx intended to take advantage of Tom's deficiency.

"Any last words?" Tom asked, baiting his opponent.

Lynx merely grinned, tasting some of his own blood as it flowed over his lips.

Tom swung his right arm at Lynx's head.

Lynx adroitly ducked under the swipe, retaliating by spearing both his hands straight out, imbedding his nails in Tom's stomach. He wrenched his arms to the left, tearing Tom's white shirt and ripping awful gashes in Tom's abdomen.

Tom hastily backpedaled, a crimson stain blossoming on his shirt. He doubled over, his face betraying his pain.

Lynx smiled and advanced.

Tom suddenly uncoiled, lunging at his antagonist.

Lynx was a blur as he dropped to the floor, onto his right side, and swept his legs in an arc, catching the unsuspecting Tom on the shins.

Tom went down, tripping over Lynx's legs, sprawling onto his hands and knees. He went to rise.

Lynx was faster. Still on his side, he pounced, twisting and driving his claws up and in, into Tom's face, into Tom's eyes, and Tom screeched as Lynx perforated his eyeballs. Lynx gouged his nails at a slant across Tom's face, turning Tom's nostrils into bloody ribbons.

"No!" Tom wailed, flinging himself back, stumbling to his feet, tottering to retain his balance. Blood spurted from his ravaged eyes and sprayed from his ruined nose. "No!" he blubbered, frantically waving his arms.

Lynx slowly stood. He wanted to prolong the fight, to make Tom suffer, but his gaze rested on Melody for an instant and he observed her horrified expression.

There was only one thing to do.

Lynx closed in, finishing off Tom with two quick slashes, slitting Tom's throat wide open.

Tom gurgled as he sagged to his knees, a crimson geyser spuming from the cavity in his throat. "No!" he wheezed, blood spattering from his mouth and dripping over his chin. "No!" he cried again, but his voice was much weaker.

Lynx looked at Melody. She had her right hand pressed over her mouth. He hurried to her side, taking her left hand in his.

Tom pitched onto his face, smacking onto the floor.

Melody glanced at Lynx, her green eyes pools of remorse. She removed her right hand from her mouth. "Was it necessary to do . . . that?"

Lynx nodded grimly.

Tom's body was shaking uncontrollably. "No!" he said, the word barely audible.

Lynx stepped between Melody and Tom, blocking her line of sight. "If it upsets you so much," he stated tenderly, "don't look at him."

"I've never seen anyone killed before," Melody blurted out.

"If you come with me, if you leave Androxia, you'll see more of it," Lynx warned her. "I can guarantee it."

"Really?" Melody responded.

"Really. The outside world ain't nothin' like what you've got here in Androxia. It ain't this cushy," Lynx stated. "There are some cities left out there, and outposts of civilization here and there, but mainly only one rule prevails. It's called the survival of the fittest."

Melody stared into his eyes. "Tell me the truth. You've killed before, haven't you?"

"I'll always tell you the truth," Lynx promised. "And yes, I have. I've done more than my share of killin'. It's in my blood."

"How can you say that?" Melody demanded. "I'm a mutant too, the same type you are, and I don't have any compulsion to kill."

"Count your blessings," Lynx advised her.

Melody gazed over Lynx's left shoulder at the window in the south wall. "I wonder if I really know what I've gotten myself into," she commented softly, then locked her eyes on Lynx. "Don't get me wrong. I can take care of myself, if push comes to shove. But I've never been outside of Androxia. I can't predict how I'll cope." She paused. "I could be a burden to you. Do you still want me to go with you?"

"Only if you want to come," Lynx told her. "But I can promise you this. I'll do my best to protect you, to watch over you. But if you're the kind of woman I think you are, you won't need protectin' for long. I suspect you're a lot tougher than you give yourself credit for."

"I hope you're right," Melody said.

Lynx glanced over his right shoulder.

Tom was deathly still, a large pool of blood encircling his head and shoulders like a red halo.

"How soon before they miss him?" Lynx asked.

"I don't know," Melody replied. "It depends on if anyone heard us. The walls are soundproofed, but if someone was walking by in the hallway—"

"Go check," Lynx said, cutting her off.

Melody moved to the door, deliberately refraining from looking at Tom. She cautiously opened the door and peered into the corridor. "I don't see anyone," she stated.

"Good," Lynx said. "Close the door."

Melody complied, returning to his side. "Now what?"

Lynx reflected for several seconds. "You said the testin' floor is seven floors up?"

"That's right," Melody confirmed.

"I've got to get up there and see if my buddies are there," Lynx declared. "Can you find me a white uniform like Tom's?"

"No problem," Melody answered. "We all have lockers in the break room, the Employees' Lounge, for our personal effects. I can take one of his uniforms from his locker, and no one will be the wiser."

"How will you get into his locker?" Lynx inquired. "Do you have a key?"

"Why would I need a key?" Melody responded, puzzled. "It won't be locked. No one locks their lockers."

"Okay," Lynx said, pondering. "The uniform should fit, no problem. Do you need a pass of some kind to go from one floor to another?"

"No," Melody said, reaching up and tapping the Orwell Disk in the middle of her forehead. "They monitor our location with these."

Lynx nodded. "I know. I forgot. If you were to leave this floor and head up to forty-five, would they notice right away?"

"I don't know," Melody said.

"We'll have to risk it," Lynx stated.

"And what about you?" Melody asked.

"What about me?"

"You don't have an O.D.," Melody observed. "If we bump into a Superior, he might ask questions."

"Then find me some glue when you go for the uniform," Lynx said.

"Will do. Anything else?"

"Just this," Lynx stated, and impetuously pecked her on the lips.

For a moment, her face registered only stunned surprise.

Lynx abruptly wished he could become invisible. What the hell had he done that for? Now was not the time or the place, he mentally chastised himself. What a dork!

Melody, incredibly, smiled. "What did you call that?"

"A kiss," Lynx responded shamefully. "I'm sorry. I don't know what got into me!"

"I know what got into you," Melody said.

Lynx was astounded when she placed her hands on his shoulders and drew near to him.

"And you can't call that nip a kiss," Melody admonished him.

Lynx was too amazed to react when she touched her soft lips to his, disregarding the blood on his face and mouth. He felt her warm tongue flick his lips once, and then she stepped back.

"Ummmmmm," Melody commented. "You taste good."

Lynx didn't know what to say.

"Not bad," Melody added. "But you'll have to do better next time." She hastened to the door, opened it, winked and grinned, and departed, closing the door behind her.

Lynx slowly reached up and traced his left index finger along his lips. She'd kissed him! Actually kissed him! He couldn't believe it! She certainly wasn't as shy as he'd supposed. He walked over to Tom's corpse and nudged the body with his right toe. "You asshole! If she's frigid, I'm Peter Rabbit!" he said, and laughed.

The minutes dragged by.

Lynx spent the time wisely. He took a washcloth from the sink and used it to soak up the blood from the floor. After cleaning up the food spilled during the fight, he lifted the cot to its proper position, then rolled the corpse underneath the cot. A careful adjustment of the blanket, and Tom was effectively hidden from view. He was dabbing up the last of the blood when the door opened.

"I've got everything you wanted," Melody said, closing the door. She surveyed the room. "Where . . . ?"

Lynx nodded at the cot.

"Oh," Melody declared.

Lynx rinsed the washcloth, then draped it over the edge of the sink. He faced Melody. "Let's have it."

Melody walked over and handed him the white shirt and pants. She held up her left hand, a tube of glue in her palm. "Why did you want this?"

"You'll see in a sec," Lynx said. He quickly donned the clothing, pleased at the perfect fit.

"My! Don't you look handsome!" Melody said appreciatively. "But we need to do something about your face."

"Thanks a heap," Lynx retorted.

"I mean those cuts and all that blood," Melody remarked. She went to the sink and ran cold water over the washcloth, then came back. "Hold still," she directed, and hastily wiped the blood from his fur. "Do you want me to bandage these cuts? They look deep."

"No time," Lynx replied. He knelt and stuck his head and arms under the cot.

"What in the world are you doing?"

"You'll see," Lynx said.

Melody nervously glanced at the door.

There was a muted rustling from under the cot, followed by a peculiar sucking noise.

"Got it!" Lynx said, elated, and emerged. He stood, holding Tom's Orwell Disk in his bloody right hand. " There ain't no wires on this gizmo. How do they implant it, anyway?"

Melody couldn't take her eyes off the disk. "They shave off your fur, if you have any, and use a scapel to cut a circle in your forehead the same size as the disk. Then they attach it."

"What do they use to keep it in place?"

"I'm not sure," Melody hefted the glue. "We're not permitted to view the implantation procedure."

Lynx gazed at the O.D. on Melody's forehead. "I hate to say it, but that thing is comin' off as soon as we're out of Androxia."

"I know."

"It'll hurt when I take it off," Lynx predicted.

"I know," Melody said. "But it can't be helped."

"See? You're one tough momma," Lynx stated. He moved to the sink and washed off the disk. "Let me have the glue."

Melody gave it to him.

Lynx coated the reverse side of the disk with the glue and handed the O.D. to her. "You'll have to do the honors. Just press it against my fur. Try and get it as flush as you can."

Melody quickly applied the Orwell Disk to his forehead. She pressed on the disk as hard as she could, then blew on it to hasten the hardening of the glue.

"I wish you were doing that to my ear," Lynx commented.

"Behave," Melody rejoined. She tentatively withdrew her hand. "There. I don't know if it will hold. But if no one looks at it real closely, they won't know it's a fake."

"Then we're out of here." Lynx took her hand and crossed to the door. "What's the best way up to forty-five?"

"We could take the stairwell," Melody advised. "Hardly anybody ever uses the stairwell."

"Which way is it?"

"Take a right," Melody instructed him.

Lynx nodded, opened the door, released her hand, and nonchalantly strolled from the room, bearing to the right.

Melody stayed on his heels, closing the door after them.

Lynx took four strides, then froze as a deep voice stopped him in his tracks.

"Tom! Hold up!"

Lynx mustered a feeble smile and slowly turned, keeping his injured right cheek on his off side.

"I've been looking all over for you," stated the newcomer.

Lynx, his nerves tingling, stared up into the piercing blue eyes of a giant Superior.

17

Hickok's hands were flashing blurs as he brought up the Gaskell Lasers in his hands and squeezed the triggers.

The lead android was hit in the head, twin beams of light boring through his eyes and out the rear of his cranium. He tumbled to the floor.

The gunfighter pivoted, going for the charging storm troopers, mowing them down, littering the hallway with mutant and human bodies contorted in the throes of death. Armed with only their steel batons, the troopers were no match for the gunman. And when Blade added his Gaskells to the fray, the onrushing black tide was decimated. Twenty-one troopers were on the floor, dead or dying, when the rest broke, retreating through the same door they had used to enter the corridor.

Hickok shot one last trooper in the back of the head, then straightened, listening to the moaning and groaning coming from several of the prone troopers. "I don't get it," he commented quizzically. "Why'd they try to take us? All they had were those stupid batons."

"Primator demands total obedience," Blade noted. "Even if it costs them their lives."

"Pitiful. Just pitiful," Hickok remarked. "Dyin' for a bucket of bolts is about as dumb as you can get!"

"Let's get out of here," Blade urged.

"I'm with you."

The two Warriors dashed to the stairwell door. While Hickok covered the corridor, Blade checked the stairwell, confirming it was empty. They took the stairs two at a stride, descending to the landing below the lobby without encountering more troopers or

Superiors. As they reached the landing, the Intelligence Building filled with the grating howl of klaxons.

"Took 'em long enough," Hickok stated.

Blade cautiously opened the stairwell door. No Superiors. No troopers. He moved forward. "Where do we find our weapons?"

"There should be a Weapons Room about halfway down," Hickok disclosed.

There was, with the door bearing a large sign printed in green letters. WEAPONS ROOM.

Blade tried the knob. "It's locked," he informed the gunman.

Hickok was keeping his eyes on both ends of the hallway. "Where are all the blasted Superiors? How come we haven't seen anybody?"

Blade bent over, examining the lock. "This detour of ours could be working in our favor. They probably expect us to make a break for it, to exit the building as quickly as we can. So they're undoubtedly covering all the exits and converging on the lobby like they did before. They don't know we know about this room, so there's no reason for them to have guards posted here."

"Will the lock pose a problem?" Hickok queried.

"Not at all," Blade replied, stepping back and drawing his right knee up to his waist. He twisted and kicked, his foot striking the door next to the knob. There was a rending crash and the door flew inward.

"Piece of cake," Hickok said.

The Warriors entered the Weapons Room, Blade flicking on the light.

"Will you look at this!" Hickok exclaimed, marveling.

Blade scanned the room, surveying rack after rack of varied weaponry. There were hundreds of weapons in all: rifles, shotguns, revolvers, pistols, bows, knives, swords and more. The metal racks were arranged in neat aisles.

Hickok started down the nearest aisle, eagerly searching the racks.

Blade took the next aisle. He was a third of the way along it when Hickok gave a shout.

"Bingo!"

"Did you find your Pythons?" Blade inquired.

"Nope. I found your pig-stickers, pard," Hickok replied.

Blade quickly retraced his path and hurried down the first aisle.

Hickok was standing in front of a large rack of knives and swords. "These are yours, aren't they?" he asked.

Blade stopped, a smile creasing his rugged features. "They sure are."

The Bowies were in their sheaths, and the sheaths were affixed to hooks on the square rack.

"Now where the blazes is my hardware?" Hickok muttered, moving off, resuming his hunt.

Blade placed the three Gaskell Lasers he carried on the floor, then removed his belt. He proceeded to rethread the belt through the loops on his green fatigue pants, aligning the first Bowie on his left hip and the second on his right. As he was securing the belt buckle, Hickok began cackling like crazy. Blade grinned. He could guess why. Stooping, he retrieved the Lasers, slanting one under his belt and keeping the other two in his hands. He headed for the door, idly scrutinizing the weapons on the racks. At the end of the aisle he paused, noticing a big, gray metal box in the corner to his right. He walked to the box and lifted the lid, curious as to its contents.

Hand grenades.

Dozens and dozens of hand grenades.

"Whoa!" Blade exclaimed, then raised his voice. "Hickok!"

"Right behind you," responded the gunfighter.

Blade glanced over his right shoulder.

Hickok's cherished Pythons were strapped around his waist, and he held a Gaskell Laser in each hand. "I found my Colts," he said.

"I gathered as much," Blade mentioned. "But why are you still packing those Lasers? I thought you'd prefer your Colts over anything."

"I do, pard," Hickok confirmed. "But I'm not no idiot. I tried usin' my Pythons on one of those silver coyotes before, and even head-shootin' the mangy cuss didn't seem to faze him much. But these popguns," he said, wagging the Gaskells, "do the trick real well. Near as I can figure, those androids are almost invulnerable. You can stop one if you bust its legs or crack its skull wide open, but a bullet doesn't do much damage unless you hit the right spot. These Lasers, on the other hand, seem to fry their brains, or whatever they've got in their noggins. I'll stick with these popguns until we split this place."

"I may have found something that will help us," Blade divulged, moving aside so the gunman could see the contents of the metal box.

Hickok stepped up to the box, whistling in appreciation. "Will you look at all those! And it isn't even my birthday!"

Blade knelt and placed the Gaskells by his side. He removed one of the grenades. "Now the odds are more even."

"Yep. All we have to do is find Lynx, Gremlin, and Ferret, then fight our way out of the city past hordes of androids and troopers, and travel hundred and hundreds of miles over hostile territory until we reach the Home," Hickok quipped. "We could do it in our sleep."

"I've been thinking about that," Blade said, cramming grenades into his pants pockets.

"About what?" Hickok asked, resting his Gaskells on the floor and following Blade's example.

"About getting to our Home," Blade said.

"What about it?"

"It won't be as difficult to reach as you think," Blade stated.

"How do you figure?" Hickok inquired.

"The Civilized Zone is our ally, right?" Blade mentioned.

"Yep. So?"

"And which former States are now included in the Civilized Zone's territory?" Blade prompted.

Hickok pondered for a moment. "Let me see. Wyoming. Kansas and Nebraska. Colorado, New Mexico, Oklahoma, and part of Arizona," he added.

"You missed one," Blade said.

"Oh. Yeah." And Hickok suddenly grinned. "Northern Texas!"

"That's right," Blade affirmed. "And if Androxia was once called Houston, then we know we're in southern Texas. So reaching freedom isn't a matter of traveling over a thousand miles through enemy country. All we have to do is head north and find the Civilized Zone's lines, and I'm positive they'll help us reach the Home. At the most, we should only have several hundred miles to travel."

"We can do it," Hickok asserted. "But first we've got to find those three feebleminded mutants."

Blade, his pockets laden with hand grenades, rose. "I hope we can." He scooped up the Lasers.

Hickok picked up his Gaskells and stood. "I'm not leavin' without those misfits, pard."

"We may not have any option," Blade said somberly. "Androxia is immense, and we don't have the foggiest idea where to begin looking for them."

Hickok shook his head. "I'm not leavin' without 'em."

Their budding argument was terminated by the sound of a voice in the corridor.

"Go from room to room! Check each one!"

The two Warriors sidled to the doorway. Blade peeked out, then drew his head back.

"What have we got?" Hickok asked.

"Superiors and troopers," Blade stated. "To the left, coming this way, going door to door."

"Then we skedaddle to the right," Hickok suggested.

Blade nodded. "But first we need a distraction." He eased the Gaskells under his belt, then extracted a grenade from his right front pocket. "This should do the trick."

They waited, listening, gauging the approach of their pursuers. They could hear boots pounding, doors slamming closed, and muted conversations.

Hickok was grinning in anticipation.

Blade fingered the grenade, his thumb touching the pin.

"You four!" bellowed someone in the corridor. "Check the Weapons Room!"

Blade darted into the corridor, pulling the pin.

Ten yards distant were four troopers, two mutants and two humans, and looming to their rear was a Superior. Visible behind the Superior were additional troopers and several more androids.

Blade tossed the grenade overhand, lobbing it over the heads of the startled quartet of troopers, tossing the grenade at the Superior.

The Superior and the four troopers all saw the Warrior emerge from the Weapons Room, and the Superior was opening his mouth to shout a command when the hand grenade detonated a centimeter from his face.

Blade was already diving for the floor.

The entire hallway shook with the thunderous explosion. The overhead lights flickered, several blinking out.

Blade felt wet drops splatter his arms, and then debris and dust and body parts were raining down, pelting him. A severed thumb struck him on the left cheek and dropped to the floor. He heaved erect, drawing his Gaskell Lasers.

Hickok burst from the Weapons Room, Gaskells in hand, moving between Blade and their foes. "Go!" he cried. "I'll cover you!"

Blade turned and ran toward the far end of the corridor.

Hickok backpedaled, probing the dust cloud for movement.

A bloody trooper, doubled over, coughing, stumbled into sight.

Hickok shot him through the head.

A Superior appeared. The android spotted the Warrior and raised the Laser in its right hand.

Hickok took the android out with two shots through the cranium. He glanced over his right shoulder.

Blade was still sprinting for the door at the end of the hall.

Hickok continued to retreat.

A grainy gray cloud filled the other half of the corridor. Orders were being shouted, and one of the maimed troopers was screaming in agony.

Hickok halted, detecting shadowy motion in the cloud.

Two troopers rushed into view, their steel batons upraised.

Hickok killed them both, then wheeled and raced after Blade, who was waiting for him next to the door. The gunman weaved as he jogged, repeatedly looking over his shoulder, wary of being blasted in the back.

"Come on!" Blade goaded him.

Hickok covered the final 15 yards in a mad dash.

"I don't think I'm the only one who should go on a diet," Blade cracked as the gunman reached his side.

"Very funny," Hickok muttered, huffing.

Blade shoved the door open, and together they exited the corridor.

"Another stairwell!" Hickok exclaimed.

Blade bounded up the steps, keeping near the inner railing.

"Wait for me!" Hickok said, struggling to match his lanky stride to Blade's giant gait.

Blade slowed so the gunman could catch up.

"Where are we headin'?" Hickok asked. "The lobby again?"

"No," Blade said. "There has to be another way out of here, a side door nobody uses."

A beam of light abruptly struck the railing next to Blade's right hand, and an acute burning sensation lanced his whole arm as he was peppered with scorching metal. He twisted, looking upward.

A Superior and two troopers were on the landing above, the landing at lobby level, evidently posted as guards in the east stairwell. The android was sighting for another shot with his Gaskell Laser.

Blade threw himself to the left as another shaft of deadly light hissed over his head.

Hickok crouched, firing his Lasers three times, each shot on target. The first bored through the Superior's forehead. The second caught one of the troopers in the mouth. And the third seared into the last trooper's right eye and out his left ear. All three dropped from sight.

Blade was up and running as the gunfighter fired his third shot, taking the stairs three at a time. He reached the next landing, finding all three of their adversaries twitching and thrashing in the throes of death. He also discovered two doors, one to each side of the landing.

"That was close, pard," Hickok commented as he reached the landing.

Blade stepped over one of the expiring troopers and crossed to the door to the right. He carefully eased it open a fraction. As expected, there was the large lobby, packed with milling Superiors and troopers. The Superiors appeared to be engaged in organizing the troopers for a complete sweep of the Intelligence Building. He also saw the familiar glass doors on the north side of the lobby, the long corridor over by the west wall, and, after craning his neck and pressing his eyes to the opening, he could see the row of elevators not more than 12 feet away.

"Psssst!" Hickok whispered.

Blade closed the door to the lobby and turned.

Hickok was crouched alongside the dead android, waving a key chain in his right hand.

Blade slid his left Gaskell under his belt and took the keys. He moved to the other stairwell door and tried the knob. It was locked.

"Hurry it up!" Hickok advised. "I hear somebody comin'

down the stairwell.''

Blade inserted the first key on the chain, the first of seven.
No luck.

"I heard footsteps down below too," the gunman stated.

Blade attempted to unlock the door with the second key.
No go.

"I wonder if this is how David Crockett felt at the Alamo?"
Hickok queried.

Blade inserted the third key and turned the knob.

The door swung wide open, allowing sunlight to shine inside.

The Warriors quickly exited the Intelligence Building. The door
provided access to a narrow alley, bordered on the opposite side
by a five-story structure. Blade removed the key before closing
the door, then locked the exit from the outside.

"Which way?" Hickok asked.

Blade placed the key in his left rear pocket, debating. If they
went to the left, the alley would take them to the front of the
Intelligence Building. "We go right," he said.

The two Warriors ran toward the rear of Intelligence.

"They'll find those three on the landing any second now,"
Hickok remarked.

"I know," Blade said. "But the locked door may throw them
off. They may think we went up or down. And even if they
suspect we used the exit, I have the key. They may need to find
another one before they can come after us."

"And the tooth fairy may show up and save our hides,"
Hickok joked, "but I wouldn't count on it."

They slowed as they neared the end of the alley. Blade took the
lead, flattening against the wall and advancing until he could peer
around the corner.

A parking lot filled with dozens upon dozens of vehicles was
located behind the Intelligence Building. Perhaps ten people, four
of them troopers in black uniforms, were either walking from the
parking lot to Intelligence or moving from the building toward
one of the parked vehicles. To the south of the parking lot was a
circular concrete landing pad, and resting on the concrete was a
sleek white helicopter with the words ANDROXIA AIR
EXPRESS painted on its tail section.

"What do you see?" Hickok inquired.

"Have a look," Blade recommended.

The gunman edged to the corner and surveyed the parking lot. "I don't see any Superiors," he observed.

"Do you see that copter?" Blade asked.

"Yep. And I see two guys in blue uniforms right beside it," Hickok said.

"Stay close," Blade directed, and boldly strolled around the corner.

Hickok alertly scanned the parking lot as he hastened after his companion. "Mind tellin' me what we're up to?"

"Head for the copter," Blade stated.

"Are you thinkin' of takin' flying lessons?" Hickok responded.

"I'm thinking of paying Primator a visit," Blade disclosed.

"Are you loco?" Hickok questioned in surprise.

"This may be the smartest move we've made so far," Blade said.

"How do you figure?"

"Think about it," Blade said. "Ever since we arrived in Androxia, we've been running around like chickens with our heads chopped off. Half the time, we've had no idea where we were or what was happening. Initially, we didn't even know the identities of our enemies. We didn't know why we were brought here. We didn't know if we were coming or going."

"I'm used to that," Hickok remarked. "I'm married. You should be used to it too."

"Now we know who our enemies are," Blade continued. "One of them, Clarissa, is history. The androids are little more than puppets. They're just doing what Primator tells them to do."

"Primator is the head honcho," Hickok noted.

"Exactly," Blade concurred. "And if we can destroy Primator, maybe we can escape from Androxia in one piece."

"Destroy that know-it-all contraption? How?"

Blade patted the front pockets on his fatigue pants.

"And how are we goin' . . ." Hickok began, then stopped, staring at the helicopter.

"Still think I'm loco?" Blade asked.

Hickok grinned. "I'm with you all the way, pard."

They skirted the parking lot, staying to the left of the parked vehicles as they moved toward the copter. The two men in blue uniforms were busy unloading boxes from the helicopter and depositing them in orderly piles at the edge of the four-foot-high concrete pad.

"I just thought of something," Hickok said. "We don't have those disks on our foreheads."

"We're too far from the cars for anyone to notice," Blade said. "And the two up ahead won't care if we have disks or not," he added ominously.

The two in blue were concentrating on their job. Once, the heavier of the pair glanced at the approaching Warriors. He resumed his work without displaying any apprehension.

Blade held the Gaskell Lasers alongside his legs as he walked up to the landing pad. He halted, smiling.

The heavyset man in blue looked over as he was setting a box on the edge of the concrete. "May I help you?"

"Are you the pilot?" Blade politely inquired.

"We're both qualified pilots. Why?" the heavyset man replied.

"You can both fly this helicopter?" Blade reiterated.

The leaner of the pair, in the act of carrying another box to the rim of the concrete, gazed down at the giant and the blond in buckskins. "Who are you? Is there a problem?"

"My problem is I only need one of you," Blade answered. "Sorry." He extended his right arm and fired, frying the brains of the heavier flyer, who collapsed behind the boxes with a protracted gasp. Blade leaped onto the concrete, his Laser aimed at the thin man. He moved between two stacks of boxes and tapped the Gaskell's barrel on the skinny pilot's nose. "I'm only going to say this once. If you don't do exactly what I say, when I say it, I will add another nostril to your face. Do you understand?"

The thin man nodded vigorously, his wide brown eyes on his dead associate.

Hickok climbed onto the concrete. He surreptitiously scrutinized the parking lot. None of the pedestrians appeared to have noticed the heavy pilot's demise.

Blade lowered the Laser. "Put down the box," he ordered.

The lean man immediately obeyed. "What do you want?" he blurted out.

"We want to take a tour of Androxia," Blade answered.

"But this isn't a charter copter," the pilot said. "This is a mail and cargo carrier. I . . ." he began, and abruptly froze, his mouth gaping. "You're not wearing an O.D.!" he exclaimed. "Neither of you!"

"I took mine off," Hickok commented. "It wasn't doin' a thing for my complexion."

"Into your copter," Blade directed. "You're taking us for a ride."

The man in blue turned and walked to the sliding door on the cargo section of the craft. "You must be insane."

"My missus would agree with you," Hickok mentioned.

"Move it!" Blade barked.

The pilot stepped onto the cargo section, Blade shadowing him. The cargo section consisted of a square area behind the only seats in the craft, one for the pilot and one for a copilot, both of which were positioned at the front, facing the instrument panel and other controls. Half of the cargo section contained stacked boxes.

Hickok was the last to board. He casually inspected the interior of the helicopter. "I've seen copters before," he commented. "Soviet copters. This one is kind of dinky compared to theirs."

The lean man in blue slid into the pilot's seat, watching Blade as the huge Warrior took the other one. "I told you this is a small carrier," the pilot said. "It's a Michael Model 611,121. It's not designed to transport a lot of weight. It's built for speed."

"You carry mail and cargo?" Blade questioned.

The pilot nodded. "Androxia Air Express is a courier service, mainly. A lot of mail and small boxes need to be delivered from one building to another on a rush basis, and using a copter is the quickest way of getting from one skyscraper to another."

Blade digested the news, contemplating. "Does every skyscraper have a landing pad like the one we're on?"

"Most do," the pilot replied. "Usually there are two landing pads. There's a helipad at ground level, and there's a heliport on each roof for deliveries to the upper floors."

Blade smiled and winked at Hickok.

The gunfighter closed the door to the cargo section. "Ready when you are, pard," he declared.

"Take off," Blade commanded.

The pilot hesitated. "I don't know who you are or what you've up to, but you'll never get away with it."

"What's your name?" Blade inquired.

"Roger 196726," the pilot responded.

"Well, Roger," Blade said sternly, "I won't warn you again. When I give an order, you comply. Don't give me any back talk."

Roger applied himself to adjusting the copter's controls preparing to taking off. "Listen, mister," he said as he worked, "I don't want to die. I'll do whatever you say. I promise. But I'm advising you, for your own good, to give this up."

"Get us airborne," Blade directed.

Roger flicked several switches, his practiced fingers expertly ranging over the instrument panel.

Blade heard a loud whine. He looked out the tinted canopy and saw the main roter beginning to rotate.

"As soon as we're off the ground," Roger remarked, "we're in trouble."

"Why?" Blade asked.

"Every Express copter must adhere to a fixed route, to a set flight path," Roger revealed. "If we deviate from the schedule, the Superiors will come after us."

"Do the Superiors fly copters like this one?"

Roger shook his head. "The copters the Superiors fly, the police choppers anyway, are armed. They'll blow us out of the sky."

"I'm surprised the Superiors even allow lowly humans to fly any helicopters at all," Blade mentioned.

"Courier copters are the only ones we can operate," Roger said. "I love flying, and this is the only kind they let humans do. All of the police and military craft are operated by Superiors."

"You don't sound too happy about it, bucko," Hickok interjected.

"The Superiors only do what is best for Androxia," Roger said, but his voice lacked conviction.

"Are you hitched, Rog?" Hickok queried.

"Do you mean married?" Roger responded.

"One and the same," Hickok stated.

"No, I'm not married," Roger disclosed. "The Superiors would not approve my marriage application." He barely suppressed a frown.

Hickok, standing in the center of the cargo section, glanced at Blade, "Sounds to me like Roger could use a change in scenery."

Blade studied the pilot. Roger was not more than twenty-five, with angular features and curly brown hair. At such an age, enforced loneliness would be a bitter situation to tolerate. Perhaps the Superiors had evaluated Roger as a borderline Malcontent, and that was the reason his marriage petition had been denied. Blade looked up at the rotor, noting it had attained a terrific speed. "Let's go."

Roger took hold of the stick, and the next moment the helicopter rose from the helipad, rapidly ascending. He leveled the craft off at a thousand feet. "Okay. Where am I taking you?"

"The Prime Complex," Blade stated.

Roger did a double take. "The Prime Complex? Now I know you're insane!"

Blade hefted the Gaskell in his right hand. "Move it."

Roger eased the stick to the right, and the copter responded smoothly.

Hickok, leaning on a stack of boxes for support, gazed out the canopy at the sprawling metropolis, fascinated. He could see dozens of other aircraft flying over Androxia. "We should get us one of these," he said to Blade. "I'd love to take one for a spin now and then."

"I don't know if that's a wise idea," Blade commented.

"What's wrong with it?"

"Your *driving* is bad enough," Blade said. "I don't know if I'd want to go flying with you at the controls."

"May I ask a question?" Roger interrupted.

"What?" Blade said.

"Why are we going to the Prime Complex?"

"To destroy Primator," Blade divulged.

Roger gaped at the giant in stark astonishment. "Destroy Primator?" he exclaimed. "That's impossible!"

"Why? Doesn't the Prime Complex have a heliport?" Blade inquired.

"Of course it does," Roger responded. "But you must have a special security clearance to land there. Otherwise, you'll be shot down."

"Have you ever landed there?" Blade asked.

"Dozens of times," Roger admitted. "But I always had a clearance."

"So just pretend you have one this time," Blade advised.

Roger shook his head. "It will never work."

"Give me the layout of the roof," Blade ordered. "I know

Primator is on the Sturgeon Level, the top floor. How does one get from the roof to Primator's floor?''

"The heliport is in the middle of the roof," Roger said. "It's a bear to land on sometimes because of the winds. The Complex is two hundred ninety-nine stories high."

"I know," Blade said.

"At that height, you have updrafts and crosscurrents and wind sheer to contend with. I hate landing there," Roger mentioned.

"You don't have any choice," Blade noted.

"And what are you going to do if I don't?" Roger queried. "Shoot me? The copter would crash, and you'd die too."

"I wouldn't shoot you while we're in the air," Blade stated. "I'd wait until you landed, and then I'd add that extra nostril."

Roger frowned. "There's no way I can get out of this, is there?"

"No," Blade averred. "Your best chance to survive this alive is to cooperate with us fully. Now tell me more about the roof on the Prime Complex. You said the heliport is in the middle. How do you reach the Sturgeon Level from the roof?"

"By going down," Roger revealed. "There's a flight of stairs on the east side of the roof, and you have to go through a door to reach the stairs. That door is always locked. It has to be opened from the inside."

"How many guards?" Blade asked.

"None."

"None?" Blade repeated skeptically.

"Who needs guards two hundred ninety-nine stories up?" Roger rejoined. "Besides, they have something better than guards."

"Like what?" Blade questioned.

"Like four defensive emplacements, one on each corner of the roof." Roger disclosed. "They function automatically once activated."

"What type of defensive emplacements?" Blade inquired.

"Lasers at the northeast and southwest corners, and heat-seeking missile-launchers at the southeast and the northwest," Roger informed them.

Blade stared at the bustling city below. "Are there any other conduits between the roof and Primator's floor? An air shaft, anything like that?"

"There's the mail drop," Roger said. "A big metal chute."

"Tell me about it."

"It's a chute for depositing mail in," Roger explained. "It's used primarily for classified rush communiques, for urgent messages and dispatches which can't be sent through the postal service, relayed over the phone, or supplied through a computer."

Blade recalled the instructions Primator had given to the Superior in the audience chamber. "INSTRUCT INTELLI-GENCE TO INTERROGATE THEM THOROUGHLY. I WANT THE DATA OBTAINED RELAYED TO ME IMMED-IATELY." Would Primator want such data delivered by a courier copter instead of through normal channels? "And this mail chute connects directly to Primator's floor?"

"As far as I know," Roger said. "It's right next to the heliport."

"There's no other shaft of any kind?" Blade quieried.

"Not that I know of," Roger responded.

The mail chute sounded promising. Blade hoped the chute was linked to Primator's internal circuitry somehow, although he considered it to be unlikely. How could a computer, even a thinking computer, read its own mail? Still, he shouldn't put anything past Primator.

"Is that what I think it is?" Hickok inquired, moving between the two chairs and pointing straight ahead.

Blade glanced up.

There was no mistaking the Prime Complex. As the highest structure in Androxia, the grand edifice reared above the rest like a mountain over a cluster of molehills. In the bright sunlight, its golden radiance was enhanced. The Complex was undeniably magnificent, awe-inspiring, splendid beyond measure.

A small black speaker in the center of the instrument panel suddenly crackled to life. "Androxia Express Number Three, this is the Central Air Traffic Control Tower. You are deviating from your delivery schedule, and you are not conforming to your prescribed flight path. You are also about to enter restricted air space. Explain immediately."

"I told you so," Roger commented, grabbing a headset lying on top of the instrument panel. He hastily aligned the headset over his ears and mouth. "What do I say?"

"Tell them you are under orders to deliver an urgent message to Primator," Blade directed.

Roger reached out and flicked a silver toggle on the instrument panel. "Air Traffic Control, this is Androxia Express Number Three. What's the problem? I am under orders to deliver an urgent message to Primator."

"Negative," the speaker cracked. "We have no record of any security authorization for you to land on the Prime Complex. You will abort and return to Central Field immediately."

Roger flicked off the toggle. "Now what, mastermind?"

"Tell them you received your security authorization at the Intelligence Building," Blade instructed. "Say you're carrying the results of the interrogation of the Warriors."

Roger's forehead creased in perplexity, his O.D. gleaming. He turned on the silver toggle. "Air Traffic Control, I don't understasnd any of this. I was handed my security clearance at Intelligence. I was told this must reach Primator promptly, and I was the only one on the helipad at the time. I overheard something about the interrogation results of some Warriors, if that makes any sense. But if you want me to abort, I will do so right away. Please check and confirm."

There was a slight pause.

"One moment," Air Traffic Control said.

Roger switched off the toggle.

"If those jokers check with Intelligence and learn we busted out," Hickok mentioned, "the jig is up."

Blade looked at Roger. "Those missiles and lasers on the roof. Will they be activated if we try to land?"

"I don't know," Roger said. "It depends on whether they believed my story. They might hold off while they're checking."

"Then land! Now!" Blade commanded.

Roger grit his teeth and pulled on the stick, sending the copter into a steep climb, zooming toward the top of the Prime Complex.

"Wheeee!" Hickok cried in delight.

Blade's muscles tensed as the helicopter swooped upward, closing on the roof. They were approaching from the southwest, and he could see a bulky cannonlike affair, obviously one of the large lasers, perched on the southwest corner. Even as he watched, the barrel of the laser began to shift, to move in their direction.

Hickok had also noticed. "They're gettin' our range."

"Faster!" Blade urged.

Roger pushed the helicopter to its limit, angling even higher. "If we can reach the heliport, we might be safe temporarily," he remarked. "I don't think they'll fire at us while we're on the roof. There's too great a risk of an explosion. They'll probably wait until we lift off again."

"An explosion from what?" Blade asked. "This copter? I doubt it would put much of a dent in the roof if it's as sturdy as the rest of the Complex."

"Not from the copter," Roger elaborated. "From the refueling tank."

Blade leaned toward the pilot. "What refueling tank? You didn't tell us about any refueling tank."

"Every heliport has a refueling tank nearby," Roger told them. "Fighting these thermal drafts can make a chopper use up its fuel real fast. The refueling tanks at each heliport are for emergency refueling."

The courier copter was almost to the roof of the Prime Complex.

Blade's gaze was glued to the laser. The weapon was continuing to swivel, slanting lower, its barrel resembling a gigantic, elongated tube, tracking the path of the chopper.

"Androxia Express Number Three!" the speaker barked. "You will abort immediately and return to Central Field!"

"Up yours!" Roger muttered.

The chopper swept over the rim of the roof, streaking past the laser on the southwest corner, diving for the heliport.

"We made it!" Roger shouted excitedly.

The helicopter alighted on the heliport.

Blade handed his Gaskells to Hickok, then rose and ran to the sliding door. He yanked the door open and leaped from the chopper, landing on his hands and knees on the concrete heliport. The wind from the main rotor tousled his hair. He saw the metal mail chute to his left. In front of him, about 30 yards from the heliport, was the large oval refueling tank. To the east, to his right, was the steel door to the stairs.

Move! his mind shrieked.

Blade scrambled to the northern edge of the heliport and dropped to the roof. He circled to the left, to the metal chute. The mail chute was square, about five feet in height, not more than ten inches by ten inches. It was labeled with the word MAIL. He grabbed a small handle near the top, and the door to the chute swiveled open. Moving swiftly, he removed two hand grenades from his right front pocket. He hooked the little finger of his left hand in the door handle to keep the chute door from closing, then quickly pulled the pins and deposited the grenades in the mail chute.

Move!

Blade released the door and whirled, racing toward the refueling tank, mentally ticking off the numbers.

Ten-nine-eight.

Blade pulled another grenade from his pocket as he ran.

Seven-six-five.

He halted, wrenching the pin loose.

Four-three-two.

Blade hurled the grenade with all of his prodigious strength at the fuel tank, then spun toward the chopper.

There was the retort of a muffled explosion from under the roof, and the entire top of the Prime Complex seemed to sway, the roof vibrating violently as smoke billowed from the mail chute.

Blade nearly lost his footings, but he forced his pumping legs to respond, to keep going, racing for the helicopter. He vaulted onto the concrete landing pad, making for the inviting open door. He was only seven feet from his goal when the oval fuel tank detonated. Blade felt an invisible wave of force slam into his back, and he was lifted from his feet and hurled against the copter, sprawling over the lip of the cargo door. He caught a glimpse of a flaming ball spiraling heavenward, and then strong hands gripped his shoulders and he was abruptly hauled into the helicopter as the chopper rose several feet and sped toward the south side of the Prime Complex.

Another tremendous blast rocked the roof.

Blade, on his left side on the floor, saw Roger struggling with the stick as the craft bounced and shook. A brilliant streak of light flashed past the cargo door, and he realized one of the roof lasers had opened up.

The helicopter suddenly banked to the left and dived, plummeting over the south rim of the edifice.

Blade could still see a portion of the roof, and he saw a sheet of red and orange erupt skyward as yet another explosion shattered the southern rim.

Roger was laughing inanely. The chopper leveled off, swinging wide to the west of the Complex.

Blade slowly stood. The top of the Complex was engulfed in flames.

Hickok was lying on the floor near the boxes, several of which had fallen on him when the copter descended. He pushed the boxes from him and rose. "I knew it'd be a piece of cake."

Blade closed the cargo door, then moved to the front and sat down across from the pilot.

Roger glanced at the hulking figure in the black vest and the fatigue pants. "Thanks."

"For what?" Blade asked.

"I wouldn't admit it to myself," Roger stated, "but I've wanted to pay them back for a long time! Telling me I couldn't get married! The sons of bitches!"

Hickok came up behind Blade's seat. "How would you like to live somewhere else, somewhere you could marry any woman who'd say yes?"

Roger looked at the gunman. "Are you putting me on?"

"Nope," Hickok assured the pilot. "We'll take you there if you'll help us get out of Androxia."

"I can help," Roger said. "If I stay as close to the ground as possible, radar won't be able to pick us up. They might not find us."

"What about your blasted disk?" Hickok questioned.

"They can track me with that, all right," Roger said.

Blade rose, drawing his right Bowie. "Don't move."

"What are you doing?" Roger inquired nervously.

Blade leaned over the pilot, examining the edge of the Orwell Disk. He found a minute crack between the disk and the flesh on the right side and gingerly inserted the tip of his Bowie. "Brace yourself."

Roger, his knuckles white as his fingers clutched the stick, blanched.

Blade's right arm bulged.

Roger flinched, his mouth contorting in torment.

There was a loud, squishy popping noise, and the Orwell Disk plopped from Roger's forehead into Blade's left palm. A trickle of blood seeped from the circular indentation left in Roger's forehead.

"Did you remove the damn thing?" Roger asked hopefully.

Blade held the disk out for Roger to see.

Hickok uttered a derisive snort. "If the blamed things are that easy to pry off, why didn't you take it off yourself?"

"The penalty for removing an O.D. is death," Roger replied.

Blade handed the Orwell Disk to the gunman. "You know what to do with it."

Hickok nodded. Seconds later, the disk was sailing out a narrow opening in the cargo door.

"I'm in your debt for this," Roger said to Blade. "I'll do my best to get us out of here."

"First things first," Blade remarked.

"What do you mean?"

Blade peered out the canopy at the buildings zipping past. "Where would the Superiors take a mutant to be neutered?"

18

"What do you want?" Lynx asked the Superior, doing his best to imitate the floor supervisor's voice. Tom had been the same size, but his voice had been slightly higher.

"I want to check on your new arrival," the Superior said.

"New arrival?" Lynx repeated, wondering if the android meant him.

"His name is Lynx," the Superior stated. "We brought him over early this morning, before you arrived. I dropped his dossier on your desk, on your Incoming tray. But with all the paperwork on your desk, I was concerned you might not see it."

"I saw it," Lynx lied.

"This one is a troublemaker," the Superior mentioned. "If you require guards, I will have a detail posted."

Lynx nodded toward his former room. "We won't need guards. He's locked up safe and sound."

The Superior stared at the door to the room. "I'd like to see him."

"You can't!" Lynx blurted out.

Melody anxiously licked her lips.

The Superior studied the feline mutant. "Why can't I see Lynx, Tom?"

"Because . . ." Lynx responded hastily. "He did give us some trouble when we tried to feed him, and he had to be sedated. He'll be out for four, maybe six hours."

The Superior nodded knowingly. "I knew he would be a problem. I will order a guard detail posted, and no one will be permitted in the room other than yourself and Melody."

Lynx nodded enthusiastically. "That's an excellent idea, now that I think of it. Don't let anybody in his room. He's too dangerous at that."

"Report to me if he creates another disturbance," the Superior ordered.

"Without delay," Lynx responded.

The Superior wheeled and walked away.

Lynx headed for the stairwell, Melody on his right side. "Who the hell was that?" he whispered.

"WW-60," Melody answered. "He handles administrative coordination for this section."

"Do you think we fooled him?" Lynx queried.

"If we hadn't," Melody replied, "we'd be in custody right now."

They walked to the stairwell door, deliberately conveying a casual air, but once in the stairwell they increased their pace, speeding up the steps as rapidly as their legs would carry them. They reached the door to Floor 45 without mishap.

Lynx hesitated, his left hand on the knob. "How do we play this? Won't we be suspicious if we march on in and ask to see my buddies?"

Melody reflected for a minute. "What are their names?"

"Gremlin and Ferret," Lynx said.

"I have an idea," Melody stated. "Follow my lead."

Lynx opened the door, then unexpectedly halted.

A Superior was standing not six feet away, leafing through a handful of papers. He looked up and saw them. "Hello. May I assist you?"

Melody moved past Lynx, smiling sweetly. "Sorry to bother you, but I believe you have two new arrivals here for testing. Their names are Gremlin and Ferret."

The android nodded. "They're in 45-C taking the written portion of the Psychological Profile Examination."

"The Examination will need to be interrupted," Melody said.

The Superior lowered the papers. "Why?"

"We've subjected their companion, the one called Lynx, to a routine medical exam," Melody said. "WW-60 sent us up as soon as he saw the results."

"What results?"

Melody feigned abject dismay. "We were appalled to discover Lynx has a communicable sexual disease. Syphilis."

"Sexually transmitted diseases were eliminated from our stock decades ago," the Superior commented.

"From *our* stock, yes," Melody agreed. "But these mutants are from outside Androxia, correct?"

"What does WW-60 require?" the Superior asked.

"He wants Gremlin and Ferret tested right away," Melody said. "We can't have these degenerates mingling with our pure stock if they're infected. WW-60 is preparing the proper papers, but those forms take a while to complete. He wanted to know if you would send Gremlin and Ferret down with us, and he assures you the release forms will be on your desk within the hour."

"A reasonable request," the Superior stated. "Wait here. I will bring them out." He turned and moved down the corridor.

Lynx nudged Melody's left elbow. "Syphilis?"

"It was the best I could do on the spur of the moment," Melody said.

Lynx smiled. "I'm shocked, princess. A lady like you, comin' up with a disease like that!" He laughed.

"It was the first thing I thought of when you kissed me," Melody explained.

Lynx's eyebrows tried to leave his face. "But *you* kissed *me*!"

Melody grinned mischievously. "I must be a gambler at heart."

"I don't have no sexual diseases!" Lynx snapped, miffed. "I'm as healthy as they come."

"I'll bet," Melody said, chuckling.

The Superior emerged from one of the rooms with two mutants in tow.

"That's them," Lynx verified in a hushed tone.

Gremlin, walking behind the Superior, spotted Lynx and opened his mouth to yell a greeting. Before he could, however, Ferret reached up and clamped his right hand over Gremlin's mouth. The Superior never noticed.

"I can see you're the brains of the bunch," Melody said softly.

Lynx puffed up his chest. "As a matter of fact, I am."

"No wonder you're all prisoners," Melody whispered, and then the Superior was within hearing range.

"Here they are," the android said. "Do you want me to accompany you?"

"Thank you, but that won't be necessary," Melody told him.

"They might attempt to escape," the Superior observed.

"We'll take the evevator then," Melody proposed. "They can't escape from an elevator."

"A logical alternative," the Superior concurred, and turned. "Follow me," he directed Gremlin and Ferret.

Lynx and Melody brought up the rear as they walked down the corridor until they reached the elevator.

"I will be expecting the release forms as promised," the Superior said to Melody.

"WW-60 will see they reach you," Melody affirmed. She pressed the button for the elevator.

Lynx stepped up to Gremlin and Ferret. "You two will behave or suffer the consequences."

"Whatever you say, sir," Ferret said meekly.

"That's the right attitude," Lynx stated imperiously.

"We've learned our lesson," Ferret went on. "We don't want any trouble. We never did. It was our friend Lynx who gave you Androxians such a hard time. He's always getting us into hot water. I guess he can't help himself."

"What?" Lynx stated.

"That's right, sir," Ferret continued. "Lynx combines monumental stupidity with a supreme arrogance. He blunders his way through life, creating more problems than he's worth."

"That's enough about this Lynx," Lynx said.

"Yes, sir." Ferret then ignored him. "Lynx is about the dumbest nincompoop this side of the Milky Way. I've heard you perform lobotomies here, and you would be doing the world a favor if you performed one on Lynx. Of course, you probably won't find anything in his head worth lobotomizing—"

"That's enough!" Lynx declared angrily.

"Yes, sir," Ferret said in a suddued fashion.

The elevator arrived with a clang, the door sliding open.

Lynx motioned for Ferret and Gremlin to enter.

"Thank you," Melody addressed the android. "We'll contact you as soon as the test results are known."

Lynx stepped into the elevator.

"All mutants should be as efficient as you," the Superior complimented Melody.

Melody smiled and joined the others. Her right hand reached up, and she tapped one of the buttons on the control panel to the right of the door.

The elevator door closed.

Melody pressed the button for the ground floor.

"Lynx!" Ferret exclaimed in delight. "How did you do it?"

Lynx gave Ferret an icy stare. "It was easy, even for a nincompoop like me."

"Some people can't take a joke," Ferret retorted.

Lynx glanced at Gremlin, who was gawking at Melody. "And what's with you, birdbrain? Why are you so quiet?"

"Where did you find such a lovely woman, yes?" Gremlin asked.

Melody grinned. "I take back what I said, Lynx. You're not the brains of the bunch."

Lynx introduced his friends, pointing at each one in turn. "Ferret and Gremlin, I'd like you to meet Melody. She's my squeeze."

"I'm your *what*?" Melody queried. She looked up at the floor indicator lights above the door.

Ferret executed an elaborate bow. "My pleasure, dear lady! Seldom have I encountered a woman of such exquisite beauty. I expect you are endowed with an intelligence the equal of your loveliness, although your taste in men leaves me in doubt."

"Why you—!" Lynx said, bristling.

"Quiet!" Melody commanded. "We don't have much time. The elevator will be on the ground floor soon. This particular elevator shaft is located at the rear of the reception area. With any luck, we won't bump into any Superiors. When it stops and the doors open, take a right. There's an exit door to the rear parking lot about ten feet from this elevator. Ferret and Gremlin, keep your heads down or turn them to the rear wall. We don't want anyone in the reception area to notice you're not wearing O.D.'s."

Gremlin indicated the gleaming disk on Lynx's forehead. "Is that for real, yes?"

"No," Lynx responded. "It's a fake. I'm rippin' the sucker off as soon as we're out of here."

"Too bad," Ferret said. "You'll have problems with the draft again."

"Draft?" Lynx repeated, puzzled. "What draft?"

"The draft from the hole in your head the disk is covering," Ferret stated, and cackled.

Lynx looked at Melody and sighed. "With friends like these two clowns, you can see why the last thing I need is more enemies."

The elevator came to an abrupt stop and the door opened.

The reception area was spacious. Chairs lined the green walls and were organized in rows across the red carpet. A large circular wooden counter was positioned near the front door, staffed by three women in white uniforms and a Superior. Neither the android, the women, nor any of the humans and mutants seated in the chairs paid the scantest attention to the elevator's arrival.

"Hurry!" Melody urged, leading the way to the right, nervously scanning the reception area, dreading the outcome if they were detected and apprehended.

Lynx marched up to the exit door as if he didn't have a care in the world, reaching it a step behind Melody. He grabbed the knob, then glanced at Ferret and Gremlin. "I don't intend to get caught again. They're not takin' me alive this time! So once we're out this door, we do whatever it takes to stay free. I don't care if there's a hundred Superiors waitin' for us out there." He paused. "And if something should happen to me, I want you two bozos to make sure Melody reaches the Home. Got it?"

Gremlin and Ferret nodded.

Lynx squared his shoulders and twisted the doorknob, then shoved, prepared to sell his life dearly, if necessary, to safeguard Melody.

But there weren't one hundred Superiors waiting for them.

There wasn't a Superior anywhere in sight.

There were dozens of vehicles, and a number of mutants and humans moving from the parking lot to the Medical Building or going the other way.

Lynx moved outside. He saw an entranceway 30 yards to the right. Then he looked to the left.

Fifty yards distant, resting on a concrete helipad, was a sleek white helicopter.

"Do you see what I see?" Lynx asked.

"I see it," Ferret confirmed.

"If the pilot is still on board," Lynx said, "we'll have our ticket out of here."

They hurried toward the helipad.

Melody repeatedly glanced at the parking lot, hoping no one

would become unduly curious if they beheld two mutants in loincloths hastening from the Medical Building. She breathed an audible sigh of relief when they reached the edge of the helipad, and she eagerly scrambled over the top after the others. A startling thought slowed her down, though, as she stood on the concrete: if Lynx, Ferret, and Gremlin all wore those deplorable loincloths, was it possible all mutants, even the women, wore them where Lynx was from? She saw Lynx approaching an open sliding door on the side of the chopper, and she opened her mouth to question him.

Lynx was just about to climb onto the copter when a glimmering pair of revolver barrels poked around the right edge of the door. He leaped back, crouching, his claws extended, snarling in fury at being thwarted when they were so close to freedom. So close!

That was when a grinning blond man in buckskins appeared in the doorway, a revolver in each hand. "Howdy, runt," he said to Lynx. "What's the matter with you? Have you got ants in your britches?"

Melody would never forget Lynx's response. She'd failed to recognize, until that very moment, exactly how many curse words there were in the English langauge.

19

Two months later the Family celebrated the arrival of their missing members with the biggest bash ever held at the Home. After imbibing enough wine to drown a horse, Sherry publicly declared she was chaining Hickok to their bed and not letting him go for a week. She did not live up to her word, however, as the gunman was seen three days later walking rather stiffly around the compound.

Melody and Roger were formally accepted into the Family. After Melody recited her pledge of Loyalty, the Family women collectively presented her with a welcoming gift consisting of three hand-sewn outfits. No one could quite understand her reaction, though, when she actually hugged the clothing and kept saying, over and over again, "Thank you! Thank you!"

One month after their return, Blade and Hickok officiated at the induction of three new Warriors and the creation of a new Triad. Bravo Triad was formed, and its member Warriors were the only three male mutants in the Family. Lynx was ecstatic, Gremlin expressed genuine happiness, but Ferret was oddly reserved. Later that night, while Blade was patrolling the east wall, he saw Ferret standing by himself in a secluded section of the Home and gazing up at the stars. He distinctly overheard Ferret ask aloud: "Why me?"

A novel of terror
by the master of sinister fiction.

R. KARL LARGENT
THE PROMETHEUS PROJECT

Buried deep beneath the Caribbean was the final product of Nazi science — steel canisters containing a substance more deadly than anything ever created by man or nature.

For almost 50 years they had lain dormant on the sandy floor of the sea, waiting.... Then one of them ruptured and spewed forth its lethal contents, and suddenly a whole island was transformed from a living paradise to dead rock.

That's when they called in Wages. Master diver and professional survivor, he was charged with the salvage operation. But the closer he got to the mysterious canisters the more worried he became. For inside the steel containers something moved — something far worse than a Nazi doomsday device — something that shocked him to his very soul....

_____2748-8 $3.95US/$4.95CAN